I0788409

HEART OF THE DEEP

THE KRAKEN #4

TIFFANY ROBERTS

Copyright © 2018 by Tiffany Freund and Robert Freund Jr.

All Rights Reserved. No part of this publication may be used or reproduced, distributed, or transmitted in any form by any means, including scanning, photocopying, uploading, and distribution of this book via any other electronic means without the permission of the author and is illegal, except in the case of brief quotations embodied in critical reviews and certain other noncommercial uses permitted by copyright law. For permission requests, contact the publishers at the address below.

Tiffany Roberts

authortiffanyroberts@gmail.com

This book was not created with AI, and we do not give permission for our work to be trained for AI.

This book is a work of fiction. Names, characters, places, and incidents are products of the author's imagination or are used fictitiously and are not to be construed as real. Any resemblance to actual events, locales, organizations, or people, living or dead, is entirely coincidental.

Cover Illustration & Chapter art by Fadhila Inès (IF_Art)

Character Portrait by Marespinosa

❀ Formatted with Vellum

HEART OF THE DEEP

HIS HUNTRESS AND HIS HEART

Larkin has spent almost a year hunting the monstrous kraken in the hope that they knew the whereabouts of her missing brother. Her efforts finally come to fruition when she and the other rangers capture three of the beasts — but the reality is nothing like the stories they've been told, and the kraken are not the monsters she expected. Dracchus awes her, captivates her, and makes her long for things she'd never dared dream. With tensions between their people escalating, can she jeopardize everything by trusting him? Is a taste of him worth her life?

HER WARRIOR AND HER REFUGE

Dracchus has risked himself countless times for the sake of his people, doing anything and everything to protect and provide for them. Between the vocal, anti-human kraken at home and the hunters prowling the seas, everything is falling apart around him. But when he meets Larkin, he allows himself hope — hope for a mate of his own, for a family of his own. She is his match, unlike any female he's ever known. To have her, he'll have to endanger her, along with all those he's come to care for. After years of self-lessness, how much is he willing to gamble to fulfill his own desires?

Dedicated to my beloved. I'll always stand with you.

Special thanks to Cindy McGriff and R. Lee Smith for their title suggestions, Deep in the Heart and Depths of the Heart, which were made as part of a contest we ran to help choose a title for this book.

CHAPTER 1

362 Years After Landing

"We're finally going to bring the fight to those slippery bastards," said Commander Nicholas Laster.

Larkin had no response for her father as she watched the workers hoist the sails and put the finishing touches on the rigging.

It was complete. After ten months of labor, which had seen almost every able body in The Watch assist at one point or another, the ship was finally complete. That fact produced a heavy weight in her stomach, a blend of anticipation and fear — she *wanted* to get out there and find her brother, Randall by any means necessary, but what if all they found was his body?

Worse, what if they never found *anything*?

There was still hope of him being alive out there, somewhere, even if it was as a captive of the monsters lurking beneath the waves.

No one had believed the rumors of sea monsters, but Larkin's father had sent her brother to The Watch over a year ago to investigate the stories. When Jon Mason, one of Randall's men, had returned to Fort Culver with drawings of the kraken and a letter from Cyrus Taylor, a longtime friend of their father's and Randall's second-in-command, attesting to the monsters' existence, the commander couldn't ignore the evidence.

The hurried journey across hundreds of kilometers between Fort Culver and The Watch had been the longest of Larkin's life. She'd never been so far from home. But the hardest part had come after they arrived in The Watch.

The locals had informed them that Randall and his entire party of rangers had been missing for months.

"She's finally ready to sail!" Michael, one of the local laborers, called as he descended the gangplank. "Might be the biggest ship ever built on Halora."

"Will the cages hold them?" Nicholas asked. He'd been adamant that a brig be included below deck for the sole purpose of containing the kraken they intended to hunt. The monster's strength was rumored to be immense.

"If they can't, nothing will."

"Good." Nicholas turned toward the rangers standing nearby. "We sail at dawn, gentlemen."

The rangers — there were twenty gathered here, with two more parties of six out patrolling in smaller ships — wore mixed expressions. Everyone had been sent out on expeditions of varying length during their time here, but these men weren't comfortable remaining in one place for so long, pretending to be shipwrights and sailors. They were restless. Demoralized. Eager for a change of pace.

Ready to kill.

"Load her up. We're due for a month's worth of provisions. Bring the equipment we pulled out from under the lighthouse, too," the commander said.

The rangers dispersed quietly.

Nicholas faced Larkin and grasped her upper arms. "We're going to find him, Elle."

Larkin searched her father's face. He was a handsome man with a wide, square jaw covered in black-and-gray stubble. His hair, also streaked with gray, was cut close to his scalp. But he'd aged too much over the last year, and the gleam in his eyes reminded her of the stare he'd worn for so long after her mother died. She feared she was losing him; it would only take one more push to send him over the edge.

He *needed* Randall to be alive.

His facial hair scraped at her palms as she put her hands on his cheeks. "Of course we are, Dad."

They'd find Randall; he *was* alive. Larkin wasn't sure how, but she'd *know* if Randall passed, she'd feel it. They'd always been close. Four-year-old Randall had declared himself Larkin's protector on the day she was born, had treated it as his duty to look out for her, and that hadn't changed even as they grew into adulthood.

He's not dead.

Nicholas smiled and kissed her hair before releasing her. "I'm going to need you out there, Elle. You're the best shot in all Halora. You going to be ready to take it when the time comes? For your brother?"

"Yes." Whatever these creatures were, she wouldn't miss.

Her father faced the ship again. The locals streamed across the gangplank and gathered briefly in a cluster on the dock, many staring back at the three towering masts as though in awe of what they'd built. The ship was massive compared to the others moored nearby.

Larkin guessed the locals' relief was equal to their awe. This project had disrupted their lives, altered their routines, dominated their town. Its completion was a chance to reclaim normalcy.

"We should head back," Nicholas said as the last of the workers walked past. "Tomorrow's an important day. We're going to find *them*, and then we're going to find your brother."

They followed the locals up the paved ramp leading into town, passing rangers hauling varied equipment toward the dock. Larkin tugged at her clothes to peel her undershirt away from the sweat-dampened skin around her collar, on her back, and between her breasts.

The lighthouse atop the promontory vanished from her view as their ascent drew them nearer to the cliffside. Larkin glanced up; the crane's cable dangled over the edge of the cliff, swaying in the breeze. Beside it stood the large warehouse in which the townsfolk stored their fish. A handful of small houses skirted the path. As far as she was aware, they all belonged to fishermen.

Larkin and her father entered the town proper shortly afterward. The setting sun created harsh highlights on rooftops and walls but blanketed the paths running between the buildings in long shadows. The homes to either side were an eclectic collection — concrete and metal structures dating to the early days of colonization, mixed liberally with new structures and additions crafted of wood and scrap.

They passed few people during their walk to the town hall at the heart of The Watch. Larkin had grown used to the open, vexed stares of the locals. She couldn't blame them — the rangers had essentially commandeered the town, its laborers, and its resources. The fishermen were the most disgruntled. They'd already given over three good boats — one of them lost at sea with Randall and his men — and countless hours of their time and expertise for what they deemed a fruitless endeavor. They wanted the rangers off their dock and out of their town.

The town hall was the largest building in The Watch and saw more traffic than any other — it operated as a pub and the center for socialization among the locals.

The din of numerous conversations hit Larkin first as she followed her father inside, but the smell that followed was more potent. Body odor, the aroma of cooking food, and the stale scent of spilled drinks combined to create an overwhelming stench that nauseated her almost every time she walked in. Tonight, the smell was strengthened by the stifling heat in the main room.

Cots and pallets lined the stage toward the rear, and there were more in the back rooms; this was the only place large enough to house all the rangers who'd come with them. A dozen tables were arranged between the sleeping area and the door, occupied by clusters of locals and rangers. More people were gathered along the bar on the left side of the room.

It was cramped and stuffy, noisy and stinky, but Larkin would deal with it for as long as necessary. They had a mission to accomplish.

"Hey, commander! Elle! You hungry?"

Larkin followed the voice to see Jason Dane, one of the rangers, standing beside the bar. Three bowls were perched awkwardly on his open hands, tottering at the end of his extended arms. He hurried toward Larkin and her father, raising and lowering the bowls as he wove through the crowd.

Somehow, he arrived without spilling anything.

"Took down a couple krull today." He smiled and jabbed a thumb at the bartender; Larkin's heart leapt, and she barcly stopped herself from lunging forward to catch the bowl he was surely about to drop. "Aiden here made a damn fine stew of them."

He passed a bowl each to Larkin and her father.

She accepted the offering and set the bowl onto the table. Steam flowed up from the mixture of meat, vegetables, and thick broth. It was a miracle the bowl had survived the trip from the bar.

Nicholas led them to one of the few open tables.

"So tomorrow, huh?" Jason asked as they took their seats. "Think the monsters are just like those sketches Cyrus sent?"

Larkin had studied the drawings many times over the last year. Most of them were parts of a greater whole — tentacles, webbed fingers tipped with long claws, eyes with strange, oblong pupils. As detailed and lifelike as they were, much was left to the imagination.

What *were* the kraken?

"Probably uglier," Nicholas replied around a bite of food. "You need to be prepared to set aside any wonderment you might experience when we find these things, ranger. We have a job to do. They are the enemy."

"You won't catch me gawking." Jason wiped his mouth with the back of his hand. "How we gonna find them?"

"We found a treasure trove of tech stashed away in the bunker under the lighthouse," Larkin said. "There are enough functioning spectra goggles that we can have three or four on each boat."

"And what do those do?" Jason asked.

There was still some old military tech in working order back at Fort Culver, but most items from the colonization had long since worn out or been lost. Beyond the command team, few rangers knew much about the old stuff, because they weren't likely to see any of it in their lifetimes.

"They provide enhanced optics," she explained. "Increased viewing distance, like a spy glass, but they can also be switched through various spectrums of light the human eye cannot detect."

"Oh."

"And they can scan for lifeforms up to fifty meters out," Nicholas said, still chewing; his bowl was nearly empty. "That's all we need them for. We know those bastards have been watching our boats. I have at least four confirmed sightings, and they all corroborate these monsters having some kind of natural camouflage that makes them *almost* impossible to see, even when they break the surface. But now we're going to know *exactly* where they are, and we'll be ready when they get too close."

Larkin scanned the room as she ate. Apart from the bar — where everyone went to make their orders — the rangers and the locals kept to their own groups. The friendliness of the townsfolk hadn't evaporated, but it was certainly worn thin after eleven months of constant ranger presence. The underlying tension between the two groups was undeniable.

When they were young, Nicholas had taught Larkin and Randall that one of the most important parts of entering a town in their official capacity as rangers was befriending the locals and setting them at ease.

You have to earn *their trust,* he'd said.

He hadn't been doing a good job of that, and it worried her. Nicholas Laster wasn't sloppy in his work. At least not before this excursion.

It didn't help that some of the townsfolk seemed to be holding a grudge against them before they ever arrived.

What really happened while you were here, Randall?

"So, what's the plan?" Jason asked. "Cyrus said these things were strong."

"Nets and tranquilizers," Larkin said. "We want them alive for questioning."

"They really talk?"

"Based on Ranger Taylor's report, they are fully capable of conversation."

"He seemed to be of the opinion that the creature he encountered talked too damned much," her father added before finishing off his stew. He placed his bowl and spoon on the table, wiped his mouth with a handkerchief, and met Larkin's gaze. "It doesn't matter what they say. You follow my orders. Understood?"

Larkin frowned. "Haven't I always?"

Nicholas matched her frown, but the set of his brows suggested annoyance. "You know what I'm talking about. Now, more than ever, I need your head in this game. We don't have room for sentimentality."

She pressed her lips together. Larkin had worked just as hard as any of the rangers, if not more so, to prove she was as capable as anyone. She'd been Nicholas's second in command for years, had remained loyally at his side even after he'd given Randall command of his own team, and she could outshoot any man here.

But her father would always see her as a little girl with too soft a heart.

Appetite gone, she pushed her half-eaten bowl forward, scooted her chair back, and stood. "I have followed every order you have ever given me, *commander*. I will do my duty."

"I don't appreciate your tone, *ranger*," he replied, "and I did not dismiss you."

Larkin clenched her fists at her sides. "Permission to be dismissed, sir."

For several seconds, he wore the hard, angry face of the commander, the man who had led the Culver Hunters since she was a little girl. A man who was to be respected and feared, who did not tolerate slights. But his eyes softened; most men wouldn't hold his gaze for as long as Larkin. Most men would never see the cracks.

He finally nodded, looked down, and waved her away. "I want everyone loaded up to depart at dawn."

Larkin caught Jason's smirk as she turned away from the table. The rude gesture she offered in response left him choking on his stew.

She held onto her sliver of satisfaction as she made her way into the back room. Several other rangers were already bedding down; some would have to wake in a few hours for their watch shifts. She wove between their pallets to the curtained area at the rear of the room. Her father had set it up to allow Larkin and the handful of other female rangers some degree of privacy.

Thankfully, the other women hadn't yet retired.

Larkin kicked off her boots, positioning them against the wall. She pulled her knife from her belt, slipped it under her pillow, and looped the belt over her boots. Ignoring the snoring from beyond the curtain, she stripped down to her tank top and underwear.

She sat on the pallet and rubbed her hands over her face before taking hold of her braid and pulling it forward. Her fingers brushed through its tip as she stared down at it.

"Where are you, Randall?" she asked softly. An ache flared behind her breastbone. Releasing her hair, she lay back on her pallet, folded her hands over her stomach, and stared up at the ceiling. Randall's absence was a physical pain she couldn't shake. She missed him, *feared* for him, but he wasn't dead. She wouldn't believe that.

"I'll find you. I promise."

CHAPTER 2

A GROWL WAS THE ONLY WARNING DRACCHUS RECEIVED BEFORE tiny teeth sank into one of his tentacles. He twisted his torso to look down at the youngling gnawing on his limb — Jace, Aymee and Arkon's offspring.

Jace scrunched his nose and growled again. The other younglings giggled.

"He got you, Uncle Dracchus!" Sarina's face was lit up in triumph. At a year and three months old, she was Jace's elder by less than half a year, but every week made a difference for rapidly developing kraken younglings.

Her birth had been a memorable event; her parents, Jax and Macy, were a kraken and a human. She'd looked so strange despite her many similarities to her kraken brethren. Her hair and nose were unique among their kind — or had been, until Jace.

One look into Sarina's bright green eyes after her birth and Dracchus had been caught.

He'd never spent much time around younglings before Sarina. Now he seemed to be surrounded by them constantly.

"He's pretending to be Ikaros again," Melaina laughed. She was the eldest of the three children present at seven years old, and looked more and more like her mother, Rhea, with each passing month.

Ikaros, stretched out on the floor beside Melaina, lifted his head and cocked it. He was a prixxir — creatures that walked on four legs while on land, with small, flexible scales, a spikey fin along their spines, and long whiskers on their faces that were constantly in motion. Like the kraken, prixxir were able to breathe both underwater and in the air.

Dracchus coiled a tentacle around Jace's middle and lifted the youngling off the floor, raising him to eye level. The child swiped at Dracchus with his tiny, clawed fingers and intensified his growling.

"You are not doing it right," Dracchus said.

Jace stopped, arms dangling, and stared at Dracchus questioningly. It was the same inquisitive look that Arkon so often wore.

"Ikaros does not bite me," Dracchus explained. "Because I do not taste good, and he likes me."

Sarina giggled and reached toward Dracchus. He bent, offering her an arm, and lifted her when she latched on. Holding herself in place with her tentacles, she placed her hands on his cheeks and blew through her siphons. Dracchus mimicked her; he'd done so once, when she was very small, and she'd enjoyed it so much that they'd done it over and over again.

"Can we go out soon?" she asked. "I want to swim."

"That is for your mother and father to decide. I will go out soon, but I must journey far away, and I cannot bring you."

She frowned. "I want to go with you."

Jace squirmed. Dracchus ruffled the youngling's hair and let him back down before returning his attention to Sarina. "You are too small. This is your place for now."

"Will there be a hunting party?" Melaina asked. Ikaros perked upon hearing the word *hunt*, whiskers sweeping forward.

"No, not this time." A hunt would've been a simple thing to explain, but very little had been simple over the last year. "We have heard of a large boat and must see that it is not a danger to us."

Sarina coiled her tentacles tighter and wrapped her arms around Dracchus's neck. "I don't want you to go."

Dracchus had never understood the bond he and Sarina had formed, had never understood why she showed him so much affection or why he was compelled to show her the same. He was too inexperienced with younglings to know if it was normal behavior. He'd accepted it as a truth and moved on.

That acceptance had led him to unexpected experiences — like the pang in his chest now, an echo of the sorrow in her voice. He didn't want to leave her, but duty called him away.

"If I do not go, your father will go, and Jace's. And I do not want them to be away from you if they don't have to be."

Sarina's hold tightened.

"Is Randall going?" Melaina asked.

Dracchus shook his head. Randall, another human like Macy and Aymee, had become one of Dracchus's most trusted companions alongside Jax and Arkon, but this task required speed and stealth underwater that humans could not match.

"Randall and Ikaros will remain, also," he said. Staying behind would allow Randall more time with Melaina and her mother, Rhea, who had become Randall's mate.

"Will you be back?" Sarina asked against his shoulder.

His brow fell, and he frowned. However well as she articulated herself, Sarina was too young to have such concerns. Life had never been easy for the kraken, but their young were usually protected from the harsh realities of survival in the endless, unforgiving ocean for at least a few years after birth.

Perhaps things were worse than he'd led himself to believe.

"I will be back."

"Promise?"

He slid a finger under her chin and tilted it up. "Yes."

Her dark hair framed her face, long enough now to brush her shoulders. She met his gaze and smiled. "I will miss you."

Dracchus smiled in return; many of his people likely believed him incapable of such an expression. "I will miss you, as well. But you are strong."

The door behind Dracchus slid open. He turned to see Jax the Wanderer enter the room.

"Daddy!" Sarina's face brightened.

Jax grinned. "Dracchus will have to learn to live with one arm if you cling to him like that all the time."

"He could do it if he wanted to," she replied. "He's the strongest."

"But your father still bested me every time I challenged him." Dracchus worked his fingers between Sarina and his arm, mindful of his claws, and gently broke her hold. "Strength comes in many forms."

"Daddy's the fastest," Sarina said, holding her arms out for Jax.

Jax accepted the youngling from Dracchus. She climbed onto his back, latching her tentacles on his shoulders, and wrapped her arms around his forehead.

"I guess I don't need to ask why you're here," Macy said as she stepped around Jax. She smiled up at Sarina before looking at Dracchus. "You spoil them."

Dracchus tilted his head. Meat spoiled if it went too long without being eaten, but he wasn't sure what that had to do with the younglings.

Macy bent down and lifted Jace into her arms. "Thank you for watching them, Melaina."

"I love to spend time with them," Melaina replied, moving forward to brush her cheek against Jace's. "Ikaros helps."

Macy met Dracchus's eyes and smiled. "He's an excellent protector." She turned back to Melaina. "Why don't we take Jace to visit Aymee in the infirmary?"

Melaina grinned. "Okay. Can we play hunters-hunted when we're there?"

"Hunters!" Sarina bounced on her father's shoulders.

Ikaros sprang to his feet at Sarina's excited tone and bounded back and forth around Jax, chirruping.

Macy laughed. "Yes. We can play." She reached for Sarina, and the youngling climbed into her mother's waiting arm. As Macy leaned closer to Jax, their eyes met, and her smile changed.

Dracchus was still learning to read human expressions and body language, even after so much time spent around them, but he knew what Macy's smile meant.

Jax's understanding was evident in his grin.

"*We* can play tonight," she said softly.

"I will not let you break that promise." A flash of maroon passed over Jax's skin, there and gone in an instant.

She rose on her toes and brushed a kiss over his lips. "Never."

"Can I play, too?" Sarina asked.

Macy pulled away from her mate with a chuckle. "It will be after your bedtime, Sarina."

"And some games are only for your mother and father," Jax added.

Sarina pouted. Jace cuddled against Macy's chest and yawned wide, displaying his small, sharp teeth.

"I'll see you later," Macy said to Jax.

"I look forward to it." His gaze followed Macy as she, Melaina, and Ikaros exited the room.

The gleam in Jax's eyes was both familiar and utterly foreign to Dracchus. Macy and Jax had far surpassed the depth of the bonds shared by most mates long ago, and their connection seemed to strengthen with each passing day.

Dracchus couldn't begin to guess what that felt like. He adored Sarina and the other younglings, but what Jax and Macy shared was much different from anything the kraken had known before she entered their lives. Their relationship had sparked something, and more pairings had followed — Aymee and Arkon soon after, and then Rhea and Randall. Everyone around Dracchus was forming such bonds, it seemed. Building *families*.

Dracchus had no mate and did not share his den, but he recognized these relationships as something worth defending. As something that could strengthen their people and help them build a future in which they wouldn't merely survive, but thrive.

"You are planning to find the new boat, are you not?" Jax asked, turning his head toward Dracchus.

"I am."

"When are we leaving?"

"I will leave with a small party in the morning."

Jax frowned.

"Your place, for now, is here," Dracchus said. "You and Arkon have younglings and mates to protect, and the Facility is not safe for them with you away."

Brows falling low, Jax scowled. "Kronus's supporters have grown bold in their anger."

"We cannot assume they have limits on what they might attempt, should we lower our guards." Dracchus released a slow breath. These events had been set into motion when he pursued his suspicions more than a year ago and had discovered Jax involved with a human — Macy. They'd come to the Facility at his insistence to face the judgment of the kraken, and that had given rise to the human-opposed group led by Kronus.

Would Dracchus have done things differently, had he known what would follow?

It was a worrying question, the sort Arkon would undoubtedly contemplate for hours and hours. The lack of a clear answer only made it more troubling. If Dracchus had never made Macy come here, these connections, this growing family, would never have formed, but the divide amongst his people would never have opened.

Was the taste of this new lifestyle worth the current strife?

"What troubles you, Dracchus?"

"Everything," Dracchus grumbled.

Is it worth it?

Yes. The kraken would rise from the conflict stronger than before, with a newfound camaraderie that would empower them to face the future.

At least he hoped they would.

"Many of our people look to you for leadership," Jax said.

Dracchus shook his head and smiled despite his concerns. "It should be you to lead us, Wanderer. I never wanted to."

"All the more reason you should. I've always been selfish in the pursuit of my own fulfillment, but you have ever put our people before yourself."

"Kronus's supporters believe I put humans before our people."

"Kronus's supporters could best serve our people by feeding themselves to a razorback," Jax said. His skin rippled with crimson; the human-opposed group hadn't been shy about threatening the humans living in the Facility, including Jax's mate.

"That would be the easiest resolution," Dracchus agreed, "but I do not want any of our people to come to harm. Kraken or human."

"The more you speak, the more you support my belief that you should lead us."

Dracchus grunted. He would do what was necessary, what was *right*, just as always, but leadership...surely there were kraken more capable than he for such a role. Kraken possessing swift minds, like Jax and Arkon, or the wisdom of experience, like the elder, Ector.

"Come," Dracchus said. "Lets us catch up to your Macy. As close as the infirmary is, she should not be alone for long."

They moved into the corridor together. Doors stood at regular intervals in either direction, all leading to rooms almost identical to the one they'd just left. Long ago, before the kraken had claimed the Facility as their own, these rooms had served as dens for the humans who'd built this place. The hallways had been empty and silent for generations but were now often filled with the laughter of younglings and the warm conversation of friends because humans had returned. Even with less than ten people dwelling here, this section of the Facility felt *alive* for the first time in Dracchus's memory.

"How many will you take with you?" Jax asked.

"Myself and four others. Two are followers of Kronus."

"And you trust them?"

"Not at all." Dracchus slowed as they moved along the tunnel that led from the Cabins to the main structure, glancing at the dark water outside through one of the large windows. "But that will be two less to bother you here, and we will have them outnumbered."

"Might as well consider it six-to-one, if they move against you."

Dracchus smiled. "Sarina did say I am the strongest. I will be fine. More important that your mate and the younglings are safe."

When they entered the infirmary, Macy lay atop one of the beds, and Aymee was examining her with a scanner — a strange device which cast light on a person and made their insides visible.

It gave Dracchus pause; he'd only seen Aymee use the scanners when people were injured or ill.

"What is wrong?" Jax hurried to Macy's side. Sarina was curled against her mother, fast asleep.

"Jax! I wasn't expecting you to come," Macy said. "I said I'd see you later, in our den."

"We just wanted to make sure you arrived safely." He leaned down, studying the images produced by the scanner. "What is wrong, Macy?"

Dracchus approached the bed for a closer look, but he didn't know enough about human insides to tell if anything was amiss.

"Nothing's *wrong*, Jax," Arkon said, watching over Aymee's shoulder. Jace dozed in his arms.

Macy glanced at Aymee, who was grinning. "Well, I guess since you're here…"

"Show him!" Arkon's tentacles writhed on the floor, but he held his son steady.

"I was going to tell you tonight, after we were sure, but…" She moved a hand down her abdomen and pointed to something low on her pelvis.

Aymee manipulated a control, and an unseen speaker played a distinct sound — rapid thumps in time with the tiny, pulsing thing Macy was pointing at.

"What is… I do not understand. Why is her heartbeat so fast?" Jax asked.

"That," Aymee said, "is the reason I am going to be looking into contraceptives."

All three male kraken exchanged confused glances with one another.

"What are contraceptives?" Arkon asked.

It was unusual — and satisfying, if petty — to know there were words Arkon wasn't familiar with.

Aymee smirked. "Something to prevent this from happening more often than we initially thought possible."

"I'm pregnant." Smiling widely, Macy framed the pulsing spot with her hands. "This is our baby."

Jax leaned forward and tentatively reached toward the image. He placed the pads of his trembling fingers just below it, as though fearful of inflicting harm on the developing youngling.

Dracchus had no words; a warm, tingling feeling spread outward from his chest, numbing his mind with wonder. The ability to *know* with such surety was nothing short of amazing.

Jax pressed his forehead to Macy's and they both closed their eyes.

Another pang struck Dracchus. Was it wrong for him to want what they had? To crave a mate and younglings of his own? Before Macy and Sarina, he'd never known the joy of interacting with younglings, had never imagined the thrill and pride of watching them learn and grow, of *teaching* them.

His mild resentment — his *jealousy* — was shameful, but it refused dismissal.

This moment belonged to Jax and Macy, and he would not allow his own longing to impede upon their joy.

He left quietly and encountered no one else as he exited the Facility. The relative silence of the ocean closed in around him. He usually found comfort in it, in the feel of water surrounding him, easing his movements, but now it only made him miss the animated conversations that took place when he was with everyone else.

He'd never yearned for companionship; he'd done his duty and mated with many females since reaching maturity, but he'd formed no attachments.

Though he recognized the value of such a change, he didn't understand it.

Dracchus swam to the flooded building that held his den, illuminating his skin to light the dark corridors inside. He entered the room he'd claimed as his own years before. It was a familiar space, but now it seemed cold, empty, and uninviting. Lonely.

Growling, Dracchus cast aside his emotions. He needed to rest. Tomorrow's search was about his people's security, and it would require all his attention.

He couldn't allow the hollow ache in his chest to distract him.

CHAPTER 3

THE SURFACE WAS LIT WITH THE VIBRANT ORANGE OF THE approaching sunset when Vasil flared out his tentacles and flashed yellow to alert the others. Dracchus followed Vasil's gestures to the dark shapes in the distance — three boats, moving in close formation.

At Dracchus's signal, the kraken turned toward the boats and increased their depth. They gained on the vessels gradually as the sky bled from orange to red, pink, and violet.

The shrinking distance made one thing clear — the boat at the center was larger than the other two, larger than any watercraft Dracchus had ever seen.

He signed to his companions, warning them to remain cautious as they neared the boats. Despite its relatively low speed, the central craft left a massive wake, and the sound of it breaking through the water vibrated over Dracchus's skin. He adjusted his pace to match the ships' as his companions fell into place in his peripheral vision, two on each side.

The large boat had to be close to fifteen body-lengths from rear to front. Dracchus studied it closely. He wasn't familiar with the materials used in its construction, but there was something different about this ship compared to the others. Its wood planks seemed smoother, fresher, lighter in color.

Were there different types of wood, or was this freshly built?

There were no nets or fishing lines trailing behind the boats, no bait in the water. That alone wasn't alarming, but Macy had told Dracchus that the fishermen from her town only worked by day. Their relatively small vessels stood little chance of surviving a sudden storm after nightfall, even with the most experienced guides. Dozens of hunts had confirmed the information — the fishing boats always turned back toward The Watch by late afternoon.

These ships were moving *away* from the town.

He knew of only one reason for humans to be at sea as night fell. They were hunting kraken.

Dracchus clenched his jaw against the sudden flare of heat in his chest. His people had been hunters throughout their existence, and he would not allow them to become prey while his hearts still beat. No one deserved to be hunted and slaughtered simply because of what they were.

That included humans.

Despite his anger, he understood. The humans were acting against a potential threat. Dracchus had often guided his people to do the same.

Glancing up at the shadowed underside of the huge boat, he cast aside his rage and reviewed the situation. Assumptions could be dangerous — he didn't *know* what these humans were doing — but his instincts rarely failed him.

Dracchus looked toward Vasil and Neo, who swam to his right; the latter was one of Kronus's and had joined this scouting trip along with another human-opposed kraken, Garon. Their presence served as a reminder that, regardless of Dracchus's wishes, none of this was simple, and none of it would be easy. The kraken were divided amongst themselves.

Gut feelings, as Randall aptly called them, wouldn't be enough to convince either side.

Neo signed with hands and tentacles, adding a few flashes of color to emphasize his impatience. *Will we follow all night?*

Dracchus shook his head. They'd gain little in trailing the boats through the darkness, but confirmation that the humans had a massive ship was too little information to take away.

What did he know?

Humans were social creatures. They seemed helpless but to speak and interact with each other. Dracchus had grown to appreciate such behavior; he was fond of Macy, Aymee, and Randall, and enjoyed their conversation, even if they used words in ways he did not understand. Could their social nature prove a benefit to the kraken?

Did the potential reward outweigh the risk of attempting to exploit human nature?

We must go up, alongside them, he signed.

Vasil flashed yellow; *danger*.

Neo grinned. He raised a hand with fingers splayed and snapped them closed into a fist, punctuating it with a flicker of red. It was a simple sign, used often during hunts.

Make the kill.

For the first time since they'd departed that morning, unease twisted in Dracchus's gut.

He signaled *no* firmly, tinting his skin crimson to make it clear that he'd accept no disagreement. Until they broke the surface, there was no guessing how many humans were in the boats or how heavily they were armed. He wouldn't lead these kraken to needless deaths.

Stay close to them. Dracchus signed, gesturing to the boats. *Watch. Listen.*

Neo scowled, but he offered no argument.

Perhaps with more time, or assistance from Arkon or one of the humans at the Facility, Dracchus might have reached a clever, covert means to obtain the information they sought, but no one was around to offer innovative solutions. Vasil and Brexes were reliable and trustworthy, but they were no more prone to unconventional thought than Dracchus.

They needed to *know* the humans' purpose.

The thickening darkness on the surface would pair well with the kraken's natural camouflage. With patience and luck, there was a chance they'd be able to return home before the next sunrise.

Dracchus directed Vasil and Neo to the rightmost boat, Brexes and Garon to the left, and looked up at the central vessel — the humans' wooden behemoth. It seemed somehow fitting for Dracchus to take it on himself.

He altered his skin to match the dark water and swam upward. His tentacles brushed along the underside of the boat. Though the wood was smooth, his tentacles sensed every tiny imperfection in the material. He was used to the sleek metal and plastic of the Facility, to the soft sand and rough stone of the seafloor. Wood seemed unnatural to him, though he knew it came from land vegetation.

He drew himself along the curved wood until his head finally emerged from the water. Vasil and Neo surfaced alongside the smaller boat to the right, which sailed several body-lengths away from Dracchus, and signaled they were okay.

Only thin, weak moonlight provided any illumination from overhead, diluted by dark clouds. When Vasil and Neo matched their skin to the boat at their backs, even Dracchus had difficulty discerning their forms; this was enough light for a kraken to see by, but Randall had explained that human sight was comparatively poor in the dark.

They would be almost invisible to the humans.

Dracchus latched onto the side of the boat with tentacles and claws, pressing himself against it, and altered his camouflage to match the wood.

The sea sounded different from above; the wind filled his ears, but couldn't drown out the hissing and sighing of the ever-moving water, or the constant rush of boats traveling over its surface. Several humans stood on the right boat, bathed in the glow of a cylindrical light which hung from a post near the front of the craft. The light's reflection shimmered atop the water but barely penetrated the surrounding darkness.

Something about it raised Dracchus's suspicions; weren't there predatory sea creatures that used natural emissions of light — Arkon called it *bioluminescence* — to lure in prey?

One of the humans reached up and rang a bell hanging from the ship's central pole. Another bell on the largest ship answered with two measured rings, a pause, and two more rings. Dracchus knew it was some sort of signal but couldn't guess its meaning.

Dracchus tilted his head. Human voices drifted to him from somewhere above him, but they were nearly swallowed by the noise of wind and sea, and he couldn't make out the words.

The kraken's current positions were risky enough, but they'd be facing danger for nothing if they couldn't hear the humans' conversations.

He lifted his gaze, examining the hull. The weak moonlight cast the smooth planks along this side of the ship in shadow. They were designed to break water, not to be climbed, but he had to get closer.

Dracchus granted himself no time to second-guess his decision. He turned to face the hull, lifted his arms out of the water, and sank his claws into the wood. The wind chilled his exposed skin as he pulled himself out of the water. Spreading his tentacles wide, he climbed higher, creeping up a handspan at a time.

The human voices grew clearer with each beat of his hearts.

He glanced down. The water speeding by below him was disorienting, but the boat rocked to the familiar rhythm of the waves, easing the strangeness.

He pulled himself closer to the top, closed his eyes, and shifted all his focus to listening.

"...do this now, sir," someone said.

"Probably more. Just let them come," said another. Both were male.

"We have a chance at five, sir. Do we want to pass that up?"

A chance at five what?

Realization struck Dracchus a heartbeat later.

"Fine. Sound it," commanded the second human.

The bell on the largest ship sounded again, forgoing the measured beats of a few moments before in favor of a rapid, bone-rattling alarm.

Dracchus signed toward Neo and Vasil — *below, to the deep!* — but the humans were already in motion.

Footsteps thudded hurriedly on the deck of the large ship, and the humans in the smaller boat were at the siderail with strange guns in their hands.

"Below!" Dracchus roared.

Two of the humans on the small boat put feet up on the rail and leaned over the side, swinging their weapons toward Vasil and Neo, hampered by the length of their guns and the awkward angle. Two more men from the same vessel aimed at Dracchus.

There was a boom from overhead. Vasil jerked against the side of the smaller boat, something small jutting from his neck.

Dracchus released his hold on the hull as the men on the other boat fired. Two heavy thumps marked the impact of projectiles on the wood just before Dracchus hit the water. He darted toward Vasil and Neo; all he could do for Brexes and Garon now was hope they'd reacted quickly enough.

Projectiles hit the water around him. He ignored them and pressed forward, aiming for the blotch of crimson ahead — Neo, his color reflecting his fury.

Another gunshot sounded behind Dracchus.

Vasil pushed away from the boat sluggishly. Neo followed,

shaking his head sharply. A projectile was embedded in his shoulder, gleaming in the weak moonlight.

The men on the boat behind the pair raised a bulky gun. It went off with a *pop,* and a torrent of bubbles obscured Vasil and Neo.

The thrashing of the two kraken weakened quickly, and as the water cleared, Dracchus realized what had happened — the large gun had fired a net around Vasil and Neo, and their struggles had only entangled them further.

Dracchus dismissed conscious thought, giving over to instinct. The humans on the boat were the primary threat. Increasing his speed, he swam past his companions and surged up, leaping above the surface.

The humans along the rail stumbled back. Dracchus couldn't tell if they were moved by surprise or fear; their eyes were covered by strange devices made of plastic or glass.

He latched onto the side of the boat before the humans could react beyond their reflexive retreat and lashed out with arms and tentacles. Catching hold of limbs and clothing, he wrenched all four humans toward him. Their lower bodies struck the wood railing, levering their upper bodies over the top. Dracchus released his hold quickly, allowing all four to plunge into the water with flailing limbs and startled cries.

The pair of humans remaining on the boat stared at him with large eyes but remained frozen in place — one at the rear, and one at the wind-cloth pole.

Dracchus twisted to look at the large boat.

More humans with guns lined the siderail, but his attention was drawn immediately to one. A female. Even in the muted moonlight, her hair, woven into a thick cord, was a vibrant red. She wore a device over her eyes, too, and her full lips betrayed no emotion.

The other humans fired, their shots hitting the hull of the boat and the water around Dracchus.

The red-haired female's gun flashed with a hollow bang.

Piercing pain erupted on Dracchus's neck. He reached up, grasped the tube-like projectile, and tugged it out of his throat. Only the tip, a thin, glistening needle, had penetrated. He dropped it into the sea.

Drawing back the bolt of her gun with practiced ease, the female loaded another projectile.

Dracchus pushed off the boat and rushed toward his companions, ignoring the four humans frantically swimming toward their vessel. A tingling sensation radiated from his neck, creeping through his shoulder and along his arms, numbing his face. He shook his head, but the numbness did not diminish.

The net was attached to the small boat by a thick rope. He grasped the tether with a hand and a tentacle, pulling it taut, and raised his claws to it. His fingers moved sluggishly, refusing to bend fully.

Another hollow bang, and something impacted his right shoulder. He felt pressure, but no pain.

His vision blurred, and his unresponsive fingers slipped off the rope. Blinking, he swung his gaze to his companions. Their struggles had ceased.

Had they been poisoned?

A fire ignited in Dracchus's gut. He turned toward the large boat and roared, forcing all his strength, all his will, into a headlong charge toward the red-haired female.

She didn't flinch. Her gun boomed.

A heavy blow forced the air from Dracchus's lungs, and darkness claimed him.

LARKIN TORE off her goggles and stared, wide-eyed, as the creature collapsed in the dark water. Her heart pounded, and she had to force her ragged breaths through a dry, constricted throat.

She'd hunted animals of all sizes, had faced down beasts that could topple trees when they charged, had stalked predators so quiet that they could only be heard in the space between breaths. She'd almost lost her life on many occasions.

But she'd never hunted anything that was intelligent enough to prioritize its actions, had never hunted anything that looked at her with such intelligent, focused rage.

Shouts rose around her, and boots thumped on the deck. A net gun fired with a low pop. The net wrapped around the dark form in the water, but even that didn't ease her; it had taken three tranquilizers to stop the creature, and they'd balanced the dosage to make each dart strong enough to knock out several full-grown men.

Larkin lowered her rifle, resting its barrel on the railing to still the tremors in her arms.

"The other two escaped, commander," one of the rangers called over the other voices. "Got out of scanner range."

Larkin turned her head in time to see her father and Ranger Dane pass behind her, heading toward the back end of the ship. She pushed away from the rail and followed them.

Nicholas spat out a curse. "Get the rest of them secured and on this boat. I want them locked up before they come to."

Rangers scrambled to fulfill his orders. There was a sense of cautious excitement amongst them; the few townsfolk from The Watch who'd agreed to come along to help operate the ships were more reserved, exchanging worried glances with each other.

Larkin frowned. The locals had told the rangers that two young women from town had been taken by the kraken, often in overly-dramatic tales of nighttime abductions during a terrifying storm, but the families of the missing women had given a very different take.

The women had gone willingly.

She'd dismissed that as a coping mechanism, a mental shield against the loss of their daughters, but if the kraken were intelligent enough to speak and reason...

Larkin shouldered through the crowd gathered at the center of the ship. At the center of the group, several men guided a dripping net down from a pulley. Four rangers anchored the rope on the other end, leaning back to use their weight to counter the black kraken's bulk. They lowered the net into the pool of seawater on the deck and opened the net.

The creature lay in a heap of tangled limbs, completely still apart from its slow, shallow breathing. Several nearby rangers pointed their rifles at the beast. It took three of them to roll the creature onto its back, using the butts of their rifles for leverage.

"Fucker is huge!" someone said.

Larkin stared at the kraken. Its skin was black, with gray stripes on its tentacles, arms, and head. Its broad shoulders led down to a tapered waist. Based on its musculature, she had no doubt it was male; she was more shocked by how *human* it appeared once she looked past the obvious differences.

One of the rangers approached the kraken with a large metal collar. Another man lifted its head, allowing Larkin a glimpse of the creature's face — a wide mouth, a hairless brow, and only a pair of holes where its nose should have been — before her view was blocked.

The collar barely fit around its neck.

A heavy hand fell upon her shoulder, startling her.

"Good work, ranger," her father said.

She turned her head toward him. The frustration had faded from his expression, but a worrisome gleam remained in his eyes. Larkin missed Randall with all her heart, but Nicholas Laster seemed obsessed.

"The couple that got away wasn't your fault," he continued. "You did your job exceptionally. Two and a half damned weeks out on this water, and it finally paid off. I'm proud of you, Elle."

A flicker of pride swelled within her at his praise, but it quickly subsided.

"What are you going to do with them now?" She looked

forward as six men grasped the net under the creature and hauled it toward the ramp leading below deck, their muscles straining.

"We're going to establish them in their new quarters and ask them some questions when they wake up." The tightness creeping into Nicholas's expression offered Larkin no comfort.

"I heard this one shout a warning to the others. Cyrus was right. They do speak our language."

"Well, we'll find out if they know more than one or two words soon enough."

"Father, what are y—"

"We're done here, ranger. Hit your bunk. You've earned some rest." Before she could say anything more, he turned and stepped away, barking orders at the others as they hauled the second net out of the water.

She clamped her teeth together to suppress her hurt. Things had changed drastically since they'd learned of Randall's disappearance, but the rift between Larkin and her father seemed to grow daily. In his quest to find his son, he was pushing his daughter away.

Larkin brushed the stray bits of hair from her face and looked out over the silver-lit sea. Despite her efforts, her gaze drifted back to the kraken.

This didn't feel like an accomplishment.

It felt *wrong*.

CHAPTER 4

A dull throbbing between his temples drew Dracchus up from impenetrable blackness. Awareness returned slowly. His mouth was dry, which he'd never experienced before, and his eyelids were too heavy to open. His aching arms were drawn up with his hands to either side of his head, held in place by metal bindings at his wrists. A larger piece of metal encircled his neck. His tentacles were also bundled together tightly by a rough, irritating material, leaving no room for them to move independently. The whole bundle felt like it was anchored at his waist.

Clenching his teeth, he forced his eyes open. His vision adjusted so slowly that he wasn't sure if the gloom was in the air around him or merely a result of his own grogginess.

Vertical bars ran in front of him and to either side. He turned his head, but the collar would only allow a small degree of movement. He tugged at his bindings tentatively; they offered no give and were likely attached to the cool piece of metal at his back.

"Finally awake, *leader*?" Neo asked. "We should have killed them. All we did was hand ourselves over to our enemies."

Dracchus shifted his gaze toward Neo's voice. The other kraken was in an identical cage on the other side of a small walk-

35

way, bound in the same manner as Dracchus. His skin was a muted red, signaling his displeasure.

The cell beside Neo's held Vasil, who maintained his normal, pale gray coloring. Vasil's only outward sign of distress was the bulging of his jaw muscles.

Dracchus counted six more cages, all empty. He hoped that meant Brexes and Garon had escaped.

He inhaled deeply, and the faint ache in his chest as his lungs swelled reminded him of the projectiles he'd been shot with. What sort of poison had they contained? How much time had passed? He recalled charging toward the large ship, recalled the red-haired woman and the thump of her gun, and then…nothingness.

"Are either of you injured?" he asked.

"Uncomfortable, but unharmed," Vasil replied.

Neo growled. "I am going to—"

An opening door cut off Neo's threat. Light flooded the room — not the flickering fire the humans had used on the small boat, but a handheld light of the sort found in the Facility. *Electric,* according to Arkon.

The intensity of the light impaired Dracchus's vision, turning the humans behind it into dark, indistinct shapes. When they shined the beam directly at him, he squeezed his eyes shut against the sting.

"Looks like they're awake," one of the humans said.

"Good. I was afraid we'd have to wait another day on the big one," said another, and Dracchus recognized the voice — it was the human who'd given the command to attack. "He took three darts before he finally went down."

The light shifted as the human holding it crouched in front of Dracchus's cell. Dracchus slitted his eyes, meeting the human's gaze through the bars.

"That's some freaky shit," the man said, scowling. "How long do you think these things have been around, commander?"

The leader stepped closer and stared down at Dracchus, his

expression hard. "Doesn't matter, Ranger Dane. They make the wrong move, and there won't be any of them left."

Dracchus balled his fists and bared his teeth.

"Does that piss you off?" the commander asked.

Clenching his jaw, Dracchus maintained his silence. He longed to act upon the fury roiling inside him. He wouldn't tolerate even the vaguest threats against his people, but the complexity of this situation extended well beyond the fact that he was currently immobilized by his bonds.

"I know you understand me," the commander continued. "I see it in your eyes. You want to kill me. Imagine how much I'd love to gut *you*, right here, right now, and force you to watch the whole thing."

Ranger Dane glanced up at the commander. His tongue slipped out and ran over his downturned lips before he stood up and backed away a step, keeping the light on Dracchus.

"Maybe I should start with your friends." The commander gestured toward Neo and Vasil.

Neo growled and thrashed against his bonds.

"Look at how red that one is," Ranger Dane said, staring over his shoulder.

"We have made no move against you," Dracchus said, calling the humans' attention back to him.

"So, you know how to speak *and* how to lie." The commander's eyes gleamed with reflections of Ranger Dane's light. "Six of my men are missing. You're going to tell me where they are."

"I only cast four into the water."

The commander grasped the bars and leaned forward. "You know that's not what I'm talking about! They came looking for *you*, and *you* know where they are now!"

"I cannot help you," Dracchus said, keeping his tone as even. Despite his restraints, his instinct was to meet this human's aggression with aggression of his own, to rise to the unspoken challenge that had been issued.

The commander gritted his teeth. "You have information about them. All of you do. And we will extract that information by any means necessary. If you cooperate, we'll be merciful. I understand the value of that. But this is your only chance for it."

"We will slaughter you," Neo snarled.

"Close your mouth," Dracchus growled. "Give them *nothing*."

"Is that how you want it to be, then?" the commander asked, looking from Neo and back to Dracchus.

Neo glared at Dracchus, lips pressed into a tight line, but said nothing more. Vasil remained silent, head slightly bowed. His siphons and nostrils flared in quiet anger.

The commander stepped back from the cage. "Ranger Dane, go get Sanson, Brock, and Altez. Our guests are tough. We might need some extra muscle to persuade them to cooperate."

With a muttered acknowledgment, the human holding the light strode out of the room, plunging the place back into shadow. The commander clasped his hands behind his back and paced between the cells.

Dracchus strained against his bindings, but without any way to anchor himself, he couldn't generate enough force to break them.

"You are without a doubt the most incredible things we've ever hunted," the commander said, boots thudding on the floor in a steady rhythm, "and we've hunted damned near everything on this planet. You're intelligent. Maybe as intelligent as a human. So, you should be smart enough to know that this isn't going to be pleasant.

"I'll ask again," he stopped before Dracchus's cell, "where are my missing rangers?"

Dracchus met the man's gaze and pressed his lips together. Anger burned in his chest, speeding his hearts, but he would not give it voice. These humans did not represent the entirety of their race any more than Neo and Kronus represented the kraken. The thought did little to ease his fury.

The Commander clutched the bars and brought his face closer. "Where is Randall Laster?"

Hearing that name very nearly startled Dracchus into betraying its familiarity. At the edge of his vision, Neo stirred, skin pulsing crimson and black; the issuance of a challenge that could not be faced.

Dracchus focused on the commander. He'd seen eyes very much like this human's many times over the last year They were Randall's eyes.

This man was Randall's sire.

The commander's intensity dwindled at the sound of footsteps near the doorway. He eased back from the bars as Ranger Dane and three burly humans entered the room, plucking something from his belt — a small, thin piece of metal with toothlike protrusions at one end. He inserted the object into a box on the door. There was a click, and the door swung open. He turned away and repeated the motion for the other occupied cages.

Dracchus wasn't sure what the tiny device was; apart from the few that required a certain pattern to be entered on a keypad, all the doors in the Facility opened at the touch of a button. Did the commander's device fulfill a similar function?

Ranger Dane stopped beside the commander, who directed each of the other humans to enter a cage. The broad-shouldered human with yellow hair — Brock, according to the Commander — loomed over Dracchus with an indecipherable expression on his face.

"Rangers, introduce yourselves to our guests," the Commander said, once again pacing between the cells.

Brock moved with surprising speed, slamming his fist into Dracchus's cheek.

The kraken's head snapped aside, forcing the collar into his neck. The taste of blood spread over his tongue; his teeth had cut the inside of his mouth.

Dracchus looked up at the human, whose large frame obscured the view of the other cells. Neo snarled and growled on the other side of the room, rattling his bindings.

"Release me and try that again," Dracchus said evenly.

Brock snickered, mouth tilting into a smirk.

"However big you are, however strong you are, *we* are the hunters," the commander said. "Give me the information I want, and we'll see about altering our relationship. Until then, you're nothing but animals in these cages. Six of my rangers went missing."

Brock hammered a fist into the other side of Dracchus's face.

"Cyrus Taylor."

A blow to Dracchus's gut.

"Hassan Stone."

Another.

"Ward Bowman. Joel Tatum. Chad Booth."

Each name was punctuated by a heavy strike.

"And Randall Laster!" the Commander concluded in a shout.

Lifting his knee, Brock kicked Dracchus in the face, his boot scraping skin. Warm blood oozed from the wounds. Flexing his abdomen, he swung his bundled tentacles toward Brock's feet. The human grabbed onto the bars, holding himself upright, and scowled.

Despite the deep aches in his body, Dracchus curled and stretched his fingers and bared his teeth, offering a challenge of his own. "Your body will break before mine, human."

"We'll see about that," the commander said, nodding toward his men. "Let's go over this again..."

LARKIN CONCEALED herself behind a stack of crates as her father and four other rangers emerged from below deck. The commander's mouth was set in a harsh line, his movements were tense, and his eyes burned. She shifted her attention to the others, and her heart stopped.

The glow of Jason's flashlight made the blood on their fists, shirts, and pants glisten.

Dad, what have you done?

Nicholas called another man over — Lance Oliver, a young, inexperienced ranger — and spoke with him quietly. Lance nodded, grabbed his rifle, and positioned himself beside the door leading down to the brig. They'd designed the bowels of the ship to keep the holding cells separate from everything else; nothing could come or go from that room without alerting the guard posted above.

Larkin waited until her father was out of sight before stepping out of her hiding place. She crossed the deck, heading directly for the brig.

Lance straightened as she approached. "Miss Laster."

"*Ranger* Laster," she corrected. As petty as it was, any guilt she might've felt for what she was about to do faded in the face of that slip-up.

"Sorry." He cleared his throat, cheeks reddening. "W-what can I help you with?"

"I want to see the creatures."

The color that had just entered his face quickly drained. "I don't think anyone's supposed to go down there right now, Ranger Laster."

"That might be true for the others, but I am Commander Laster's second, and I want to question them myself."

Swallowing, Lance swung his gaze from side to side, as though her father would materialize to sort this all out.

"You know the commander places high value on respect for the command structure, Ranger Oliver," she said. "Do I need to report your insubordination to him?"

"N-no!" Lance licked his lips and squared his shoulders. "Please, just be careful down there. Those things are *strong*."

"I will." She placed her hand on Lance's forearm and smiled at him. "Thank you."

His blush returned, but he otherwise maintained his composure.

She walked through the wide entryway; the door had been left open since the creatures were hauled below and would likely remain so while the weather was fair. Her fingers trailed along the wall as she moved down the ramp into the room below. A single electric lantern hung on the wall, illuminating the door into the brig, which was secured with a thick wooden bar.

Larkin raised the bar, swinging it aside and latching it in an upright position. She paused. A strange sense of foreboding filled her chest, amplifying the beating of her heart. Taking a deep breath, she pushed the door open and stepped inside.

The metallic scent of blood hit her nose immediately, mixing with the briny air and the odor of recently treated wood to create something overwhelming.

Father, what *have you done?*

The room was dark; the lone window, high on the wall opposite the door, allowed only a sliver of moonlight inside. She stepped back to remove the lantern from its hook and reentered the brig. The white lantern light reflected on the metal bars, which cast wide, vertical shadows on the creatures inside the cells.

Two kraken were caged on her right — the first two she'd hit with tranquilizers. The closest cell held the gray one; the creature hung limp in its bonds, eyes closed, blood and saliva oozing from its mouth.

Larkin! frowned and stepped closer, raising the lantern to shift the shadows away from the kraken's face.

The creature in the next cell snarled and thrashed in its bindings. Larkin leapt back, hitting the bars behind her. Dark splotches of drying blood stood out against the kraken's crimson skin.

For all its fury, its struggles quickly weakened, and its head finally lolled back as it sagged in its cuffs. Its skin faded to brown, and its chest heaved with short, shallow breaths.

Despite her startlement, Larkin's heart ached for the creature. She looked between the two kraken. It was easy to imagine them as humans in those cells, with their heads bowed and their tentacles bound. Her stomach clenched; her father had done this.

Something released a low growl behind her.

Larkin moved away from the cell at her back and turned, holding up the lantern.

The largest of the three kraken was inside, the one with the black skin and pale stripes. Though its amber eyes were narrowed, they glowed with reflected light, and its intense gaze was directed at her.

Not *it; him.*

His coloring made it difficult to assess his condition, but the glistening patches on his cheeks and lips indicated open wounds. She leaned closer, and as the light shifted the shadows over him, she realized that parts of his face were swollen.

"You have come to relish your victory?" His voice was a deep rumble that raised gooseflesh on her skin, but his words were slightly slurred.

"My victory?"

"Your shots brought me down."

She pushed away her pang of guilt. The kraken were the only lead, the only hope of locating Randall and the others. The tranquilizers had ensured these creatures survived capture.

"They did," she agreed, "and both your companions."

He closed his eyes and curled his hands into fists, but seemed otherwise relaxed. His position couldn't be comfortable. She suspected that all three kraken had been hit with lower doses of tranquilizer in an attempt to keep them docile.

"Leave," he grumbled. "Enjoy your victory while it lasts. The next will be mine."

Larkin ran her gaze over him. She didn't doubt that men would die if he broke free. She'd seen him leap onto the other boat and pluck four men over the railing with little effort, had witnessed the ferocity of his charge despite having been hit with two tranquilizers.

Powerful wasn't an adequate description of this kraken.

"Did you tell the commander where the rangers were?" she asked, refusing to back down.

"Leave," he repeated.

She stepped closer to his cell, gripping the bottom of the lantern to hide the trembling in her arms. "Did you tell him where Randall is? Is he alive?"

The tube-like protrusions on the sides of his head opened wide as he released a long, slow breath.

"Is Randall alive?" she asked again, trying to keep the desperation from her voice.

"Leave me!" he roared, opening his eyes as crimson flared over his skin. His huge muscles flexed, and veins bulged; the whole ship seemed to groan.

Larkin stumbled back. Without another word, she walked out of the room, closing the door behind her and slamming the wooden bar into place. She leaned back against the door and closed her eyes, chest heaving with rapid breaths.

She couldn't deny her fear, though that wasn't what had made her run. Her exit had been fueled by guilt and grief. Randall was still missing, they weren't any closer to finding him, and a year of that uncertainty, that *need* to know, had taken its toll.

That familiar pain had paired well with the new — *Larkin* had put the kraken in those cages. They weren't mindless beasts, they weren't sources of food. The kraken were *people*. And the big one blamed her, acted as though she relished her actions.

Her father had told her they would be hunting monsters.

These were not monsters. Though they were clearly capable of viciousness, these were not the ferocious, unreasoning creatures Cyrus's report had depicted.

This was no different than hunting, caging, and beating humans from any village on Halora.

The krakens' blood was on her hands just as much as it was on her father's.

CHAPTER 5

Ranger Dane swung his bucket, splashing its contents through the bars and into Dracchus' face. The water was cold, refreshingly so, but the kraken would not express gratitude. The humans were not doing this out of kindness; it was a simple matter of preserving Dracchus and his companions until they gave up the information the commander was after.

Vasil gasped when another bucketful of seawater hit him. His siphons gaped open and closed. Streams of bloody water poured down his face, trickling over his neck and chest. One of his eyes was swollen shut, and his lips were split in two different places.

Dracchus bore similar wounds, and they stung as seawater ran over them. If nothing else, the sting confirmed he was alive.

Time had become strange for him; he knew this was the second day since waking in this cage, the second day of *questioning*, but his mind couldn't reconcile the time that had passed. How could two days feel like years?

The Commander stood in the space between the cells, wiping blood from his knuckles with a rag. He'd joined in the beatings today, moving between the cages to assist Brock, Sanson, and Altez in their work.

Despite the punishment they'd endured, none of the kraken — not even Neo, whose rage was growing as his body flagged — had given up any information. Dracchus was proud of them. They were remaining strong in the face of this pain.

He didn't let his thoughts dwell on the notion that his pride meant nothing now.

"I am disappointed and impressed," the commander said as he folded the bloody rag. He extended his fingers, staring thoughtfully at his split knuckles. "We'll see if you break tomorrow."

Neo fought against his restraints. "We will break *you*, human!" he shouted as the humans, without a backward glance, walked out of the room. "We will gut you! Feed upon your—"

The door slammed shut, and Neo's words ended in a snarl. The kraken's voice was raw, but that hadn't stopped him from making his threats.

Did Neo realize that the humans were intelligent enough to see through his fury and recognize the distress beneath the surface?

"Save your energy," Dracchus said.

"Every one of them will die!" Neo growled. "First those on this boat, then on the other two. We will return to the Facility and slaughter those humans as well. It is because of that *slit* Jax brought back that this is happening!"

"I will not tolerate threats against them." Dracchus narrowed his eyes at Neo, ignoring the sharp pain as a cut on his forehead widened.

"How can you defend them after this?" Neo shouted.

"They are not responsible for the actions of others," Vasil said quietly.

"Now you speak? Now you have something to say?" Neo flashed his color in challenge at Vasil. "You haven't uttered a word to these humans, but now you will speak against me?"

"You would allow your hate to bring you to kill innocents," Vasil replied, looking at the angry kraken. "Where is your honor?"

"Honor is—"

"The way of our people," Dracchus said. "You and your lot claim to uphold our traditions, but you have lost your honor. You are no better than the humans holding us."

Neo growled threateningly but said no more.

Dracchus closed his eyes. With the swaying of the ship, he could *almost* imagine himself riding the waves, could almost taste the salty breeze. The sound of water against the hull was still strange to him, but at least he *knew* it was the sea. That had to be comfort enough for now.

Breathing slowly, he reviewed the day's wounds, exploring each pain individually. The damage inflicted on the first day had healed overnight. He expected today's damage would be nearly gone by the next morning, leaving what Arkon would call a *blank canvas.*

He missed Arkon and Jax. It was a strange feeling for him, especially after years of conflict with them, but he couldn't deny how much he wished they were near. They'd proven more dependable than anyone else he knew. They'd become his friends.

They were where they belonged, defending what was important to them, what was important to all kraken — the future.

The sound of the door drew Dracchus out of his contemplative state. He opened his eyes to see a dark figure enter the room — a human carrying a light. The cord of red hair hanging over the figure's shoulder was the first detail to come into focus as his vision adjusted.

What blame should he place upon this female? She'd fired the shots that incapacitated him, Neo, and Vasil. She'd been essential to their capture. He should've hated her.

But there'd been something in her voice the night before that had given him pause.

Every kraken hunting party was led by an individual, and that individual's decisions were to be obeyed for the duration of the hunt. That had been the kraken way for as long as anyone could remember. What if it was the same amongst the humans?

The commander led this massive hunting party. The female had followed his orders, had carried out his plan. She was an enemy to the kraken, but were all enemies equal? Was it possible for her to be an…unwilling enemy?

The female closed the door and raised her lantern to look at Vasil; he simply turned his head away from her. Neo snapped his teeth when the light touched him. Dracchus averted his eyes from the harsh glare when she drew closer to him. Pausing, she placed the lantern on the floor — turning it so it did not shine directly upon him — and approached his cell.

She stared at him in silence for a long while; Dracchus felt her gaze lingering even after he tipped his head back and shut his eyes.

"Did you tell the Commander where the rangers are?" she asked.

"Why do you assume we know?" Dracchus replied.

"We received a report about your kind from one of our own, Cyrus Taylor. He dispatched another ranger to our base of operations right before he and his group left The Watch in search of kraken. They never came back."

"They're dead," Neo said.

Dracchus opened his eyes and met Neo's gaze; all their people knew what had happened in the Broken Cavern, when Jax, Arkon, and Dracchus battled the rangers. They knew that only one of the rangers had left that place alive.

Neo looked up at the female, who had turned to face him. "And you will join them soon."

"Are they dead?" she demanded. "All of them?"

With a malicious, blood-stained smile, Neo looked away from her.

She grasped the bars of Neo's cell, posture tense. "Answer me!"

The kraken's only answer was to widen his grin.

She turned back to Dracchus's cage and banged a hand on it. He finally looked up at her; she stood with her forehead against the metal, face downturned, one hand grasping a bar above her head. She remained that way for a while, silent and unmoving. Her breaths stirred the small strands of hair that had fallen from her braid.

"What is your name?" she asked.

Dracchus studied her features. Delicate red brows, a shade darker than her hair, were furrowed above her closed eyes. Long, black lashes rested on her pale cheeks, and now that she was closer to him and he was no longer consumed by his anger, he realized that her skin was dusted with tiny, light brown specks, most prominent across her nose and cheeks.

None of the humans he'd seen up close were like this one. Her hair was vibrant, her skin unique, and he found himself strangely drawn to her. What did she look like in full light? How would it change her coloring; would it make her hair shine?

Though he was intrigued by her, he offered no answer to her question.

She sighed. "My name is Larkin. Elle to my friends and family. Not that I have many." Her eyes opened and met his.

The clear, piercing blue of her gaze was familiar to him. They were the same as the commander's. The same as Randall's.

Elle.

This was Randall's sister.

Dracchus's mind was empty for an instant. He opened his mouth to say something, but could not find words.

"Do you have family?" she asked.

"Yes," he replied, though he was only distantly aware of his response.

She searched his face and frowned. "Sometimes you will do anything to protect the ones you love. Go to any extreme. But that doesn't always make it right."

Dracchus had the sense that she was speaking as much to herself as to him.

"What can I do?" she asked.

"About what?" Dracchus couldn't read her expression, and it made her seemingly simple question difficult to unravel.

"You can free us, you filthy human slit!" Neo snarled.

She was unfazed by Neo's outburst. "I can't do that."

"Water," Vasil said.

She met Dracchus's eyes, as though for confirmation.

He nodded. How had Arkon explained it? "We *hydrate* by being in water. Seawater."

LARKIN PUSHED AWAY from the bars and looked toward the barrel standing in a shadowed corner. She was already disobeying her father's wishes by being in here; pushing her defiance a little further couldn't make things any worse. She *couldn't* stand for this.

She walked to the barrel and raised the lid. The briny scent of saltwater struck her as she glanced at the big kraken. "I can't get into your cell to help you drink this."

"Splash it on us," the grey kraken said.

"Okay." Setting the lid aside, she picked up one of the nearby buckets and dunked it into the barrel. She carried the filled container to the gray kraken's cell, took hold of it in both hands, and splashed the water through the bars.

The tubular protrusions on the sides of his head flared with his deep breath.

She repeated the process for the crimson kraken, ignoring his insults and aggression. He couldn't fulfill his threats.

At least not now.

After filling the bucket for the third time, she went to the black kraken's cell. He'd watched her the entire time, silent and calm.

He held Larkin's gaze for a moment before she threw the water into his cell.

She returned the bucket, slid the lid back into place, and gripped the rim of the barrel with both hands. Leaning on her arms, she looked at the kraken with her brows drawn.

The red one had calmed, and his color was back to the brown she'd seen the night before, but he continued glaring at her. The gray kraken had closed his eyes and tilted his head back against the wall.

"It is too late to win us with kindness," the black kraken said. Despite his imprisonment and his visible wounds, his strength and bearing seemed undiminished. Her father had inflicted pain on this creature, likely great pain, but had not broken him.

"I know," she replied. The shame she felt for her part in all this wouldn't provide these creatures any comfort.

"Then what do you seek to accomplish?"

"I'm not sure." Larkin wanted answers, but that hadn't been her sole motivation in coming here again. She couldn't watch this suffering and remain inactive. "I'm sorry. I know it doesn't mean anything to you, but I am. This...this is not how I thought it would be."

What had she expected? Her father had been trying to capture kraken for months, growing increasingly desperate as the search for Randall and the lost rangers remained fruitless. Nicholas Laster hadn't been in his right mind — perhaps for longer than she cared to admit — but the idea had appealed to Larkin, too. Randall was alive *somewhere*, and the chance was as good as any that he had been taken by the kraken, like the two local women.

Capturing a kraken and squeezing information out of it was their way to find Randall.

But that had been before she knew anything about these people. Before she'd understood how intelligent they were, how *human*. Even after receiving Cyrus's report, the kraken had remained a myth, something that any rational person couldn't quite believe. But now that she'd seen them up close, *spoken* to them…they were so much more than she could've imagined.

And they were being tortured. Why hadn't her father told her this was his plan?

He knew I'd fight him.

She would have seen the wrongness of this immediately, even if the kraken weren't thinking, talking creatures. Nothing deserved to be caged and tortured.

The black kraken frowned, his amber eyes surprisingly thoughtful despite the swollen flesh around them.

Larkin looked away and pinched the bridge of her nose. If she released the kraken — she didn't have the key, but the locks, although sturdy, were simple — she'd be giving up her only chance of finding Randall. Though they'd yet to give up any information, these kraken knew *something*. She felt it in her bones.

But how can I condone this?

She needed to speak to her father. There had to be another way, they just had to figure it out.

Larkin dropped her hand and barely contained a sardonic laugh. Commander Laster would likely take this opportunity to throw her bleeding heart in her face.

Pushing away from the barrel, Larkin approached the black kraken's cell and bent down to retrieve the lantern. She felt his gaze on her back like it was a physical thing as she rose and walked to the door. She reached for the door.

"I am called Dracchus," the black kraken said.

Larkin paused, fingertips on the handle.

"Thank you…Dracchus." Without looking back, she exited the room, closed the door, and gently lowered the bar into place.

At the top of the ramp, she offered Lance a smile. He hadn't questioned her when she'd come to the brig this time; he'd greeted her, flashed a smile, and told her to stay safe. If Nicholas knew about any of this, Lance would be reprimanded — not only for allowing Larkin to see the kraken, but for flirting with her.

As the commander's daughter, Larkin was off limits. That hadn't stopped men from displaying interest — the knowledge that they could enjoy a woman's body without risking any *complications* was tempting for some, even when the potential *consequences* involved dealing with her father afterward.

After bidding Lance a good night, Larkin crossed the deck, boots thumping hollowly on the planks. She stopped at the door to her father's quarters and lifted her hand to knock when she heard voices inside. Lowering her hand, she leaned closer to the door.

"...heal too quickly. We need to take this to the next level," Brock said from inside.

"It's good they heal quickly," replied Nicholas. "Doesn't do us any good if they die before they break."

"My hands are fucking killing me, sir," Sanson grumbled. "We don't heal like they do. We got to shift our tactics."

"At least let us use some blades, or clubs, or *something*," Brock urged. "They know they'll just heal from a few cuts and bruises. Maybe if we threaten them with something more, they'll talk."

"We don't want to give them the satisfaction of seeing us too banged up to beat on them, do we?" Altez asked.

Nicholas grunted thoughtfully.

Larkin could picture him standing at the window, focused on a point of nothingness near the watery horizon, hands clasped behind his back. That he was considering any of those suggestions made her stomach twist into knots.

"No," he finally replied, and his pause after that word was long enough to instill Larkin with false hope, "we don't want that. Not even the smallest victory for them to latch onto. We'll explore new options tomorrow. See what kind of damage they can take."

Larkin lifted the latch and shoved the door open. It banged against the wall.

"How could you do this?" she demanded, stalking into the room. The men inside swung their eyes toward her; Brock,

Sanson, Altez, and her father. Nicholas Laster indeed stood at the window, hands clasped at the small of his back, gazing at her over his shoulder.

"Were you eavesdropping?" Altez asked, scowling.

"You three are dismissed," Larkin said, not looking away from her father. They didn't move, but the commander didn't object. Fury filled her. "I said you are dismissed!"

Averting their gazes, Brock, Sanson, and Altez shuffled out. Larkin slammed the door behind them and dropped the latch into place.

Nicholas turned to face her. "I'll give you thirty seconds to explain just what the hell you think you're doing, ranger."

"What are *you* doing?" Larkin advanced until only the desk separated them. "Blades? Clubs? *See what kind of damage they can take?* You're torturing them!"

"I'm doing whatever is necessary to find your brother!" He slammed his fists on the desk.

Larkin didn't flinch; she held his gaze. "This isn't the way!"

"And who are you to tell me that? To judge me? My son, your *brother*, and you're going to tell me not to look for him?"

"I'm not telling you not to look for him, but torture isn't the way. They are *people*! How can you not see that?"

He jabbed his finger toward the door, the cords of his neck standing out. "They are *monsters*! How can *you* not see that? They'll tell me where Randall is before I'm done, and when we get him back, we'll hunt down every last one of those abominations."

Larkin stared at the man, this *stranger*, before her. "The only monster I see is you."

His jaw muscles bulged. "What did you just say to me, girl?"

"My father would never hurt another human being. Would never inflict such needless suffering. Whether you believe it or not, they are people. You're just too blinded by anger and desperation to admit it."

"You are speaking to your commanding officer," he said

through gritted teeth, "and you don't know anything about necessity. You don't know anything about this world! I gave you a good life, you and your brother both. And this is my payment for it? I did everything I could to make you strong, to make you a survivor, and what is there to show?

"You're going to shed tears for those monsters, for our enemies? You're going to turn against me and abandon your brother?"

Larkin slapped her hand on the desk. "I want him found just as much as you, damnit! But this is not how we're going to accomplish that!"

"If that was true, you'd be helping me, not fighting me every step of the way."

"I have done everything you asked!" she screamed. "*Everything!* But *this*, I will not do. I will not make myself into the monster you've become!"

Nicholas shoved himself around the table and loomed over her, grabbing the front of her shirt. "You will recant that statement and apologize to me *immediately*."

Larkin glared at him. "No."

"Maybe I've been too easy on you. Sheltered you too much. Maybe I should show you what's supposed to happen when you oppose your commander."

"What would Mother think if she saw you now?"

"What did you just say?" The unstable gleam in his eyes intensified.

"This is not the man she loved," Larkin said, throat tight. Despite her anger, tears filled her eyes. "This is not my father."

His face reddened, and he raised his free hand, curling his fingers into a fist.

Something in Larkin broke. Her father had never raised a hand to her, would never have considered it. He'd always been a hard man, but he'd never been cruel. She mourned for the man she'd known.

Seconds passed; she didn't know if he'd follow through and hit her, but she didn't care. He needed to see what he'd become reflected in her eyes.

After what felt like forever, he shoved her back, releasing his hold, and turned away. "Get out of here before I do something I'll regret." His voice was low, quivering with anger.

Larkin stepped back until she reached the door. She opened it and paused.

"You should already regret the things you've done," she said quietly before exiting. She pulled the door closed behind her.

There was a crash on the other side, followed by a furious yell.

CHAPTER 6

LARKIN CLOSED HER BAG AND SLUNG IT OVER HER SHOULDER. NIGHT
had fallen, and her father and his men had finished their *questioning* long ago. Her stomach clenched as the conversation from
the night before replayed in her mind. Had her father followed
through with his plans?

She held onto a shred of hope that she had changed his mind,
but it was a foolish hope; she didn't think he was so far gone as to
be beyond reason, but his pride was still strong enough to crush
his conscience. He'd always avoided displaying weakness in front
of his rangers, and men like Brock, Sanson, and Altez seemed to
think mercy was a weakness.

She hated that her father cared more about his pride than his
humanity.

Larkin left her room, closing the door quietly behind her, and
made her way up to the deck. Strong gusts of wind battered the
ship, rustling the partially raised sails and whistling through the
rigging. She swept loose strands of hair out of her face, wishing
she'd braided it, and shivered against the biting chill.

The deck was empty save for a few men from The Watch, a

goggled lookout at each end of the ship, and Lance Oliver, who stood guard at the entrance to the brig. The young ranger's half-lidded eyes and slouching stance suggested he was close to falling asleep.

He stood at attention as Larkin approached. "Ranger Laster. You're out late tonight."

"I couldn't sleep. I keep thinking about Randall and his men, and how close we are to finding them."

"We'll find them." Lance offered a kind smile. The genuineness of the gesture caught Larkin off guard.

"Thank you, Lance," she said, stepping closer to peck a kiss on his cheek. It was low of her, using such tactics. "I'll be right back up after I'm done questioning them."

He stared at her, wide-eyed, as he blushed; even his ears turned red. "Be careful, Larkin."

Below deck, she retrieved the hanging lantern and carried it into the brig. She squeezed her eyes shut as the scent of blood mixed with the other ship smells. The little girl inside her feared what she might find and refused to believe that her father was capable of such brutality as he'd threatened.

Steeling herself, she walked to Dracchus's cell and placed the lantern on the floor.

His slitted amber eyes rose to meet her gaze, but she shifted her attention to his dark skin, searching for the lacerations and stab wounds she expected to find. Despite his slow, labored breathing, the only open wounds she could see were on his face.

"Did they use weapons today?" she asked, barely keeping her voice from trembling.

"No," Dracchus grunted.

She grasped the bars of his cell to prevent herself from collapsing in relief.

He didn't do it.

It was a small, bitter victory; the kraken had been beaten badly enough that a human suffering the same punishment would've been recovering for weeks, but at least their flesh hadn't been sliced up.

"Would you like some water?" She slid her bag off her shoulder and set it down beside the lantern.

"For them first." Dracchus flicked his gaze toward the kraken behind her.

She splashed each of them twice, starting with the gray kraken. The water was tinted red with their blood as it streamed down their skin. The brown kraken's angry eyes followed her throughout.

After Larkin was finished, she replaced the bucket, closed the barrel, and crouched beside her pack. She took out her tools and set to work on the lock. Within a minute, it clicked open.

"What are you doing?" Dracchus asked.

"What I can," she replied, swinging the door open as she stood up. She collected her bag, stuffed her tools inside, and was stepping through the entry when she halted abruptly. "May I approach you?"

He spread his webbed fingers slowly, displaying open palms over the thick shackles around his wrists. "I have little choice in that."

"I'm giving you the choice."

He frowned, studying her with quizzical eyes, and finally nodded.

She stepped closer, moving her gaze from his tentacles, which were tightly bound in netting, to the defined muscles of his abdomen. Sculpted muscle filled out his chest and arms. He was bigger than any man she'd ever seen.

Kneeling beside him, she set her pack down and removed a jar of salve. "I'm going to put this on your wrists and around your neck. It might sting."

His eyes narrowed infinitesimally, dipping briefly to the jar. He didn't voice whatever suspicion he harbored; instead, he tilted his head back as far as the collar around his neck allowed, offering her his throat. In a primal sense, it was a submissive gesture, but she knew that understanding didn't apply now. This wasn't his submission, it was a modicum of trust.

She stared at his neck for a moment; it had to be as thick as her thigh.

Unscrewing the lid, she dipped her fingers into the jar, gathered a glob of salve, and dabbed it along the raw flesh beneath his collar. The cords of his neck twitched, but he made no sound.

"Tilt your head down," she said.

When he complied, she leaned closer, slipping an arm behind his head. She frowned at how tightly the collar fit; no wonder he could barely move his head.

Larkin paused when his warm breath disturbed the loose hair hanging before her chest, tickling the skin left exposed by her shirt.

Dracchus inhaled, slow and deep.

Was he...*smelling* her?

To her shock, gooseflesh broke out over her skin and her nipples hardened.

He made a strange, low sound in his chest, somewhere between a hum and a grunt.

She drew back quickly and scooped more salve from the jar, shifting to either side to apply it to his wrists. When she was done, she removed a wax paper bundle from her bag and unfolded it. The aroma of cooked fish rose above the room's other scents.

"I know it's not much," she said, breaking off a piece and holding it to Dracchus's lips, "but it's more than you've had in the last couple of days."

"I cannot."

"Why? It's not poisoned. I'll take a bite if you need me to."

"I will not eat if they do not," he said, looking at the other kraken, "and I do not think they will accept your food."

"You need your strength, why would you refuse to eat?" Furrowing her brow, she looked at the others. "I brought plenty."

"I will eat," the gray one said.

Larkin looked at the brown kraken. His eyes bore into her own, and the corners of his lips curved up into a grin comprised of pointed teeth and maliciousness.

She would deal with him when the time came.

Larkin returned her attention to Dracchus. "Eat. I will help them after."

He shook his head again. "They must eat first."

She opened her mouth to explain again that there was enough food, but she released a long, slow sigh instead. He was putting his companions before himself. She could respect that.

Larkin rewrapped the fish and moved her bag into the walkway. She made quick work of the lock on the gray kraken's cell and brought her supplies inside.

She'd just finished applying the salve when he spoke.

"My name is Vasil."

Larkin sat back on her heels as Vasil lifted his head to meet her gaze. His eyes were gray, like his skin, and bore a weary gleam. Guilt constricted her chest.

"Thank you for telling me," she said.

He nodded. "Thank you for the reprieve."

She wished she could do more.

They lapsed into silence as she fed him one of the fillets she'd taken from the galley. When it was gone, she folded the paper, stood, and exited his cell, closing the door quietly behind her.

She moved to the brown kraken's cell and stared down at him. Dark eyes burned.

"Are you not coming in?" he asked.

Refusing to be intimidated, she picked his lock, opened his cell door wide, and entered.

"May I approach?" she asked.

"Come," he said, too eagerly.

Larkin had taken two steps into the small cell before her feet were suddenly swept out from beneath her. She hit the floor hard, taking the impact on her shoulder and hip. Pain pulsed through her body. Gritting her teeth, she lifted her head, and the brown kraken struck her across the face with his bound tentacles. Though his restraints prevented him from producing much force, the sheer weight of his limbs was enough to daze her briefly.

She tasted blood; the inside of her lip had been smashed against her teeth.

He drew his tentacles back for another blow, but this time Larkin was ready.

GROWLING, Dracchus clenched his fists, straining fruitlessly against his bonds.

This female was his enemy, part of a group that had caged and beaten Dracchus and two of his kind. Seeing her brought low should've brought him some satisfaction. Instead, the fires of rage erupted in his gut, their heat an intensity growing with each passing moment. The target for his fury was not Larkin.

He understood why Neo had attacked her. If there'd been no legitimate reason for his hatred of humans before, Neo had one now. That did not lessen Dracchus's anger toward him.

Helplessness tensed every muscle in Dracchus's body as Neo swung his bundled tentacles at Larkin again.

She rolled onto her back and spun around, bending her knees so they nearly touched her chest. Her boots caught Neo's tentacles. She slid a handspan backward, braced herself against the side of the cage, and then heaved, extending her legs fully. Neo's tentacles were forced into the bars on the opposite side, twisting his midsection awkwardly against his stationary upper body. The kraken hissed, wincing.

Without a moment's hesitation, Larkin swept up her bag and the bundle of food and rolled through the doorway. Grasping a crossbar with one hand, she pulled herself to her feet and gently closed the door.

Hair a tangled mess, cheeks red, and hands white-knuckled, she stood in the walkway. Her shoulders rose and fell with three deep breaths. Finally, she walked back to Dracchus's cell.

"Guess he's not hungry," she said. "Are you?"

Her voice betrayed none of the emotion she must have felt in that moment. Her collected reaction to Neo's attack was impressive; not only had she handled a male who was larger and — despite his weakened state — much stronger than her, but she'd done so without further retaliation. Dracchus wouldn't have blamed her if she'd rained blows upon Neo after regaining control.

She was a huntress.

And he wanted her. When he escaped this cell, this ship, she would be his. It didn't matter that she was his enemy. She'd make a worthy mate.

"I am," he replied.

She closed the distance between them, set her bag on the floor, and knelt in front of him. Opening her small bundle, she offered him a piece of fish. His lips brushed her fingertips as he accepted the food, granting him the tiniest taste of her.

Though he'd not eaten in days, he barely noticed the food's flavor; he devoted all his attention to her as he chewed.

Larkin kept her gaze averted, eyes obscured by her tousled hair. She hadn't looked at him since entering his cell. His fingers burned with the unfulfillable desire to brush the red strands away from her face. His nostrils picked out her scent from the myriad smells in the air — distinctly human, with hints of earth and the sweet vegetation he'd encountered during his foraging trips with Jax in the jungle.

"Why did you come to the boats?" she asked after feeding him another bite.

Though he longed to answer, he couldn't reveal any information to her. His instinct said to trust her, but the possibility that she was simply using these small kindnesses to interrogate them couldn't be dismissed.

"Why did you come to sea?" he asked.

"For my brother," she answered without hesitation.

The dedication and sorrow layered in her voice struck Dracchus harder than any blow from Brock, Altez, and Sanson. Harder than any he'd taken from one of his own kind. He clenched his jaw until his urge to console her eased.

"How did you know we were there, Larkin?"

She met his gaze when he spoke her name. Her bundle of food crinkled as she tightened her grip on it. "Tell me why you came to the boats, and I'll tell you how we knew."

It seemed a favorable exchange of information — the knowledge he would gain was by far more valuable — but he paused to consider it. He'd told his companions to give the humans nothing. He had to hold himself to the same expectation.

She nodded as though she'd heard his thoughts and offered him more food.

Through hours of pain, he'd not felt the slightest urge to provide any information to the commander. Why was he so tempted to answer Larkin's questions now?

"Why are you doing this?" Dracchus asked.

Larkin wiped her fingers on the empty wrapping, folded it up, and returned it to her bag. "Because you're people." She winced as she stood up. "No one deserves this."

She'd spoken not with passion, but practicality; it was a simple communication of something she viewed as an indisputable fact. That made her words more genuine to Dracchus than if she'd shouted them with fire in her eyes. She wasn't trying to convince him.

"We came to learn what your people intend to do with this ship," he said.

"And you found out," she said, waving her hand to indicate the cages. Her frown deepened while her gaze lingered on the metal bars all around. Finally, after many moments of silence, she gathered her bag and exited his cell, closing the door softly.

"We have spectra goggles. They're old military tech, with multiple modes of enhanced vision. One of them uses some kind of energy field to scan for lifeforms in a limited range and converts the data into visual form. We knew you were tailing the boats for a while."

A year and a half ago, her explanation wouldn't have meant anything to Dracchus. But Arkon and Randall had taken their time to explain the functionality of the diving suits often used by the Facility's humans. What Larkin had described sounded similar to the masks on those suits; Randall had used their vision enhancements to great effect while hunting with Dracchus.

But Randall, Aymee, and Macy hadn't thought the other humans had access to such devices.

If these hunters had goggles that could see the kraken despite their camouflage, even underwater, and bullets that could make a kraken sleep, what else would they use against Dracchus's people?

"It's late." Larkin glanced at Dracchus over her shoulder. "I..." She sighed and turned her face away. "Rest, if you can."

When she looked away, his gaze followed her red hair down from her shoulders, pausing on the curve of her backside as she bent to retrieve the lantern. Legs were still strange to Dracchus, but he suddenly understood some of their appeal. Were his tentacles free, he'd gladly run them over her body, scenting, tasting, discovering if the little brown spots on her skin felt any different than the rest of her.

She exited the room, plunging it into darkness. There was a thump as something fell into place on the other side of the door, and then only the ship's sounds remained — creaking wood, howling wind, lashing waves.

"I should have known you would give in to the first human slit they dangled before your face," Neo said, "just like your traitorous friends."

"When we return home, Neo, I will accept your challenge. And I will enjoy crushing you."

Neo growled, but said no more.

CHAPTER 7

A sudden impact woke Larkin; she'd landed hard on her side. Pain radiated through her already bruised hip. She twisted to look up at the bunk she'd been in a moment ago. Before she could comprehend what had happened, her stomach lurched, and the floor tilted wildly. She slid across the steeply angled floor, clawing wildly to slow herself, but her momentum was too great. She rolled into the far wall, hitting her head.

"Fuck!" She pressed a hand to her throbbing temple.

Objects fell from the nearby table, scattering around her.

The world tilted again, this time in the opposite direction. A crack of thunder shook the floorboards.

She shoved herself to her feet and grabbed her boots, leaning against the wall for stability as she tugged them on. She stumbled to the door, threw it open, and hurried to the stairs. The wild motion of the ship battled her every step. Grasping the rail with both hands, she hauled herself up.

When she lifted the latch at the top of the steps, the wind blasted the door open, nearly knocking her back down the stairs.

Lightning streaked across the sky. Its illumination granted her a fleeting image of the chaos before her. Men shouted orders over the din, scrambling to secure the sails. Others were tying themselves down to keep from being swept overboard by the crashing waves that crested the siderails.

Thunder boomed immediately after the bolt of lightning. The wood beneath her feet rumbled.

Someone pushed Larkin from behind. She caught herself on the wall beside the door as men rushed from below deck to join the efforts.

She hurried to a group of men struggling with the rigging. Taking hold of the thrashing rope, she leaned back with the others until her muscles strained and her ass nearly hit the deck. Rope fibers bit into her palms, scraping flesh as the rope slipped.

"Heave!" one of the men yelled.

Larkin gritted her teeth, planted her boots, and pulled.

A gust of wind swept into the sail. Larkin cried out as the rope was yanked from her hands. She hit the planks hard enough to crack her teeth together. Men fell around her, a few partially atop her, cursing and sliding in the seawater on the deck.

There was a blinding flash and a deafening boom. Slivers of wood exploded from the central mast.

Turning her face away, Larkin threw up her arms for protection. The men nearby cried out in pain, their bodies taking the brunt of the splinters.

"Look out!" someone shouted.

Larkin looked up as the upper half of the mast pitched forward. Bright flames spread rapidly across the sails and crept along the rigging. She dragged herself from beneath the men, scrambled to her feet, and ran. The entire boat shuddered as the mast hit the deck. Larkin stumbled, catching herself against the wall near the stern.

The men's' shouts grew more frantic. "Fire! Fire!"

She stared with wide eyes at the damage. Coaxed by the wind, the flames spread quickly. The foremast and sails were ablaze within moments.

Realization crept up her spine, icy in the wake of the fire's heat — the ship was burning, and the people aboard would burn with it unless they dove into the sea. But how could anyone last in those violent waves? They'd have to choose between drowning or burning alive.

No.

She wouldn't accept that.

The kraken!

The churning ocean wouldn't be a problem for them, but they didn't stand a chance against the fire while they were locked in those cages. She needed to free them.

A light off the side of the ship caught her attention. She battled the tilting deck, leg muscles burning, to take hold of the port rail and peer over it. One of the smaller boats bobbed on the swelling waves nearby, cast in lantern light made eerie by the surrounding darkness.

"Larkin!"

She turned to see her father running toward her.

He gripped her arm when he reached her. "We need to get everyone to the other boat!"

"I know," she called over the wind, looking back toward the light. Anyone who attempted to reach it would drown.

Unless they have something to guide them…

But throwing a rope to the other ship in the dark, with this wind, would be nearly impossible, and they didn't have time to attempt it.

When the idea hit her, she didn't waste time.

"Wait here!" she yelled as she hurried away from her father. She didn't stop when she heard him shout her name.

The harpoon guns — meant as the back-up plan if the tranquilizers didn't work or there were more kraken than they'd anticipated — were still mounted along the outside wall of her father's cabin. She tugged one down and rushed back to him. The weapons were old tech, from the days of the colonization, each with a bundle of line attached.

She could only hope the line was durable enough — and long enough — for what she needed.

Her father took a single look at the harpoon gun, met her eyes, and nodded. She knew the expression on his face. It was one she'd seen too little as of late. *You've got this, Elle.*

Stabilizing herself against the rail, she raised the gun and took aim, focusing on the small boat. Distance, wind, the weight of the harpoon, the movement of the two ships; all were factors in whether she'd succeed. She only hoped she wouldn't hit one of the men on board.

She took in a single deep breath, released it in a slow exhale, and pulled the trigger. The harpoon flew from the gun with a *thump*, and she lost it in the darkness. She couldn't hear an impact over the wind; her grip tightened on the gun.

The line went taut. Her father grabbed onto it as it tugged her forward, throwing his weight backward to counteract its pull.

The light on the other ship flashed, and, distantly, a bell rang.

Larkin ran off some slack, and together they lashed the line around the nearest mooring post. Once it was tied off, she wedged the gun against the railing for good measure.

"It's secure!" she said.

Her father barked orders over the storm. Several men gathered at the post — far too few. Had some already abandoned ship or been washed overboard?

"We need to send everyone across, now," Larkin said. "That boat's going to get full, but we don't have a choice."

"Go, Elle!"

Larkin stared up at her father. A dozen emotions flickered across his face, cast in an orange glow and harsh shadows by the growing flames, though his expression changed little from the stern mask of the commander. The sorrow and pain in his eyes, the hint of desperation, almost broke her resolve.

"Go!" he repeated. "I'm not letting you do anything stupid, damnit!"

Larkin threw herself at him, taking him into a tight embrace. "Get them off the boat," she said as she slipped the keys off his belt. "I'll be right back."

She turned and ducked between two men, squeezing through the frantic press of bodies to emerge on the other side. She raced across the deck toward the brig, not slowing when her father shouted her name. The entryway was open and unguarded; she hoped Lance was safe, but there was no time to search for him.

Hands on the wall to maintain her balance, Larkin hurried down the ramp and grabbed the lantern at the bottom. She lifted the bar and shoved the door open.

The ship lurched as she crossed the threshold, pitching her forward. She twisted to protect the lantern, hitting the metal bars of Dracchus's cell with her shoulder.

She groaned, gritting her teeth against the pain in her limbs, and clutched the bar behind her as the ship righted itself.

Once the floor was somewhat stable, she turned and fumbled through the keys until she found the one that fit the lock. She flung open the cell door and moved inside, dropping to her knees in front of Dracchus.

His amber eyes were alert as they met her gaze. If he was fearful, he sure as hell wasn't showing it. "What is happening, Larkin?"

"The ship's on fire," she said, nearly dropping the keys as she unlocked his collar.

"Should you not leave?" he asked.

"I'm not going to leave you here to die." She moved to his wrists next, freeing them one at a time.

He lowered his arms stiffly and groaned as he straightened his elbows and curled his fingers. The popping of his joints was audible even over the fury of the wind and sea.

Reaching into her boot, she pulled out a small knife and cut the netting around his tentacles.

Dracchus sagged onto his side, catching himself on an arm that nearly buckled beneath his weight. He kept his head down as his broad back rose and fell with several deep, shaky breaths. He spread his tentacles once she'd cut enough of the netting, tearing apart what remained.

Larkin clutched the bars for support as she stepped out of Dracchus's cell. She hung the lantern on the wall before making her way toward Vasil. Once his cell was open, she set about releasing him from his bonds.

He moved with the same sluggishness as Dracchus, limbs trembling, as he slowly dragged himself toward the door.

The ship creaked and moaned, and thunder boomed, rattling wood and metal all around. Larkin turned to exit Vasil's cell but stopped abruptly as she nearly collided with a black wall of muscle.

Dracchus loomed in the space between the cells, erect on his tentacles. She'd thought him large while he was restrained, but she hadn't understood the breadth of him; her eye level was at his chest and his shoulders nearly spanned the entire walkway.

She'd known men with commanding presences, but Dracchus *dominated* this space.

"Here." She shoved the keys and the knife into his huge hand. "Free your friend and get off the ship."

His brow furrowed when he looked down at the items on his palm. "I will not leave you to die, either."

"My father is waiting for me above deck. There's another boat. Just get yourselves to safety."

Dracchus frowned.

She heard Vasil move behind her and glanced over her shoulder. He wasn't as large as Dracchus, but he still towered over Larkin. Being surrounded by them made her uncomfortable; they could tear her apart effortlessly. After what her father had done, what reason did they have to spare her? Why would they be selective if they chose to take revenge on the humans aboard these ships?

Finally, Dracchus closed his fist around the knife and keys. He shifted aside, opening a narrow path for her. "Go."

As she moved through the gap, her chest brushed his abdomen. She stilled and stared up at him. "Hurry, Dracchus. Before the fire traps you down here."

His gaze held her in place, enveloped her, deeper and more mysterious than the ocean. Nostrils flaring, he leaned his face closer to hers. "We will survive. See to yourself, Larkin."

She lingered, searching his eyes. Common sense returned a moment later. She raced through the door and up the ramp.

The heat of the blaze hit her like she'd run into a wall at the top of the ramp. Her first breath had her coughing as the wind wafted smoke into her face.

Lifting her hand to shield her eyes, she stumbled toward the spot where they'd tethered the harpoon. Her father's form materialized in the haze. As he assisted a man onto the line, he turned his head, squinting through the smoke until he caught sight of her.

She ran to him.

"Where the hell were you?" he demanded, grabbing her wrist and pulling her closer. Beads of sweat coated his skin, glistening in the firelight. He seemed to have aged years while she was gone.

"There was something I needed to do," she said.

"Get your ass to that boat, Elle." His tone indicated there'd be a tongue-lashing for her later.

She didn't fight him. Throwing her leg over the rail, she gripped the rope and looked across the water, visible only because of the vibrant, reflected flames on its surface. The smaller boat was a ghostly glow twenty or thirty meters away. A man's head bobbed in the water as he pulled himself toward the other ship, clutching the line desperately.

The waves swelled, lifting the smaller boat high and drawing the tether suddenly taut. The man was flung out of the water, losing his hold on the line, and disappeared under the surface when he came back down.

Larkin gritted her teeth. How many had they lost so far?

"You *will* make it across," Nicholas said behind her. "You're not getting out of the ass chewing you have coming."

"Maybe give me something to look forward to?" She attempted a smile and failed.

Her father placed his hands on her waist, steadying her as she lifted her other leg over the rail. She grasped the line with both hands, wrapped her legs around it, and crossed her ankles before she lay on her belly. Dark water churned below her, too close for her comfort.

Larkin glanced over her shoulder. "See you on the other side, Dad."

"Damn right you will, Elle."

The line sagged when she pulled herself forward, and Larkin's stomach twisted into a knot. She squeezed the line with her thighs as she swung upside down. The thrashing water was less than a meter beneath her, its impenetrable black highlighted by the hellish glow of the burning ship. The roar of the waves was deafening.

She pulled herself along the rope, hand-over-hand, as harsh winds and angry waves competed to see which would break the pathetic little human's hold first. She squeezed her eyes shut and turned her face away from the leaping water. An eternity passed in the span of a few seconds, but she kept moving.

She *would* make it to the other boat.

The roiling ocean swelled again, forcing the two ships closer together.

Larkin clung to the rope as she plummeted into the chilly water. She kicked to the surface, disoriented and sputtering, and swung her gaze to the first thing that caught her attention — the burning ship.

Gunshots sounded over the cacophony, and her heart stuck in

her throat. A dark figure hurtled over the railing, tentacles trailing in the air as it came toward her. She caught a hint of crimson skin just before the figure slammed into her.

The immense weight forced her underwater and broke her hold on the rope.

THE HUMAN MALE beside the commander writhed on the deck. His hands could not stem the flow of blood from his shredded abdomen; he'd taken the brunt of Neo's charge toward the commander.

Dracchus didn't know if Neo had been hit or not. The commander had drawn a gun from his belt and fired several quick shots. It hadn't been enough to drop the kraken, but it had forced Neo to dive over the side and into the sea below.

Now the commander leaned over the railing, aiming his weapon at something in the water, the cords on his neck standing out as he shouted.

Vasil moved forward.

Dracchus caught him by the shoulder, forcing him to turn. "Get to safety." He gestured to the opposite side of the boat. "Return home and warn our humans that Neo is a threat."

Vasil's muscles tensed under Dracchus's palm. He glanced at the commander. "Ending him will protect our people, Dracchus."

"I will deal with him. You have witnessed much, and you will tell our people the tale without bias. That is your role. Now go. Dive deep and swim quickly."

With a nod, Vasil darted to the railing and dove over.

"Larkin!" the Commander's voice rose over the roaring fire, wind, and sea.

Dracchus's hearts pounded. Was Larkin in the water when Neo leapt down?

He rushed across the deck, reaching the commander as the human was climbing over the side. Dracchus caught the back of the human's shirt and dragged him back. The commander's legs slipped out from beneath him, but Dracchus didn't allow the man to fall. Dracchus reached forward and closed his free hand over the pistol, tearing it from the human's grasp. He threw the weapon into the flames.

"Let me go, you son of a bitch!" the commander yelled, struggling to free himself. "My daughter's down there!"

Dracchus shook him hard, stunning the human. "Your daughter is *mine* now. That is the price for your life." He thrust the commander away.

The man's cry of rage and anguish was cut off as he tumbled over the wood planks.

Dracchus turned and vaulted over the railing, dropping into the water.

The sea was chaos — waves thrust upward like jabbing spears and fell again with equal force, crashing into one another and pulling away. The sound was overwhelming. The light of the fire barely penetrated the water's surface, but it was enough to illuminate the tangled shapes of Neo and Larkin.

Neo held Larkin underwater, hands wrapped around her throat and skin pulsing crimson. Larkin clutched his forearms and kicked wildly, but her blows had little effect; she couldn't match his strength.

Wisps of blood streamed from several small cuts on Larkin's arms and face, mingling with more from unseen wounds on Neo's body. The clouds dissipated casually, unconcerned with what was going on nearby.

Larkin's struggles weakened. Bubbles flowed from her mouth; she was running out of air.

Though she was an enemy, though she was human, Larkin was *his*.

Dracchus surged forward. He directed all his momentum into a single blow, slamming his fist into Neo's jaw.

Neo's grip on Larkin loosened as he tumbled sideways. Dracchus forced himself between the two and broke Neo's hold. Despite his dazed state, Neo raked his claws across Dracchus's back, creating fresh trails of agony.

Dracchus wrapped his arms around Larkin and pushed to the surface.

She sucked in a huge, ragged breath, and then fell into a coughing fit. Her body shook, and the force of her coughs rattled through Dracchus. He placed a hand on her hair and tilted her head back, checking her neck; watery blood flowed from several minor cuts, and bruises were forming on her pale skin.

She struggled in his arms, dragging her blunt claws across his skin, hitting him with boots, elbows, and knees. Dracchus tightened his hold on her.

"Be still, Larkin," he rumbled.

Her frantic gaze lifted to his face as though seeing him for the first time, and she ceased her struggling. She shivered against him.

Neo surfaced a moment later, a body length away. Dracchus turned, shifting Larkin to one side to keep himself between her and the other kraken.

"Even after what they have done, you defend them?" Neo shouted over the roaring ocean.

"They have done no worse than you would, if given the chance," Dracchus replied.

"I demand her death!"

"You will demand nothing. Be thankful you have your life."

Nero snarled, baring his teeth as he advanced. "You threaten me, *your own kind*, while you protect that filthy human slit?"

Larkin stiffened. The warm, steady flow of her breath against his neck intensified.

Where was the honor in this? Neo, Kronus, and their fellows claimed to uphold the ways of their people, but attacking a defenseless female violated all those traditions.

"Cry off, Neo, or I will—"

A loud boom sounded over the other noises, interrupting

Dracchus's words. Something hit the water with a hissing splash in front of Neo.

Not thunder.

Dracchus turned his head toward the smaller boat in time to see another gun-flash and hear the next boom. Another round struck the water, spraying mist into Dracchus's face.

Neo growled and vanished below the surface.

"Hold your breath," Dracchus said.

"What? No! The boat is there. Just let me go." She loosened her hold on him.

Turning away from the boats, he swam, adjusting his rhythm to account for his hold on her. "Hold your breath, Larkin."

Another gunshot. Dracchus didn't know if they were firing normal bullets or the sleep bullets Larkin had used to capture the kraken, but he didn't intend to find out.

"Dracchus, no! Take me—"

He dipped down, and before the water closed over their heads, he heard her deep inhalation.

CHAPTER 8

THE RAIN BEGAN SHORTLY AFTER THEY LEFT THE SHIPS BEHIND, silencing Larkin's repeated demands to be returned to her comrades. She offered no resistance when he shifted her onto his back to free his arms. Her body was soft and warm against him, and the feel of her hold around his neck and shoulders was surprisingly comforting.

He'd never been one to feel lonely — not until recently — but he was grateful for her nearness amidst the restless, impossibly dark waves, which were illuminated only by occasional flashes of lightning.

When the storm finally broke and the water eased, a hint of dawn loomed at the edge of his vision.

The sunrise gave Dracchus a target — the sun always came up over land, and they needed land to rest and recover from the night's ordeals. He swam toward the light on the horizon, not allowing himself to slow as the gloomy gray of early dawn gave way to red, orange, and finally gold. The sun was fully visible over the ocean when he spotted land in the distance.

Relief flooded him. It was a small island, its shore covered in pale sand.

With a concrete destination, he pushed hard, straining his weary, battered body. Were he not so worn, he'd have scouted the area before making landfall.

He swam until the water was too shallow for it, and then dragged himself by hands and tentacles onto the beach. Larkin released him and slid off his back, landing in the sand beside him. She crawled on hands and knees to the grass beyond the tideline and collapsed on her back in the shade of a large tree.

Dracchus did not allow himself to halt until he was beside her. His arms finally gave out, and he relaxed his tentacles, laying on his stomach with his head turned toward her.

This was his first glimpse of her in natural light. Her hair was even more vibrant than he'd realized, a deep red-orange, and the sunshine highlighted the little brown spots on her white skin. Her dark pink lips were full, and her delicate features belied the strength beneath the surface.

Her shirt left her arms, neck, and upper chest exposed, and she had several small, shallow cuts on her pale skin, accompanied by blue and purple bruising on her throat and temple.

He growled. His instinct shouted to claim her, keep her, protect her.

Her eyes were shut, her breathing slow and even in slumber. He'd have to wait at least a little longer to see the sunlight make her brilliant blue eyes sparkle.

Dracchus slid closer to her and draped a tentacle over her waist.

He closed his eyes. Every muscle in his body ached, especially his arms and shoulders, which had spent days in an unnatural position, and the spots where his beating had been particularly intense — and where Neo's claws had raked his flesh — were still tender. Hunger gnawed at his gut.

Where were they? Where was the Facility, or The Watch?

Dracchus dismissed those questions; exhaustion was the most immediate issue. He'd face everything else after he rested.

He gave into his exhaustion, and sleep claimed him within moments.

∾

PAIN WAS Larkin's first sensation as she floated toward consciousness. Her body felt like one giant bruise, and she was sure even her hair would hurt, were it possible.

Her brow furrowed, and her fingers twitched. The sound of waves was immediate and loud. Not unusual on a boat. But where was the steady rocking motion to which she'd grown accustomed?

Larkin's eyes fluttered open. She squinted against the bright sunlight, and several realizations struck her — she was lying atop soft vegetation on solid ground, not on her bunk in the ship; it was daytime; there was a warm body pressed against her.

She slowly turned her head. Her eyes widened as her gaze settled on Dracchus. His face was close to hers, nearly tucked in her hair, and his large body was curled around her. One of his arms was draped over her stomach and his tentacles were coiled around her legs. His shoulders rose and fell steadily, and his eyes were closed.

All traces of the abuse he'd suffered on the ship were gone; his cuts, bruises, and swelling had healed completely.

Larkin found herself studying him. His features were relaxed in sleep, and the daylight displayed them with a clarity she'd never seen in the brig.

He had a wide, defined jaw and full lips, high cheekbones and a heavy, expressive brow. In the shadows below deck, she'd thought he lacked a nose, but she saw now that it was simply less pronounced than a human's — it sloped so gently off his face that it was difficult to make out from the front. His face was striking, handsome both because of and despite its differences.

Horizontal, light gray stripes ran from his forehead toward the back of his head. The same pattern repeated on his shoulders, upper arms, and tentacles.

Larkin frowned as her grogginess faded and the events of the night before came roaring back — the storm, the blazing fire, her attempt to reach the smaller boat. She'd been on her way toward it when the line slackened, dropping her into the water…

And the red kraken had attacked her.

She'd stared up at him, water stinging her eyes, as he held her below the surface. He could've killed her with just a bit more force, but he'd chosen to make her suffer. He'd chosen to watch the life fade from her eyes. His visage had been hellish, silhouetted by the burning boat behind him.

If Dracchus had been even a few seconds slower in breaking the other kraken's grip, she would've drowned.

Larkin shoved away from Dracchus, untangling her legs from his tentacles. She rolled over the grass until there was some distance between them and then pushed herself to her feet. Her legs nearly gave out; she stumbled forward, extending her arms to either side to catch her balance. The ache and stiffness in her limbs would pass.

What she saw around her was the more distressing problem.

The wind blew hair into her face, and she swept it back. Countless kilometers of water stretched in all directions. Where the hell were they?

"What is wrong?" Dracchus asked. She glanced at him over her shoulder; he was upright and alert, and if she hadn't known better, she would've guessed he'd been awake the entire time.

"What's wrong?" she repeated, turning to face him. "*What's wrong?*" She marched toward him, ignoring the discomfort of her wet boots. "You took me away and brought me *here!*"

"You are alive and safe." He tilted his head to the side very slightly, brow dipping.

She jabbed her finger at him, opened her mouth to admonish

him only to snap it shut, gritting her teeth. With a frustrated growl, she stormed past him, heading for the higher ground a little farther inland.

He's right, damnit! How can I be angry at him for that?

Because he refused to take me back.

The sound of vegetation flattening under his tentacles as he followed her was whisper-soft, especially against the wind. He didn't have any right being so quiet on land. He didn't have any right to follow her, either. She pressed her lips into a tight line and continued up the small rise. The grass and trees yielded to bare rock. Her muscles ached in protest as she climbed.

By the time she reached the top her chest was tight, her breath ragged, and her limbs weak. She swallowed, bringing fresh discomfort to her dry throat.

"What are you doing?" Dracchus asked.

Larkin ignored him as she shaded her eyes with a hand and surveyed her surroundings. She stood on a small island, perhaps two hundred meters from one tip to the other. Rock, sand, and grass dominated the landscape, broken by several scattered copses of windblown trees. The shallows around the island teemed with sea life. That meant potential food, but without rain, there'd be no fresh water.

She could improvise a primitive means of collecting rainwater in the meantime, but no immediate access to water and adequate shelter would quickly take its toll.

Dracchus's hand — massive but surprisingly gentle — settled on her shoulder and guided her to turn toward him.

"What are you looking for, Larkin?"

She lowered her brows. "Why are you here?"

"I swam here," he said without a hint of irony, "with you."

"You know what I mean!" She shrugged his hand off. "Why are you here? I released you. You should be gone." Her anger returned in a flash. "You should have taken me back!"

"Your people were shooting at us."

"You could have waited. I could have called out to them and they would have stopped."

He shook his head, frowning. "The sea would have swallowed your voice, and then taken you, too."

"Then take me back now," she said.

"If your people captured me again, do you think any would let me free?"

"Take me to the mainland, then. To The Watch."

He turned his head toward the far beach, setting his gaze on something far off. Larkin squinted as she searched for what he was looking at.

Her heart leapt. A lumpy sliver of blue-gray lay along the horizon; it *had* to be the mainland. Though distance was difficult to judge on the open ocean, she guessed it was at least six or seven kilometers away.

Larkin couldn't stay here, but she wasn't foolish enough to believe she could make that sort of journey. She wasn't the strongest swimmer to begin with, and attempting to cross such a distance through open water was suicide.

But *Dracchus* could make it.

"Take me there," she said.

He was silent, amber eyes fixed on her.

"Damnit, Dracchus, I can't survive here!" She swept her hand outward. "There's food, but that's it. No shelter, no drinkable water. Between the sun and thirst, I'll be a scorched husk in two days."

"If I bring you there, you will attempt to return to your people."

Larkin scowled. "Of course I would. Why wouldn't I?"

"I cannot allow that to happen."

She held his gaze, silently fuming, but worry licked at the fringes of her mind. "What do you mean?"

"You are a great danger to my people while you are with yours." He spoke matter-of-factly, without any emotion in his voice, but there was something she couldn't place in his eyes. "It is too great a risk to us."

"I know nothing more than what the others already know."

"Not what you know. What you can do."

Larkin shoved her hands into his chest. He didn't budge, which made her angrier. "I let you go! Why would I help them capture you again after what they did? You knew I didn't agree with it once I realized what you are!"

"You did it because it was your duty, and that duty will be no different when you return to them."

"To hell with them! I can damn well say no if I want to. It's called free will."

"Did you not possess that when you first captured us?"

"I thought you were monsters! All I've thought about for the past year was getting my brother back, and you were supposed to be the key. But it wasn't until they hauled you on deck and I *saw* you, *conversed* with you, that I understood differently."

Tears stung her eyes, and she hated herself for them. She refused to cry, especially in front of him. She pressed her finger and thumb to the inside corners of her eyes. "I just want my brother back safe. Now, I don't even know if my father's alive."

Dracchus gently grasped her wrist and guided her hand down. His gaze moved over her slowly, appraisingly, while his front right tentacle slid restlessly over the ground.

"We have saved one another's lives," he said finally, "and you showed kindness to myself and my companions despite the situation. That is meaningful to me. I have learned much more about compassion from your people than I have about hate. I will answer for you now what I could not on the ship."

The pad of his thumb brushed along her forearm, making her skin tingle. He looked into her eyes. "Your brother is alive."

Larkin's heart stopped. She stared up at Dracchus, waiting for a sign that this was a malicious joke or a trick to gain her compliance. "He's...alive?"

"He has lived with my people for the last year."

"No." She shook her head and took a step back. "You're only saying that so I cooperate with you. He wouldn't... He wouldn't just leave us."

Wouldn't leave me.

Dracchus maintained his grip on her wrist; it wasn't painful, but she knew she couldn't pull free unless he allowed her to.

"He had no choice."

Those words filled her both with relief and anger. "Why? Because he saw you?"

"He was wounded—"

"Did you hurt him?" She yanked her arm, but he didn't release her. "I swear if any of you—"

"One of your own shot him," he said. "He was betrayed by his hunting party."

The air fled her lungs. No, that couldn't be right. Randall was loved by his men, by all the rangers. They looked up to him.

Despite the warmth of the sun, a chill crept across Larkin's skin and worked its way into her bones.

"I-I don't believe you. I can't believe that."

"He will tell you the same." Dracchus's frown deepened. "But I cannot allow you to return to your people."

"Is he safe?" she asked.

"As safe as he can be."

"If you are telling me the truth, and Randall is really with your people, then bring me to him."

"I cannot. The journey would kill you, and I am unfamiliar with our current location."

"Then...what are you going to do with me?"

His jaw muscles ticked as he swung his gaze around the island, finally halting it on the horizon. He stared in silence for a time, his face unreadable. She knew, in her heart — that soft, soft heart her father so despised — that Dracchus wouldn't kill her. He wasn't the monster he'd been made out to be. Why would he have saved her otherwise?

"I will take you there," he finally said, lifting his chin toward the mainland, "but you will not attempt to return to your people. Once I can determine where we are and where my home is, I will obtain the means to take you to your brother."

Larkin's brows rose, and she took a step closer. "You will?"

Dracchus angled his head down to meet her gaze. "Yes. But hear me — if you return to your people in the hope of rescuing Randall from us, you will never find him. He is beyond the reach of humans. But he is safe. He is…happy."

Those last three words silenced the harsh reply she'd been prepared to make.

Randall was *happy*?

A twinge pierced her chest. She raised her hand to absently rub the spot. Larkin and her father had spent over a year searching for him, tearing their hair out with worry, never know if whether he was dead or alive. She was relieved to know he was safe, but she couldn't help feeling betrayed. It was a selfish emotion, and she couldn't deny it. While her world had crumbled, he'd been *happy*.

Had he ever thought about her while he was with the kraken? Had he ever wondered where she was, or what she was doing, or if she was all right?

"He has spoken of you often," Dracchus said, as though he knew her thoughts. "When you revealed your name, I knew who you were. Your eyes served as confirmation. They are like his."

"I won't run," she vowed. "Just bring me to him."

He nodded. "It will take time. You are sure you will be able to survive if we move to the mainland?"

Larkin narrowed her eyes. "Don't insult me, kraken." She was a damned ranger; she *lived* in the wilds.

Dracchus's lips shifted upward, into an almost-smile, and the light in his amber eyes softened. "Then come, human." He turned and moved toward the far shore, leading her by the arm.

"I can walk without you holding my hand," she said, hopping down from a larger rock.

Dracchus paused, twisting to look back at his hand on her wrist. He released her with a strange combination of reluctance and confusion and moved on without a word. She remained in place, head cocked, and watched him *walk*.

The play of the toned muscles in his back and arms was certainly enticing, but she was more mesmerized by the motion of his tentacles. They stretched and contracted, pushing and dragging him simultaneously. He didn't leap down from the rocks; he flowed over them, seeming to stick to their sides in defiance of gravity on his way down.

She climbed down behind him, her feet squished inside her boots, and caught up with him on the beach. Here at sea level, the mainland was no longer visible.

"Climb onto my back." He spread his tentacles, sinking into a crouch.

Larkin peered toward the horizon and sighed.

"You will be able to swim on your own when I take you to your brother," he said.

"How?"

"You will know when it is time."

Larkin rolled her eyes and stepped over his tentacles — his long, *thick* tentacles. "You're so damn cryptic, you know that?"

He glanced at her over his shoulder, brow low. "That sounds like a word Arkon would use. What does it mean?"

"It means you aren't speaking plainly." She sidled closer to his back. They'd traveled like this for a time on their way to this island, but she'd been so exhausted that she hadn't put any thought into it. Now, however, she was fully aware of her proximity to the muscled expanse of his back, to his broad, powerful shoulders, his huge arms...

He grunted and faced forward. "It *is* an Arkon word. *Cryptic.*"

Larkin settled her hands on his shoulders, sliding them around his front until her arms were around his neck. His sea-kissed scent filled her nose as her chest pressed against his back. His skin was velvet-draped steel, surprisingly soft over solid muscle. Heat flowed into her through every point of contact.

He rose, and her feet left the ground. She lifted her legs instinctively, squeezing her thighs against his sides, and he looped his arms under her knees to guide them around his waist. He was big enough that her feet couldn't touch on the other side.

"Who is Arkon?" she asked.

"One of my people," he replied as they entered the water. The rhythm of his movement reminded her of the way the ship had moved while the sea was calm. "He uses words the way humans do. *Cryptic.*"

"And you don't?" She tightened her arms and legs around him as the water rose above her midsection. It was cold at first, but she quickly adapted to it.

"I do not toy with words."

She felt it when they lifted away from land. The shock and exhaustion had left their previous journey a blur in her memory, but now she was alert and attentive. His method of movement in water was just as strange as on land, creating a similarly odd rhythm. He spread his tentacles wide and forced them back together, propelling them forward. Their burst of speed slowly deteriorated until he repeated the process.

She leaned forward, touching her cheek to his as water lapped around her shoulders.

He pulled his face away from that first contact, tension thrumming through his body, but it was short-lived. He soon relaxed and moved his head back to its original position.

Eventually, the distant mainland emerged from the horizon, growing steadily larger and more defined. Larkin focused on it, ignoring the feel of Dracchus's body. What good would it do her to watch the muscles of his arms stretch and relax, or to brush her fingertips over his shoulders as they moved?

Randall was all that mattered.

She didn't know where he was, but if there was even a tiny chance Dracchus was telling the truth — and, crazy as it felt, she didn't think he was lying — she *had* to take it.

CHAPTER 9

Branches and leaves snapped and crunched around Dracchus as he followed Larkin through the dense vegetation, announcing his presence to all creatures within earshot. The destruction in his wake left a visible trail.

Everything was strange to him on land — the colors, the smells, the tastes and sounds. Living and dead plants, while essentially the same thing, possessed entirely different textures and scents, and even the ground had no consistent feel from place to place. The thick, hot air held only enough moisture to tease Dracchus and make him long for the sea.

The vegetation seemed to claw at him as he passed, like it recognized he did not belong. Everything in the jungle felt so *close*.

Larkin, by contrast, moved silently and effortlessly, slipping between plants and walking over the cluttered ground as easily as Dracchus could swim.

"Are you always this broody?" she asked.

Dracchus looked up. Larkin stood on the crest of a small rise, looking down at him over her shoulder. Her damp clothing clung to her body, particularly around her breasts and backside, accenting her curves. He trailed his gaze over her body slowly; it was easier than answering her question, which had only confused him. A brood was a group of younglings. Did she think he was acting like a youngling?

Larkin turned to face him, one brow arched. "What are you doing?"

"Studying your body."

She frowned and crossed her arms over her chest. There was a hesitance to her action that spoke of uncertainty; was it because he was a kraken?

Her attempt to hide her breasts only pressed them together and pushed them upward, granting him a more enticing view.

"What is wrong?" he asked. Why were humans always so intent on covering themselves? Even Randall, a fit, confident male, wore clothing that covered most of his body. Dracchus understood that humans were more sensitive to cold than kraken, but how could *any* creature find this air cold?

"Well, most men don't just admit to ogling women." She shifted her weight onto one leg, cocking her hip to the side. "They like to think they're subtle about it."

Dracchus glanced down at himself. "I do not think I am capable of being subtle."

The corners of her lips twitched before finally lifting into a grin. "I guess not."

He'd not seen her smile in the brief time he'd known her, and the expression lit up her face like he couldn't have imagined. For an instant, he saw Larkin without worry, without pressure, with nothing but a bit of joy. And she was beautiful.

"You're doing it again," she said, grinning wider.

Dracchus nodded. He'd spent considerable time with a small group of humans over the last year, so their features were not particularly new or unusual to him. Yet he couldn't help staring at Larkin, even with so many unfamiliar things surrounding him.

She turned away and lowered her arms. "Come on. We need to find a source of water and a place to shelter before it gets dark."

He moved up the rise and fell into place behind her as they continued through the jungle. Occasionally, she paused, crouching to study the ground nearby or reaching up to run her hand over a thick vine.

Before long, she seemed to find whatever it was she'd sought. She stopped at a cluster of vines, touched them with palm, and kneeled, drawing a knife from her boot. The weapon was similar to the one she'd handed him on the ship. Standing up, she cut a notch high on the vine and crouched to sever the plant completely near the ground.

She leaned back and lifted the open end of the vine, holding it a hand's span over her mouth. Water dripped from the severed plant to land on her waiting tongue.

When the flow of liquid slowed, she tipped the vine up and looked at him. "Do you need some?"

"No," he replied. "Is there anything humans don't do with plants?"

"What do you mean?"

"You eat them, and Arkon said you use them to make clothing, shelters, colors to paint things. You drink from them, too?"

"Most plants have a use." She shrugged. "I guess humans are just...resourceful. We make do with what we have."

Dracchus grunted; the kraken had made do with the Facility for generations, using what had been left after their ancestors claimed the place. But that didn't quite match what Larkin had displayed.

The kraken, as a people, could stand to be somewhat more *resourceful*. Their home would not last indefinitely, and they needed to think beyond what they had now. Arkon was good at it, and sometimes Jax, but the rest — Dracchus included — seemed to show little ability for it.

And yet, they were part human. Did that not mean they were all capable of innovation to some degree?

He went to the severed vine and lifted it, glancing at the open end before looking back at her. "So, we will shelter here, where there is water?"

"I think we're close to a larger water source. I've been following a krull trail for a while now, and they usually walk particular paths to get to the water."

Larkin resumed the journey, and Dracchus followed, dropping his gaze to the ground. He swept his eyes back and forth over the jungle floor, looking for the *krull trail* she'd spoken of. The plants, both living and dead, were too similar for him to differentiate, and he had no idea what a krull was.

He glanced at her boots. As she lifted a foot, some of the dead vegetation came up, and he noticed a depression in the ground below matching the bottom of her boot. Tilting his head, he searched the area nearby. Not far from her boot print, he noticed a more defined mark in the dirt — a cluster of three oval shapes, the central one straight with the outer two angled away.

His gaze shifted forward, and he spotted another track half-covered by rotting leaves.

Understanding dawned on him; this was the same technique his people sometimes used to locate the dens of the hard-shells dwelling on the seafloor. The creatures left visible pathways when they crawled over the loose sand on the bottom.

"So...this Arkon sounds intelligent," she said.

"Yes, when he is not being foolish."

"Aren't we all a little foolish?" Larkin brushed aside a low hanging branch and suddenly leapt back. The branch sprung back into place, but something dropped into the brush below. "Move back," she commanded.

Dracchus held his position as she backed up. Though he was unfamiliar with land creatures, he would not retreat.

She glanced at him over her shoulder for an instant. "Damnit, do you *want* to die? I said move!"

The creature emerged from the thicker vegetation. It had a long, thin body with rough-looking skin that resembled the outside of the nearby trees. The creature lifted its front off the jungle floor, rising unsteadily so its head swayed at the height of Larkin's waist. Tiny legs tipped with claws lined its belly. The creature opened its mouth, revealing two long, thin fangs.

It advanced slowly, matching the pace of Larkin's retreat, and hissed each time its head lurched forward in a mock attack. Larkin seemed to be its sole focus.

Dracchus growled and moved in front of Larkin, pulsing his skin red and black. He reached behind him with a tentacle to guide her away, holding eye contact with the strange, aggressive beast.

"What the hell, kraken?"

He spread his tentacles, positioning them to intercept a potential attack, and eased sideways. The creature followed his movement, twisting the upright section of his body to keep him in its vision. It continued its lunges, darting forward and swaying back. Dracchus sensed that this was little more than posturing — like the dancing that began a challenge between two kraken — but he didn't lower his guard.

The distance between kraken and beast shrank. Dracchus tensed, preparing for the imminent strike.

Larkin moved around him suddenly, swinging a large branch downward and bashing the creature's head into the ground. She pressed her attack, hitting the creature repeatedly, mercilessly.

"Krullheaded—"

Whack.

"—foolish—"

Whack.

"—thick-skulled—"

Whack.

"—kraken!"

She adjusted her hold on the stick, spreading her hands wide for better control, and jabbed the fork-shaped end over the creature's neck. Its body writhed, legs scrambling in the rotting leaves. Larkin pressed a boot onto its body, just behind the stick, and drew her knife. She sliced the creature's head off in one quick motion.

Larkin stumbled back, shoulders heaving and cheeks red, and blew the hair out of her face.

Dracchus knew she was skilled with guns, but that had only given him the smallest glimpse of her capability. This female wasn't merely a huntress, she was a *warrior*.

And she would be his.

Warmth spread through him, and his shaft pressed against the inside of his slit.

She bent forward and plucked the still-writhing body off the jungle floor. Her blazing eyes met his. "The next time I tell your ass to move, you *move*. This is a vorix. One bite, and you'd be dead before nightfall." She tossed the carcass to him. "That's dinner."

Larkin was already walking away, using the stick like an extra leg, when he caught the creature. He took a single glance at her kill and grinned. He'd provided for many females during his life. This was the first time a female had provided for him.

Dracchus followed her, though now she seemed to make little effort to keep a pace that didn't have him crashing through the vegetation. Branches and exposed rocks poked his tentacles and scratched at his skin. They were a minor irritation, irrelevant compared to his main focus — the swaying of her hips, the swing of her long hair against her back.

He wanted this female more than he'd ever wanted any other. His previous pursuits of females had been fulfillments of duty first, a means of pleasure second. If the kraken did not mate, they would not produce younglings, and their people would die out.

He knew all the females he'd mated, though the details of their time together had faded from his memory.

They'd done their duty. What more had mattered?

Were he a more contemplative individual, he might've reflected upon the reasons for his attraction to Larkin. Might have explored and analyzed those reasons, might've determined their root causes and learned something about himself in the process. But this was a simple situation for Dracchus — he wanted her, and he would have her. *Why* made no difference.

He knew, somehow, that his time with her would not be forgotten. She would be burned into his memory forever, granted more thought than any of his kills and conquests.

Larkin stopped, tilting her head to the side. "Do you hear that?"

Dracchus halted behind her and listened. Wind whispered through the leaves, and countless unseen creatures made their calls. Somewhere in the distance, a branch cracked, producing a clamor as it crashed to the jungle floor.

Then he heard it — not the rumbling of the sea he'd known since his earliest days, but a lighter sound, rushing water trickling over rocks and stones.

"Water," he said.

She grinned. "Damn right it is."

Larkin broke into a run with a *whoop*. Unwilling to let her out of his sight, Dracchus gave chase. She was a formidable hunter, and she'd not yet claimed him as a mate, but instinct drove him to protect her at all costs.

He used trees and their large, tangled roots to propel himself forward, following Larkin and the strengthening sound of water. When he broke through the final barrier of plants, he found himself beside a natural pool. Water poured into it from elevated land on one side, sending up a fine, cool mist that was a welcome refreshment after the stifling jungle air. Sunlight poured through the leaves above to create shimmering rainbows in the mist.

"Finally!" Larkin said.

Dracchus swung his gaze to her and stilled.

She toed off her remaining boot, dropping it beside the other, and lowered her hands to her waistband. She unbuttoned her pants and shoved them down, revealing her supple thighs and shapely backside; the latter was covered only by a scrap of cloth.

Had he thought clothing an unnecessary before? The covering on her pelvis teased him, offering a maddening hint of the plump petals of her sex. This clothing had purpose — to drive him wild with desire.

His cock strained against his slit, and he clenched his jaw against the discomfort. He wouldn't embarrass himself by extruding and spilling his seed like an adolescent experiencing his first look at a female.

Larkin straightened, and Dracchus couldn't take his eyes off her as she stepped to the edge of the pool, the light setting her red-orange hair aglow. She leapt into the water.

Dracchus's tension eased. He groaned, pressing the heel of his palm to his slit to lessen the lingering ache of his hardened cock.

After all the challenges he'd faced, would it really be this little human female to bring him low?

To his own surprise, Dracchus didn't mind. The challenge of conquering his huntress would be the greatest of his life.

LARKIN SLID the last piece of vorix flesh onto a sharpened stick and propped it over the fire. The aroma of cooking meat made her mouth water, and her empty stomach clenched with hunger.

They'd worked hard after locating the stream earlier that afternoon. She'd strained her already sore body even further, but it had been the sort of work she appreciated.

She'd found several thick, hollow reeds to use as water containers, and they'd located a suitable spot to camp that was near both the stream and the sea. Despite the repeated trips over uneven ground and through thick vegetation, Dracchus hadn't uttered a single complaint. He helped without having to be told, asked questions to clarify what she needed before he made mistakes, and seemed to have limitless endurance.

His assistance was the only thing that enabled her to get a shelter up before dark — not only was he well equipped to tear down large branches and haul heavy loads to their campsite without tools, but his extra limbs were invaluable in combining those pieces into a functional whole. He was able to hold numerous components in place simultaneously while she secured them with thin vines.

Larkin turned her head to look at him. The firelight cast a soft glow over his dark skin, reminding her of how she'd first seen him within the brig. But he wasn't restrained by manacles and netting now; he was free to recline in all his splendor beneath the large lean-to they'd constructed, leaning on an elbow with his tentacles stretched out to one side.

She'd expected him to be uneasy around the fire. He'd gone to the sea while she built it, and she couldn't imagine an aquatic species having much to do with flames, but he displayed no discomfort. Rather, his gaze repeatedly crept toward the cooking meat, gleaming with poorly concealed hunger.

Larkin gathered the first three sticks she'd set up and held them out to him. The meat on their ends continued to sizzle, dripping juices. "Here."

He shook his head. "You eat first."

"Are you always this noble?" she asked.

"I do not know *noble*. You made the kill. The first share is yours."

"To humans, it's rude to turn down an offering."

"And?"

Larkin rolled her eyes. "Krullheaded kraken," she muttered, snatching the meat from one of the sticks and slipping it into her mouth. "There," she said around the food, shoving the other two sticks into his hand.

"Is that not rude, also?" he asked as he accepted the sticks, gesturing toward her mouth. "Macy tells the younglings not to speak while they are chewing."

She lowered her eyebrows. The rangers always attempted to be polite and personable within settlements, but the field was a different story. What did etiquette matter when you were hunting wild beasts in the middle of nowhere?

Still, she chewed and swallowed before speaking again.

"Macy. She's that missing girl from The Watch. The one who was taken by a kraken last year."

"She was not taken." He bit the entire chunk of meat off one of his sticks and proceeded to talk with the food in his mouth.

Jerk.

"She went by her own choice," he continued, "aided by her friends and family."

"Why'd she leave?" Larkin picked up another skewer and took a small bite, breathing around its heat.

"She was mated to a kraken."

Larkin choked. Dracchus shifted toward her with concern on his face, but she waved him back, shaking her head. She coughed, clearing her throat. "I think I misheard that. She *what?*"

"She was mated to a kraken."

Her gaze traveled down his body, pausing on his pelvis, right above the start of his tentacles. There was nothing there but smooth, black flesh.

"Is that even possible?" she asked.

He followed her gaze downward and frowned. "We do not extrude at all times, like your males."

Larkin was glad she hadn't taken another bite of food; her shock would've choked her to death. "*Extrude?* You mean it's...*in* there?"

"Where else would it be?" His brows fell to enhance his frown.

She couldn't tell if he was confused or insulted. Perhaps a bit of both?

Still, she found some humor in this. He'd shown no shame in examining her. Smirking, she turned her face away. "Must be small, to be tucked away like that."

Dracchus was suddenly in front of her; he'd moved with a speed he shouldn't have been capable of, and her heart leapt. He pushed her down onto her back and loomed over her, filling her vision entirely, amber eyes reflecting residual firelight.

"I could take that as a challenge, female." His voice vibrated through her belly, straight to her core. Her sex tightened as desire flooded her. "One that you cannot handle."

Larkin stared up at him, confused by her body's reaction. How could something — some*one* — that wasn't entirely human affect her in such a manner? Despite the familiar structures of his face and torso, so much about him was alien. And, somehow, his dominating presence — the press of his lower body against hers, his arms caging her in, the sound of his voice, and the intensity in his eyes — was exciting.

She knew at that moment that any control she held over the situation existed only because he allowed it to. The realization should've been frightening, but deep down, in a part of herself she'd never acknowledged, it thrilled her.

Her heart hammered against her ribs. She raised her chin, keeping her eyes locked with his. "I can handle anything you got, kraken."

His gaze dipped, sliding over her body with more heat than the nearby fire. Tentacles moved over the outsides of her legs, curling over her thighs, and his nostrils flared with a deep inhalation. He released the breath with a rumbling growl and smirked, giving her a brief glimpse of his pointed teeth.

"Perhaps you can, female." He rolled aside, returning to his original position.

She laid there for a moment, quietly catching her breath.

What has gotten into me?

When she sat up, Dracchus offered her a pair of sticks with cooked meat on their ends as though nothing had happened.

Larkin took them and ate in silence, forcing her attention onto *anything* but Dracchus. All the while, she felt his gaze upon her, and the hollow ache between her legs only worsened.

CHAPTER 10

Larkin woke to the sound of waves against the shore. She rolled onto her back, opened her eyes, and turned her head. Dracchus's place under the shelter was empty. Drawing in a deep breath, she sat up and stretched her arms over her head, scanning the campsite.

Dracchus was nowhere to be seen.

The fire had died out, leaving nothing but the charred, crumbled pieces of a log and pale ash. The vorix meat had made a good meal, especially after going a while without food, but it couldn't have provided enough sustenance for the big kraken. At best, it had whetted his appetite.

He'd be back. She knew it with instinctual certainty, and she refused to think about it any deeper than that; she wasn't ready to admit to herself that she *wanted* him back. Now.

Larkin grabbed her boots and pulled them on, groaning appreciatively as she wiggled her toes inside; her footwear was finally dry.

She drained two of the reeds to slake her thirst. The water was cool and clean, a welcome refreshment in the already warm jungle air. After wiping her mouth with the back of her hand, she gathered the empty reeds and carried them into the jungle, heading toward the nearby stream, stopping briefly to empty her bladder along the way.

Crouching beside the stream, she filled the reeds one at a time, propping the full containers against a rock. She let her eyes wander as she worked.

Morning sunlight streamed through the canopy, shafts of it hitting the water to make it sparkle in small patches. Everything was full of life — the thick vegetation was varying shades of green and violet, with a few hints of red and blue scattered amidst it. Countless sounds filled the air, creating the rhythmless music from which she'd always drawn comfort. The jungle had been her favorite place as a little girl. She knew all the animal calls and had always been fascinated by the variety of wildlife on Halora.

Larkin had been ecstatic when her father had deemed her old enough to start learning about survival. She'd felt so big and proud following her brother and parents through the jungle, learning to spot trails, to make traps, to locate sources of water and which plants were safe to eat. At six years old, it had all seemed so huge and wondrous, and her parents seemed to know *everything* about all of it.

A pang of loss struck her chest. Larkin rubbed her breastbone, frowning. Her relationship with her father had been strained since they'd learned of Randall's disappearance. Nicholas Laster had been in pain, but he refused to let Larkin in, choosing instead to turn his hurt into anger. That's all that had fueled him over the last several months.

The pain in her chest intensified as she recalled their argument on the ship.

No matter what he'd done, he was her father. She didn't love him any less, even though he'd lost his way.

Had he made it off the burning ship? Had he survived long enough to reach one of the other boats?

All Larkin could do was hope he was safe, just as she'd hoped for Randall.

She carried the armful of water-laden reeds back to camp, standing them in small holes she'd dug to prevent them from tipping over. That done, she busied herself by collecting wood and kindling for their fire. During her search, she found several piles of krull dung, and gathered them in large leaves; they would burn longer and cleaner than wood.

After collecting adequate fuel, she picked up the stick she'd used to kill the vorix and followed the stream toward the sea. When she finally stepped onto the beach, she tilted her head back and let the cool ocean breeze flow over her. Her skin was already sweat-dampened, her clothes already sticky, and she was grateful for the relief.

She scanned the shore as she walked along the soft, dry sand. Still no sign of Dracchus.

"Where the hell are you, kraken?"

The waves continued teasing the land, flowing over the sand and receding back in an endless game as old as time. It was a beautiful sight, and the constant sigh of the sea was surprisingly soothing. She'd been too distracted in The Watch to appreciate the scenery.

She climbed onto a large, flat rock, which stood about a meter over the sand and stretched into the water. Several depressions on the rock were still filled with seawater, and small sea creatures had sheltered in the many nooks and holes to await the high tide. Empty shells and the remains of Halorian lobsters were scattered amidst drying stalks of seaweed.

Larkin moved to the edge of the rock, kicked aside a broken shell, and sat down. Water rushed around the stone below, nearly flowing over her dangling feet. She drew her knife, laid her stick over her lap, and began sharpening the points of its fork end.

Her thoughts strayed to the large kraken as she worked. She could still recall his weight pressing lightly over her, the feel of his skin, the closeness of his thick arms, and the way his voice had dipped an octave when he spoke. She was getting wet just thinking about it.

"Ugh!" She squeezed her thighs together, but that only seemed to worsen her discomfort.

She glared out at the open water. How could she be attracted to him? He wasn't human, and his kind had taken her brother and likely killed the other rangers.

But Dracchus had said Randall was betrayed by his men. If that was true, they'd deserved any punishment the kraken had inflicted…

She found herself glancing up from her task repeatedly, anticipating a glimpse of his dark, damp skin glistening in the sunlight as he rose from the surf.

DRACCHUS SPREAD HIS TENTACLES WIDE, slowing his forward momentum. He'd spent half the day swimming along the coast, searching for a familiar feature by which to determine his current location. Despite the comforting embrace of the sea, it was too much time away from Larkin. She was tough and capable, and he no longer doubted her ability to survive in the jungle, but he did not trust land or the creatures dwelling upon it.

He scanned his surroundings. The coastal cliffs to his right gave way to a gentle, rocky slope at their base, which in turn flowed into patches of seagrass, towering stalks of seaweed, and large, colorful chunks of coral. He wasn't far from their camp, and the abundance of life in this area would likely provide a meal with minimal effort. He'd not yet hit his physical limits, but lack of food pushed him closer that much faster.

He smiled as he sank toward the bottom. Larkin would want to cook anything he brought back. Though it wasn't his preference, he'd eat cooked meat without hesitation just for the opportunity to share her company.

Warm, gentle currents flowed around him, and he drifted into one, letting it carry him forward.

The feel of Larkin's body and its increasing warmth beneath his had not faded from his mind since the night before, and his skin tingled with the remembrance. He'd nearly claimed her then and there — the perfume of her arousal, though faint, had swept over him and made him dizzy with lust.

Dracchus dropped out of the current, changed his skin to match the sand, and crept along the bottom.

Such distractions were unlike him. He'd always been able to disconnect himself from worries — even through the turmoil his people had faced over the last year — and focus on the task at hand. Food was a *necessity*. That meant setting aside everything else to fulfill the more pressing need.

He acknowledged all of this, understood it, but couldn't shake Larkin from his thoughts.

Larkin's brother had proven himself an excellent hunter and a trusted companion, and Dracchus had no doubt she would be the same. He longed to see her skill at work in his native environment. Female hunters went against the traditions of the kraken, but what did that matter? Human females were not like kraken females — they weren't nearly as rare and weren't designed to have difficulties reproducing. That didn't make human females expendable, but one putting herself at risk would not endanger the existence of her species.

Larkin was a worthy mate. She'd not back down from any challenge, and she'd never accept a place in the Facility amongst the females and younglings even if he commanded it.

Dracchus turned slowly onto his back, spreading out his tentacles beneath him, and lay still. Gradually, the surrounding creatures seemed to decide the new mound of oddly-shaped sand wasn't a threat.

Did humans ever lay in wait like this to ambush their prey? They seemed relatively clumsy and conspicuous in the water, so obviously out of place that Dracchus couldn't imagine them using such tactics, even on land.

Then he recalled the silent ease with which Larkin had moved through the jungle, and he knew he was foolish to doubt their abilities in any way. Humans were nothing if not surprising.

Thoughts of her movement led to thoughts of her backside and legs, which in turn summoned images of her peeling her pants off to reveal her pale, lithe limbs. Dracchus longed to slide his tentacles over her bare flesh, to peel the scrap of cloth away from her slit and taste her there. His blood heated, pulsing into his shaft.

He clenched his jaw against a wave of desire and discomfort.

Only a massive surge of willpower forced his attention back to his surroundings. The thumping of his hearts had grown louder than the ever-present sound of water, and heat gathered low in his gut. He resisted the urge to dig his claws into the sand and thrash his tentacles restlessly, but his limbs itched with the need to move, to release some of his sudden tension.

Fish swam by above him — some long and sleek, some short with powerful tails, some with flexible growths protruding from their bodies, or reflective skin, or oversized mouths. The kraken had names for some, but many types weren't important enough to warrant naming because they either weren't a good source of food or weren't a danger.

Humans seemed to name *everything*, regardless of importance. How did they avoid getting confused?

A large spinefish entered his field of vision, and he cast aside his other thoughts. The fish's body was longer than Dracchus's arm, and the spikes jutting from around its head were nearly half its body length. It would provide enough meat for he and Larkin to enjoy a filling meal together.

Dracchus tensed his muscles as the spinefish neared, its flat tail swishing from side to side with an easy rhythm. Predators large enough to prey upon these fish were low in number, and their long, hard spines deterred all but the most precise attacks.

The spinefish glided directly over Dracchus. He waited, watching for the vulnerable section behind its head.

Dracchus darted off the bottom. Surrounding fish scattered at the sudden burst of movement, but the spinefish was too close to flee. Two of Dracchus's tentacles coiled around it just behind its head. Despite its thrashing, it could not break his hold, and the angle of its spines prevented it from inflicting any damage.

Without pausing, Dracchus drew the fish closer and jabbed a claw behind its skull. Its thrashing ended in a series of uneven spasms. When it was still, he snapped off each one of its long, bony spines, gathering them into a small bundle; Larkin might have use for them.

He continued his return trip.

Dracchus emerged from the water shortly after, carrying the spinefish by its mouth. The sun blazed directly overhead, marking midday. His search would have to resume tomorrow, and he'd need to push longer, farther, if he wanted to figure out where they were. But he didn't want to leave her alone.

That he would even consider delaying was foolish. *Because I wanted to be near you* was no good reason for it. Larkin wanted to see Randall; her patience would only hold out for so long.

Dracchus's self-control would only go so far, as well.

Besides, he needed to know what was happening in the Facility. Had Vasil warned them? Had Neo already tried something, forcing Jax and Arkon to defend mates and younglings? Dracchus cared about all the kraken, and he'd accepted Macy, Aymee, and Randall as his kind. As his family. He couldn't bring himself to feel shame for holding those closest to him above all the rest.

As he moved up the beach in the direction of their camp, shouting from Larkin caught his attention.

He hurried toward her voice, rounding a bend to find her

standing atop a flat rock. The tide splashed against the stone on three sides. She clutched her long stick, her gaze shifting between four slowly advancing prixxir.

They were full-grown beasts, slightly larger than Ikaros and longer than Larkin was tall, with thick, strong tails.

Ikaros had been a youngling when Randall began caring for him; he was fiercely protective of Randall and Melaina, but never showed aggression without provocation.

Dracchus doubted these prixxir had been provoked.

The prixxir produced undulating growls, and the foremost beast lunged, snapping its jaws near Larkin's feet — only then did Dracchus see the pair of fish laid out on the rock before her. She took a step back and jabbed her stick at it. The beast scurried back into place beside its companions.

Passing the spinefish to a tentacle, Dracchus rushed forward and hauled himself onto the rock beside the pack of prixxir. The closest two spun about to face him, long whiskers flattening with uncertainty, but another charged at Larkin.

Without slowing, Dracchus swung his arm upward, catching the attacking prixxir in its side and heaving it off the rock. The beast chirruped and splashed into the incoming tide. Dracchus turned to face the others immediately. All three had assumed low stances, baring their teeth and growling, hind legs bunched as though ready to pounce.

Dracchus flared his skin red and roared, advancing toward the creatures.

The prixxir ducked their heads and scrambled off the rock. Dracchus watched as they swam back out to sea, eventually dipping beneath the waves and vanishing from sight.

"You're quite fierce," Larkin said from behind him.

He eased the tension in his muscles, reverted his skin to normal, and turned to face her. There was no fear in her expression.

Smirking, she tilted her head. "Had the humans seen you like that, they'd have pissed themselves."

Dracchus grunted. "Yes, and then shot me anyway."

Larkin winced. "Yeah, probably." She shifted her gaze, staring in the direction the prixxir had gone. "Thanks for that."

He nodded. "Prixxir do not normally come ashore during the day in search of food. Either they believed your catch to be an easy meal, or a larger predator frightened them out of the water."

Larkin laughed as she bent down to retrieve her fish. "A larger predator definitely scared them *into* the water."

The sound of her laughter caused warmth to bloom in his chest, and he smiled. Though they'd spent less than two days together, they were falling into an easy companionship he'd not experienced often in his life. Having his words turned around on him used to infuriate Dracchus, at least when he'd been able to recognize the mockery, but there was no malice in Larkin's demeanor now.

His female was teasing him. He'd learned from the humans in the Facility that such could be a sign of affection.

"Are you hurt?" he asked, looking her over.

"No. You came in time. Any later and I might've been prixxir food." She jumped down from the rock.

Dracchus followed her down. Prixxir preyed on small creatures — fish and hard-shells, mostly — but they were capable of inflicting significant damage when provoked. "They would have left when they got your catch," he said.

"I went through a lot of trouble catching those fish, and I have a kraken to feed. They could have caught their own."

He glanced at her as they moved toward the jungle.

I have a kraken to feed.

It was still a strange thing to Dracchus. He'd been a provider since he was old enough to go on his first hunt; it had been his duty to feed everyone else. And now this little human was attempting to provide for him. Kraken females did not hunt. A tangled mess of emotions rose in him, too chaotic, too raw, for him to sort. Should it hurt his pride, or make him proud of her?

He dismissed the question as more foolishness. His pride in her only increased with each passing moment. She put others before herself, and that was a quality Dracchus admired.

"I brought food, as well," he said, bringing the spinefish forward. "I have a human to feed."

Larkin grinned at him over her shoulder. "Looks like we'll have full bellies tonight."

CHAPTER 11

ON HIS THIRD DAY OF SEARCHING, DRACCHUS FINALLY FOUND WHAT he'd sought — a distinct, recognizable feature on the sea floor, a place he *knew*.

Here, the coastal cliffs sloped gradually at their bases until they eventually leveled out, and the bottom was mostly exposed rock with sand and vegetation gathered in countless crevices. It was a common enough underwater seascape, but one thing made this area stand out.

The Ring.

It was a huge circle of sand amidst the stone. Tall, thin rocks stood at random intervals and conflicting angles around and within it, and the sand was broken by sparse clumps of vegetation. Many of the smaller stones were undoubtedly sandseekers, buried in the sand as they awaited the passage of prey overhead. Coral growths and clusters of sea creatures surrounded the ring with vibrancy and color, enhancing its contrast with the dark stone even further.

Dracchus knew the place well; it was one of several locations where the kraken regularly hunted sandseekers, and he'd been here more times than he could count.

His first instinct was to swim to the Facility immediately. He needed to ensure his friends were safe, and the sooner he obtained a diving suit for Larkin, the sooner he could bring her to Randall.

The sooner he could share a den with her.

But it had taken him nearly half a day's swim to get here from their encampment, and it would take just as long to reach the Facility from the Ring. By the time he returned to her, he'd have been gone all day and an entire night.

After their encounter with the vorix and her stand-off with the prixxir, he was hesitant to leave her alone for so long without a word.

Was informing her of his intention worth losing a day to unnecessary travel time?

Dracchus turned toward the Facility and swam, pushing himself hard. Water rushed past him, stone and sand sped by, and his hearts thumped rapidly.

He was growing used to feeling conflicted; ever since he'd discovered Jax with Macy, Dracchus had started questioning everything he'd known. Few things were as simple as he'd once believed. But he didn't have the luxury of prolonged consideration every time he was presented with a complicated matter. His internal conflicts couldn't be allowed to prevent him from making necessary decisions.

Larkin was practical. She would understand his choice.

He kept low, gliding just above the bottom, avoiding the likeliest places for sandseekers and other predators to lurk. The seafloor was a blur, its familiar features reduced to indistinct shapes and blotches of color by his haste. His alertness was instinctual, fueled by a lifetime of experience.

For all Dracchus's speed, the journey felt too long. Part of his mind remained with Larkin, back on land, imagining all manner of terrifying beast stalking her through the dense jungle. Another part had shifted ahead to anticipate the worst back at the Facility

— that Neo and Kronus had made a move and harmed Dracchus's family.

The dark shapes of the Facility's clustered buildings were a relief when they finally came into sight, but the feeling was short-lived. He'd rarely been so aware of the passage of time, even when dealing with other urgent matters. Every moment felt essential, important, valuable, and though they passed with agonizing slowness, they seemed only increasingly inadequate in number.

He swept his gaze across the front of the Facility as he approached. No net hung from the exterior light posts, meaning no hunt had been organized. That was as troubling as it was fortunate — it meant less chance of encountering Kronus's followers inside the main building, but it also signaled a potential disruption to the kraken's lives.

Obtaining food had always been dangerous work, but the humans had presented a new threat, one beyond the understanding of most kraken — technology.

He pressed in the button sequence at the primary entrance and entered the pressurization chamber. His preoccupation deafened him to the computer's voice; he reacted only to the light over the interior door shifting from red to green, reaching forward to slap the button and open the entryway.

Dracchus hauled himself through the corridors, using every available handhold to increase his speed. He passed the chamber in which he'd hidden most of the diving suits and guns after Randall had been brought to the Facility. Larkin needed a suit, and a weapon would grant her another layer of security. Ferocity alone would not save her from a razorback or a sandseeker.

He would return to the room as he departed the Facility.

He hurried through the tunnel into the Cabins, where Macy, Aymee, and Randall kept dens with their kraken mates and younglings.

Jax and Macy were in their den, the latter playing some sort of game with Sarina involving colored squares and little round pieces.

Sarina sat across from her mother at the table, staring down at the game with her little tongue sticking out between her lips. Her gaze flickered up to Dracchus and fell again as she reached for one of the pieces. Her hand stopped in mid-air and she looked at him again, wide-eyed.

"Uncle Drak!" She bumped the table as she leapt off her seat, rattling the game pieces, and darted toward him.

The youngling jumped at Dracchus. He caught Sarina and wrapped his arms around her as she squeezed his neck, ignoring the tightness in his chest; it was likely the result of overexertion and lacking nourishment.

"Thank God!" Macy hurried over with Jax close behind. She threw her arms around Dracchus's waist and embraced him. "What happened to you? When the others returned, and you—"

"He's the strongest," Sarina explained as though it were a given. "Nothing can stop him."

"Has Vasil returned?" Dracchus asked.

"Two days ago," Jax replied.

"And Neo?"

Macy frowned, and Jax's features darkened.

"Yesterday." Jax encircled Macy with his arms when she stepped back from Dracchus, drawing her close. "Vasil had already given an account of what happened. Neo's story was similar, but he was far more vocal about the cruelty of the humans on board, and the *war* between our people. It worked Kronus and the rest of their followers into a frenzy. They have made more threats, but there's been no violence thus far."

Dracchus nodded. Having seen Neo's state the night they escaped the ship, Dracchus's only surprise was that the enraged kraken hadn't yet acted on those threats. "I trust Vasil was truthful."

"This situation is moving beyond a point at which we can

maintain our tenuous control." Jax leaned his head down and pressed his lips to Macy's hair.

Dracchus had fault in that — he'd already been involved, even before Larkin, but his recent actions had likely heightened the tensions. He would not stand down. Change was difficult, uncomfortable, and taxing, but it was the only means of securing a future for the generations to come.

"Is Arkon in his den?" Dracchus asked. "We three must speak."

"He and Aymee were resting while Jace naps," Macy replied, "but I can go get them. Everyone's going to be so happy to see you home safe!"

"No." Dracchus's voice halted Macy as she was moving toward the door. She met his gaze with concern in her eyes. "No one else must know. Not until I return."

"Everyone was ready to go out and rescue you," she said, "to risk themselves to save you. Now you don't even want them to know you're okay? And what do you mean not until you return? You're leaving again?"

Her words hit him with surprising strength, creating an ache in his chest. Dracchus hadn't expected anyone to come for him, hadn't *wanted* them to; all the individuals he cared about most had mates and young to look after. He was not worth putting the safety of females and younglings at risk. That they'd even consider searching for him had never crossed his mind.

"I am going to bring the human who shot us with sleeping bullets to the Facility. She is Randall's sister."

Sarina climbed along Dracchus's arm and shoulders, seemingly oblivious to her parents' stunned silence.

"Bring Arkon," Dracchus said, "but *only* Arkon. I will tell you all I can before I leave, but haste is necessary."

Jax opened his mouth only to close it a few moments later without uttering a word. He nodded and drifted out of the room.

Little Sarina mounted Dracchus's shoulders, wrapping her arms around his forehead, and rested her chin on his head.

"She's the one you saved from Neo," Macy finally said. "He wants to…" She looked up at her daughter and frowned.

"He will end every human he can find, if he has his way," Dracchus said.

"Why are you bringing her here? The kraken are more divided now than ever, and Kronus's group will want to harm her even more than they do the rest of us."

"She released us while the ship was burning. The other humans would have left us in those cages to die."

"Why not let her return home? People already know about the kraken, but none of them know how to find this place. Once you bring her here…that's it, isn't it? She can't leave."

"She wants to see her brother again."

Macy frowned. "And you trust her?"

"With my life," he replied without hesitation.

Macy's eyes widened, and even Dracchus was surprised by what he'd said.

He'd only known Larkin for a short while, but he'd come to trust her unquestioningly.

"She will be mine," he said.

Macy's mouth gaped. She shook her head and laughed, prompting laughter from Sarina. "Leave it to you to choose the greatest challenge."

Jax returned with Arkon a few moments later.

"You have returned!" Arkon said, and the lingering grogginess in his eyes cleared rapidly. "You will have to tell me everything you can about these goggles the hunters used, and—" He fell silent when he noticed Macy's incredulous expression. "What is it?"

"You're not going to believe this," she replied, shifting her gaze back to Dracchus. "Dracchus picked a mate."

"You were correct. I do not believe it," Arkon replied.

Dracchus turned to face Arkon and Jax, producing another chuckle from Sarina, who clung to his head like he was a wild sea creature attempting to buck her off.

"Come on, you," Macy said, pulling Sarina down from Dracchus's shoulders. The youngling put up a bit of resistance before finally relinquishing her hold.

"What is this all about, Dracchus?" Arkon asked. "I hope you do not mind my saying, but you don't look particularly happy to be back."

"It is a complicated situation, Arkon. The sort you enjoy puzzling out," Dracchus replied.

He told them everything, starting with the human boats. Fortunately, Arkon seemed to sense Dracchus's urgency and refrained from asking a torrent of questions. When he was done, everyone stood in silence save Sarina; she had returned to the table, where she was moving the game pieces around, stacking them atop one another and making strange little sounds as she played.

"What do you need?" Macy asked. "Anything we can do to help. Jax and Arkon can escort you, and—"

"No, Macy," Dracchus said gently. "Jax and Arkon will remain here. We cannot leave any of you vulnerable."

"But that's such a long way to travel alone, Dracchus."

Larkin's words rose to the forefront of his mind. *We make do with what we have.*

"We will make do," he said. "Given the current situation, none of you will go unprotected."

"We should tell Randall, at least. He will accompany you," Arkon said.

"Randall must not know until I bring her here."

"Do you not trust him?" Jax asked.

"I trust them both. But I do not want to give Randall the chance to do something stupid. He is better off here, helping to defend all of you."

"I won't speak a word, then," Macy said. "But there has to be something we can do to help you, Dracchus."

He tilted his head back and turned it slowly, running his gaze over the walls and ceiling. "Prepare a den for us, here in the Cabins, with anything she might need to be comfortable." He paused for a moment. "One beside Randall's."

Something wrapped around his tentacle. Dracchus glanced down to see Sarina clinging to him, staring up with big eyes.

"Are you leaving again?" she asked.

"I must," he replied, lifting her up. "But I will return tomorrow."

She pressed her forehead against his and blew out of her siphons. He did the same.

"One day, you will be big and strong enough to accompany us, Sarina." He flicked his gaze to Jax; the Wanderer wore a warning expression. "So long as your parents allow you to."

"Let's not get ahead of ourselves," Macy said. "She doesn't need to grow up any faster than she already is."

Jax moved forward and pried Sarina from Dracchus's tentacle. She giggled and climbed up her father's arm, searching for a new place to perch.

"Go and do as you must," Jax said, placing a hand on Dracchus's shoulder. "We will await your return, and once she is here, we will do all we can to protect your female."

Dracchus nodded. Jax's steady, deliberate gaze conveyed his understanding of all that was at stake — this went beyond a single human, beyond a single female. Supporting Dracchus in this, in protecting the human who'd been integral to the capture of three kraken, would be declared the ultimate betrayal by Kronus's supporters.

This would all but eliminate the chance for the kraken to resolve their disagreements peacefully.

CHAPTER 12

LARKIN STARED OUT INTO THE DARK JUNGLE FROM BENEATH THE shelter, spear resting on her lap and knife on the ground beside her. The fire cast eerie, dancing shadows on the trees around her. She should've been asleep, but sleep had refused to come. Her gaze darted toward every sound, moved not by fear, but anticipation.

Dracchus hadn't returned from his search. He'd returned before sunset on the other days, but night had fallen hours ago. She wasn't sure what to think. What had happened?

Had the rangers recaptured him? Had he been attacked by another predator?

No, she wouldn't believe any of that. She knew, wherever he was, he had a good reason for not returning. That knowledge offered no comfort.

Dracchus was more than a means of seeing her brother again. She'd enjoyed his company over the last few days and found a kindred spirit in him. He was practical, tough, and dependable, and had no problem admitting when he didn't know something. Though most of her jokes seemed to go over his head, he'd accepted them with endearing nonchalance. Even his stubborn streak had grown on her.

Being around him felt natural, comfortable, liberating. She could be herself instead of the commander's daughter. She could just be…Larkin.

She opened her eyes, sitting up abruptly. The faint, gray light of predawn tentatively prodded the canopy. When had she fallen asleep?

Her grogginess dissipated quickly; she'd been woken by a noise — rustling vegetation, like something large was approaching. She grabbed her spear and leapt to her feet. The fire was low, meaning it would be of little aid in scaring away most jungle creatures.

A huge black figure emerged from the foliage, towering over her, amber eyes reflecting the faint light.

"What the hell, kraken? Where have you been?" she demanded, lowering her spear.

He lifted something in his hand — a black bundle — and unfolded it, removing what appeared to be a curved piece of glass from its center. He held the black fabric up, revealing some sort of suit that looked to be sized for a child.

"Today I will bring you to see your brother," he said.

"Really?" she asked, eyes wide as she looked between him and the suit. "You found it?"

"Yes." He handed her the suit and the piece of glass and sank down next to the fire.

She'd set aside several pieces of cooked fish for him, wrapped in thick leaves to mask their scent. He unwrapped them and ate ravenously, scarcely allowing himself time to breathe. Had he been traveling all day yesterday and through the night?

Larkin frowned.

"If we leave with the dawn, we will arrive before sunset," he said.

"Rest, Dracchus," she said, stepping away to study the suit. The material was strange, unlike anything she'd ever seen. A hexagonal pattern covered the black fabric, which felt far too thin to be as durable as it seemed.

He slipped a final piece of fish into his mouth, chewing it to one side, and gestured at the remaining bundles of food. "You need to eat before we leave, female."

"Once you finish, I will. Eat as much as you need."

Dracchus shook his head. "What's left is yours. Thank you for saving it."

Larkin arched a brow. "Kraken, you should know not to argue with me by now. You've been out all day and night while I've just been sitting around. Eat."

He stared at her with a creased brow and swallowed the bite he'd taken. Finally, after a long pause, he opened the remaining bundles and wolfed down the meat.

"How does it work? Will it even fit?" she asked, eyes back on the suit, shifting it in her hands.

"It will stretch when you pull it on. The circle piece is the front."

She held the suit up by the shoulders and turned it, locating the plastic-looking chest piece. She couldn't deny her skepticism; the thing was way too small. But a lot of the old tech — the good stuff, anyway — was so advanced that it seemed more like magic than technology.

Bending down, she raised a foot and pushed it into the suit.

"You have to remove your other coverings," Dracchus said.

She turned her head toward him, brows drawn. "What?"

"Macy said you have to remove your coverings," he said, gesturing to his torso as though he had a shirt on, "or else the suit will not work properly."

Larkin scowled. "Of course," she muttered. "Turn around, kraken, and no peeking."

He frowned and tilted his head.

"I'm not joking," she said.

Dracchus shifted his lower body, sliding his tentacles around to twist away from her.

Once she was certain he wasn't looking, she placed the suit on the ground and unbuttoned her pants. Hooking her waistband and underwear at once, she pushed them down her legs and kicked them aside. Her tank joined them soon after, leaving Larkin as bare as the day she was born.

Picking up the suit again, she tugged it open and shoved her feet in one at a time.

As Dracchus had said, the material stretched as she pulled, far more than she'd imagined possible — so much so that it threw her off-balance.

She stumbled backward, waving her arms to right herself, and spun as her heel caught on a stone. She pitched toward the fire.

Dracchus's hands encircled her waist from behind, halting her downward momentum. For a moment, she stared down at the low flames, breathing heavily. He lifted her off the ground like she weighed nothing and set her back down away from the fire, turning her to face him.

Larkin's fingers curled around his forearms as she looked up at him, wide-eyed, but he only briefly met her gaze. His eyes dipped. She remembered suddenly that she was naked above her knees. His amber irises darkened.

She stood there, frozen — unable to cover herself, to look away, to breathe. Her heart fluttered, and her awareness of him intensified. His hands on her waist were firm, but gentle, and she could feel the small pricks of his claws pressing lightly against her backside. Her nipples tightened beneath his lustful gaze, aching to be touched. Desire coursed through her.

His eyes moved lower, and he scowled. He brushed the pad of his thumb over the large, rough scars on her lower abdomen, and tension pulsed through his hands.

Larkin stiffened, an icy chill chasing away the heat that had suffused her.

"What is this?" he growled, nostrils flaring with a heavy exhalation.

She attempted to step out of his grasp, but his hold tightened. She covered her breasts with an arm and narrowed her eyes. "Let me go."

"Did someone do this to you?" he demanded. His skin had taken on a crimson tint. "Tell me who, and they will know vengeance."

Larkin's brows furrowed. "What? No one did this. It was a hunting accident." She pushed at his chest. "Now let go."

Her shove didn't budge him at all. He searched her face, his rage giving way first to confusion, and then reluctant understanding. His gaze fell to her stomach. "What happened?"

Glowering, she slapped her other hand over her scars. "I was stupid and paid the price for it."

If only the scars had been the sole consequence of her bleeding heart on that long-ago day.

She pressed her lips together and looked away from him. She was used to looks of discomfort and disgust from the few people who'd seen her scars; most men she'd been intimate with had turned away from the sight of them and seemed to avoid touching them as though they were contagious. They were jagged, pink and puckered, poorly healed — the only treatment available when she was injured had been improvised in the field, and the infection that followed hadn't helped.

But she'd never seen anyone get angry about the scars. Her father had averted his gaze, unwilling or unable to acknowledge their existence or what they represented, and Randall's expression always fell when he caught sight of them. She'd taken to wearing longer shirts beneath her usual clothes so her beltline would remain hidden.

Unlike everyone else, she couldn't pretend they didn't exist. She'd live with the reminder for the rest of her life.

"Just let go of me, Dracchus." Tears welled in her eyes. Even all these years later, those emotions were still raw. She'd accept the irreversible damage that had been done to her own body without complaint if she could have her mother back.

She wouldn't let those tears fall. Not after holding them in for so long.

His hands lingered on her waist, and his thumb brushed over the exposed tip of the scars. Then he released her and backed away.

Larkin faced away from him and hurriedly yanked the suit on, thrusting her arms into the sleeves. She trembled, but she wasn't sure if it was her body coming down from her prior arousal, the adrenaline rush of her anger, or the emotional pain she always suffered when reminded of what had happened.

She heard Dracchus move farther away from her.

Larkin closed her eyes and took several deep breaths to calm herself. He wasn't at fault. She just... She was tired of being looked at as though she were damaged, as though she were less than a woman, as though she were unworthy. She wanted to matter in someone's eyes. To have someone look at her and not see her scars and what they represented, but to see *her*. To want her. *All* of her.

The back of the suit gaped open, exposing her skin to the already warm air.

"How do I close this?" she asked.

"Slide your fingers around the edge of the round piece."

She glanced down at the plastic chest piece and lifted a hand to it, running her covered fingertips along its outside. She nearly shuddered as the suit sealed itself up her back; it was amongst the strangest sensations she'd ever experienced.

"The hood will need to be raised," he said.

Reaching behind her neck, she caught hold of the hood and drew it up, tucking her hair beneath it. That done, she looked down at herself, turning her hands slowly. The suit clung to her like a second skin, though it wasn't uncomfortable.

When she turned toward Dracchus, he extended an arm, offering the piece of clear glass. As she accepted it, she noticed a thin, black border around the edges.

"This…is for my face, right?"

He nodded.

"How do I put it on?"

Dracchus spread his fingers and lifted his hand to his face. "It will seal itself." His frown hadn't eased, which only made her regret the way she'd spoken to him.

She held the mask in both hands and stared down at it. Though it was large enough to cover the entire opening in the hood, there were no visible means to fasten it in place. Still, he'd been right so far. She raised the mask, leaning her head down to meet it. The sudden, soft hiss startled her, and she felt the weight of the mask lift off her hands as it connected to the hood.

"Hello," said a pleasant voice, "I am Sam, your system assistant and monitor. Field generator active." A tingling sensation pulsed across Larkin's skin, gone as quickly as it had come. "Automatically adjusting vision for poor lighting conditions."

Larkin's eyes widened as everything in her field of view brightened; it was like the sun had fully risen in an instant. This tech was more advanced, but it was similar in function to the spectra goggles the rangers had found under the lighthouse.

"You will have to learn the feel of the suit while we travel," Dracchus said.

She looked up at him and frowned. "You just got back. Shouldn't you rest?" Her voice sounded strange, its tone slightly altered by some sort of audio transmitter in the mask.

"I will rest when we have reached the Facility."

"What facility?"

"It is the name of my people's home." He held out his hand to her, palm up. "Come, female. We have a long journey ahead, and I am eager to see its end."

Larkin stared at his hand; if he were anyone else — excluding her brother — she would have slapped it away, offended. She didn't need her hand held. She'd proven herself, had earned her place. But Dracchus wasn't offering because he thought her weak. It was a gesture of reassurance; they were about to enter territory wholly unknown to Larkin, and he would be with her the whole time.

She placed her hand in his and was immediately disappointed — she wanted to feel his skin against hers, but the suit prevented that.

He closed his fingers around her hand. Instinctively, Larkin stepped closer.

"We will not be able to communicate once we are below." There was that hint of worry on his brow again, the ghost of a frown tugging at the corners of his mouth. "You must remain close at all times."

"I will. Do we need to bring anything?" she asked, looking down at her spear, knife, and clothing.

"There are human clothes in the Facility you may use, and I brought a weapon for you. It is closer to the beach."

Larkin nodded, anticipation chasing away any anxiety she might've felt. She'd see Randall again soon. "Let's get going, then."

"YOUR HEART RATE HAS ACCELERATED," Sam said, his voice breaking through the stifling quiet. "Do you require assistance?"

"No, Sam," Larkin replied distractedly. "I'm fine."

His voice was the only one she'd heard for hours. Her fascination had split her attention between the suit's functions — she'd asked Sam countless questions while she swam alongside Dracchus — and the alien world around her. She'd never imagined such vibrancy and variety underwater.

Though the suit greatly eased her movement, she was unused to the motions; she'd spent years hiking through rough terrain, but swimming taxed muscles she didn't often put to use. Dracchus patiently kept pace with her, stopping when she needed time to rest, his gaze ever-watchful.

Her weariness crept toward exhaustion with the waning sunlight. As they swam farther and farther from land and steadily increased their depth, fear crept out of Larkin's subconscious to assail her.

She was trapped — submerged under thirty meters of water and surrounded by an unfamiliar landscape that grew more indistinct as the light faded. All that protected her from that looming abyss was the too-thin fabric of the suit and the small piece of glass over her face. It didn't matter how advanced the gun Dracchus had given her was, it couldn't protect her from drowning.

She breathed deep, willing herself to calm. Weakness suffused her limbs, but she'd dealt with it before — she could push through it. This was Dracchus's third time making this trip without any rest. Larkin sure as hell wasn't going to give up or ask for help on her first attempt.

And Dracchus was there with her. That knowledge held firm beneath her fear, beneath her weariness, and it helped to know she wasn't alone.

Eventually, darkness conquered the water, leaving only the faintest shimmers of starlight on the surface far overhead.

Larkin's speed faltered, slowing until she came to a stop.

"Your heart rate has accelerated. Do you require assistance?" Sam asked again.

"No!" she snapped, turning her head from side to side, scanning the darkness. "I just...need a moment."

Sam possessed multiple vision functions to compensate for the darkness, but she couldn't recall their names through the tired, fearful haze that had settled over her mind, and there wasn't anything to be seen in that darkness because it was impenetrable, impossible, infinite...

Now that they'd stopped, her limbs refused to move again. She didn't know if it was due to panic or exhaustion.

Dracchus was a nearby shadow, barely discernable from the surrounding black. Her eyes detected his movement, but she was only sure of his presence when he wrapped an arm around her waist and drew her body against his. Her arms instinctively encircled his neck.

"I'm not like this. I swear I'm not." He couldn't hear her, but she needed to say it. Despite what other people thought, she'd always excelled due to her own efforts. Her father had never coddled her, and she'd pushed herself harder because she would *not* let the others be right when they said he was the only reason she'd reached her position. Larkin had *earned* everything she had.

But when all the layers were peeled away, she was only human, flawed and vulnerable. She knew her own limits.

Dracchus's hold on her was firm but not painful, and though his size should have made her feel smaller and weaker than she already did at that moment, she felt *safe*. He was solid. Real. Dependable.

He guided her legs around his waist. The suit diminished her sense of touch, but she felt his muscles flex and relax as he swam.

Points of soft blue light appeared on his skin. At first, she thought she was seeing things, but the light really was coming from him. It cast a gentle glow on his features, making him the only thing she could see in the darkness.

Larkin's eyes widened as she studied the glowing stripes on his head, which followed the outline of his neck to his shoulders. Lightly, she traced the markings on his arms. "How are you doing that?"

If he knew she'd spoken, he made no indication.

Their forward motion continued in his unique rhythm. The darkness surrounding them gradually lost its menace as she focused on Dracchus's light, and soon she rested her head on his shoulder. His hold on her tightened.

Sometime later — she could've asked Sam how long it had been, but it seemed unimportant — Dracchus tapped her lightly on the shoulder. She lifted her head and met his gaze. He nodded toward something over her shoulder, and she twisted around to look.

The darkness ahead was broken by a cloud of illumination, and huge shapes loomed in the light.

Buildings, she realized with wonder.

There were at least three, each easily a hundred meters from one end to another, but it was the foremost that drew her attention. The outside wall was bathed in cones of light from fixtures on its exterior, all of which were spaced at almost even intervals — a few gaps indicated that some of the lights had failed.

She counted at least six windows, though all but one was dark. As Dracchus brought her closer, the details of the structure grew more distinct — there were large-but-subtle geometric patterns on the wall, lines and rounded rectangles breaking up what might otherwise appear monotonous and bland.

As they approached the building, they swam between a pair of functioning light posts that stood free on the seafloor. Dracchus directed them toward a metal door with a red light over the top of it and a keypad at its side.

"Do you require entry?" Sam's voice startled her.

Larkin glanced at Dracchus. "Um, yes."

The light above the door switched to green. The door opened.

"Sam, what is this place?" she asked.

"This is *Pontus Alpha*, an Interstellar Defense Coalition research base built with the assistance of Tureon Industries, Incorporated."

Dracchus carefully swam through the open doorway, angling himself to prevent Larkin from bumping into anything. Once they were inside the chamber, she watched over his shoulder as he raised one of his tentacles and pressed a button on the wall behind him. The door slid shut.

"Re-pressurization sequence initiated," Sam said.

"Well, hell. And no one knew about this place? How is that possible?"

A low hum pulsed through the water around them, just strong enough to be noticeable. Larkin tightened her grip on Dracchus, glancing around the room.

"Pontus Alpha is a classified base," Sam said. "Only authorized personnel are briefed on its location and functionality. Please contact your commanding officer with further questions."

As the waterline fell, her body felt heavier. It made holding onto Dracchus harder, but she worried that she'd collapse the moment her feet were beneath her.

"This is your home? The facility you told me about?" she asked.

"Pressurization complete," said a feminine voice from somewhere overhead as soon as the water was drained. "Welcome back, diver six-two-zero."

"Yes," Dracchus said. Larkin felt one of his tentacles brush the side of her leg, and another door whispered open behind her. "You may remove the mask. It is safe."

"Oh." She reached up and tugged on it; the mask didn't budge. "Um, Sam, how do I remove the mask?"

"The mask can be released by utilizing your wrist controls, or through a simple verbal request," Sam replied cheerfully.

"Sam, remove the mask."

There was a faint hiss, and the mask sagged forward into her waiting hand. She lowered it and drew in a tentative breath; the air was surprisingly clean, with only the faintest scent of brine.

"I guess I should let go of you now," Larkin said, smirking at Dracchus.

"If you wish it," he said. "Your weight is slight." The glint in his eyes suggested he didn't want her to let go.

She found that she didn't want to, either. She liked this closeness with Dracchus. Their evenings together had given her a sense of who he was — someone who'd shield her from anything but who'd never belittle her. His strength didn't make her feel inferior; it empowered her to have him at her back. She had the sense that he'd never treat her as lesser, despite his prowess.

Larkin's thoughts gave her pause; these were sentiments people felt toward loved ones. They'd known each other for less than a week, and she'd helped to capture him, had enabled his torture. There couldn't be anything between them — she was human, and he was kraken. Larkin and her people had brought suffering to Dracchus and his.

She lowered her legs from his waist, welcoming immediate pain. Knees wobbling, she released her hold on him.

Dracchus reached for her as she lost her balance, but she caught herself against the wall and held up a hand to stop him, shaking her head.

"I got it," she said. After hours in the water, her body felt as heavy as lead but as unstable as jelly, while her head felt like it floated in an unseen current.

With a frown, Dracchus lowered his arms and backed away, keeping his amber eyes upon her.

Larkin took a deep breath. She'd been carried back into Fort Culver only once, despite dozens of injuries over her time as a ranger, and the circumstances of that occasion had been far worse than this. Dracchus had already carried her enough. Gritting her teeth, she straightened, grateful for the waist-high handrail along the wall.

"Then come, female," he said, not unkindly, and ducked through the interior doorway.

She forced her legs to move and followed him into a long corridor, which looked to be in excellent condition despite the bits of seaweed, sand, and other debris along the floor. Though this space was larger than the walkway between the brig's cages, Dracchus seemed to fill it completely.

"So, you really live here?" she asked, peering into dark rooms through open doorways. "A place made by humans?"

He glanced at her over his shoulder. "It is fitting that we live in the place where our kind was created."

Larkin's steps faltered. "What? What do you mean *created*?"

Dracchus turned to face her, hands at the ready, but he didn't reach for her. "My kind were created by humans long ago. Arkon can explain more, in terms beyond my understanding. But we should not delay here long."

She frowned; her mind was still mulling over what he'd just said, but the warning in his tone couldn't be ignored. "Why shouldn't we delay?"

"Because some of my kind are not friendly to humans. Neo is especially hostile, after his time on your ship."

Larkin scowled. "The one that tried to drown me."

Dracchus nodded. "I will break him if he lays hands upon you again," he said, and Larkin's heart gave a funny little leap, "but I would rather avoid him altogether. You and I are in need of rest, and you'll want to see Randall."

"You're taking me to him now?"

"Is that not what I told you I would do?"

"Yes! Let's go then." She flicked her hands, urging him onward.

He tilted his head, eyes dipping to her gesture, but he turned and continued on without comment.

Reinvigorated by the thought of seeing her brother, Larkin walked beside Dracchus. Her aches were temporarily relegated to the far reaches of her awareness, each step a bit easier than the one before it. They turned down a few intersecting corridors.

Even in her excitement, she picked out visual inconsistencies to use as markers in her mental map — a spot where something claw-like had scraped away the paint; a dim light in a hallway, third from the end; a missing section of grating in the floor grooves.

One of the turns lead them into a tunnel that was glass on all sides, allowing her to stare out into the ocean; all she could see were the other buildings, bathed in their artificial light, but her mind summoned images of cerulean water lit from overhead by the midday sun.

"This place is amazing," she said, trailing her fingertips over the glass.

The entryway at the far end of the tunnel was marked *CABINS*; they passed through it and into another long hallway. Its contours were smoother, softer, and more comforting than the hallways before the tunnel. Doors lined both sides, identical to one another save for the numbers on their faces — odds on the left and evens on the right.

Dracchus led her through two similar hallways before finally stopping in front of a door. Anticipation and anxiousness filled her. He raised a hand, but Larkin caught his arm before he could knock. Frowning, he looked down at her.

"Do you think he'll be happy to see me?" she asked quietly.

What if her coming here changed things for him? Dracchus had said Randall was happy here, and what if she disrupted the new life he'd made?

"He will be happy to see you." The confidence with which he spoke eased her nerves.

After so long apart, after traveling so far and going through so much hardship just to learn if he were alive or dead, how could she be nervous to see her brother? Randall was her only true friend. The only family she had left, besides her father.

She released Dracchus's wrist and stepped back.

Dracchus banged his fist on the door three times in quick succession, producing three dull *thunks*; there were doors in Fort Culver that made a similar sound when struck. Her father sometimes called them blast doors.

Were these strong enough to keep kraken out, or could Dracchus force his way through if he wanted to?

The door made a soft *whoosh* as it slid open. Larkin's position kept her from seeing inside.

"Dracchus?"

Larkin's heart skipped a beat; that was Randall's voice. To hear it after a year of worry made her knees weak. Her brother was alive. He was *here*.

"You look like Ikaros just dragged you in off the beach," Randall said. "Where the hell have you been? We thought you were captured ag—"

Larkin launched herself between them and threw her arms around Randall. The suddenness of it caught him off-guard, and he staggered backward.

"What the hell?" Randall steadied himself, placing his hands on her shoulders.

A pair of growls — one low and undulating, the other oddly human — sounded from somewhere behind him, but Larkin ignored them. She tightened her hold on him, pressing her face against his bare chest, failing to stem the flow of tears from her eyes.

"You're alive." The words clawed their way out of her tight, dry throat. She wanted to tell him that she'd known he was alive all along, that she'd never doubted it, but a small part of her had always feared him dead — a part that had become harder to ignore as time passed and their father grew increasingly obsessed with the search.

"Elle," Randall choked out her name, wrapped her in a crushing embrace, and rested his cheek on her hair.

Larkin cried harder. She hadn't realized how much she'd missed his hugs.

Something pressed against her leg, and Larkin glanced down to see a prixxir sniffing at her calf. She started, pulling her leg away from the beast. It lifted its head and met her gaze questioningly.

"Who is this?" asked a woman from behind Randall. There was an edge to her tone that, while not necessarily hostile, hinted at the potential for aggression.

Randall looked over his shoulder. "Rhea, this is my sister. This is Elle."

Larkin peered behind Randall and her eyes widened in surprise. Rhea was a *kraken*.

Rhea returned Larkin's stare, but curiosity replaced the threat in her gaze. Her features and frame were delicate compared to her male counterparts, belying the subtle muscle tone of her arms and abdomen, but Rhea's sturdiness and strength were unmistakable. Larkin had no doubt this female kraken could easily overpower her.

Like Dracchus, Rhea had no visible hair.

And she was *naked*.

Her small, firm breasts were on display, but Larkin couldn't discern any genitalia below her belly. Were her *parts* hidden, like Dracchus's?

The female kraken approached. The motion of her tentacles, paired with her posture, created a surreally graceful image.

"Randall has told me much about you," Rhea said, tilting her head.

"You are Elle?" came a second voice, softer, and more childlike. Another female kraken — a child, standing as high as Larkin's chest — came out of hiding to join them. Her features were similar to Rhea's, and her smile was warm despite being filled with sharp teeth.

Larkin looked into the room beyond them — to the rumpled bedding, the shirt draped over the back of a chair, the boots stored under the table. She released Randall and took a step back. "This is your home."

Why did she feel so betrayed by that?

Randall looked at Rhea and the child before returning his attention to Larkin. His brow was furrowed. "Yeah, it is."

"And you're happy?"

"Despite everything that happened, yes. I am." He took a step toward her. "Please, Elle, don't look at me like that."

Larkin retreated, bumping into the solid wall of flesh that was

Dracchus, who'd entered the room behind her. She pressed her lips together and slowly released a breath through her nose. Her chest felt strange, *tight*, as though the words she couldn't get out had lodged inside her, and the pressure behind them was rapidly building.

Why was she acting like this? She should be happy for him. Why was she *spoiling* this reunion?

Because I thought he was dead, but he's been here all along, making a home. Making a family. A new family.

All at once, her exhaustion hit her. Her legs wobbled, her knees buckled, and only Dracchus's hands curling around her arms kept her from collapsing. She leaned into him gratefully.

Randall frowned, expression darkening. "What's going on?" he asked, and the confusion in his voice was quickly laced with anger. "Why the fuck did you bring her here, Dracchus? With everything that's going on, why *here*?"

Pain pierced her heart quick and sure, as true as any bullet. "What?"

He clenched his jaw and turned his head as though she'd slapped him. "That's *not* what I mean, Elle."

"There was nowhere else to go," Dracchus replied.

"Don't try to feed me that krullshit!" Randall advanced, eyes locked on Dracchus, as though he stood a chance against the kraken. He jabbed a finger toward the hallway. "They'll want her *blood*, damnit! They already told the story. Elle's the one that captured the three of you. Neo and Kronus would tear her apart at the first opportunity."

"They will not touch her." Dracchus's rumbling voice vibrated through Larkin's back. His hands tightened infinitesimally on her arms. "She is *mine*."

All the breath left Larkin in a rush. She turned her head to stare up at Dracchus; had she heard him correctly? Had he just...*claimed* her?

"What do you mean she's yours?" Randall demanded. His eyes

rounded, and then his face fell into a furious scowl. "What the fuck did you do to my sister?"

Randall was close enough now that Larkin was able to extend her arm and press a hand to his chest, halting his approach.

"He hasn't done anything!" she said. "Not that it's any of your business."

"Larkin, this is—"

"I can barely stand, Randall. All of this is too much for me to take in right now. I just… I need to rest. To think."

Randall clenched his jaw again, and his throat bobbed. Unmasked hurt gleamed in his eyes, but, as hard as it was to do, Larkin brushed it off. This wasn't how she'd expected their reunion to go, and it was her fault. Dwelling on it wouldn't change what had been said, but she wouldn't stand here and let things get worse. Especially not when she wasn't thinking clearly.

He searched her face, and for the first time seemed to realize the state she was in. She could only imagine — bags under her eyes, hair a tangled mess, blotches of red skin where she'd been sunburned.

Larkin slid her hand to his shoulder, brushing over a small patch of rough, raised skin. She looked down to see a circular scar.

"What happened?" She ran her gaze over his torso, finding a similar mark on his abdomen. "Was it true what Dracchus said?"

Randall looked at Dracchus and narrowed his eyes. "What did he say, that I was betrayed by my own men?"

"Cyrus did this?" she asked.

"He only pulled the trigger once, but yeah. He did this."

Shock stole Larkin's breath. She hadn't wanted to believe what Dracchus had told her. She'd never cared for Cyrus Taylor — he'd always possessed a cruel streak — but he was a knowledgeable ranger and their father's closest friend, and he'd been part of their lives for as long as she could remember.

"Why? Why would he do this?"

"We'll talk about it after you get some rest," Randall said, only then meeting her gaze. He took her hand and gently tugged her toward him. "You can take the bed, Elle."

"She will share a den with me," Dracchus said, holding her firm.

"Fuck that!" Randall exploded.

Rhea's tentacle wrapped around Randall's waist, drawing him back into her waiting arms.

"Be silent, human," she said, her lips next to his ear. She looked from Randall to Larkin and Dracchus. Her expression was heavy with meaning that Larkin couldn't decipher. "It is for a female to choose, is it not?"

Dracchus grunted, and Randall looked ready to tear out of Rhea's hold and charge.

"I'll be fine, Randall. We've shared a camp for the last few nights, and Dracchus hasn't hurt me," Larkin said.

"Elle—"

"I can take care of myself. You take care of your new family."

He flinched. Somehow, Larkin kept a straight face, but inside, guilt twisted through her like barbed wire. He hadn't deserved that.

Randall composed himself and looked up to Dracchus again. "You and I are going to have words, kraken."

"We will, human," Dracchus replied.

Rhea gently coaxed Randall back toward the bed as Dracchus steered Larkin into the hallway. The prixxir, who'd been sitting silently, chirruped. Larkin turned her head toward it. The kraken child was beside the creature, staring at Larkin with wide, curious, innocent eyes until the door closed.

CHAPTER 13

THE ROOM DRACCHUS HAD LED LARKIN INTO WAS SET UP LIKE Randall's — its bed was of similar size, the furniture stood in the same places, even the colors were the same. But this room felt cold. How long had it been since anyone lived in it? A hundred years, two hundred years? More? Despite its disuse, it was clean, and it was the nicest place she'd ever stayed, including her room back home.

She turned toward the soft *swish* of the door closing and got an eyeful of dark skin and muscle. She'd been aware of his presence behind her while she surveyed the room, but she hadn't realized he was so close. Dracchus had become her living shadow.

Tilting her head back, she met his gaze. "Thank you. For bringing me here, and for the room."

He offered a soft grunt in response and regarded her with a frown. She was beginning to understand that his grunts were a language all their own, but she hadn't yet decoded their meanings.

Larkin shifted her weight to one leg as he stared. "I'm sure you're ready to be back in your own bed, or whatever you sleep in, so, um, goodnight."

"This is our den," he replied.

"What?" Her brows creased. "I don't think I—"

"This is *our* den." Though he didn't raise his voice, his tone left no room for argument.

"Okay, hold up," she said, lifting her hands, palms toward him.

She will share a den with me.

Her tired mind hadn't quite registered what Dracchus had meant when he said that to Randall. Had he been serious?

She is mine.

Oh shit, shit, shit!

What had she gotten herself into?

Larkin cleared her throat and retreated a step. "Is this your room? Cause if it is, I'll gladly take another and leave you to it."

"I know humans do not often speak plainly, but do you also have trouble understanding plain speech? This den belongs to both of us. We will stay here together."

Larkin bristled. "I have no fucking trouble understanding, but maybe *you* should speak more plainly. Why do we need to share this room? There are a dozen other rooms in this hallway! I understand we shared a campsite, but haven't I proven myself trustworthy yet?" She advanced toward Dracchus, glaring up at him. "Do you seriously think, after everything, that I am going to try anything to harm your people?"

He held her gaze, and a fire sparked in his amber eyes — but it wasn't anger. "You will share this den with me because of the harm my people may try to inflict upon *you*," he said evenly. "You are under my protection, and I can only fulfill my duty by being near. You, more than any of the humans here, have earned the hatred of some kraken."

One of his tentacles slipped around her waist and drew her closer. "And you are *mine*, female. This is your place now."

Larkin's breath hitched at his words. The heat of his body seeped through her diving suit, and his tentacle was like a brand around her waist, deliciously hot and as sturdy as a shackle. She put her hands on his chest and pushed, tilting her upper body away from his. He didn't give at all; she wasn't going anywhere until he allowed it.

"What do you mean by yours?" she asked. "Am I your prisoner now?"

"No." He cupped her jaw with one of his big hands and leaned closer. The fire in his eyes intensified, its heat scorching Larkin to her core. "You are my mate."

She stared at him, her breath rapid and heart racing.

What right did he have to decide that?

"Fuck that!" She jerked her face away from his hand and pushed against his chest. "You can't just do that! I'm not going to…to *mate* with you!"

"Why?" he asked, drawing back and narrowing his eyes. "I have seen the way you look at me. I have not hidden my interest in you."

Larkin's jaw gaped. "You're serious, aren't you? I thought you were just curious because I was human. Not that you wanted to… Fuck!" She turned her face away. Despite her anger, she couldn't deny her body's reactions to him, even now, and that only heightened her frustration.

He guided her face back toward him. She didn't bother resisting; one of his fingers was probably stronger than her entire arm.

"You are a worthy mate," he said. "My equal. Your strength is to be admired, but it is made into something amazing when paired with your compassion. You are a hunter, a fighter, a *warrior*, selfless and fearless, adaptable, unconquerable. But I *must* face that challenge. I will conquer you, or you will conquer me. Either way, I will have you."

He brushed the pad of a finger along her jaw. His gaze held her, and she didn't want to escape it; she wanted to sink into those amber depths and lose herself. "We will share this den, and I will protect you. That will be all for now. In time, I will persuade you to make your claim."

He gently withdrew his tentacle from her waist and lowered his hand. "There are clothes in the dresser, and that room—" he pointed toward something behind her "—has fresh water, if you want to clean yourself."

Larkin swallowed, unsure of what to say. She turned to look at the open doorway behind her. Suddenly, the entire world crashed down on her. Her body was heavy with exhaustion, her eyes swollen and sensitive from crying and strain, her chest raw and throat dry, but she couldn't crawl into bed in her current state.

She glanced back at Dracchus. "This conversation is far from over."

To her annoyance, he simply nodded. How could he seem so confident, so *reasonable*, about this? He'd just decided they were mates and that was supposed to be it?

Krullheaded kraken.

Exhaling heavily through her nose, she walked to the dresser, tugging open the drawers to see what they contained. To her surprise, they were filled with dozens of articles of clothing, all folded neatly. She ran her fingers over a shirt. Her callouses snagged on the soft material.

Why would anyone need so many clothes?

"Where did all this come from?" she asked, picking out a long, loose, shirt and a pair of pants.

"From the humans who lived here before," Dracchus replied.

"Are there any still here?"

"They were all killed by the kraken many generations ago."

Larkin raised her brows and looked at him. "All of them? You killed everyone?"

"My ancestors." His gaze was steady, and there wasn't a hint of shame or remorse in his voice. "I cannot deny the past, but I have done what I can to prevent it from repeating."

"And I made it worse, haven't I?" she asked, frowning. "Bringing me here… What will that do?"

The muscles of his jaw ticked, and his shoulders sagged infinitesimally under some unseen burden. "It will continue to force my people to face the truth of our situation. Change is occurring. It is necessary. And it will not stop."

Larkin held the clothes against her chest as she stared at him. The truth of his words was discomforting, but she couldn't deny it. Change was happening. The very existence of the kraken altered Halora in ways that no one fully understood; the decisions made now, the actions taken, would affect generations to come — human and kraken alike.

As long as they didn't kill each other off.

"Our people have a lot in common, it seems. We thought you were monsters." She ran her gaze over him slowly, and a spark ignited within her that she could not deny. Dracchus's form was appealing to her. He was a kraken, yes, but he was still a *man*. "We weren't wrong. Your kind are capable of being the monsters we imagined, but humans tend to forget we are, too."

After all, hadn't a man her father trusted tried to murder Randall? She'd seen Cyrus's cruelty emerge from time to time on hunts, but she'd never guessed he would direct it toward another human. Just more proof of how naturally humans took to deception, masking their malicious intent behind attractive, friendly faces. The kraken, on the other hand, bore sharp teeth, claws, and tentacles, but seemed — at least in her limited experience — far more honest about their intentions.

Especially when they wanted to kill you.

Dracchus had shown her respect, had fought one of his own to protect her, and had kept to his word. Everything she'd seen from the kraken spoke of an underlying humanity, for better or worse — humans weren't all rainbows and sunshine, either.

"Go and do as you must," he said, nodding toward the washroom. "You need rest, as do I."

A flash of guilt flowed through her. Dracchus had pushed himself for days to find this place, bring her here, and reunite her with her brother. They could talk later.

"Don't wait for me," she said gently.

She entered the washroom and was stunned by what she found inside. She knew the fixtures — a toilet, a sink, and a shower — but they looked so different from everything she'd seen in Fort Culver and the other towns scattered across the mainland. This equipment was top-quality, built to last, with a sleekness that wasn't present in the colonies topside. She'd never seen so much functional technology in one place.

Closing the door, she set her clothes down beside the sink and peeled off the diving suit. As she kicked it aside, she caught sight of herself in the mirror and cringed. Her nose and cheeks were red from the sun, her freckles more pronounced, and her eyes pink and puffy. Her hair was a tangled mess of red frizz.

Dracchus wanted *her* as a mate? After seeing a female kraken, Larkin couldn't believe he'd find her attractive — especially now — when he could have one of his own kind.

She opened the shower door and turned on the water. Taking a few quick breaths to prepare herself for the cold, she stepped under the showerhead. To her shock, the water was *warm*. She braced her arms on the wall and let the heat cascade over her body and ease her aches. She moaned appreciatively.

I might not want to leave this place.

DRACCHUS HEARD the sound of running water through the interior door as he moved deeper into the room. Pausing beside the table, he glanced down at the bowl of fruit that had been placed atop it. He plucked out a piece of fruit and studied it, running the pad of his thumb over the smooth-skinned bumps on its surface.

Biting into the fruit would be a strange experience — strange enough to distract him from his confused thoughts. But the thought of eating plants was unappealing, despite his hunger, and he wouldn't take food that had been set aside for Larkin.

He returned the fruit to its place and released a measured breath through his siphons.

Twisting to stare at the closed bathroom door, he focused on the sound made by the water, a constant stream broken by splashes that could only be her moving beneath it. His mind summoned the stolen glimpse he'd had of her naked body when she'd first put on the diving suit.

What did she look like now, with water flowing over her bare skin? What would she feel like?

Taste like?

Arousal heated his blood, and his shaft twitched behind his slit. He was not behaving in a manner his people would approve. Females were meant to have the choice, and he was leaving no choice for Larkin — he'd have her, in the end, and it would only be by her choosing because he'd make himself the only option. Whatever guilt he might have felt for it was a small price to pay for claiming her.

His thoughts shifted again, this time to the interaction between Larkin and Randall. They were family, and their affection for one another had been apparent, but they'd descended into arguing within moments of seeing one another.

Why? Why was Dracchus's female hurt and upset? Why had Randall stared at him with such intensity and challenge? Dracchus expected such from male kraken attempting to establish their place, but Randall's competitiveness had been good-natured during his time here. He'd always been content so long as he could hunt, contribute, and spent ample time with Rhea, Melaina, and Ikaros.

The Facility presented new dangers to Larkin, but that didn't seem reason enough for Randall's change in demeanor. All the humans living here were in constant danger — Larkin wasn't unique in that, and Randall knew it better than anyone.

Was it because of Dracchus's claim on Larkin? That didn't make sense; Randall already had a female of his own, and Larkin was his sister. Who better to keep her safe than Dracchus?

The bathroom door opened. Larkin stepped out, eyes meeting Dracchus's immediately. Her cheeks were flushed, and her wet hair hung around her shoulders, no longer a mass of tangles.

His gaze dropped to her loose clothing, and disappointment rippled through Dracchus. He'd come to enjoy the form-fitting coverings she'd worn over the last few days. These were almost maddening, offering little hint of the body beneath. He found himself battling the urge to peel her new clothing off her one piece at a time.

"Now I know it's not just curiosity that has you staring at me," Larkin said.

"I never pretended that it was." His eyes rose — *slowly* — to meet hers again.

"I suppose not." She looked away from him, but not before Dracchus caught a hint of uncertainty in her expression. Walking to the bed, she bent forward, pressed her hand atop the blanket, and smoothed her palm over it. "So where are you sleeping?"

Dracchus lowered his eyes — her position pulled the fabric of her pants taut, accenting the curve of her backside. He gritted his teeth. His willpower would be tested this night. However tired he was, his body awakened when she was near, fueled by the possibilities offered by her anatomy.

Kraken females could only be entered from the front, but that was not so for humans.

He moved closer, balling his fists to keep from reaching for her. "There is room enough in the bed for both of us."

Larkin straightened, turning her head to look him over. "You sure about that?"

Drawing back the blanket, threw herself onto the bed, spread her arms and legs wide, and moaned. The throaty, sensual sound nearly had Dracchus spilling out of his slit.

"I don't think I'll ever be able to move again," she said.

Dracchus moved around to the far side of the bed. The short journey did nothing to cool his blood, but he could not act on his desires. Not yet. Dracchus was a hunter before all else, and he knew this prey would require ample time and patience to lure out. Brute force would not win this contest.

Though it took only a few moments, Larkin's breathing had slowed, and her eyes were closed by the time he reached the bed.

Despite himself, he could appreciate the humor in the situation — females had thrown themselves at him in the past, had clung to him with insatiable appetites for mating. And now, the one female *he* had chosen had fallen asleep within moments of reclining.

Carefully, Dracchus shifted Larkin's limbs aside to make space for himself on the bed. He climbed atop it slowly. The material moved around him, adjusting its support to accommodate his weight. He was unused to the feeling; the sense of weightlessness afforded by water was by far more familiar and comforting. Once he was in place, he slipped his arm around her shoulders and drew her close.

She groaned, eyes fluttering open sleepily, but she didn't push him away. "What are you doing?" she mumbled.

"Resting with my female," he said, turning his body slightly toward her and coiling a tentacle around one of her calves. The tip ended at her ankle, where his suction cups lightly kissed her skin.

"Hmm," Larkin hummed as she drifted back to sleep.

Her scent and taste had been altered by her shower, but the underlying aroma and flavor remained, the parts that were uniquely *her*. The pressure behind his slit increased as her warmth flowed into him. He appreciated the way the diving suit had sculpted to her body, but it hadn't allowed him to feel her — her softness, her heat, the play of muscles beneath her skin.

Exhaustion closed in gradually on his awareness, creating a

dark, encroaching cloud at the edges of his vision. He was beginning to understand the risks that Jax and Arkon had taken with their mates. Now he knew a bond could form between two people that was worth facing any danger. He would fight to his end for the people he cared about...and somehow, for Larkin, he'd continue fighting beyond that.

CHAPTER 14

Larkin shifted uncomfortably on her chair, looking between Macy and Aymee — the missing women from The Watch. They weren't acting like they'd been abducted by monsters. They were happy.

That they'd chosen to stay here with the kraken — with their kraken *mates* — was clear by the sparkles of joy in their eyes and their easy laughter. These women were at home with one another, comfortable with their surroundings, and at ease with the kraken.

It only highlighted Larkin's discomfort; she didn't belong here, with these people. Only Randall's presence helped ground her.

She hadn't known what to expect when someone knocked on their door that morning. Was it Neo, come to make a second attempt on her life? Randall, ready to either apologize or rekindle their argument?

Dracchus had opened the door to reveal a large group outside the door, holding plates of food — Macy and Aymee, Randall, Jax and Arkon, and two kraken children — and welcomed them all inside.

Larkin had been shocked upon realizing the children possessed features she hadn't seen on any other kraken thus far —

hair and defined noses. She'd swung her gaze between the children and Macy and Aymee, and the resemblance, despite the alien cast of the little kraken's features, was undeniable.

When Dracchus had told her that human females had mated with kraken, she'd never imagined *this* was a possibility.

Her startlement faded as she watched the children. Their laughter brightened the room, and their sweet smiles sent a bittersweet pang through Larkin's heart. Despite their appearance, they were no different than human children — they played and giggled and bugged their parents like any other kids would. One in particular — Macy and Jax's daughter, Sarina — clung to Dracchus like he was her whole world.

Larkin would never have this. She'd never know the feeling of carrying a child, of feeling a new life growing within her. She'd never hear the laughter of her own child. That had been taken away from her.

Her attention fell on Dracchus as he lifted Sarina high into the air. The little girl's tentacles latched onto his wrists, and she cupped his face when he brought her close. She blew through her siphons and giggled when Dracchus did the same.

Something cold closed around Larkin's heart and squeezed. Dracchus adored Sarina, and he was so laid back and gentle with all the children.

And he wants me to be his mate.

His declaration still had her off-balance. She'd gone from hunting creatures she believed were monsters to saving them, and then to enjoying her time spent alone with one. Larkin and Dracchus had worked well together while camping on the edge of the jungle. He was often quiet, but when he spoke it was always with honesty and purpose. His directness could be unsettling, but she'd come to appreciate that he was open with her. He'd didn't treat her any differently because she was a woman.

He praised her, respected her, supported her.

Despite all that, she was confused by her desire for him.

Larkin's gaze fell to Dracchus's tentacles. This morning, she'd woken to them curled around her, with the tip of one having slipped up the bottom of her pants to touch the sensitive flesh behind her knee. She could barely recall climbing into bed, much less Dracchus joining her, but she'd somehow ended up encircled by his arms, tucked against his side. Being next to him had felt so…right.

She'd slept with a few other men and had never much enjoyed being held by them afterwards. Those casual couplings, usually in the field, had only served one purpose — mutual release. The *cuddling* following those acts always seemed hollow. Sex didn't necessitate a relationship, and they always parted with the dawn. Why pretend it was any more complicated than that?

None of those experiences could compare to what was happening now. Dracchus wasn't looking for simple release; he *wanted* her, and even if she thought he'd come to that decision much too quickly, she found comfort and security in his arms.

Why was it different with him? Why hadn't she felt this way toward anyone else, toward a human man?

"Larkin?"

She tore her gaze away from Dracchus to find Macy, Aymee, and Randall staring at her. Her cheeks heated. She wasn't often caught off-guard. How long had she been staring at Dracchus?

"Sorry, what was that?" she asked.

"We heard that you helped the kraken escape," Aymee said. "What changed your mind?"

Larkin glanced at Randall, who sat on her right. "They weren't the monsters they were made out to be, and they didn't deserve what was being done to them."

Aymee smirked. "She's quicker than you, Randall."

"Never said I was the smart one," he replied, though his smile was forced. His eyes flicked toward Dracchus for an instant.

"What do you mean, Aymee?" Larkin asked.

Grinning, Aymee shifted her legs, smoothing the material of

her skirt over them. "It took a lot of convincing to get Randall to see the kraken as people. He refused to take my word for it, though I can't blame him for that."

Larkin tilted her head. "Dad wouldn't say it was because I'm smarter. He'd blame my *bleeding heart* and call it a weakness."

"It's not a weakness, Elle," Randall said, clasping her hand. "Our father isn't the best judge of character, anyway."

She frowned and squeezed her brother's hand. They'd come close to losing Randall, but not by any kraken's doing. "I'm sorry for the things I said."

He dropped his gaze. "Shit's been rough. I get it. I would've sent word somehow, if I had a way. But with everything that happened…" He shook his head, and the tip of his tongue slipped out to wet his lips.

"We're not prisoners," Macy said, "but we can't risk going back. The kraken are family to us, and we can't take the chance of exposing them, especially with all the hunters around."

"I see that now," Larkin said, running her gaze over the kraken in the room. When she met Dracchus's eyes, she quickly looked away, returning her attention to Randall. "It hurt at first, knowing you've been here this whole time, making another family, while Dad and I were searching, desperate to know if you were even alive…but I understand."

"I've thought about you every day, Elle," Randall said. "Missed you every day, but at the same time, I wished that Jon would never make it back home. I knew if he did, Dad would come looking. And that he wouldn't leave you behind."

He turned his head to look fully at Dracchus. "They killed everyone else. And I don't feel much of anything for that, because those men threatened innocent people and supported Cyrus when he tried to murder me. Dracchus spared my life, but only because Aymee persuaded him to."

"You saved Jax," Aymee said. "If you hadn't shot that other man, Jax might've been killed."

Macy paled, settling a hand on her stomach as she looked at Jax; he met her gaze from his place on the floor, where he was playing with Jace, and frowned.

"It was a mess," Randall continued. "And Dracchus made it clear that if anyone else came looking, he would end them. I didn't ever want you to come, Elle, and that's why I got so upset last night. But now you're here, and…"

"And you're the one who captured three male kraken," Aymee said.

"Some of these kraken hate us. Doesn't matter what any of us have done to help them out. Just like some of our people will hate the kraken no matter what." Randall turned back to Larkin. "But there's always the threat of danger here, especially for you."

"What do we do now, then?" Larkin asked.

"Just *live.*" Macy glanced down at the hand over her midsection. "We can't let fear rule us."

Larkin's eyes widened. The woman was *pregnant.* She tightened her grip, forgetting she was holding Randall's hand.

Randall leaned closer, resting his shoulder against hers and tipping his head to settle atop her hair gently. "I'm sorry, Elle," he whispered, and she knew he wasn't apologizing for his behavior.

She closed her eyes and drew his hand into her lap, taking it in both of hers.

"We'll let you guys catch up," Aymee said.

Larkin opened her eyes and returned Aymee's smile.

"It was nice meeting you, Larkin," Macy said, standing up. "We'll come visit again. If you need anything, just let us know."

Jax gathered Sarina and moved to Macy's side.

"Thank you. I would like that," Larkin replied, meaning it. She'd spent little time in female company throughout her life, but despite her earlier unease, Macy and Aymee had been nothing but welcoming and kind.

Dracchus looked between Larkin and Randall as the others

filtered out of the room. "I will see them to their dens and return shortly." His tone almost turned it into a question.

Larkin nodded.

"Are you okay, Elle?" Randall asked after Dracchus departed.

"I am. I'm worried about Dad, but I'm all right."

"What's going on between you and Dracchus?"

Larkin frowned and drew away from Randall, turning her head to face him. "Did he do something to you?"

"No, he didn't do anything to *me*." Randall leaned back, wearing a frown of his own while he studied her. "I want to know what he's done to you. You're my sister, Elle, and—"

"I'm a grown woman."

"And I'm your older brother."

"And I love you," she squeezed his hand again, "but you need to trust me, as much as I trust you." She glanced down at their hands and swallowed. "Do you trust him?"

Randall sighed after several seconds of reluctant silence. "With my life."

"Then you know that I'm safe. Everything else," she smiled sweetly, "is none of your damn business."

He grinned and shook his head, eyes glistening. "Fuck, I missed you."

Tears prickled her own eyes, and she hugged him. "I missed you, too."

Randall returned the embrace. They clung to each other, and for a few moments, everything else faded away, leaving only Larkin's relief and love for him. Finally, he pulled away — whether the hug had lasted for ten seconds or ten minutes, it was too brief — and offered her a smile.

"I'm going to go find Rhea and Melaina. They'll probably get back with Ikaros pretty soon, and he gets anxious when I'm not around."

"Okay. And Randall?"

He stood, and she released his hand. "Yeah?"

"I'm happy for you."

"Thanks, Elle. Despite everything, I'm glad you're here."

Dracchus was standing in the hallway when Randall opened the door, facing away from the room. The kraken turned to face the human.

"I'm not mad at you," Randall said, his voice deliberately measured, "but if you hurt her, I will fuck you up."

"Randall!" Larkin yelled.

He glanced at her over his shoulder and then looked back at Dracchus, jabbing a finger at the kraken. "*After* she fucks you up, because she's a grown woman. I'll see you later, buddy."

Larkin covered her mouth with one hand to hide her mirth as Randall exited the room. That was *not* what she'd meant.

Dracchus furrowed his brow, staring after Randall down the hallway before he finally entered the room. "What was that?"

She lowered her hand; she'd contained her laughter, but couldn't keep a broad grin from her face. "He's being protective."

"But I already told him that I would protect you."

"He's protecting me from *you*."

He tilted his head, nostrils flaring with a slow exhalation. "I have not done anything to harm you, Larkin."

"I know that. It's…a big brother thing." She stood and walked to the table, picking up one of the fruits Aymee and Macy had brought. The table was laden with food — fish, lobster, winefruit, naba, and daruk nuts — all harvested from either the jungle or the sea. "To Randall and our father, no man is worthy of having me."

Dracchus closed the distance between them, holding his gaze upon her. "That is for you to decide, female."

She turned toward him. "I seem to recall a certain kraken laying claim on me already."

"Because I know you will make the choice, in time."

Larkin smirked. "Are you so confident in that?"

He stopped mere centimeters away from Larkin and ran his gaze over her slowly, without shame, devouring her with his eyes.

Heat radiated from him, warming her suddenly sensitive skin. "Yes."

Larkin raised the winefruit to her lips as his low voice reverberated through her, making her core tighten with desire. Her heart sped, threatening to burst out of her chest, but she didn't look away.

Damn her, but she was convinced by his confidence, too.

DRACCHUS PAUSED beneath a flickering overhead light in the hallway, tilting his head back to look up at it. Though he'd never spent much time in this building before Macy and the other humans had come, he was familiar with which lights worked and which did not. This pulsing was the start of a new failure.

How long before everything in the Facility stopped working? How long before this place, the only home his people had ever known, became little more than another dark, underwater cave?

After they'd shared a meal, Dracchus had taken Larkin to visit Randall, Rhea, and Melaina. Ikaros's presence had nearly given him pause — the memory of Larkin fending off a pack of prixxir was still fresh — but Dracchus had hunted alongside Randall and Ikaros for months. Larkin was safe with them.

Reluctantly, Dracchus had left her with her brother, freeing himself to traverse the Facility. He greeted as many kraken as he could on his meandering path; they needed to know he'd returned, needed to know Kronus was in no position to claim dominance or leadership. Though most kraken operated independently, they had always relied upon one another for mutual survival, and often looked to the most capable males for guidance.

Kronus could not be allowed that sort of influence.

Hushed voices drifted to Dracchus from somewhere further along the corridor. He'd seen Vasil and Brexes already, and old

Ector, and dozens of others, but a certain group had remained unaccounted for.

Dracchus moved toward the voices, rounding a corner to follow another long corridor nearly to its end. He stopped in the doorway of a room that reminded him of the Infirmary — this chamber was much smaller and had no beds, but the cabinets, counters, and equipment were similar.

Kronus and Neo were inside, accompanied by two of their supporters — a male named Orphus and the female, Leda.

"We must, as quickly as possible!" Neo said.

"That is not how this matter should be resolved," Kronus warned. "They will continue—" His eyes darted to the doorway, and he scowled. "Dracchus."

Clenching his jaw, Dracchus entered the room.

The other kraken turned to face him, Neo's skin bleeding to crimson. Dracchus had faced open hostility many times, but the intensity in the air now was at a new level. He was outnumbered four-to-one.

Part of him hoped they'd try.

"You are not welcome here," Kronus said.

Neo growled. "Take your treacherous skin out—"

"The humans are under my protection," Dracchus said. Neo snapped his mouth shut. "Jax, Arkon, Melaina, Sarina, Jace, and all our people who disagree with you. They are all under my protection."

"You come to threaten us, Dracchus?" Leda asked. Her half-lidded eyes moved over his body, lustful despite the situation.

"Only to remind you. My patience has thinned as of late. You will not be afforded the courtesy of a threat, going forward."

"Siding with those *humans* over your own kind." Kronus moved closer, catching Dracchus's eyes. "Threatening your own people. What have you become?"

"If you wish to fight, Kronus, the decision is yours," Dracchus replied, "but you will fail. Change will not await your acceptance."

"This change will not be accepted. Humans have no place here, and they will leave no matter how hard you battle it."

"You do not need to make them your enemies, Kronus. I made that mistake already and warn you of its folly."

"After all they've done, you take their side?" Neo advanced, skin scintillating, his anger apparently having overpowered his fear. "You choose them over your own? They kept us in cages and beat us for hours each day. Starved us. Where has your pride gone, Dracchus, your backbone, that you defend those who brought you low?"

Dracchus's stomach twisted, and a heavy weight sank in his gut — built not of fear, or shame, but remorse. These were his people, but they would not be reasoned with. Kronus had been bested in numerous challenges and had yet to be deterred. At some point, this would escalate into true violence, something far worse than two kraken in a challenge. When that point came, Dracchus would not hesitate to put an end to it.

Dracchus didn't raise himself on his tentacles, didn't draw in a deep breath and flex his muscles, didn't even change his color. He just stared unflinchingly into Neo's blazing eyes.

"All the humans in the Facility are my people. Anyone who violates that and attempts to do them harm is no longer kraken to me and will be crushed." Dracchus shifted his gaze to Kronus, then Orphus, and lastly Leda. The time for threats had indeed passed; this was a promise.

The female smirked and approached him, arching her back to thrust her breasts forward. "You will not touch me, Dracchus, unless it is to mate me." She extended an arm, trailing a finger over one of his shoulder stripes. "You would not risk the punishment for doing me harm and leave your human slits unprotected."

He caught her wrist and forced her hand away. "Should you make it necessary, Leda, Rhea would gladly put you in your place."

Leda's expression darkened into a scowl. Dracchus allowed her to snatch her arm away.

Despite their behavior, he didn't want to hurt any of these kraken. Not yet. But he knew they were capable of treachery, and that at least some of the human-opposed kraken were willing to follow through with their threats.

"We are not through," Kronus growled.

Neo remained close to Dracchus, lips tight. His shoulders heaved with strained breaths.

"For your sake, you had better be." Dracchus held Neo's gaze, allowing the ensuing silence to emphasize his words, for several heartbeats.

When no one offered a reply, Dracchus finally turned — secretly hoping they'd mistake his exposed back for a vulnerability and attack — and left the chamber.

He heard no more voices as he made his way toward the Cabins.

That Kronus and his followers were in a random, functionless room so close to the human dwellings was an unspoken threat, one they'd made frequently over the last year. Apart from the Mess, where the kraken met to organize hunts or for the rare occasions warranting a group discussion, few of the males spent time in this part of the Facility. The group's only purpose here was to ensure the humans could not travel the halls safely.

Randall and Rhea's door was closed when Dracchus reached it. Rather than disturb them — he *still* wasn't entirely sure what was wrong with Randall — he went to the den he shared with Larkin.

Inside, the bathroom door was closed, and the unmistakable pattering of water in the shower drifted from behind it.

He moved to the bed and ran a tentacle over the sheets. Her scent lingered on them. He closed his eyes for a moment, casting everything aside to focus on the aroma. His attraction to her didn't need to be understood, only accepted; it just *was*. With everything around him rapidly descending into chaos, he needed something simple, powerful, and pure to hold onto, and Larkin provided that.

The water shut off. Dracchus turned toward the bathroom door, easing himself partly onto the bed, and waited.

The door opened. Larkin emerged from the bathroom clad only in a towel, held in place by one of her hands. The cloth was wrapped around her torso, covering her from chest to mid-thigh, leaving tantalizing portions of her pale, brown-flecked skin exposed. Her hair hung wet and loose around her shoulders.

She stopped short when she saw him. "I wasn't sure when you'd be back."

He couldn't prevent himself from surveying her bare flesh. His blood heated, and his prior frustrations faded away, forgotten in a haze of desire. "So you came out to await me in your towel," he said.

Larkin coughed, her skin flushing. "Actually, I just forgot to grab some clothes." She turned away from him and walked toward the dresser.

He moved in the same direction, stopping behind her. He settled his hand over hers as she reached for the drawer and gently guided her to turn toward him. She tilted her head back and met his gaze.

"Your skin has changed color," he said, running the back of his finger lightly down her cheek, along the side of her neck, and over her shoulder. She shivered.

Her tongue slipped out to wet her lips. "Yours, too."

Dracchus hadn't done so consciously, but she was correct — his skin had shifted to maroon, an open sign of his want. He hooked a claw onto the edge of her towel, where the fabric bridged the shallow between her breasts. "Are you pink beneath this, as well?"

Her breath quickened, and her breasts strained against the towel. "Dracchus, what are you doing?"

He slid a tentacle up Larkin's bare leg. She flinched but didn't withdraw. Easing the limb farther up, he coiled it around her thigh. A tremor ran through her, but there was no fear in her eyes.

Her skin tasted clean and sweet and bore a hint of something more, something alluring. He leaned closer and inhaled, drawing in her intoxicating scent. Her arousal.

"Seducing my mate," he replied in a low rumble.

She pressed a hand to his chest but didn't shove him away. "I'm not your mate."

"You are," he said, cupping her cheek and running the pad of his thumb across her lower lip, "you just have not admitted it yet."

Larkin kept her hand clasped over the towel, resisting the gentle pull of his claw. Her body heat increased. "Dracchus…"

He leaned down, moving his mouth near her ear. "I ask nothing more than to see you. To touch you. To *feel* you."

She released a shaky breath and loosened her grip on the towel. The cloth unraveled, sliding away at Dracchus's light tug, and pooled at her feet.

Dracchus drew back and groaned deep in his chest as he lowered his gaze. His cock strained against his slit. Her skin was pale, as pale as the faces of the moons at night, sprinkled with those little brown spots on her chest, arms, and shoulders — they were as unique as the markings of any kraken. More so, perhaps, because they belonged to her.

And she was *his*.

Her breasts were small and high, tipped with pink nipples which hardened beneath his gaze. His eyes traveled down the smooth expanse of her stomach, over the jagged, puckered scars of her pelvis, to settle on the bright red hair between her legs.

He slid his tentacle higher, curling its tip around the back of her thigh and over her hip to brush over the uppermost hairs on her pelvis. His suction cups sampled their first taste of her arousal. His mouth went suddenly dry; he craved a *real* taste of her on his tongue.

Larkin gasped, eyes widening as she looked down. She dropped her hand from his chest, grasping his tentacle, while the other covered her scars.

"You don't want this, Dracchus," she said, stepping back into the dresser. "You don't want me. Not really."

He followed her, keeping his tentacle on her thigh, and took hold of her arms. She struggled as he spread them apart, sliding his hands down to hers and intertwining their fingers as much as possible. "These are yours," he said, brushing the tip of another tentacle across her scars, "and they are beautiful. Do not be ashamed of them. They are proof of your strength, your courage."

She stared up at him, pupils large, blue irises so bright they were nearly lost in the whites of her eyes.

Dracchus lowered his head, leaning close enough that her nipples brushed against his chest, and brought his mouth close to hers. He longed to kiss her as he'd seen Jax and Arkon do with their mates, wanted to experience it for himself, but only with her, only with Larkin.

"I'm human," she said, as though it were a reason to stop, but there was no conviction in her words.

He ran his tentacle over the hair between her legs to stroke her slit. Her hips jerked, and her lips parted as she emitted a soft cry.

Dracchus groaned and released one of her hands to curl his fingers around the side of her neck, tipping her chin up with his thumb. "I want you, human."

He slanted his mouth over hers. Her lips yielded to him, inviting him to deepen the kiss, and he caressed them with his own — tentative, learning, craving more and more of her. When she looped her arms around his neck, he leaned forward and placed his hands on her sides. He trailed his palms down, cupped her backside, and squeezed the soft flesh, drawing her pelvis against his slit.

The pressure within him built to new heights as she undulated her hips on his tentacle. The heat of her core flowed into him, her oils coated him, and her scent enveloped him, consuming his senses.

She moved her mouth beneath his, and her tongue flicked

against his lips, his teeth, his tongue. The kiss deepened with their mutual desire, matching Dracchus's hunger and then amplifying it. He allowed her to take the lead before mimicking her actions, delving into her mouth with his own tongue.

Larkin panted, her sounds rising steadily in pitch as Dracchus increased the speed of his tentacle over her sex. She clutched at him, dull nails biting into his back, and writhed in his hold. Her reactions pushed him onward as she relinquished control.

His hearts thundered, his skin tingled with want, and his shaft screamed in protest at its confinement, but he would not allow it to emerge. If Larkin was not ready, he would respect that. For now, her pleasure was enough.

As he continued stroking, a suction cup caught on a hard pebble at the apex of her sex.

Larkin's body stiffened, and she threw her head back. "Oh fuck! Dracchus!"

Her words gave way to desperate, breathless moans, and she squeezed her eyes shut as liquid heat flowed from her slit. He inhaled her scent, tasted her sweetness, and yearned to have it on his tongue.

Biting her bottom lip to quiet her release, she clung to him. Dracchus didn't relent until her trembling ceased and she sagged in his arms.

He reluctantly unwound his tentacle from her leg and trailed it down the outside of her thigh. "Are you pleased, female?"

Larkin tensed. She drew back quickly, glancing up to meet his eyes for an instant before she ducked out of his arms and snatched up her towel. She moved beyond his reach and hastily covered herself, holding the towel in place with an arm across her chest.

"We shouldn't have done that," she said.

Dracchus ached with need; he craved release almost as much as he craved the feeling of her body reacting to his touch, almost as much as he wanted another taste of her. Larkin's inner thighs glistened with the evidence of her own desire.

"Why?" he asked, trying unsuccessfully to ignore the throbbing behind his slit.

She clenched a fistful of the fabric over her pelvis and pressed her lips into a thin line, cheeks paling. "This is moving too fast. I just found out that krakens existed and now I'm practically having sex with one." She spun away from him. "What the hell is wrong with me?"

"Nothing." He moved closer but hesitated as he reached toward her. Humans touched often, but he'd seen enough of their interactions to know they didn't always want to be touched. He wished he knew how to tell when that was the case.

"There is plenty wrong with me," she said. "I'm not what you want, Dracchus. You just haven't realized it yet."

He moved closer still, extending an arm, but she shrugged away from his hand.

"I'm getting back in the shower." She tugged open one of the dresser drawers and rummaged through its contents.

Dracchus stilled, heartbeats stuttering. He took her by the shoulders and forced her to turn toward him.

"I don't know where they are," Larkin said with a glare, "but I will kick you square in the balls if you don't let go."

"Are you so disgusted by my touch that you must wash your-self again?" he demanded. His lingering, painful arousal had mingled with the hurt of her words, turning into a jumbled, nauseating mess in his chest.

Any anger she'd displayed vanished within the next instant. "No. That's not what I... Fuck." She looked away. "It's not you, Dracchus. I'm not...disgusted." Her grip on the towel tightened. "I just need some space to figure this out. I'm not...good with this kind of thing."

He was uncertain of whether he felt reassured by her answer, uncertain of whether she'd *meant* to be reassuring. At his core, he understood he wasn't good at things like this, either. He didn't

even know what exactly *this* was, apart from totally new to him...
but he wanted it nonetheless.

Dracchus released his hold on her shoulders and moved back.
His limbs felt oddly heavy and unstable; if a body could be
strengthened by rage, it made sense that it could be weakened by
sadness or doubt. Still, it was an unfamiliar sensation, and that
unsettled him. Had Jax and Arkon gone through similar feelings?
How had they coped?

"I will grant you space," he said. "At least for a short while."

"Thank you." She offered him a small, grateful smile and
turned back to the dresser.

For a few moments, he watched her, unable but to notice the
curve of her backside against the fabric covering it. Then he
forced himself to turn away and move toward the door. He'd only
just returned to their den, and he'd no desire to leave it — to leave
her — but if it was what Larkin needed, he'd grant her request. It
was for the best. Despite this exchange, his blood was still hot, his
desire still overwhelming.

He could not trust himself around her. Could not trust himself
to ignore his desires and respect her wishes.

He entered the corridor and leaned beside the doorframe after
the door slid shut. The hallway was silent save for the gentle,
familiar, barely perceptibly hum present throughout most of the
Facility. Arkon called it the *whirring of hidden machinery*.

Dracchus didn't care about machinery, hidden or otherwise.
Larkin's taste lingered on his suction cups, her scent clung to his
skin, and his shaft ached. She was driving him dangerously close
to casting aside all the ways of their people. He needed to have
her, had never wanted anyone or anything more.

But he knew now, more than ever, that he could not make the
choice for her, and he could not force her to choose. She needed
to come to him of her own free will.

CHAPTER 15

LARKIN WRINKLED HER NOSE AND LOOKED AROUND THE LARGE room. Lockers stood along two of the walls, and various pieces of equipment — most of which she didn't recognize — were stacked beside a third wall. In the center of the room was a huge pool of clear water; it had to be at least sixty meters from one end to the other, and half that across.

"What is that smell?" she asked.

Dracchus shrugged. The gesture was almost comical given his size. "Chemicals, Arkon says. I am not sure what that means, but he insists that is the source."

"Chemicals for what? Are they dangerous?" Their smell sure as hell implied they were.

"I do not believe so." He stared into the pool, one corner of his mouth turned down. "Kraken have entered the water before, and none have come to harm for it."

"It's coming from the water?" Larkin stepped to the edge and looked down. Her eyes widened at what she saw.

The bottom of the pool was covered by countless little stones, their differences in color creating intricate, swirling patterns that flowed into each other so naturally it seemed impossible.

"Who made that?" she asked.

"Arkon, over many weeks. I used to think that was time wasted."

"It's beautiful. Why would you think it's a waste of time?"

"Because it did nothing to contribute to the survival of our people," he replied, shaking his head. "But you are right. It is pleasing. I cannot decide what its value is, only that it is of some value."

Larkin tilted her head, tracing the patterns with her gaze. "We'd spend days, sometimes weeks, out in the jungle, tracking our prey. It was hard work. Tedious work. And the whole time, I knew in the back of my mind that most of our food came from farms, anyway. But when we got back into the fort with our fresh kills, there'd be music, and dancing, and a feast to celebrate. People were happy because of what we'd done. Even if the farms produced more food, we'd added something more to their lives.

"That's what this is. It's about making people feel something, about...entertainment. A full belly is great, don't get me wrong, but people need more than that sometimes to be happy. Life needs to be lived, and there *is* value in the small things, the things that might not seem important, like this," she waved at the stones. "You gain pleasure, just from looking at it."

Dracchus folded his arms across his broad chest released a slow breath. "For the kraken, it has been survival. For generations, that is all we've known."

"That's not so different from us," she said, facing him. "Humans have had to work hard every day since the colonization to carve out our place on this world. We just have the tools and experience to make our survival more efficient. But even when things are rough, we take time to enjoy life."

"So I have seen since our humans came," Dracchus said.

The tone with which he'd said that — *our humans* — was so affectionately possessive that Larkin couldn't help but smile. Whatever their differences, Dracchus had accepted the humans in the Facility as his people. Would it really be so bad to be part of that?

To be his mate?

Larkin fought a shiver as she recalled what he'd done to her last evening. She'd stood in the shower for at least half an hour afterwards before her body finally came down from the heights of pleasure to which he'd raised her. Even then, it hadn't been enough. She'd craved more.

She'd wanted *him*.

This isn't about what I want. It's about what I can't give him.

Her smile fell, and she cleared her throat. Better not to think about it. She forced her thoughts elsewhere, focusing on the tour Dracchus was giving her.

She'd seen more rooms than she knew what to do with, and she'd had few good guesses as to what most of them were for. Before they'd gone anywhere else, he'd taken her to a small chamber that had once been some sort of office, where he'd opened a hidden panel on the wall to reveal an assortment of rifles, harpoon guns, pistols, knives, all neatly stored. At least ten diving suits lay on the shelf below with their accompanying masks.

He'd shown her the button to open the panel, handed her a belt, and directed her to take a blade and a pistol. The trust he'd shown her in that moment was almost flooring, and the quality of the weapons — their *condition* — was astounding.

"So we've seen offices, labs, an infirmary that puts the one at Fort Culver to shame, the mess hall and the kitchen, a room full of functioning computers, and this place." She looked back into the pool and narrowed her eyes; its walls were lined with windows all the way around. "What was this place used for anyway? This building is surrounded by water."

"To train human divers and test their devices." Dracchus turned his head to look at her. "The open ocean was too dangerous for those functions. This was a…" His brow dropped as though in deep concentration. Larkin found it endearing. "*Controlled environment*. They tested their suits and equipment near bits of halorium. Arkon said it was to learn how to prevent halorium from disrupting their *electronics*."

"What is halorium?"

He looked at the pool and raised his arm, extending a finger. "In the center."

Larkin followed his gesture, shifting her gaze to the pattern on the floor of the pool. She wasn't sure what he intended for her to find — all the stones were small and only varied slightly in color — until her eyes caught on the middle of the design. The center stone no bigger than any of the rest, but where the others were smooth and rounded, this had sharp, crystal-like planes. It glowed a steady, soft blue; the same glow she'd often seen from jungle plants after dark.

The same glow Dracchus had emitted.

"That rock?" she asked.

"Yes. It makes old human machinery fail when it is near."

"Why did they want it, then?"

"Because it holds great power. It is what has kept the Facility alive for all this time."

"Krullshit," she said, looking back to Dracchus. "That little thing?"

"Not *that* one. There is a… I cannot recall the word Arkon used. Some machine at the heart of this place, in the Underneath, that harnesses the energy in halorium. It is why the kraken were created."

Larkin arched a brow. "Humans created you…for that?"

"Halorium is safe to touch," he said with a frown, "but it turns off the diving suits when they are too close. My kind can collect it safely. Yours cannot."

"So, what happened?"

"The kraken were treated like slaves by the humans here. We were not people to them. So my ancestors rose up and seized the Facility by force." His frown deepened, but there was no apology in his expression. "They killed all the humans and claimed this place as their own."

"How was it no one on land knew about you?" Larkin shook her head, unable to wrap her mind around it. "Fort Culver was the central command for the military on Halora. They *had* to know. They had communications everywhe—"

Realization silenced her abruptly. Though the records were difficult to access now, and most of the computers back home had long since failed, all the rangers knew the final order issued to all military personnel. It was what had defined their mission over the subsequent generations.

Hold the line against anything that might come. Defend the colonists to the last man.

"They *knew*," she said, scowling. "The IDC knew what happened, knew what they'd done, and they kept everyone in the dark about it. The final order they issued was about your people."

"I do not understand, Larkin. What do you mean?"

"Before communication was severed with the Interstellar Defense Collation, they contacted every military base on Halora and…" She sighed and shook her head, glancing at the pool then back at Dracchus. "You know what? It doesn't matter anymore. Those people are dead, and we're here. It's in the past."

He seemed to search her face for a time, and his unreadable expression made it difficult to determine what he was thinking.

"And it is up to us to shape the future," he finally said. "To prevent the same events from occurring again."

"Right." Larkin lifted one side of her mouth in a half-smile. "We haven't been doing all that great a job so far, have we?"

"The two of us have done well." He offered her the ghost of a smile in return. "Most everyone else is the problem."

Larkin studied him. His body was tense, but his shoulders slumped as though beneath a heavy burden. She'd seen from the beginning how he put his people before himself, and bringing her here had only caused more strife amongst the kraken. That strife was undoubtedly the weight he carried on his back.

She stepped closer to him and raised her hand, hesitating for a moment before settling it on his arm. "There is only so much one person can do. You make the best effort you can, you stand your ground, and you fight for what you believe in. Good people will see that, and it will inspire them to stand with you."

He glanced down at her hand, and she felt his muscles shift beneath her palm. "Will you stand with me, Larkin?"

"Against the humans?"

"Against anyone who threatens the potential peace between our people."

She lowered her gaze, watching her thumb as she brushed it over his skin, and furrowed her brow. If she said yes, it meant potentially going against her father and every ranger under his command — people she'd grown up with and had known all her life. But how could she condone the things her father had done? The torture of intelligent beings, of *people*?

She hoped that, when the time came, her father would listen.

"Yeah. I'll stand with you, Dracchus," Larkin said, meeting his gaze.

He raised his free arm and covered her hand with his. The gesture reminded her again of the immense strength he possessed and how much control he demonstrated over it.

"I do not want violence because of any of this," he said, "but it will come. From kraken, from humans, or from both."

"I'm prepared for it." She shifted her hand, sliding her fingers between his and squeezing them gently. Her skin strongly contrasted his in a mingling of light and dark. She also couldn't deny how *right* his touch felt.

Cheeks flushing, she pulled her hand away and settled it on the grip of the knife on her belt. She stepped back with a smile. "Why don't we get out of here? I think the smell is getting worse."

His nostrils flared with a deep inhalation, and she waited for him to disagree with her; if anything, she noticed the smell less, now that her nose had adapted to it. But he only nodded, and they moved back into the corridor together.

She drew in a deep breath of the clean, filtered air as she walked, detecting only the faintest hint of the chemical odor.

"Where is your room?" she asked.

"My den was in one of the flooded buildings," he replied.

"You sleep in the water? Does it bother you to sleep in the air, then?"

"Only after long periods of time. Being out of the water for days on that ship was unpleasant."

Larkin frowned. "I'm sorry. If I'd known befo—"

"Do not apologize. You did what you thought was right at the time." He turned his head toward her, and his signature frown had returned. "When I first encountered Macy, I thought it right to bring her to my people, to show them what Jax had done. I dragged her into the water, assuming humans could breathe underwater. I nearly killed her. At that point, humans were nothing more or less than my enemy. She proved me wrong when she came by her own choice to face the kraken."

"Brave of her," Larkin said. "And she was the first human since the revolt?"

"Yes."

She shifted to walk partially behind him as they passed into another hallway, careful not to trip over his tentacles. She hadn't determined the exact layout of the place, but she was sure they were moving back toward the cabins.

"When I told you Randall was here, I took way your choice, did I not?" he asked.

"Well, not really. What would you have done if I hadn't come here?"

"I would have found ways to make our camp more comfortable."

Larkin chuckled. "It was a nice little camp."

"I was interested only in the company, not the place." His tone was so matter-of-fact that she couldn't help but laugh again. She'd grown up around gruff, blunt men, but Dracchus's forwardness and lack of shame made all the others seem sheepish in comparison.

They turned another corner, entering another corridor that looked very much like all the rest. Movement ahead caught Larkin's eye.

Dracchus halted, extending his arm to bar her passage. He used that arm to gently guide her behind him, but not before she saw a pair of male kraken at the other end of the hall. One was orange-brown with dark stripes, similar to Jax in size and build. The brown one beside him was familiar to her — Neo, the kraken who'd attempted to drown Larkin while the ship burned.

"I have not seen that human before," the orange one growled.

"Why are you here, Kronus? You have no business near our dens," Dracchus replied.

"Your den? Since when do you den with the humans?" Kronus demanded.

Dracchus's muscles tensed and his skin lightened, displaying a crimson tinge. "Since you decided to threaten their lives."

"They don't belong here!" Neo snarled.

Something curled around Larkin's waist and yanked her backward. She pulled her knife instinctually as another tentacle encircled her legs, lashing them together, and a clawed hand wrapped around her neck. She twisted and raised her arm, pressing her blade to the unknown kraken's throat. He growled and tightened his grip.

"All it takes it one flick of my wrist, and you'll bleed out in seconds," Larkin grated.

DRACCHUS TURNED, looking back at Larkin, and his hearts froze. Orphus held her firmly, and she had her knife at the kraken's throat. A drop of blood oozed from beneath her blade.

"That is the human slit from the boat!" Neo shouted. "Kill her!"

"You'll die, too," Larkin said. Her voice was strained, her face slowly reddening, but she didn't show any fear.

Pressure built in Dracchus's chest, pushing against his ribs and constricting his hearts, threatening to explode. He had no misconceptions about the fragility of humans — her life was in immediate danger.

Dracchus chanced a glance toward Neo and Kronus; they were advancing down the corridor, Neo's skin crimson.

Fire burst through Dracchus's veins, roiling and unbearably hot, and ignited the pressure within him. He roared. The sound rattled his chest and reverberated off metal and plastic to become something deafening.

Kronus and Neo halted, flashing yellow with eyes wide.

Dracchus turned toward Larkin, muscles aching with unreleased fury. Orphus still held her, but he wore a fearful expression. Even Larkin's eyes were rounded.

Twisting, Dracchus slammed his fist into the wall. The metal buckled with the impact, and the wall panel sagged, its fasteners partially torn out.

"Release her," he growled.

Orphus abruptly withdrew his tentacles and backed away. Larkin stumbled forward, and Dracchus took her in his arms immediately. His hand trembled as he cupped her cheek and tilted her head back, checking her neck for injury. It was red where Orphus had gripped her, with two small, shallow puncture wounds from the kraken's claws.

It was less damage than Neo had done the night they escaped the ship.

That knowledge did nothing to calm Dracchus.

"What is this?" a familiar voice demanded from beyond Kronus and Neo.

Dracchus looked over his shoulder to see Jax and Arkon moving toward him.

"Why did you bring that slit here?" Neo asked, baring his teeth. "She is a hunter! The one who captured us!"

"She needs to die. We can't allow her to remain here," Orphus replied, glaring at Larkin. "She is our enemy, even more than the rest."

Jax and Arkon shoved past Kronus and Neo, stopping beside Dracchus. Dracchus turned his back on Orphus, moving Larkin within the shelter of his arms. He bristled with rage, but he'd never let it be his master where she was involved, would never do her harm. He met Arkon's gaze.

"Take her to Randall's den," Dracchus said.

Arkon's eyes rounded with innumerable questions; he voiced only one. "Are you sure of this?"

Dracchus nodded.

"What's going on?" Larkin asked, drawing his attention down to her.

"You betray your own kind!" Neo growled. Kronus hissed something to his companion, but Dracchus couldn't make it out.

"A challenge," Dracchus replied. "Go with Arkon. I will come to you soon."

Larkin grabbed his wrist, her fingers barely wrapping halfway around it. "I stand with you, remember?"

She was a warrior, a huntress, formidable and fierce in her own right. But this was not her fight.

"Trust me, Larkin." He placed his hands on her shoulders and guided her to Arkon.

"Damnit, kraken, no!" she said, attempting to pull from Arkon's hold.

Arkon held her firm, shifting to shield her body from Kronus and Neo with his own. "He will be fine, Larkin. Jax will remain at his side."

Larkin growled, jabbing a finger at Dracchus. "You better come back in one piece, or I'll tear the rest of you apart myself."

Only the flames rampant inside Dracchus prevented him from smiling; their heat was scorching, uncomfortable, driving. The last thing he wanted was to have her out of his sight, but he could not adequately protect her and settle this matter at the same time.

Jax served as a living barrier between Arkon and the other kraken as Larkin was escorted past them. Neo scintillated red and black, and Kronus physically restrained his companion as the others went by.

Soon, Arkon and Larkin turned the corner. She glanced back once, face hard with anger and concern, before she was out of Dracchus's sight.

Dracchus's skin prickled; he could *feel* Orphus behind him, could feel the hatred in Neo's glare.

"You will all pay the price for betraying us!" Neo yelled. "You will die the deaths of traitors, and then every human will—"

"Orphus. Neo. Kronus." Dracchus's deep voice cut through Neo's shouting, silencing the angry kraken. "You received your final warning. I issue my challenge."

Jax eased closer, arms spread slightly and claws at the ready. "None of you seem to learn."

"You have disrespected the ways of our people enough," Kronus spat. "Your challenge is no longer valid."

"My challenge is not optional."

The air behind Dracchus shifted, whispering across his back. He lashed out with his rear tentacles, wrapping them around Orphus's waist, and slammed the other kraken into the wall.

Before Orphus could recover, Dracchus spun and hammered his fist into his foe's face.

Bone crunched, and metal groaned. Orphus sagged. Dracchus grasped him by the neck and arm, swung him around, and threw him toward Kronus and Neo.

Caught off-guard, Neo was too slow to do the same. He and Orphus tumbled to the floor in a tangle of limbs.

Kronus caught himself against the wall before he could be dragged down with his followers. He clenched his jaw, eyes blazing, and turned red. Bunching his tentacles, he sprang at Jax. The Wanderer was ready, meeting Kronus's ferocious assault with equal speed and intensity. Blood splattered the wall and floor from fresh cuts.

Dracchus advanced on Neo and Orphus as they pulled themselves up, the latter moving unsteadily.

Neo recovered as Dracchus drew near, and launched into an attack, pushing off the wall with his tentacles to speed his charge.

Dracchus accepted the full force of Neo's strike. Claws sank into his sides, and he swayed back slightly, but remained upright. The sharp pain of his wounds strengthened his focus; Neo wouldn't have hesitated to bury these claws in Larkin's pale skin, wouldn't have shown her any mercy.

Growling, Dracchus wrapped his arms around Neo's chest, clasped his hands together, and squeezed.

Neo's hands scrambled in panic, raking fresh gouges over Dracchus's ribs and back. His tentacles curled, battling to wedge under Dracchus's arms and pry them open. Dracchus flexed his muscles in response. When Neo exhaled, Dracchus tightened his hold.

The captive kraken's struggles weakened.

Orphus, steadying himself against the wall, shook his head sharply. Blood trickled from one of his nostrils, and his eyes were glassy, but he staggered forward all the same.

Jax and Kronus continued their battle at the edge of Dracchus's vision; more blood seemed to glisten on the skin of the latter than the former.

Fingers curled, Orphus lunged, swiping at Dracchus. His claws caught the big kraken's shoulder. Warm blood flowed over Dracchus's skin.

Dracchus roared and heaved Neo to the side, slamming him into Orphus like an oversized, unwieldy club. Orphus fell toward the opposite wall, halting himself only by latching two of his tentacles around one of Dracchus's.

Dracchus widened his stance and gripped the floor and wall with his suction cups, anchoring himself as he dragged Neo away from Orphus. Neo renewed his struggles, jabbing his claws into Dracchus repeatedly.

When Dracchus swung this time, he released Neo, launching him directly into Orphus. The pair hit the wall together, Orphus losing his grip on Dracchus's tentacles.

Without a moment's hesitation, Dracchus raised himself up and reached over his head, grasping the ceiling rails. He swung back and, using his arms to add momentum, hurled his lower half at his foes. He spread his tentacles wide just before impact, closing them around Neo.

Neo fell to the floor, arms pinned to his sides and tentacles restrained. Dracchus settled all of his weight onto his captive and shifted his attention to his remaining foe.

Orphus pushed off the wall in another off-balance lunge, putting all his weight behind a wild punch.

Dracchus batted Orphus's blow aside with his forearm and followed the deflection with a cross, catching Orphus's cheek with his fist. The already dazed kraken went down hard.

"I will rip out her eyes and—" Neo's threat ended in a pained grunt as Dracchus's tentacles coiled tighter.

For good measure, Dracchus pounded his fists — right, left, right — into Neo's face in quick succession.

"She is the only reason we did not burn on that boat," Dracchus growled.

The captive kraken groaned, head lolling to the side, but he retained consciousness.

Dracchus turned to Jax; the Wanderer had restrained his opponent in a similar fashion, save that Kronus was face-down, neck bent at an awkward angle to glare up at Dracchus.

Kronus's skin changed to yellow. "You have bested us, traitors. We yield."

"I grant your lives as a gift on this day," Dracchus said. A little more pressure, a little more time, and he'd crush Neo's body. "And I give you a choice: live here in peace with *all* the Facility's inhabitants or leave forever. My tolerance for your hatred has ended."

Neo raised his head, baring his bloody teeth, and began to speak. Dracchus silenced him with a blow strong enough to make Neo's head bounce off the floor.

"No more words," Dracchus said. "Your actions have spoken loudly enough. Hold your tongue and remain here in peace or seek refuge in the open ocean. Do *not* give me the satisfaction of killing you."

Neo's head lolled again, and the tension in his body eased. Dracchus slowly released his hold and pushed himself up. Orphus, sprawled on the floor nearby, remained unmoving.

Once Dracchus was up, Jax freed Kronus. The defeated kraken propped himself up on his arms, head bowed, and did not revert his skin to its normal shade.

"You have chosen *them* over us," Kronus said. Blood dripped from numerous cuts on his body; Jax wasn't in much better a state.

"I have chosen us at every turn," Dracchus replied. "Perhaps you will come to understand that, in time."

He and Jax turned away together and moved down the corridor toward the Cabins.

Rage gnawed at Dracchus's gut; he'd not satisfied his urge to destroy, to *kill*, and its lingering intensity was worrisome. He'd have battled to defend any of the humans here, any of the kraken, especially when they'd done no wrong, but this was beyond the straightforward defense of a friend.

They'd threatened his mate directly today. Dracchus had forgiven much in his life, but *this* would not be forgotten.

"They'll only be angrier, now," Jax said as they passed through the tunnel.

Dracchus grunted. "Should they choose to act upon it again, I will show them what true anger is.

CHAPTER 16

LARKIN PACED ACROSS THE SMALL FLOOR SPACE OF RANDALL'S room, shooting glares at Arkon and her brother, who stood sentry at the door. They'd refused to let her go help Dracchus. It felt like she'd already waited an eternity, though she knew in her heart that only a few minutes had passed.

The others — Rhea, Aymee, and Macy — sat in the back of the room with the children, talking nonchalantly, but their expressions bore hints of their worry.

She rounded on Randall and Arkon. "I told him I would stand with him! What help am I in here?"

"You've seen what they can do, Elle," Randall said. "Unless you were going to start shooting—"

"And if I was?"

"Our numbers are relatively few," Arkon said with a frown. "Despite the difficulties some of our brethren have caused, Dracchus does not want to kill anyone."

"I didn't say I would kill them." Larkin scowled. "But I could have done *something* to fend them off."

"There's nothing we can do," Macy said gently. "Not against them."

205

Larkin clenched her fists. "It's my fault he's having to deal with it to begin with."

"Damnit, Elle, you know this isn't your fault." Randall's frustration was clear; despite the tension between him and Dracchus since Larkin's arrival, they appeared to be close friends, and he couldn't be any happier about waiting here idly than she was.

Dracchus and Jax could be fighting for their lives out there.

"You are not responsible for the actions of others." Arkon's voice was calm, but he turned his head toward the door often, as though listening for some sign. "The blame lies solely upon Kronus, Neo, and Orphus in this case."

Halting, Larkin ran a hand through her hair. She hated feeling so damned useless. "Just...let me out. Let me help him."

Jaw clenched, Randall turned away.

Arkon settled his thoughtful gaze on her and, after several moments, exhaled through his siphons. "He will not be happy about it."

"No!" Randall shouted, spinning to face Arkon. "The whole point of this is to keep her safe, it has nothing to do with him!"

"I can protect myself," Larkin said.

"Listen to me, Elle." Randall closed the distance between them and grabbed her hand, desperation strengthening his grip. He pointed at Arkon. "He was shot three times, and he was still able to tackle Cyrus and rip him to shreds. I'm friends with these kraken, and I still have fucking nightmares about how quickly they took apart those rangers. For them, it's just a brawl at the pub. For us, it's life or death."

Larkin glanced from Randall to Arkon, frowning.

"He is not alone," Arkon said. "Jax is there, too, and he is the only one who's ever bested Dracchus. They will not lose now."

"Uncle Dracchus is the strongest, and Daddy is the fastest!" Sarina declared.

"They are," Macy agreed.

Sarina's words eased Larkin somewhat, but the tightness in

Macy's voice was unmistakable. Until Dracchus was here, alive and well, for her to see with her own eyes, Larkin would be restless. She cared about the big kraken. A lot.

"Come, human." Rhea gestured for Larkin to join them. "We must wait. Your male will conquer."

My male.

Larkin trailed her gaze over everyone else. There was no question of the affection they all held for one another. This was a family born not of blood, but circumstance, its bonds only strengthened by its origins.

And they'd made her one of their own.

They passed the time in tense silence, which was broken only by the innocent sounds of the young ones playing. Unable to sit still, Larkin paced throughout, drumming her fingers against the holster at her hip.

Someone pounded on the door three times in rapid succession. Larkin's heart fluttered in anticipation, but her tumultuous emotions weren't enough to make her careless.

She drew her pistol. Randall pulled his own and fell into place beside her. Grasping the firearm with both hands, she watched as Arkon opened the door.

Jax entered first. At least a dozen cuts glistened on his blood-smeared skin, but his movements seemed unhindered.

"Jax!" Macy leapt up with Sarina in her arms, ran to him, and wrapped an arm around his torso without hesitation.

Both Larkin and Randall holstered their weapons. Randall exhaled shakily as Larkin crept forward, awaiting a glimpse of Dracchus.

"Daddy's hurt," Sarina said, looking at her father with huge, sad eyes.

Jax embraced his mate and child. If the movement hurt his open wounds, he made no sign of it. "I am fine."

The trio moved aside to allow Dracchus entry.

The big kraken's chest swelled with a slow inhalation, and

fresh blood oozed from gashes and puncture wounds on his sides. His gaze fell upon Larkin immediately, blazing with intensity; for an instant, they were the only two people in existence, and her breath caught in her throat.

The depth in his eyes compelled her to move closer.

She stopped in front of him, running her gaze over his many wounds, and her heart pounded. So much blood. Many of his injuries would require stitching. She looked up and raised her hands, cupping his jaw to draw him down.

Meeting her gaze, he allowed her to guide him.

"Don't you ever, *ever*, send me away again," she said.

He closed his eyes and leaned his forehead against hers. "I will do as I must to keep you safe, female."

She felt suddenly like she'd come home, like all her life before had just been a lead up to this moment, and *this* was where she was always meant to be, where she belonged. With her big, fierce, krullheaded kraken.

But all too soon, he pulled away.

It's for the best. I can't...I can't let myself care too deeply.

He wrapped a tentacle securely around her waist, as though he couldn't bear to sever contact with her for long, and drew her close as he straightened to face the others.

Jax, Macy, and Sarina remained nearby, but Arkon had moved to Aymee and Jace, and Randall sat on the bed beside Rhea and Melaina, with Ikaros curled on the floor in front of them.

"You are all my people," Dracchus said, "my *family*, and I will no longer allow anyone to threaten what is mine. I have given Kronus, Neo, and Orphus a choice today. Live with us in peace, leave this place forever, or die. Their next attack will be their last."

"Dracchus—" Arkon began, but Dracchus silenced him with a look.

"The time for diplomacy has passed. Words will no longer suffice, Arkon."

"He's right," Jax said, glancing down at Macy and Sarina.

"Their hatred has pushed some of them too far. Kronus no longer has control, because even he is too moderate for their taste. Neo would have killed us all if he could have. Do we wait until one of them succeeds?"

"One has tried," Rhea said, "and we cannot allow it to continue."

"This is a big step to take, isn't it?" Randall asked. "Killing your own…that's a threshold you don't get to return from." He wore the pain of his experiences on his face, and Larkin's heart ached for him.

"All of this because you saved me," Macy said, closing her eyes and laying her head on Jax's shoulder.

"I would do it again, given the choice. I have no regrets." Jax placed a soft kiss atop her head.

"And saving you may have saved our people," Arkon said, taking Aymee's hand. "Violence is the last thing I wish, but when they endanger our mates, our younglings… We cannot remain placid."

Larkin looked up at Dracchus. "I already said I would stand with you."

"There are many more of our people who would also side with you," Rhea said. "The humans have helped our kind greatly. They have endangered themselves to defend us, to protect our younglings, and to provide for us. They are part of us, and have brought joy to our lives."

Dracchus lifted a hand and settled it along Larkin's jaw, brushing the pad of his thumb over her cheekbone. Heat bloomed in her chest in response to the simple, tender touch.

"We have all made our choices," he said. "Now, the choice is for Kronus and his followers to make. I only wanted all of you to know what may come. To be prepared. I do not want any of you to come to harm."

"Are you all right, Dracchus?" Aymee asked.

"I will be fine." The confidence in Dracchus's voice seemed in direct opposition to his wounds. Larkin knew the kraken could take a beating, but how much was too much for them? "Come, Larkin. Let us return to our den as we had intended."

"Uncle Drak!" Sarina called.

He turned his head toward her, and a warm smile spread across his lips. He puffed his cheeks and blew air out of his siphons. Child mimicked him, flashing a bright smile afterward. Larkin's chest felt suddenly, painfully hollow.

"I need some rest, little one. We will play another time," he said.

They said their goodbyes and Larkin followed Dracchus into the hallway, watching him closely. His movements had taken on a stiffness she didn't care for, and blood still seeped from several of his wounds.

"You should have asked Aymee to look at those," she said.

Aymee was a doctor; why hadn't she pressed the issue?

"I will heal." He opened the door to their room and shifted aside to allow her in first.

"If you don't bleed out first," She stepped inside and turned to face him. "Most of those look like they need stitches."

He passed through the doorway and closed the door behind him. Larkin observed his breathing; his ribs expanded slowly, only to abruptly draw back in with twitch of his muscles, as though his wounds were being stretched too far.

"We should get Aymee," Larkin said, walking past him.

Dracchus caught her arm, halting her before she reached the door. "No. She does not need to be troubled by this. Do what you can, and it will be enough."

"Give me something to shoot at and I'll hit the target pretty much every time, but *this*..." She stared at one of the deeper gashes, which still oozed blood. "I'm not good at this."

"You need only stop the bleeding, so I do not soil our den. I will heal." He drew her closer and brushed the backs of his fingers over her cheek. "I require only the attention of my mate."

Why does he have to say things like that?

Larkin wanted to deny his claim, to give him all the reasons why she was a horrible choice, but the words lodged in her throat.

She took his hand in hers and lowered it. "Sit down, and I'll see what I can find in the bathroom."

He nodded, grunting softly as he released her and moved toward the table. Despite the situation, she couldn't help but find some humor in him pausing in front of a chair and staring at it quizzically before he finally slid it aside and squatted on the floor.

She entered the bathroom and rummaged through the cupboards beneath the sink. After pushing aside everyday toiletries — hair cleaner, shaving cream, razors, and various bottles — she found a still-sealed first aid kit. She set it on the sink and turned to gather as many washcloths as she could from the small closet.

She returned to Dracchus with her arms full of supplies and set the items on the table beside him.

"Are you sure about this?" She removed her belt and carefully set it, along with her knife and pistol, next to the first aid kit.

Once again, he nodded.

"Okay." Larkin broke the seal on the first aid kit and opened the lid. She ran her gaze over the items inside; she'd never seen many of them, and several of the names on their packaging were foreign to her.

There was no need to overcomplicate this. After a brief search, she plucked out a bottle of disinfectant, poured some of the liquid onto a washcloth, and faced Dracchus. Even in his crouch, he was taller than her.

"I imagine they are in far worse shape than you," she said as she applied the cloth to one of his wounds and gently wiped the blood away.

He grunted, and his muscles twitched. "I was merciful. This time."

"Why do they hate us so much? I mean, I know why they hate *me*, but the others."

Dracchus shrugged. "I do not know. Arkon says they are threatened. Jax thinks they believe humans make us weak. We were all raised on that old hatred — humans were our enemy, since the birth of our people, and that could never change. It is not so easy a thing to let go."

Larkin steadied herself with a hand on his back and bent down to clean some of the larger gashes. She bit her lip as his muscles spasmed in response, but he didn't make a sound.

"But you let it go," she said. "Jax and Arkon, too."

"When I first discovered Jax with Macy, I saw her as my enemy. But she never threatened any of us. Never moved against us in any way. She stood beside Jax through everything, and she saved Melaina from a razorback, nearly losing her life in the process." He released a long, slow breath through his nostrils. "Why would an enemy risk herself for one of us?"

"Because she was never an enemy to begin with." Setting the cloth aside, Larkin picked up one of the tubes. The name written on its side was meaningless to her — she doubted she could even pronounce it — but the words *Laceration Sealant* written in smaller letters below told her all she needed to know. She looked from the tube to his wounds; the small amount of sealant wouldn't go far, given the scope of the damage. "We've all made a mess of things."

"Another trait our people have in common," he said and turned his head to look at her hand. "No more of those liquids. They sting."

Larkin smirked. "There's another commonality. No matter how big they are, human and kraken men all whine when they're hurt."

He furrowed his brow and lifted his arms, glancing at the gashes on his sides. "I am not whining. But should I choose to, I have earned the right."

She chuckled and shook her head, placing a hand on his arm to guide it back down. "It's a joke. But I *am* going to use this on your shoulder."

Dracchus didn't resist as she sealed the gouges on his shoulder, pinching them together with her fingers and squeezing the liquid over the cuts. She blew on them gently, and the sealant hardened within seconds.

He rotated his arm at the shoulder. Despite the movement, the wounds remained sealed. "I can feel it there, though I cannot see it."

Larkin raised the tube and scanned the tiny print on the back. "It should dissolve once the wound heals." She used the remaining sealant on a few of his other wounds, and then picked up a roll of bandages, pressing the end to his stomach. "Hold this here."

He pinned the material in place with two fingers as she wrapped it around his torso. Due to his size, she was forced to walk around him, passing the roll from one hand to the other as she looped it beneath his arms.

Being so close, she couldn't ignore the heat of his skin, and his scent soon replaced the metallic tang of blood.

She cut the bandage and tied off the end. Taking a step back, she looked him over. The worst of his wounds were sealed or bandaged, but his face and head were splattered with blood.

"All done, except…" She reached past him to pick up another cloth, splashing it with some disinfectant. "Bend your head down for me."

Without question, he sank lower and tipped his head forward, as though ceding power to her. Larkin smiled. It seemed unlikely that he assumed this position very often. She placed her hand on his jaw and turned his face to one side. Gently, she dabbed away the drying blood, thankfully finding no wounds beneath.

Still, Larkin took her time, skimming her fingertips over his flesh to learn the feel of him. Moving closer, she slid her hand upward along his jaw until his siphon was nestled between her forefinger and thumb. She turned her face toward him and grazed his brow with her lips.

Dracchus inhaled deeply. His siphon shifted gently against her fingers as he wrapped a tentacle around her ankle, working its tip into the leg of her jumpsuit.

His touch sent a thrill through her. Dracchus was alien to her, but he wasn't frightening or off-putting. He was pure male — confident, strong, and in control. She felt a powerful, instinctual pull toward him, had felt it even in the beginning, while he'd been a captive on the ship.

And if she chose to accept whatever was growing between them, this male would be *hers*.

Larkin focused on the feel of his tentacle caressing her ankle. She warred within herself; there was nothing wrong with fun, nothing wrong with *pleasure*, but he wasn't interested in casual fucking. He wanted a mate. He wanted family. It would be so easy for Larkin to take what she wanted — *him* — but she could never give Dracchus what he wanted, no matter how much she yearned to.

His hands fell to her hips, fingertips brushing her backside, and a fire ignited beneath her skin. Her core clenched as heat flooded her. Releasing a shaky breath, she closed her eyes. The cloth fell from her fingers as she smoothed her hand up his shoulder to cup the back of his neck.

"I love the scent you make for me," he growled, tightening his grip as he drew her closer. He lifted his head and pressed his lips to her neck. Her skin tingled where they touched.

She knew in the back of her mind that she should've been shocked that he could smell her arousal, but it only turned her on more. She squeezed her thighs together and shifted as though it would alleviate the ache growing between them.

"Dracchus…"

His lips followed the line of her collarbone until he reached the other side of her neck, where he gently nipped. Driven by instinct, Larkin turned her face toward him and caught his mouth with hers. Their lips clashed in a flurry of passion, unable to get close enough to one another.

His groan pulsed through her, pearling her nipples, as he lifted her off the floor and carried her to the bed. Larkin deepened the kiss and wrapped her legs around his torso, giving herself over to his touch, his taste, to *him*. He stole her breath, her essence, her soul, and returned it with part of his own. She drowned and lost herself within him.

Dracchus laid her on the bed and followed her down without breaking the kiss, caging her with his arms. Her thighs spread wider to allow his body to settle between them. She welcomed his weight. His muscles were hard beneath velvet-soft flesh as her hands roamed over his shoulders and back. A tentacle slid up each of her legs, beneath her clothing, to coil around her calves and stroke the backs of her knees.

She felt a prick of pain and tasted a hint of blood as one of his teeth graze her lip, but she didn't care. It couldn't compare to the desire coursing through her veins, which scalded her from inside out. Her jumpsuit scratched against her overly sensitive skin. She needed to feel him against her, to feel his flesh on hers, to eliminate every barrier between them.

Dracchus reared back, breaking the kiss. Lips swollen and tingling, Larkin dropped her arms to either side of her head and stared up at him. He looked upon her with ravenous eyes. His chest heaved with ragged breaths as he moved his hands to the front of her jumpsuit.

He grasped the fabric and wrenched it apart, tearing the zipper open like it was made of paper. Cool air caressed her bared breasts, and Dracchus growled in approval. He wasted no time in removing the garment from her completely, shredding the fabric with his claws and peeling it off her arms and legs, tentacles sliding down to remove her shoes.

The chill was fleeting; as Dracchus leaned down again, his heat flowed into her, flaring when he closed his mouth over her nipple. Larkin arched, pleasure shooting straight to her core. Her sex throbbed. She cupped his head with her hands as he sucked and teased her breasts.

His tentacles slid higher, over her thighs, and slipped between their bodies to brush along her sex. Larkin inhaled sharply.

Dracchus groaned. "I will taste you on my tongue, female, before I am maddened by your scent."

He moved down her body, trailing kisses along the way. When he reached the scars on her pelvis, Larkin suddenly went cold, instinctively covering them with her hands.

"Don't," she rasped.

He caught both her wrists in one hand and drew her arms away, looking up to meet her gaze. "They are part of you, and so they are beautiful."

He dipped his head and kissed them. "My brave—"

His lips moved lower. "—strong—"

Larkin shivered as his chin brushed over the hair between her legs.

"—mate."

His mouth pressed against her sex, and his tongue ran over it from bottom to top; she nearly leapt out of her skin when it flicked her clit. Pleasure shot through her, and she released a throaty groan, letting her head fall back onto the bed. When he released her wrists, she dropped her arms to take handfuls of the bedding.

Dracchus's appreciative growl vibrated through her core. He twisted, moved his shoulders behind her thighs, and wrapped his arms around her legs, grasping her knees as he greedily lapped at her sex.

She writhed in his hold, but he didn't relent. Her moans turned into gasps, which became pleasured cries. She held nothing back.

Soon, his hands moved up, leaving his tentacles to hold her

legs parted. He covered her breasts with his palms, stroking and squeezing them as he made love to her with his mouth and tongue.

Larkin shut her eyes and bit her lip as the sensation built within her. Her feet arched, toes digging into his back as her hips undulated beneath his mouth, mimicking the act of sex; she was desperate to reach that pivotal moment.

Then he latched onto her clit and sucked.

Stars burst behind her eyelids, and she screamed. Liquid heat flooded Larkin, and suddenly, Dracchus's hands were under her, grabbing her backside and lifting her off the bed and against his face as he drank from her like he'd just crossed a desert without water. Every stroke of his tongue sent her higher and higher, and when she finally crested the peak of her euphoria, he brought her back down slowly, gently, his presence offering her a solid place to land.

She lay there staring at the ceiling, limp and panting, a light sheen of perspiration coating her skin and dampening her hair. Dracchus gave her a final lick before he kissed the top of her sex and raised his head. He drew himself over her once again, licking her essence from his lips. It was such a naughty thing, but it sent a jolt of desire right back through her.

No one had ever done that to her before. She'd never realized how intense it could be, how *good* it could feel. Despite coming, she craved more, craved it *now*.

"I will drink from you often." He brushed the backs of his fingers over her open sex and brought them to his mouth to lick clean. "As often as you make this scent for me."

Larkin licked her lips, staring at his mouth — a mouth full of sharp teeth that had been nothing but gentle as he brought her to climax. "That might be too often, even for you."

Especially after this. It'll be all I think about.

Dracchus grinned. "I accept your challenge, female."

He turned onto his back and pulled her into his arms. He

inhaled deeply, then released a satisfied hum. When he did nothing more than hold her, Larkin frowned in confusion.

"What...about you?" she asked awkwardly. Men usually did nothing without reciprocation, and considering what Dracchus had just done, she'd expected him to demand something in return.

"I must rest so my wounds will heal. Tonight was for you." He smoothed his palm down her arm, and his tentacles shifted, drawing the blanket over her before twining with her legs. "You gave more than you realize in return already."

"I did?" she asked, slowly slipping her arm around his chest. When she'd woken alone this morning — having gone to bed alone the night before — she'd found herself longing for his presence. She liked him beside her, holding her.

Making her feel safe.

"Yes. You have woken a new craving in me, and I will never be sated in my lust for your taste."

Larkin's skin heated in a blush. She shouldn't have been shocked by such blunt speech, not while living among men all her life, but the promise in Dracchus's tone was beyond anything she'd ever heard. She squeezed her thighs together, her sex clenching with the memory of his mouth and tongue.

As though reading her mind, Dracchus growled, low and deep in his chest. "Sleep. When you wake, it will be with my tongue between your thighs."

CHAPTER 17

Larkin wandered around the infirmary, picking up various items for inspection. She'd seen some of it back home, though much of the old tech in Fort Culver was no longer functional. Many more items, however, were unfamiliar to her.

Advanced technology was a luxury humans had learned to live without over the last few generations. Many of the old devices and machines had failed over the years. Tinkering and improvisation only went so far when sophisticated pieces required replacement — the colonies had never reached the point of being able to manufacture their own parts.

While she wouldn't argue the fact that technology made life easier, Larkin found something gratifying in simple tasks like starting a fire without advanced tools. It was comforting to know that humans had the skills to carry on and survive when technology failed.

Without a doubt, the Facility was the most technologically advanced location she'd ever seen. The building itself was integrated with an interactive, talking computer, was powered by glowing *rocks,* and was bristling with gadgets and weaponry that the rangers would kill to have.

She hoped they never found this place.

A rapid, steady sound pulsed through the room, drawing Larkin's attention. She turned her head to look at the others.

Macy was reclining on one of the beds, shirt pulled up and tucked between her breasts as Aymee directed the scanner over her belly. Jax held Macy's hand, gaze flicking between his mate and the life growing inside her. Arkon was beside him with a wide smile. And Dracchus...

He'd positioned himself a bit behind them, holding Sarina and Jace — one child per arm.

The sight was at once heartwarming and heart-wrenching.

Larkin swallowed her emotions. She couldn't allow it to affect her every time she saw a child. She'd accepted her reality a long time ago.

So why did it bother her so much now?

Because I never had someone I wanted to share a life with until now.

Larkin watched Dracchus, admiring his easy manner with the children. No one would look at him and think, even for a second, that he had a soft side, but he showed it often to those he cared about.

Could he be content with her? Could he take her as his mate without regret?

As she'd lain with him the night before, cradled in his embrace and feeling more loved than ever before, she'd allowed herself to believe there was a *chance* he could be happy with her. That belief, initially so innocent and mild, had shifted into a hope, into a *craving*, when he'd kept his promise and woke her with his tongue this morning.

Blushing, she tore her gaze away from Dracchus. Now was not the time to think about such things — especially considering Dracchus could scent her arousal. It'd be even more humiliating if the other kraken could, too.

"How far along?" Macy asked, running her hand over her slightly rounded stomach.

"I believe three to four weeks," Aymee replied.

Larkin frowned, brows lowering as she stepped closer. She knew little about pregnancy, but women weren't supposed to show so early on. Macy looked closer to three *months* along, not three weeks.

"Is something wrong?" Larkin asked.

"Nope, everything looks perfect, and the baby has a strong heartbeat," Aymee replied with a smile.

"Then why is she so…big?"

Aymee turned off the scanner and pushed it up. "Kraken were genetically designed to have a low birth rate, but their gestation cycle is much faster, even when carried by a human mother. A kraken fetus is fully formed in about four months. It was all part of their plan to keep the kraken's population under control while continuing to produce able workers."

"It seems that it was only the females that were altered, as the males have no problem getting us pregnant," Macy said, looking at Jax with a grin.

"We have been fortunate," Jax said, settling a hand on her belly.

Aymee snorted. "If by fortunate you mean virile."

Macy laughed.

Arkon flashed violet and cleared his throat. "We cannot help that we're drawn to our mates."

"Which is why," Aymee stepped away from the bed and walked to the counter behind Larkin, "we're going to start using contraception." She picked up a small vial and held it between her finger and thumb.

"You have said that word before. What does it mean?" Dracchus asked, seemingly unbothered by Sarina and Jace climbing on his head and shoulders.

"Whatever problems were designed into your females, kraken sperm has no problem finding its way to human eggs."

"That does not answer my question, Aymee."

"It means, we won't get pregnant," she replied.

The air suddenly filled with tension, and all three male kraken fixed their gazes on Aymee.

"Why would that be necessary?" Jax asked, his voice laced with apprehension.

Macy picked up his hand and brought it to her mouth, placing a kiss on its back. "I love the family we are making together, Jax, but I don't want to go through a pregnancy a year for the rest of my life."

Jax's brow lowered. He opened his mouth to reply but closed it without speaking.

"We have always struggled to sustain our numbers," Dracchus grumbled, "and knowing that, you will simply cease to have younglings? You have given hope to the kraken. Will you forsake that so easily?"

"Is that all we are?" Aymee asked, anger in her tone. "Just a means to repopulate your race?"

Arkon approached her from behind and settled his hands on her shoulders. "That is not what he means, Aymee."

"Isn't it?" she asked, scowling at Dracchus.

Larkin stared at him, awaiting his answer. Her hands were clenched, palms clammy, as she shifted them absently toward her scars.

Despite his clear frustration, he was gentle as he removed the children and placed them on a nearby bed. "Our females do all they can to ensure we will have future generations. They would not so casually give up such a gift."

His words were a kick to Larkin's gut.

How could I have thought he'd be happy with me? How could I think he wouldn't regret choosing me?

Just watching him with the children that first time should have been answer enough for her.

"We are not giving it up," Macy said.

Jax drew her hand closer to his chest. "But that is what Aymee just spoke of."

"It wouldn't be permanent."

"I've already researched this through the computer," Aymee said. Her voice was more controlled, but her expression made it clear that she wasn't backing down. "The effects are temporary. If, or *when*, we are ready to conceive, we either wait for it to wear off or use a different shot to neutralize it."

"I still do not understand why you would choose this," Dracchus said.

Aymee closed her eyes and inhaled deeply. "Dracchus, I understand what these children mean to you, that you're thinking of the kraken's future, but we are not broodmares."

"It's not wrong for us to want control over our bodies," Macy said. "To live and enjoy life."

"Not to mention, it's unsafe," Aymee added. "The equipment here is likely the best in the world, but if things go wrong — and they often do, with pregnancies and childbirth — there's not going to be a whole lot I can do. Especially if it's *me* in one of these beds."

Arkon's skin paled, and Jax's features tightened. As tough as the kraken were, Larkin guessed that neither male had ever considered pregnancy could end in tragedy.

"We're not giving up this gift," Macy said. She wrapped her arms around Sarina as the child climbed up onto the bed with her. "We know how much this means to you, to all the kraken, and our children mean the world to us, too."

Larkin's chest tightened.

We know how much this means to you...

"But with a gestation cycle this short, we could potentially have three babies a year. While we share the same DNA, *our* bodies are not made for that. Hell, our minds aren't, either," Aymee said.

Dracchus's expression was one of deep, troubled thought — a creased brow, eyes dark, and a heavy frown. He swung his gaze to Larkin, and his attention dipped to her hands.

Larkin quickly shifted her hands to her sides, wiping her damp palms on her pants.

His brow dropped further. Confusion gleamed amidst the darker emotions on his face.

"If it is what my mate chooses, she has my support," Jax said.

"As does mine," Arkon added.

Dracchus grunted, turning his head toward the others. "I will respect your choices." There was a hint of something left unsaid in his words, and that wasn't like the kraken Larkin had come to know. He'd faced physical confrontation and pain without blinking, but this situation had him off-balance, and that only worried her more.

"Let's return to our den," Jax said, helping Macy from the bed.

Aymee put the vial away as Arkon gathered Jace.

"We'll talk again soon, Larkin," Macy said, offering her a smile and a wave.

Aymee joined Macy. "We'll have a picnic in the Mess."

Larkin waved back, forcing a smile. "I would love to."

"What I wouldn't do to have a picnic outdoors again…" Macy's voice faded as they left the room, moving down the hallway.

Larkin looked at Dracchus to find him watching her.

"Come, female," he said, extending a hand. "I have shared you enough today."

Larkin's breath shallowed, but the warmth his words instilled within her couldn't push away her pain.

It would be so easy to love him.

Her hand itched to take hold of his as she walked toward him, but she didn't give in to the urge. Caving to her desires would only make what was to come more difficult. She'd already given in too much.

THE TRIP back to their den was short, but Larkin was silent throughout, walking in front of Dracchus without looking back a single time. When they arrived, she moved to the center of the room and folded her arms across her chest. She kept her back to him.

Dracchus approached, settling a hand on her shoulder and wrapping a tentacle around her waist to draw her close. They hadn't been alone since early morning, and he needed to touch her.

Larkin shrugged off his hand and pushed his tentacle away. She stepped beyond his reach, her body rigid, and turned to face him.

He frowned; this was not the Larkin who had awoken to his attentions this morning, not the Larkin who'd been pliant, appreciative, affectionate. Not the woman who'd begged for more of his touch.

She'd been uncharacteristically quiet in the Infirmary, but this was well beyond silence. He'd thought they moved past this days ago, during their time on the beach.

"What is wrong?" he asked, moving closer.

Larkin held up her hands, halting Dracchus. "I don't want to share a room with you anymore."

Her words repeated in his mind several times before he understood what she'd said. "I do not find humor in your jest."

"This isn't a joke, Dracchus."

"What has changed since this morning?" he asked. This had to be some sort of human trick like Randall often tried to play. But Dracchus's chest constricted all the same, and uncomfortable heat spread through him.

"Nothing has changed. I told you from the beginning that I didn't want to share a room with you. Rhea said the female chooses, and this is me making my choice."

He advanced on her, not stopping until she extended her arms and pressed her palms to his chest.

"Back up," she warned.

"No. You will explain your reasoning to me, so I may explain to you why you are wrong."

"I don't need to explain myself to you." She pushed against him.

"You are *my mate*," he growled, coiling a tentacle around her waist and tugging her closer. She locked her elbows, keeping her torso angled back to preserve what little distance remained between them.

"I'm not your damn mate!"

"*You are!*" he said through bared teeth. "And I will not give you up!"

Larkin glared up at him, shoulders heaving with angry breaths. "I'm not," she said, slapping his chest. The sting was nothing compared to the pain caused by her words. "I'm not, I'm not!"

She struck him again, and then twice more, but not before Dracchus saw moisture glistening in her eyes.

He caught her wrists in his hands. The tightness had spread from his chest to his throat, a discomfort unlike any he'd ever known. "Speak to me, Larkin. What has changed? Have we not been honest with one another from the beginning?"

Larkin squeezed her eyes shut and turned her face away, tears rolling down her cheeks. "*Nothing* has changed. I told you, I'm not what you want. You just refuse to listen."

Dracchus released one of her arms and took hold of her chin, gently guiding her face back toward his. "Why? Why are you not what I want?"

"Because I'm broken." Fresh tears streamed from her reddened eyes. She pushed against his chest again, and he let her go. Grasping the hem of her shirt, she yanked it up to reveal her scars. "Because of *this!*"

"I have told you they are nothing to feel shame for," he said, mind spinning. How had those scars sparked this situation? "I have countless of my own. They are the past, nothing more."

"They are my past, my present, and my future. I will *never* have a child."

He lowered his gaze to her scars, and wished he had the quick mind of Arkon, wished that he understood. "Is it because of...*contraception?*"

"No. This...this is permanent. I will never conceive, Dracchus. I *can't*." She wiped her cheeks with her hand, eyes locked on his as she lowered her shirt. "I'm broken. Useless."

The torrent of emotions swirling through Dracchus at that moment was too overwhelming; he stared at her abdomen numbly, unable to form words, unable to form coherent thoughts. Images of Sarina, Jace, and Melaina flitted through his mind, followed by half-realized imaginings of the younglings he'd hoped to one day sire, who he'd hoped to nurture and teach.

Those imaginings faded, leaving only the tightness in his chest and throat, so strong now that he could scarcely breathe.

She'd told him her scars were the result of a hunting accident. That she'd done something stupid and paid the price. His hearts ached for her; he would never have thought *this* would be the cost. Dracchus couldn't guess how she'd felt in the infirmary listening to the other females speak of younglings and contraception. Listening to *him* speak.

He absently lifted a hand to his chest, pushing against the ache as though that would somehow alleviate it.

"Say something." Larkin's voice was tight, and her words ended in a sob.

His brave, strong, capable female, who he'd only seen cry once before — when she was reunited with her brother after a year of not knowing whether he was alive or dead — was in terrible pain.

He didn't know what to say to her. Didn't know anything other than the raw, indecipherable emotion blazing through him. She was upset, *devastated*, and how could he possibly fix that? How could he take the pain away from her?

"I...I need to think," he finally rasped.

She stared at him mutely, fresh tears spilling from her wide, blue eyes, and something inside of Dracchus shattered.

He turned away from her, his entire body tense as he moved toward the door. He didn't want to go, didn't want to leave her behind, but he needed to gather his thoughts. He'd never been good with words, not like Arkon, or Jax, or any of the humans who'd come to live here. He'd never had a friend until the events surrounding Macy's arrival.

And what he'd been building with Larkin was far more complex, far more meaningful, than any relationship he'd ever had. Her revelation changed that, but *how*?

Dracchus opened the door and entered the hallway. Just before the door slid shut, she released a sobbing wail that pierced him to his core; it was the desperate cry of the hopeless, of the abandoned, and it was because of him. Because he'd left her.

Body trembling, he pressed a hand to the wall beside the door, taking what little stability he could from it. He hung his head and squeezed his eyes shut. Immense pressure gathered within him, sending tremors through his entirety. His throat burned, and his insides tumbled and twisted into knots.

He dragged himself along the corridor, jaw clenched.

Sarina's excited smiles flashed through his mind, followed by Jace's inquisitive stares. The sound of their giggling echoed in his head. But images of Larkin rose next — bold, confident, compassionate. A forever mate, a female to be proud of. A female to be earned.

A female to love, and to love him in return.

What did he want more? What was truly important to him?

Could he give her up?

CHAPTER 18

THE BED DIPPED BEHIND LARKIN, STARTLING HER AWAKE. SHE reached beneath her pillow for a weapon that wasn't there. Before she could turn to face the intruder, the heavy but familiar weight of a hand settled on her shoulder. It slid down the length of her arm, moving beneath the pillow to cover her hand and twine its fingers with hers.

Larkin held still, afraid to breathe, afraid she was dreaming. She stared at the powerful arm; it was nothing but a shadow, and if she moved it would dissipate into the darkness. But then Dracchus's body pressed against her back, warm and solid, and she knew this was real.

He'd come back.

She tensed, pushing aside her grogginess. "What are you doing here?"

She'd never been caught so unaware. She also hadn't cried that hard since her mother died.

"I have returned to our den." His voice was a low, gruff rumble. He settled his chin on her shoulder, touching his cheek to hers. "To my mate."

Larkin closed her eyes against the burn of tears. She tried to pull her hand away, to put distance between them, but he held firm.

"My choice has not changed, Larkin."

"But I'm—"

"My choice has not changed," he repeated. "You are my mate." His hand moved to her stomach, and she stiffened as he slipped it beneath her shirt to touch the skin of her lower abdomen. He carefully traced her scars with the pad of a finger. "You are not broken or useless. You are *mine*."

Her throat tightened around a sob. She covered his hand, closing her fingers around it. "You'll regret it. You'll regret me. I can't… I can't give you what you want."

"Say that you choose me, and you will give me all I want." He rose up behind her and placed a finger beneath her chin, gently turning her face toward him. The dim light reflected in his eyes, making them glow faintly.

"What about—"

"I choose *you*, Larkin. Say you choose me."

She searched his face, though it was shrouded in shadow save the amber of his eyes. Scalding tears ran over her cheeks and into her hair. Hope blossomed in her chest, almost too painful for words. Raising a hand, she cupped his face, holding his gaze.

"I choose you," she said softly, then more firmly. "I *want* you."

"Say that you are my mate." The reflections in his eyes might as well have been flames for their intensity.

She brushed her thumb over his cheek, exhaling shakily. "I'm your mate."

He leaned down, sliding his fingers to her hair. "I decided you would be mine while I was caged on that boat. That I would have you, whatever it took. And now that you are here, now that I have seen your bravery, your strength, your heart, I will never let you go."

He gently turned her onto her back and pressed his forehead

to hers. "You are my mate, Larkin, and your worth is beyond measure."

Larkin's heart felt as though it would burst. Dracchus had chosen *her*. He knew of her scars, knew she couldn't bear him children, and still wanted her to be his.

Moving her hand to the back of his head, she pressed her lips to his fervently. That was all it took for the barriers between them to crumble. He gathered her in his arms and held her close, slanting his mouth to deepen the kiss. She tasted the salt and the sea, tasted *him*, and craved more.

"Dracchus," she rasped, breaking the kiss to brush her cheek against his, "make love to me."

Dracchus clutched his mate to him, burying his face against her nape, and breathed in her scent. Her words hit him like a harpoon, tethering he and Larkin together irreversibly, finally completing the bond he'd longed for. A forever mate.

He released her and reared back, reaching for her clothing; he needed to feel her skin against his. Larkin was faster. She grasped fistfuls of her shirt and yanked it off over her head, her motions thrusting her chest against his. He lowered his face to her breasts and captured one in his mouth, sucking the hardened peak, careful of his teeth. She moaned, hands skimming his shoulders, sending small jolts straight to the tips of his tentacles.

Dracchus settled his hands on her sides and slid them down, tracing the curves of her hips and backside as he hooked her pants with his thumbs. He dragged the garment toward her feet, reaching up with two tentacles to finish removing it. His nostrils flared as the heady scent of her arousal permeated the air.

He raised his head and looked upon his mate. *His*. Her red hair was spread around her on the bedding, with tendrils of it draped over her pale, slim shoulders. His gaze drifted down her body, over her beautiful breasts, her flat stomach, and stopped on her scars. She had suffered, but he would allow her to suffer no longer; he would do everything in his power to make her happy. Everything to make her understand that, even in her lowest moments, even when she doubted herself, he would always believe in her.

Everything to make her understand she was the most valuable thing in his world.

His eyes dipped to the patch of hair between her legs, already damp with her desire. Curling his fingers around the inside of her thighs, he pried her legs apart. The glistening petals of her sex opened to him.

Dracchus groaned, clenching his teeth, and tilted his head back. His cock burst from his slit, throbbing, aching, eager to fill her. He wedged himself between her thighs, the bedding rough as coral to the oversensitive skin of his shaft.

"Oh, wow," Larkin breathed.

He looked up to see her propped on her elbows, peering down the length of her body, her wide eyes locked on his cock.

"So that's where it's been? How the hell did it fit in there?"

"Female, now is not the time for such questions," he growled with a smirk.

"I think now is definitely the time. And what are those…those things?" She leaned forward, extending an arm, and brushed her finger along one of the feelers at the base of his shaft.

Dracchus shuddered as pleasure flowed through him. He placed a hand on her shoulder and forced her back onto the bed, looming over her. The head of his cock slid between the wet folds of her sex. He gritted his teeth. It took every bit of his willpower to avoid thrusting against her.

"You will find out soon enough," he said, voice strained.

Larkin opened her mouth as though to ask another question, but he silenced her with a kiss. She moaned into his mouth, matching the caress of lips and tongue, and undulated her hips to glide her sex over his shaft. Tearing his mouth from hers, he hissed through his teeth and clawed at the bedding. He took hold of her hip with one hand and pinned her to the bed.

"Not yet." He lifted his torso and slid his pelvis back, breaking the contact between his cock and her sex. He needed to be inside her, but she wasn't ready to receive him.

He smoothed his palms along her inner thighs, spreading them wide, and wrapped a tentacle around each of her calves. He lowered his face, stopping just before her sex, and looked up. Larkin watched him intently, her eyes hooded with desire. She shivered when he exhaled. He didn't look away as he dipped his head, took in her scent, and slid his tongue over her silken folds.

She closed her eyes, tilted her head back, and released a throaty sigh as her fingers clutched at the sheets.

Fierce need swept through him. Her reactions drove him to give her more, to learn every sensitive point on her body and discover how best to touch them, how to caress them, how to worship her. His cock ached, and he forced it against the bed to alleviate some of the pressure.

His tongue explored her; it delved between her folds, dipped into her channel, and teasingly flicked the small nub that seemed to send her into a frenzy. He drank from her, unable to get enough of his mate's unique taste. It was his, and his alone.

"Dracchus," she breathed, cupping her breasts and kneading them as her hips rocked against his mouth.

The sight of Larkin touching herself sent his desire to new heights. His seed seeped from the tip of his cock.

He clenched a fist, ignoring the bite of his claws into his skin.

Not yet.

"I'm so close," she moaned.

Dracchus closed his lips around her nub, sucked it into his mouth, and growled. Her entire body tensed as she filled the room with a cry of pleasure. Her back arched before she sat up suddenly, wrapping her arms around his head, and pressed her sex hard against his mouth.

He grasped her backside with both hands and lashed her nub with his tongue and lips. Larkin screamed, her blunt nails biting into his skin, as a rush of hot nectar flowed from her.

He lapped at her until the involuntary undulation of her hips eased, until her cries diminished into panting breaths and her hands glided soothingly, lovingly, over his neck and shoulders. Before she could settle fully, he resumed his attentions, bringing her to another crest — slowly, leisurely, coaxing every tiny reaction he could from her body.

He brushed his lips over her inner thigh and worked his way up to her lower stomach, tenderly kissing her scars. Her abdomen tensed, but she relaxed it quickly, running her fingers over his head. Dracchus drew himself up, pushing her gently onto her back again. He shifted his tentacles up from her calves, wrapping them around her thighs and under her knees, and guided her legs to encircle his hips.

"I want you," she said, brushing her hand down his chest.

Dracchus fisted his shaft, angling her hips up with his tentacles so he could press the head into her entrance.

"You have me," he said, pumping her back and forth upon him, sinking a little deeper with every small thrust. She was tight, soft, and hot, and her oils mingled with his to ease his entry. Dracchus clenched his teeth as her sex gripped him.

Her body tensed. She released a whimper that she immediately cut off by biting her lip. Panting, she reached up to grasp the top of the bed.

"Fuck me, Dracchus," she said. "I need you *now*."

He released a hissing breath through his teeth. It was too much, she was too tight, and he was too large. Moving his hands to her hips, he met her gaze.

"Forgive me, female." Dracchus forced his pelvis forward, simultaneously pulling her toward him.

Larkin gasped and squeezed her eyes shut. The muscles in her forearms stood out as she clenched the bed.

Dracchus stilled save for his ragged breaths. Every tiny flutter of her inner walls was a delicious torment, crashing over him like a wave, impossible to ignore, but his only concern was Larkin. Her discomfort, her *pain*. He leaned forward, propping himself on an arm, and began to withdraw from her body.

Larkin opened her eyes and glared at him. "Don't you fucking dare." Her thighs tightened around him, holding him in place.

He furrowed his brow. "You are getting no pleasure from this."

"Just...give me a moment." She rocked her hips. Her slow, shallow pumps coaxed a groan from Dracchus.

Tiny changes crept across her features; the tightness in her mouth and brow gradually eased, her eyelids relaxed, seeming to grow heavy, and finally, her lips parted.

Dracchus found the rhythm of her movements and matched it, pressing himself deeper with each measured thrust. The feelers at the base of his shaft brushed her sex, providing him another taste of her, and he licked his lips to sample the lingering essence of her pleasure.

He dropped his gaze to watch as he entered and withdrew from her body. It was primal; dark and light, hard and soft, the bridging of two worlds that might never have come together.

Larkin moaned, tugging her hands through her hair before running them down her body. "Yes," she breathed. "Now, fuck me now." Her eyes met his. "Claim me."

Dracchus stretched two tentacles behind him, curling them under the bed. "Tell me who you belong to," he growled.

"You. I belong to you. My mate."

He extended two more tentacles to grasp the bed's front corners, anchoring himself. "And what does my mate want?" he demanded.

"You," she panted. "All of you!"

Heat blazed through Dracchus's veins as he slammed into her. Her mouth opened in a silent cry, and she dug her heels into his back to pull him deeper.

Instinct swept over his mind, and he relinquished control to it; he'd desired her for too long — denied himself for too long — to resist any further. He set a frantic pace, pounding into her, and she met each of his thrusts with equal ferocity. Her cries mixed with his grunts of pleasure.

The world fell away, leaving nothing but the two of them, their joining, their ecstasy. They gave freely and took greedily of one another, and the pleasure was so intense it bordered on painful.

He felt the changes in her — the fluttering of her channel as it tightened around him, a surge of heat — before her body stiffened and she came with a choked cry, his name bursting from her lips. He maintained his hold on her legs and hips as she writhed beneath him, but the sudden clamping of her inner muscles sent him over the brink. He came with a roar and fell forward, catching himself on an arm, pressing into her as deep as he could go. Shudders racked his body.

Dracchus squeezed his eyes shut; in the darkness, he felt her; her heat, the perspiration on her skin, the play of every tiny muscle. The scent of her arousal mingled with his own to create something new, something *theirs*. Larkin's breaths, ragged and forceful, flowed over his chest like a familiar ocean current.

This was pleasure at its purest. Pleasure shared with his mate.

He opened his eyes when he felt her hands glide over his sides, smoothing up toward his shoulders. For the first time in his life, he cursed his size; he was too long to kiss her, to look upon her face, without withdrawing from her.

He savored the feel of her a moment longer before he regretfully pulled from her body with a groan, immediately rolling to the side and gathering her limp form in his arms. He drew her back against his front and twined his tentacles with her legs. His slick cock brushed her thighs.

Dracchus slipped one arm beneath her head, bending it to press a hand over her heart, and draped his other arm over her hips to cover her scars with his palm. His hearts pounded. She settled her hands over both of his and eased into his embrace.

They were both silent as their bodies gradually descended from the heights of pleasure they'd achieved.

Larkin shuddered. A warm drop of moisture trickled over his arm.

Dracchus frowned. "Larkin?"

She sniffled, and her body shook anew. "I never thought I'd have this."

"It upsets you?"

She lifted her hand from her chest and wiped her face. "No. It's just… Other men always saw my scars, knew of the accident, and all they saw was a body to fuck without consequences. I used them, as well, but it still always hurt to know they'd move on because I was damaged goods. Useful to scratch an itch and nothing more. There was never a future."

Dracchus held her a little tighter at the thought of her with other males. He hated the pain she'd endured, but he was glad she'd been rejected — that rejection had ultimately led her to him. A pang of guilt struck him. It was a selfish thought, but he couldn't deny it.

"There is a future for us," he said, sliding his hand down to gently cup her sex, "and I will not give you up. You are *mine*, female. Forever."

She laughed, turned her face into his arm, and kissed it. He felt more tears, but her body shook with joy rather than sorrow. "I never imagined sex with a kraken would be so *dirty*."

Dracchus wasn't quite sure what she meant by that, but her tone didn't imply anything negative. He stroked a tentacle lazily up and down one of her legs and returned his hand to her stomach. His fingers traced the scars, and his chest swelled with pride and contentment when she didn't stiffen or flinch away.

"What happened, Larkin?" he asked.

She rested her head on his arm and took a deep breath. "Twelve years ago, when I was fifteen, we were hunting a predator that was killing livestock near a town called Gordons Ridge. The loss of food was bad enough, but it was getting too close to the humans who kept the herds, and we didn't want some little kid to become its next meal. The tracks we found near one of the attacks belonged to a tiger. A big one."

"What is a tiger?" Dracchus's few experiences on land hadn't acquainted him with much of the wildlife, and neither Arkon nor any of the other humans had ever mentioned *tigers*.

"They're large animals, with bodies shaped a bit like a prixxir. If prixxir were covered in black-and-purple striped fur and lived only on land. They have manes, which is a lot of long fur around their heads, and long ears and tails, but their tails are thin. The claws on a full-grown tiger are as big my finger. I guess the early colonists thought they looked like a creature from Earth, so they gave it the same name. Extremely aggressive. They don't usually hunt humans, but once they get a taste...

"Anyway, we tracked it into the jungle and split off into pairs to cover more ground. My mom and I..." Larkin paused, taking in a shaky breath. "We heard it roar, and then another animal bleating. We raced toward the sound and found the tiger attacking a baby opik. It turned on us, ready to attack because we threatened its kill, but we were faster. Me and my mom fired at the same time. It went down before it took two steps.

"After we made sure it was dead, my mom went to check on the opik. It was still alive. We thought that maybe, if we acted fast enough, we could stop the bleeding. Give it a chance to survive. So, we called for the rest of the rangers and got to work. But then...its mother came."

Larkin covered his hand and pressed it down on her scars, as though it could relieve her pain. "Opiks are big when they're adults. Taller than most humans at the shoulder, maybe as long as you. Thick necks, with heads low to the ground, and…horns. It didn't give a shit that we were helping its baby, just that we were *there*. That we had its baby's blood on our hands. And big as they are, they're damned fast.

"I had enough time to get to my feet, but I couldn't bring up my rifle fast enough. I don't think shooting it would've made any difference, but maybe if I'd been a little quicker…"

Fresh, hot tears flowed over Dracchus's arm. His chest ached for her. He couldn't find words.

"It hit me first. Lifted its head, and I just felt this *pressure*," her fingers clenched over his hand, digging her nails into his flesh, "and then I was in the air. I hit a tree, and my vision went black, but I could hear my mom yelling to get the opik's attention, heard it clomping through the undergrowth. Heard her screams. Then shouting, and gunshots.

"I remember everything getting so quiet that my heartbeat filled my ears. Then my father wailed, and I knew…she was gone. Randall was frantically calling my name, and I think I felt his hands on my face, but I must have passed out, because there was nothing else.

"I woke up later in agony. I was hot all over, sick to my stomach. My dad and brother were at my side, holding my hands, and I'd never seen them so pale, so strained. I'd never seen either of them cry, but they were crying over me. My mom was dead, and they were afraid they'd lose me, too. I was so torn up inside, and they stitched me up as best they could, but we were so far away from home. We didn't have supplies to perform surgery, and I probably would've died if they took me all the back to the Fort.

"An infection set in. I don't remember much of that, either, except that my father was there every time I opened my eyes. He refused to leave my side. They said it was five days before my fever broke. Someone had run to the nearest town and scrounged up a booster, some antibiotics, and a doctor, and eventually, they were able to bring me home so I could recover. It took a long time, and there was so much pain, and my mother was just *gone*, and I'd never hear her voice again, or see her smile, or be hugged by her."

Larkin swallowed. Her face trembled against his arm, and her body shook with her sobs. Finally, she released a long, unsteady breath.

"There was no goodbye. No last *I love you*. But I know she sacrificed herself for me. The doctor at Fort Culver performed surgery to repair as much of the damage as was possible, but even with all the equipment we had available, she could only do so much. After I'd woken up from the anesthetic and shaken off the grogginess, she came and told me that I would never conceive a child. The damage had been too extensive. Just one more kick while I was still down."

"Larkin," Dracchus rumbled, gently turning her face toward him. He brushed the tears from her cheeks and stared into her bright blue eyes. What could he say to take away that pain? To make it better?

The answer came to him suddenly, constricting his hearts. *Nothing.*

This pain belonged to Larkin alone, and he could never take it from her, no matter how much he wished he could. But he could ease her burden by showing her how he felt. By making her feel her worth every day. This event had shaped her into the woman she was, into his mate, but he could show her that there was more to life, that there was more to *her*.

He dipped his head and kissed her, tasting the salt of her tears, and smoothed his palm over her scars. She turned her body toward him and wrapped her arms around his neck without breaking the kiss, without breaking his embrace.

"Thank you," she whispered against his mouth, pressing her forehead to his.

He guided her head to his chest and held her as she cried. His hearts swelled with joy and hope, ached with her sorrow, and pulsed with the strength of the bond he and Larkin had formed.

Dracchus trailed his hand down her back and kissed the top of her head. "I am yours. Forever."

CHAPTER 19

LARKIN SMILED AND OFFERED SARINA A SLICE OF WINEFRUIT. THE girl took it daintily between the claws of her forefinger and thumb and shoved the entire piece in her mouth.

Juice dribbled down her chin as she grinned at Larkin. "Another!"

"Sarina, what do you say?" Macy called from the kitchen.

Sarina lifted herself up on her tentacles, craning her neck to look at her mother through the window between the mess hall and the kitchen. Then she turned back to Larkin with big eyes. "Please?"

"For being polite, I will give you two," Larkin said. She offered two slices, which promptly disappeared into the little girl's mouth.

Sarina hurried to Jax and raised her arms expectantly.

He frowned down at her. "Did you forget to say something else to Larkin?"

Her brows furrowed in confusion, and she raised her arms higher.

"Sarina," he said in a warning tone.

She blew out of her siphons and looked at Larkin, though there was no anger. "Thank you."

"You're welcome," Larkin replied, bringing up a hand to hide her grin. Sarina was just like most human children — formalities were a low priority when there were so many exciting things to do next.

"Daddy, I want up!" she begged.

Jax lowered his torso and took her into his arms.

"Tamed by not one, but two females," Arkon said as Jace crawled up his back and wrapped his tentacles around the blue kraken's face.

"I heard that!" Aymee called from the kitchen. It was followed by laughter from both her and Macy.

Arkon opened his mouth to reply, but Jace stuffed the tip of a tentacle inside, silencing his father.

"I like your youngling more each day, Arkon," Jax said with a smile, seeming to ignore Sarina's little fingers prodding his cheek.

Larkin chuckled as she peeled another winefruit; the violet-red insides divided naturally into wedges, which she added to the nearby bowl. She'd managed, somehow, not to drip any of the dark juice onto the blanket beneath her. The floor wasn't the most comfortable place to sit, but she'd agreed with Aymee and Macy — a picnic didn't feel right if you weren't sitting on blankets. The human women all would've preferred the blankets spread on a sunny beach, or in an open field, but the mess hall was good enough.

It was more about the company than the location, anyway.

It'd been a week since Larkin agreed to become Dracchus's mate, and she and the big kraken had grown closer every day. She was happy, happier than she'd been in years. She had a mate who cared for her, had her brother, and had *real* friends. She'd found it impossible not to like Macy, Aymee, and their kraken families once she'd come to know them. The only shadow in her heart was the thought of her father.

Had he survived?

She'd gone through the pain of uncertainty concerning Randall for the last year, but the experience didn't make it any easier to bear now. She had to believe he was alive, and she knew, if he was, he'd be hunting. Not just for Larkin and Randall, but for the kraken who'd taken his children.

"Do you need help?" Melaina asked, squatting down next to Larkin with her tentacles curled around her.

"Sure," Larkin said, handing Melaina a winefruit.

The young kraken dragged a claw over the skin, slicing it open cleanly, and peeled the outer layer like she'd been doing it all her life.

"In the bowl, Melaina, not your mouth," Rhea said as she lowered herself beside her daughter. She placed another bowl next to the winefruit. It was full of chopped naba stalks, all peeled to reveal their sweet, white, spongey interiors.

Only Dracchus and Randall were missing, having joined a hunting party. As much as Larkin would've loved to accompany them, she'd already promised to come to the picnic. She didn't regret it; she was enjoying herself with people she was beginning to see as family.

Larkin glanced between Rhea and Melaina — her sister and niece-by-joining. It was still strange to think of them that way, but it felt good. They'd brought about a change in Randall. He laughed easier, and his smiles were more genuine. He'd always been good at putting on a friendly face, but after their mother had died, he'd forced it more often than not.

"Where is Uncle Dracchus?" Sarina asked.

"On a hunt with Randall, Ikaros, and a group of kraken," Jax replied.

She coiled a tentacle around his wrist. "When can I go hunting?"

"When you are fully grown. *Maybe.*"

"A female hunt?" Rhea asked with a frown. "You mean to allow her out there?"

"I said *maybe*." Jax frowned deeply. "Should it not be a female's choice, like so much else?"

"It has… It is not done," Rhea said.

Melaina deposited another fully peeled winefruit into the bowl. "I would like to hunt."

"No!" Rhea snapped. "You will not. It is too dangerous."

"It is dangerous," Larkin agreed. Melaina, Jax, and Rhea all looked at her. "But life is about risks."

Arkon tugged Jace's tentacle out of his mouth, eyes wide with excitement. "See! That's what I have been saying!"

"And your risk brought the hunters to us," Rhea said.

Aymee stepped into the room, carrying a steaming platter. "But it also resulted in a mate." She beamed at Arkon.

He smiled back at her. "For myself, and for you, Rhea."

Rhea frowned, eyes softening slightly. "It is still too dangerous. Especially for a female."

"It's equally dangerous for males," Larkin said gently. "More so, sometimes, because they tend to make decisions based on how big they think their—" She snapped her mouth shut as Aymee, in the process of seating herself beside Arkon, widened her eyes and shook her head. Larkin cleared her throat. "Sorry. Men do stupid things sometimes because they have big egos. They think it proves they're somehow superior to each other."

"That is accurate." Jax held an arm out, and Sarina, dangling from it by hands and tentacles, slowly pulled herself toward his hand.

"I suppose it is," Arkon agreed. "That's essentially the purpose of all these challenges that get thrown about, isn't it? Is this the same case for human males?"

"All the time. They challenge each other any chance they get, they just don't do it as formally as kraken do," Larkin said, dropping the last wedge of fruit into the bowl. She wiped her purple-stained fingers dry on a cloth.

Sarina dropped to the floor as she reached Jax's hand and made her way toward the platter of fish Aymee had brought. She grabbed a chunk and ate it before anyone could stop her.

Macy came out of the kitchen carrying a similar tray. Larkin frowned. The normally radiant woman looked pale, perhaps even a little green. She held the tray out in front of her as though the very sight of the fish atop it sickened her.

Jax met her before she'd made it halfway across the room and took the tray from her. "Are you well, Macy?"

"I'm fine. Just a little morning sickness, I think. The smell of the fish is just really getting to me today," she replied.

They moved to the blanket together, and Jax guided her to a spot on one end before taking the tray to the opposite side and setting it down.

"Let's dig in!" Aymee said.

No one needed to be told twice; they heaped portions of fish, fruit, and vegetables on their plates, though the adult kraken avoided all but the meat. Melaina and Sarina giggled as they traded food back and forth, and Arkon attempted to feed naba to Jace, but the little boy took the pieces and held them to his father's mouth while stealing the fish from Arkon's plate.

Larkin smiled as she ate. Arkon wouldn't have anything for himself, at that rate.

"You are a hunter, Larkin, are you not?" Rhea asked.

"I am," she replied, shifting a bit of fish to one side of her mouth. There was a strange taste to the meat; not unpleasant, but wholly unfamiliar. "My parents taught me how to hunt and survive when I was really young."

"See!" Melaina piped, though ducked her head at Rhea's glare.

Rhea turned her strange eyes back toward Larkin. "Randall said you were the best shot."

There were other rangers — full-grown men, older than her

by years — who were still upset about that, but, thanks to the encouragement of her family, she'd never let them make her feel ashamed. "I am."

"Did your males teach you?"

"My parents both did — and Randall, too — but it just kind of came naturally to me. It wasn't long before I surpassed my brother, though." Larkin grinned. "You should have seen his face the first time I hit three targets dead-center in a row, beating him and his friends. I was only seven."

"I'm seven!" Melaina announced.

"Melaina," Rhea warned.

Macy laughed as she chewed on a piece of bitterstock. "Melaina is a free spirit, like Jax."

"I am sorry if that's true, Rhea," Jax said with a smile, "because if it is, she will only push harder as you set firmer boundaries."

Rhea sighed and looked at her daughter. There was worry in her eyes, but they softened as though with understanding. "I know this. I just…"

"It's hard to let them go," Larkin said. "My dad was — *is* — protective of me. No matter how old I get, or how often I prove myself, I don't think that will ever change."

"It is true," Rhea agreed.

"Aymee is a good shot, too," Melaina said as Larkin took a bite of winefruit. "She shot Randall."

Larkin inhaled and nearly choked. She coughed, brows furrowed, looking at the young kraken girl. "What?"

"He didn't tell you?" Aymee covered her mouth with her hand, cheeks turning red.

"No. He never said anything. I mean, I knew that he was shot twice, once by Cyrus, but… You?"

"It was an accident." Aymee swallowed the food in her mouth and lowered her hand. "It was the first time Randall saw Arkon, and Cyrus turned it into a fistfight on the beach. I picked up a gun to try to get them to stop, and when Cyrus hit me...the gun went off. I never meant to shoot him."

The anger flaring inside Larkin wasn't directed toward Aymee; it was reserved entirely for Cyrus Taylor. There was no reason to doubt Aymee's story; why would Randall be on such friendly terms if the shooting had been anything other than an accident? And it fit well with Randall's cryptic words about having received his wounds from Cyrus.

He only pulled the trigger once, but yeah. He did this.

"I'm glad you didn't kill him," Larkin said, offering Aymee a smile.

Aymee's shoulders sagged in relief. She returned the smile. "Me, too."

Sarina pressed a hand to her stomach. "Daddy, I don't feel good."

Jax leaned down beside her, placing his palm on her back. "What's wrong, Sarina?"

"My tummy hurts."

"She looks pale, Jax," Macy said, frowning.

Jax's brow lowered. "Maybe she has eaten too—"

Jace suddenly leaned over Arkon's arm and vomited. Arkon jerked back, though securely kept hold of Jace, his skin flashing yellow.

Aymee's eyes widened, and she leapt up, plate falling out of her lap as she hurried to Arkon's side. A second later, Sarina dropped to the floor, arms folded over her middle, and heaved, emptying her stomach.

"Sarina!" Macy cried, rushing toward her daughter.

Jax hesitated in reaching for the child, who looked so tiny and meek before him, as though fearful he'd make it worse.

"My stomach hurts, too," Melaina said, features drawn.

"We need to get to the infirmary," Aymee said, raising her son's eyelid and feeling his forehead. "Now. *Everyone.*"

Larkin stood, heart racing, when a sudden cramp twisted her belly. She gasped and pressed a hand to it.

"What is happening?" Rhea asked, helping her daughter rise. She watched with wide eyes, skin turning yellow, as Melaina bent over and vomited onto the blanket.

Cold sweat beaded on Larkin's skin; Aymee's skin glistened, too, and she'd taken on a sickly pallor.

"Aymee, what's going on?" Macy asked, scooping Sarina up off the floor and cradling her in her arms.

"Need to move," Aymee grated.

The trip to the infirmary was frantic. Macy, Arkon, and Jax led the way, followed by Rhea, who carried her daughter. Larkin had her arm around Aymee, bearing most of the woman's weight as they ran through the hallway.

Within the infirmary, the children were placed upon beds, all looking limp and lifeless. Fear closed its icy claws around Larkin's heart. Kraken or not, these were innocent children, suffering and afraid, motionless save for when their bodies doubled over in pain.

Larkin's legs were unsteady as she assisted Aymee to Jace's bed. Every few steps sent a fresh wave of agony through her abdomen. She staggered forward, and a strong arm took hold of hers and kept her from falling. She wasn't sure who had helped, but offered them a muttered thanks.

Macy stood next to Sarina, holding the girl's face in her hands. Tears streamed down her cheeks. "Sarina, keep your eyes open, sweetheart. Please. Oh God, Jax…"

Jax stared at Sarina with helplessness gleaming in his eyes. He held one of her hands, and it looked so tiny against his. Both he and Rhea had turned a pale gray, their tentacles moving restlessly beneath them, and their bodies shook with occasional shudders.

His muscles tensed, and his nostrils flared with quick, heavy breaths for several seconds.

Were they sick, too?

"Arkon, get the blood analyzer." Aymee's hair hung in her face, and her body trembled. Larkin guessed the woman was only on her feet because she was leaning most of her weight on the bed.

Arkon, who looked shaken but otherwise unaffected, crossed the room and opened a wide drawer. He looked from side to side twice before finally pulling out a small device and hurrying back to Aymee. Before he reached her, she bent to the side, clutching the bed rail with one hand, and vomited.

"Aymee," Arkon breathed.

"Jace," she said between retches. "Use it on Jace."

Arkon leaned over the bed, back turned to Larkin. She couldn't see him use the analyzer, but it didn't matter; she forced all her attention, all her willpower, toward withstanding the pain of the next cramp, clutching her stomach.

"Aymee, what is going on? What's happening?" Macy asked desperately.

"A toxin," Arkon replied. "The scanner is reading a toxin in Jace's bloodstream, matching the venom of the *blue needler*."

"*Poison?*"

Cold fear filled Larkin.

"We do not hunt blue needler," Jax said, eyes shifting between the occupied beds. "All kraken are taught it is poisonous when we are younglings."

"Does it list an antidote? Or antivenom, antitoxin, anything like that?" Aymee's voice was ragged. She sagged against the bed.

Tense silence reigned, save for the thunder of Larkin's too-fast heartbeat.

"Yes, it does," Arkon said.

"You and Macy, go to the cabinet and—" Aymee groaned, the sound drawing out until it ended in a quivering whimper.

Arkon dropped the device onto the bed and sank down, wrapping an arm around Aymee's waist to support her. His skin had gone yellow again. "Aymee?" He brushed her hair back from her face.

"Go find it," she replied weakly.

He clenched his jaw and scooped her into his arms, laying her gently on the bed beside their son.

Macy grabbed the scanner and hurried to the cabinet alongside Arkon. Though Larkin couldn't see its contents, she heard the clattering of what had to be dozens of bottles and vials as they searched.

Another wave of cramps hit her. She raised her hand to her mouth as though it would stop what was coming. She turned away from Jace and Aymee as every muscle inside her contracted, forcing out the contents of her stomach. Acid burned her throat, and the cords of her neck strained.

Everything hurt, but she couldn't stop, couldn't hold it in.

Melaina's cries broke through the haze of pain.

Larkin wiped her mouth with the back of her hand and turned toward the young kraken.

Rhea held Melaina atop a nearby bed, her features tight with worry. Her wide eyes darted from Melaina to Macy and Arkon.

Larkin stepped toward Rhea, legs threatening to buckle beneath her.

Not going to fall, damnit.

Rhea turned her panicked gaze to Larkin. "I cannot lose her," she said frantically. "I cannot." She shivered as she drew Melaina closer.

Larkin put her arms around them, offering what little comfort she could. She forced her breathing to slow and clenched her teeth against the poison's effects on her own body.

"We found it!" Macy exclaimed. There was no response. "Aymee?"

Larkin felt herself fading. Impossible heat suffused her, undiminished by the chilled sweat coating her skin, and the room seemed to be spinning around her. But she held on to Rhea and Melaina. She couldn't do *nothing*. She couldn't…

"Aymee!" Arkon roared.

"We'll be okay," Larkin whispered. "She'll be okay."

Larkin slipped into darkness.

CHAPTER 20

The season of storms usually meant chaos beneath the waves, even when the skies were clear, but the sea was surprisingly calm today. The sun shone bright, casting thin, faint, dancing shadows over the seafloor, and the currents flowed no stronger nor weaker than normal. Sea creatures carried on with their lives all around while plants and grass swayed lazily with the constant motion of the water.

Dracchus frowned and shifted his gaze to Randall and Ikaros, who swam side-by-side a few body lengths in front of him. The human moved his head in constant search, and the prixxir had its long face tendrils — *whiskers*, Randall called them — extended in all directions.

Larkin would have loved to be out here, to be doing *something* to contribute. Dracchus had seen the sparkle of excitement in her eyes when he'd mentioned the hunt. Her excitement had soon faded; he couldn't be sure whether she'd noticed some hesitance in him, but she'd told him she couldn't go. Macy and Aymee had planned their indoor picnic for today, and Larkin had promised the younglings she would attend.

It had saved Dracchus the trouble of denying her, much to his relief — though that relief wasn't without accompanying guilt.

He looked to the kraken swimming in loose formation ahead of Randall and Ikaros. Some, he trusted — Vasil had not been broken by their ordeal on the ship and hadn't allowed himself to be consumed by hatred, and Brexes, though rarely vocal, had spoken several times with Randall and made no effort to hide that he enjoyed hunting alongside the human.

Neo swam in the leader's position at the center of the formation, with Kronus to his left. Until Neo had organized the hunt that morning, Dracchus hadn't seen him or any of his followers in the Facility's main building since the confrontation over a week prior.

Kronus had been civil, but strained, while the hunting party formed in the Mess. Neo, however, had been in a strange spirit. He'd offered no false friendships and made little effort to mask the hatred in his eyes, but his rage had been replaced by an odd smugness. He'd insisted that Dracchus, Jax, and Arkon participate in this hunt, claiming they had neglected the needs of their own people for too long.

His goading hadn't worked; Jax and Arkon had remained behind. Despite the diminishment of outward hostility, they would not leave their mates and young unprotected. Larkin would be safe with them.

Neo signaled the group to slow as they neared a wide stretch of sand on the ocean floor, broken only by irregular, jutting stones. While the surrounding rock formations and bits of coral teemed with life, few creatures crossed the open ground. For now, it was braved only by small, solitary fish and a few slow, segmented crawling creatures.

The next signs came rapidly.

Down. We await, in the old way.

The kraken spread out in a half-circle around the open ground, dropping into positions in the rocks, harpoons and spears at the ready. Randall took a spot beside Dracchus, and Ikaros dropped onto his belly beside the human.

Dracchus frowned as he watched the surface shadows flutter over the sand. Neo was aware of the new techniques Arkon had improvised for baiting sandseekers, which had saved kraken hunting parties countless hours of unnecessary waiting over the last year. Was he ignoring that method out of spite? Neo had formed the hunt, and Dracchus would not challenge his leadership unless circumstances became dire, but Dracchus couldn't ignore his rising suspicions.

At a glance, this decision supported claims from Kronus and Neo that they were working to preserve kraken traditions currently threatened by humans and human thought, but that stance had always been superficial. Neo, Kronus, and their followers had ignored the traditions that hindered their true goal — removing humans from the Facility.

Randall waved, drawing Dracchus's attention. The human was on his side, harpoon gun laid on the rock next to him. He moved his hands and arms in a series of signs.

Why are we waiting?

With Arkon's help, Dracchus and Randall had discovered detailed information in the computer on human sign language. Much of it was vaguely familiar to the kraken, and Arkon guessed their ancestors had adapted the visual language to incorporate their more expressive tentacles and color changes.

Dracchus had developed a working knowledge of the human version, and Randall could decipher all but the most complex kraken signs.

Don't know, Dracchus replied.

Randall's signs were slightly forceful, conveying his frustration. *Many fish nearby.* He swept his arm in an arc, indicating the creatures all around. Just one school of fish driven in the right direction would be enough to bait out some sandseekers.

Frown deepening, Dracchus glanced up. The surface wavered

and sparkled only a few body lengths above. Pure sunlight streamed through the water, cast by a sun positioned directly overhead.

Waiting like this, they might be out past sunset.

Dracchus had once waited out a hiding rocksnapper for three days without losing his patience. He'd been tempted many times to enter its den and drag it out, but he'd refrained. Now, the thought of even a few hours' wait made him restless.

He understood Jax and Arkon's impatience when they'd been eager to return to their mates. Had Dracchus known what it felt like to *miss* someone so deeply on those occasions, he might've been more compassionate toward both males.

But this was his duty to his people, kraken and human alike. To protect and provide.

We do not lead this hunt, Dracchus signed. *We must be patient.*

Randall frowned behind his mask, undoubtedly concerned for Rhea, Melaina, and Larkin.

The human rolled onto his stomach and faced the hunting grounds, sliding the harpoon gun to lay before him. He absently scratched Ikaros's chin when the prixxir nudged his hand. A few moments later, he held up three fingers before gesturing toward three small rocks jutting out of the sand.

Three lurking sandseekers, detected by the technology in Randall's diving suit. Once this hunt ended, the kraken would need to abandon this location for a time to allow the beasts to repopulate.

The sun crawled gradually overhead, altering the shadows cast by the rocks, plants, coral, and fish. Dracchus scraped a claw on the stone beneath him; it was the only outward sign of impatience he allowed himself. He focused on the subtle flow of currents over his skin, on the constant sound of water in motion, on the open ground. All the while, his hearts pounded steadily, and a tiny spark burned in his chest.

Anticipation.

His body was ready for action, *eager* for it. However long the wait during a hunt, the burst of activity at its climax was infinitely more memorable, more powerful. Hours or days of patience collapsed into a few seconds of thrilling action. Dracchus wasn't interested in the *biochemistry* at play during those moments, though he admired Arkon's interest in such knowledge. The kill brought an undeniable rush, regardless of the underlying workings of that sensation. But something else entirely outshone that instant of life and death.

Dracchus was more excited for the aftermath. Not tending to the kill, or hauling it home, but the gratefulness and appreciation of the other kraken when the hunters brought in fresh food. Knowing that his brethren would not suffer hunger, if only for a short while, made the whole process worthwhile.

He pictured Sarina's smile upon his return and imagined Larkin's joyful greeting. Imagined how he would show his mate how much he'd missed her.

Ikaros lifted his head suddenly, drawing Dracchus's attention. The prixxir's whiskers were perked, dark eyes fixed on something in the distance. Ikaros's uncertain chirrup came to Dracchus through the water; a series of drawn-out clicks that rose in pitch as they faded.

Dracchus narrowed his eyes. Ikaros was staring at a pair of approaching objects. The sunlight shimmering on the water's surface silhouetted their forms, but Dracchus knew they were boats.

He flashed yellow in warning. The boats were closing in rapidly, and due to the position of the sun, cast no warning shadows ahead of themselves. The kraken could outswim the vessels, but only if they reacted quickly.

He gestured toward the boats when the others looked in his direction. Their expressions turned grim. Vasil's fingers curled around the haft of his spear, and he pressed his lips into a tight line.

Dracchus glanced at Randall. The human's face was strained, with brows angled down toward his nose, jaw clenched, and eyes wide.

Are you with me? Dracchus signed.

Randall stared at Dracchus for several moments, his heavy breaths briefly fogging the inside of his mask. Taking his harpoon gun by the barrel, he nodded.

Dracchus glanced at their surroundings. The water here was relatively shallow, but not nearly enough so to restrict the movement of the boats, and the rocks would provide no cover from attacks from above.

To the deep, Dracchus signaled.

Neo flared crimson and rose from his waiting place. The stiffness of his motions spoke of an underlying fury. *No! We fight this time,* he signed, and then spread the fingers on one hand and snapped them back together.

Make the kill.

Memories of the night they were captured flitted through Dracchus's mind. The kraken were armed this time, but what good would it do when their view beyond the surface was naturally obscured, while the humans could see down unhindered?

We must go, Dracchus signed.

The others looked between Neo and Dracchus, seemingly torn on who to obey. Their duty bound them by honor to follow the hunt leader, but at least a few of them must have understood that, however weak and fragile humans appeared, this battle would exact a heavy price.

This is not worth our blood. Dracchus removed his eyes from Neo for only a moment to glance at the boats; time was nearly up.

Kronus touched Neo's shoulder, calling his attention. He mimicked Dracchus's signs with strengthened emphasis.

This is not *worth our blood.*

The red of Neo's skin deepened, and he bared his teeth in a scowl. He thrust a finger in the direction of the boats and swung his gaze over all the other kraken, challenging them to disobey, to oppose his decision. On the edge of Dracchus's vision, Randall moved closer, harpoon gun in both hands, and Ikaros raised his spine fins defensively.

Before anyone could offer a response, the humans launched their attack.

A powerful *thunk* from the surface sent ripples outward from the nearest boat. A large harpoon, longer than Dracchus's arm, hit the water and sped toward Neo and Kronus in a torrent of bubbles.

Neo darted aside. The harpoon hit Kronus low on his abdomen, shearing through to emerge from his back and *clack* against the rock behind him. Dracchus surged forward, flashing yellow. He wouldn't allow this to happen again. No kraken would be taken.

Another *thump*.

Something punched Dracchus's tentacle hard enough to push him to the bottom, kicking up a cloud of loose sand. The pain was distant, but the pressure extended clear through the affected limb. He glanced down as the sand cleared. A harpoon jutted from one of his rear tentacles. A fine mist of blood drifted into the water.

The ground beneath him shifted, and he snapped his head to the side to see a sandseeker erupt from the bottom. The creature's mandibles spread wide, revealing its toothy mouth, as its small, paddle-like legs propelled it toward Dracchus.

Dracchus rolled aside as quickly as he could. The harpoon grated against his torn flesh, but he ignored the agony. He felt the impact of the sandseeker beside him, felt the displacement of water as the creature thrashed in search of the prey it had so nearly captured. He dragged himself away as the sandseeker burrowed into the sand.

He swung his gaze toward Kronus as the water cleared. The ochre kraken scrambled to grab hold of the rocks as the harpoon tether went taut and dragged him toward the boat. Neo held the line in both hands, battling its pull.

More projectiles hit the water, trailing small streams of bubbles behind them. These lost momentum before making it halfway to Dracchus, lingering briefly until their paths reversed and they drifted toward the surface. The little objects were familiar to Dracchus.

Sleep bullets.

Neo stared up at the new projectiles, and the crimson of his skin wavered. Releasing the tether, he fled toward deep water. Several other kraken scattered at the sight of his panic.

Dracchus buried his claws in the seafloor and pulled himself toward the struggling Kronus. Resistance against his forward momentum began suddenly, increasing the pressure on his wound. His claws raked across the sand as the tether dragged him backward. He couldn't find the purchase to anchor himself in place.

A weight settled on his back; the soft, pliable scales could only belong to Ikaros. Dracchus looked over his shoulder to see the prixxir close his mouth around the tether. Ikaros swung his tail to counteract the tension on the line, granting Dracchus a bit of slack.

Randall sped by, swimming toward Kronus. The ochre kraken held onto the bottom only by his hands, arms stretched and muscles straining.

Dracchus's gut clenched in fear. Kronus had made no secret of his hatred for humans. What would he do when Randall neared?

Without hesitation, Randall grabbed hold of Kronus's tether and drew a knife from his thigh. He set the blade to the line, sawing frantically. Strands of the tether snapped with metallic *twangs* that resonated through the water.

Brexes arrived at Kronus's side and took hold of the rocks with his tentacles before reaching up to grasp the tether, leaning back to alleviate some of the pressure.

Vasil rushed toward Dracchus from the right. His spear glinted in the sunlight as he moved behind Dracchus and set to work on the tether. Vibrations pulsed through the line, along the harpoon, and spread into Dracchus's limbs, producing twinges of new, unique pain.

Dracchus was freed a moment after Kronus's tether broke.

Brexes helped Kronus flee, trailing blood behind them, as the severed tethers sped toward the surface. Vasil grasped Dracchus's arm and helped the big kraken right himself. Ikaros charged to Randall and gently closed his mouth around the human's arm, tugging.

Randall stared up at the boats for another heartbeat before turning away. He and Ikaros fell into place beside Dracchus and Vasil, and the four began their hurried trip home.

Dracchus focused on his pain, on the uncomfortable weapon still embedded in his tentacle, on the thundering of his hearts.

He couldn't allow himself to acknowledge his rage.

Not yet.

A LONE KRAKEN WAITED outside the Facility's entry door, tentacles moving only to maintain his position, when Dracchus and the others arrived. Dracchus frowned when he realized it was Ector, the elder. One of the hunters who'd taught him all he knew as a youngling, many years past.

Ector's wrinkled face was grave as he surveyed the returning party. Dracchus and his companions had caught up to Brexes and Kronus during the journey, and the speed with which they'd moved would have taxed any of them even before they were injured.

Kronus's skin was pale. He had one hand wrapped around the harpoon protruding from his gut, arm trembling.

Opening the door, Ector ushered them inside. Dracchus wasn't sure how they all fit — five kraken, a human, and a prixxir — but the room drained quickly.

"Where is Neo?" Dracchus growled as soon as his head was out of the water.

"I have not seen him," Ector replied. "But you have something more pressing to attend."

"My injury can wait."

"That is not what I mean, Dracchus. We must go to the infirmary at once."

There was a gentle hiss as Randall removed his mask. "What's going on?"

Ector's eyes shifted to look beyond Dracchus. "It is best you see for yourselves before rash judgments are made."

Something in the elder's tone gave Dracchus pause — an uncharacteristic hesitance, an unfamiliar weariness. He glanced over his shoulder, following Ector's gaze.

Brexes and Vasil supported Kronus, one on each side, and blood still seeped around the shaft of the harpoon impaling him. Behind them stood a pale-faced Randall with Ikaros at his feet. The expressions in the room were difficult to read — shock, distress, fear, anger; all were represented.

"Kronus needs aid," Brexes said. "Someone should seek out the human healer and have her meet us."

"She is already there," Ector replied.

A chill swept through Dracchus's blood, strengthened by the contrasting heat of his rage.

The instant the light turned green, he opened the door and rushed through, pulling ahead of the others despite his injury. If Ector insisted they go to the infirmary, and Aymee was already there, it couldn't mean anything good. He didn't allow himself to consider the possibilities. He couldn't bring himself to face them.

He entered the infirmary without slowing. A sharp, sour odor struck his nose. Several of the beds were occupied, but his attention moved to the one directly to his left.

Dracchus froze. His hearts stopped.

Macy sat next to the bed, elbow on her knee and face propped on her hand. Her hair hung in front of her face. Her other arm was draped over the side of the bed. Jax, bearing a sickly pallor, stood behind her with his body bent to rest his head on the bed beside its tiny occupant.

Sarina.

She was utterly still apart from the shallow rise and fall of her chest.

Macy turned her face toward him, her eyes tired and filled with worry. Then she looked past Dracchus. A fierceness like he'd never seen lit within her eyes. She leapt up from her chair and ran toward him, face contorted in fury.

"You monster!" she screamed, shoving past Dracchus. He turned in time to see her slam a fist into Kronus's face. "You evil fucking monster! How could you do this? You hate us so much that you'd kill innocent babies?" She struck him again, and then grabbed the shaft of the harpoon and yanked upward on it.

Kronus cried out in pain, sagging against Brexes and Vasil.

Jax was there an instant later. He pried Macy's hand off the harpoon and wrapped his arms around her, dragging her back. Despite Jax's superior size and strength, she nearly broke his hold several times, shouting at Kronus throughout.

"Macy!" Jax called. "Macy, look at me!"

She turned her face toward Jax, and her anger dissipated in an instant. "He could have killed them, Jax! All of them. All of us." She threw her arms around him and buried her face against his neck as tears flowed down her cheeks.

"What the fuck?" Randall asked, stepping farther into the room. Ikaros followed close behind, whiskers up, and released a trembling whimper.

Dracchus looked over the other beds. Aymee lay curled on the bed beside Sarina's, a sheen of perspiration on her grayish skin, with Jace in her arms. Arkon stood beside them. The next bed over held Melaina. Rhea leaned over her, stroking the girl's cheek soothingly. The color of both females was muted, just like Jax's.

His heart stopped when he saw the occupant of the fourth bed. Larkin was in the same state as Aymee, hair damp and plastered to her face, skin glistening with sweat.

Randall ran toward the last two beds. His gaze shifted between his sister and his mate, torn between the people he loved. He brushed his palm over Larkin's forehead and frowned before turning to embrace Rhea.

Ikaros stood on his hind legs, propping his front paws on the bed to lay his face next to Melaina. She reached up weakly and patted his head.

Dracchus moved to Larkin's bedside and sank down to put his head at her level. He reached forward and placed his hand on her cheek. Her skin was cold and clammy. Her brows drew together at his touch, and her eyelids fluttered open.

"Dracchus," she breathed when she saw him. "They're okay." Her eyes drifted shut again.

His hearts constricted with a combination of relief and dread. She was alive, but how poor was her condition? Why had he chosen to leave her behind? He'd allowed this to happen to his mate, to his *people*. His *family*.

"What the hell happened?" Randall demanded.

"Blue needler venom," Arkon said, undisguised anger in his voice. "It seems likely that the fish we had today was contaminated."

Blue needlers were amongst several dangerous, venomous sea creatures that could kill even a full-grown kraken.

Dracchus looked over his shoulder, fixing his gaze on Kronus. "This is your doing?"

Kronus lifted his head; it bobbed with his rapid, shallow breaths, but he held Dracchus's gaze. There was a gleam of sorrow in his eyes. "I had no part in this."

"Liar!" Macy shouted. "Who else would do something like this? You've hated us from the beginning, and what have we ever done to deserve that besides *exist?*"

Drawing in another labored breath, Kronus winced. "Your kind has no place here. We claimed it, long—"

"I don't care! Stop living in the damn past! This is now." She pulled away from Jax, though the kraken kept a tentacle around her waist. "And right now, that's my child on that bed, my *baby*. Arkon's baby, Rhea's daughter. Your own kind! Look at what your hatred has done!"

"I want you gone from the place my people have called home for generations," Kronus said through clenched teeth, "but I will not stoop to harming kraken females and younglings to see that happen. Our kind can thrive without you, but we will not survive if we are killing one another." His gaze shifted toward the beds, and something in his expression softened. "There is no honor in this. Poisoning is a coward's tactic."

"So what, you'd rather just stab us while we're looking?" Macy demanded.

"I would look into the eyes of my enemies, yes. Treat them as though they are my equal, even if they are not."

"When are you going to realize that we are not your damn enemy, Kronus?" Macy turned away from him, into the shelter of Jax's arms.

Kronus looked first to Randall, and then the harpoon in his gut. Features strained, he bowed his head and said no more.

"Take him to a bed," Aymee said, voice raw, as she pushed herself up on shaky arms.

Arkon placed his hands on her shoulders and guided her back down. "I will tend to him. You've taught me much, and you need to rest. At worst, it will only be as much of a mess as I made of Macy's leg." He twisted to watch as Brexes and Vasil lifted Kronus onto a bed, positioning the ochre kraken on his side. "Perhaps a bit worse."

Arkon pressed a kiss to Aymee's head before joining Kronus and Brexes. Vasil moved away from them and came to a halt when his eyes caught on Melaina. He stared, silent, his brow lowering and mouth falling into a deep frown.

Finally, Vasil shook his head. "I will go and keep watch."

Dracchus returned his gaze to Larkin as Vasil departed. She hadn't stirred since first opening her eyes. "Will they recover?" he asked, gritting his teeth once the words were out. Part of him didn't want to know, fearing the answer would be too painful.

"It will take time," Aymee said. "Being kraken is all that saved the children. Had they been human, they would have died before they received the antitoxin. And if Macy had eaten…"

A chill ran up Dracchus's spine. The thought of losing the younglings, of losing Sarina, and Macy's unborn babe, of losing Larkin — it was too much. Larkin was here, right in front of him, suffering, but what could he do? The poison that had harmed her wasn't something he could fight. His prowess meant nothing in the face of this.

A hand settled on his shoulder.

Dracchus turned his head to see Ector just behind him.

"They are strong," Ector said. "Much stronger than they look. And your mate…she is a warrior. She rests now, but she will be ready to battle soon. We must ensure that the ones who did this — the real ones — are the only ones who pay for it."

"What good is my strength if it cannot help them now?" Dracchus looked back at his mate and brushed her hair away from her face, carefully hooking it behind her ear with a claw.

"It's a different sort of strength they need from you now, Dracchus," Ector said gently, "but it is one you have in abundance. Be here for them now. Do not yet act upon your anger. That is not what will help them through."

My anger?

He hadn't allowed himself to feel his anger, hadn't allowed the full force of it to rise from the depths and crash over him like a wave. Dracchus believed that Kronus had nothing to do with this. He'd seen the attempts, as of late, to restrain Neo and the others. Just before the humans had fired upon the kraken hunting party, Kronus had attempted to sway Neo from attacking.

Kronus was misguided and hateful, but he had shown no desire to throw away kraken lives needlessly.

This was Neo's doing. He'd insisted on the hunt, having never led one before. He'd insisted on waiting out the sandseekers rather than using bait. And he'd abandoned his comrades once he realized the danger to himself.

A cry broke the quiet of the room. Though he'd never heard her in such pain and discomfort, he knew it had come from Sarina, and it was as relieving as it was heart-wrenching. Dracchus twisted to look toward them, watching as Macy soothed the youngling, but Larkin's shivering drew his attention back to his mate.

Her eyes were open, clearer than they'd been the first time. She covered his hand with her own. "Best picnic ever," she murmured, "apart from the poison. Are you okay?"

"I am fine," he replied.

"He has a harpoon through a tentacle," Ector said.

"*What?*" Larkin raised her head.

Dracchus guided her back down, casting a glare at the elder. "It is nothing."

"I will join Vasil," Ector said. He departed quietly.

"Why is there a harpoon in your tentacle?" Larkin asked.

"Rangers," Randall replied, approaching Larkin's other side. He placed a hand on her arm and squeezed. "They went a little crazy on the fishing gear."

"Dad?"

Randall's face fell, and he dropped his gaze. "Don't know. Could've been."

Larkin turned her head toward Randall. "He probably thinks we're dead."

"If he didn't think I was dead that whole time, Elle, he's not going to start thinking it now."

She glanced past Randall. "How are Melaina and Rhea?"

"They're getting by. Just got Rhea to finally lie down. She's almost as stubborn as you sometimes."

Larkin's chuckle was cut short; she winced and pressed a hand to her stomach.

Dracchus frowned and leaned over her, covering her hand with his. "You need to rest, female." He looked at Randall. "No more *jokes*."

A pained snarl cut off whatever response Randall might've made. Dracchus's gaze followed the sound to Kronus's bed.

Arkon handed a blood-smeared harpoon to Brexes, who wrapped it in a cloth and set it aside. "That was the easy part," Arkon said as he shifted the overhead scanner into place. "It might be best if you don't attempt to retain consciousness." He folded another piece of cloth several times and held it to Kronus's mouth. "Bite down on this. It will help, if only a little."

"Just do it," Kronus growled before clamping his teeth over the cloth.

"Think Arkon purposely forgot the anesthetic?" Aymee muttered.

Kronus's muffled cries of pain might once have brought a twisted sort of satisfaction to Dracchus, but now they only grated on him, vibrating through his bones and constricting his chest. If asked a few days ago, he would've said without hesitation that Kronus deserved to suffer.

Here, now, that seemed like the wrong answer.

"What's going to happen now?" Randall asked.

Vengeance. Bloodshed. A reckoning...

No. Ector's wisdom had been sound; those things would not help Larkin and the others, not now.

"We rest," Dracchus said, running the pad of his thumb over Larkin's cheek, "and recover. Together. Once we are well, we will call all our people together. This treachery will not go unpunished."

CHAPTER 21

In all his years, Dracchus had never seen the Mess so full. The room had always seemed spacious, even with a few dozen gathered inside, but now it felt small and cramped. His mind wanted to dismiss the number of kraken in the room as some sort of deception, as an illusion, an impossibility.

But these were his people. Not all of them, but more than had ever come to such gatherings. Even the females had come in great number, many clutching younglings — of which there were still too few.

Uncertain silence gripped them, broken only by the occasional, indecipherable murmur. Many of them knew what had happened by now — that two human females and five kraken, including three younglings, had been poisoned — but none had been told the purpose of this meeting.

Larkin moved to his side, pressing a warm hand to the small of his back. "They're here."

His gaze followed hers down the narrow path leading to the doorway. Kronus entered first, a telling distance between him and the kraken who once followed him. The only evidence remaining of his harpoon wound was a puckered scar.

Neo and his supporters came after, in a tight cluster, faces drawn in suspicion as they took in the crowd.

It'd been six days since the incident. Six days of worry spent at Larkin's side as she recovered, six days of feeling powerless to help the people he cared about. That time had been broken only by a brief trip to the kitchen with Randall and Ikaros. The prixxir had shied away from the meat in the cold storage room, and Arkon's scanner had confirmed it was all tainted. They'd disposed of it all, disposed of dozens of hours' worth of hunting and gathering, forcing a small party of trustworthy kraken — led by Vasil and Brexes — to go catch more fish.

The afflicted had eaten little during that time. Dracchus glanced at Larkin and frowned. She tired easily and still looked paler than normal.

Despite his gentle efforts, it had taken three days for her to agree to eat anything. After she'd vomited up those bits of food, she'd gone another full day before her next attempt.

Her appetite had yet to recover — even now, when she did eat, it was in portions tiny enough to scarce satisfy a newborn.

Thankfully, the younglings had made a more complete recovery. Jace and Sarina were likely to forget the incident. Melaina, on the other hand, was old enough to remember what had happened. To remember that her own people had done this. Dracchus could only hope she'd develop the wisdom to understand that those who'd done her harm were part of a small group that did not represent all kraken.

Kronus moved to a place opposite Dracchus and stood with his head bowed, oddly calm and quiet. Neo flashed crimson as he glared at Dracchus's companions, but it was Garon who spoke.

"Why are the humans here?"

"Because they are our people," Ector said, the voices around them lowering as the elder kraken spoke. He was positioned in the center of the open area along the wall — Dracchus's contingent occupied the space to his right, while Kronus and Neo's group filled in the left. Ector was flanked by three other elder kraken, two males and a female.

"They are not kraken," Neo growled. "They do not belong here."

Ikaros stepped forward with a low growl, but Randall placed a hand upon the prixxir, calming him. "Stay."

"Take your place," Ector said to Neo calmly, waving his hand to the left. "Grievances will be presented soon."

Dracchus locked his eyes on Neo. He concentrated on not allowing his skin to change color, on keeping his expression neutral; it was among the most difficult endeavor's he'd ever undertaken. Rage roiled inside him like the sea thrashing during a storm.

They'd been mistaken to think Kronus was the true threat. Kronus had lost control.

Kraken gathered behind Neo; Orphus and Garon foremost, with Leda slipping in beside them. Kronus remained apart from them, alone until Aja, another female, moved to stand with him.

"What is this about, Dracchus?" a male kraken asked from the crowd.

"You have not heard?" another replied.

The female elder, Ceres, raised her arms. "All shall be told," she called, and the crowd fell into silence. She looked at Ector.

"I have seen three generations of kraken grow to adulthood in my time," Ector said, moving forward, "and I have taught count-less males how to hunt, how to survive, and how to conduct themselves with honor. Never in all those years have I borne witness to anything so cowardly and vile as what happened six days ago.

"There are many opinions about the humans who have shared our home. I understand the wariness. We have been taught they are our enemies since before our grandsires were birthed. But the majority of us agreed that they have done nothing but good for our people."

Ceres moved to Macy and placed a gentle hand on her shoulder. She smiled at her. "The human who saved a youngling by slaying a razorback on her own. She nearly lost her life in the act."

The next elder, Faro, approached Aymee. "The human who defied her own people to protect ours, and saved the lives of *two* kraken—" he paused to look meaningfully at Kronus "—with her healing. She has worked selflessly to ease our injuries and ailments over the last year."

Parus, the final elder, moved to stand before Randall. "The human who fought his own kind in defense of our people and has worked as hard as any of our hunters to provide us with food and security."

Ector's movements weren't as powerful or smooth as Dracchus remembered as he moved to Larkin; the years — and the last few days — were taking a toll upon him. "And this huntress. She was the one who captured Dracchus, Vasil, and Neo, but she was also the one who brought them food and water. The one who risked fire and the fury of a storm to set them free when she realized that our peoples should not be enemies."

Ceres motioned to the children in Macy and Aymee's arms. "Two younglings have come, and a third grows inside Macy. Kraken younglings."

The elders returned to their original places, with Ector at their front.

"These are our people," Ector said. "We have declared it many times, and they have earned their places. They have brought laughter and joy to these corridors and have shown us new ways."

"They violate everything we are!" Neo growled.

"How?" Dracchus demanded. His hearts thundered, and his throat was tight, but somehow, he kept his voice steady. "These are not the humans who were enemies to the kraken, and we are not our ancestors."

"Two of them hunted us!" Garon said, moving forward. "She was the reason you were put in a cage and beaten!"

Neo's skin pulsed red at the reminder, but he didn't look away from Dracchus. "What does this have to do with us, elder?"

"You know," Dracchus said.

"We have made no secret of our dislike for humans, just as Kronus voiced when the first of them were brought here." Neo's gaze flicked briefly toward Macy. "Is our stance no longer valid? Have we no right to wish for the preservation of the ways of our people?"

"You are a coward who cares nothing for the ways of our people," Dracchus replied.

Brow falling low, Neo shifted to crimson.

"And so we come to the reason for this gathering," Ector called. He looked at Dracchus and nodded.

"Six days ago, the meat we store in the kitchen, the meat eaten by our humans, their mates, and their younglings, was poisoned." Dracchus kept his gaze locked on Neo, who wore the same smug smirk he'd displayed while the last hunt was being organized. "Aymee and Larkin fell ill. Jax and Rhea fell ill. Melaina, Jace, and Sarina fell ill."

A shocked murmur rippled through the crowd. Though most had heard the news beforehand, how many had believed it? How many kraken could imagine that one of their kind would do such a thing?

"Despite her suffering, Aymee was able to guide Arkon and Macy through treatment. Had they not acted so quickly, we would have lost the younglings." Dracchus lifted an arm and pointed toward Macy. "Had she eaten the tainted food, we would have lost a youngling-to-be."

The muscles of Neo's jaw ticked.

"All the food, wasted," Dracchus continued. "Eight lives nearly taken." He swung his arm forward, pointing directly at Neo. "And it was his doing."

"You have no proof of this!" Neo shouted, tentacles writhing around him. "I led the hunt that day, I could not have—"

"The hunt you insisted Jax and Arkon partake in. The hunt during which you ordered us to wait, rather than utilize methods that would increase our chances of a fast, productive encounter. The hunt during which you abandoned your fellow kraken to save yourself."

Several kraken turned their heads toward Neo, anger in their eyes.

"I did all I could," Neo growled.

"Randall is the one who saved Kronus after you fled. One of the humans who has been a target of your hatred. Arkon repaired Kronus's wounds using Aymee's teachings, and she would have done it herself, were she not poisoned. If not for humans, Kronus would have died."

"Dracchus commanded us to the deep," Vasil said. "To safety, without needlessly confronting the humans. Even Kronus agreed. But Neo insisted upon attack." Vasil's gray eyes fixed on Neo. "I suffered at the hunter's hands as much as you, Neo. I was held in the cell beside yours." He glanced fleetingly at Larkin. "But I have seen great kindness from humans, far more than I have seen cruelty."

"They are our *enemies*, and I was leading the hunt! It was a betrayal that you all defied me." Something gleamed in Neo's eyes; was it a spark of desperation?

"You placed our people in danger," Dracchus said.

"I wanted to face our foes, to fight! But all of you are honorless cowards who wanted to flee."

"You accuse us of being honorless when you sought to poison our mates? Our younglings?" Jax snarled, moving forward. "I will accept that lack of honor if it means I can tear your guts out and force you to experience every moment of a slow death!"

Dracchus extended an arm to the side, blocking Jax's path. Despite Jax's bristling fury, he stopped. He held his glare on Neo for several heartbeats before returning to his mate's side.

"This prejudice has gone too far," Ector said calmly, looking at Neo.

"There is no proof I did anything to them," Neo said. "Wild accusations should not hold so much weight."

"I am proof." All eyes went to Aja as she spoke. "I, too, have allowed my anger to mislead me. To distrust the humans who have lived among us." She looked at Neo then swept her gaze over the crowd. "I was there when Neo spoke of his plans to kill the humans and their offspring. He said that if Dracchus, Jax, and Arkon did not join them on the hunt, then they deserved to die alongside their humans."

She bowed her head and closed her eyes. "I did not think he would do it. It is to my own shame and regret that I did not speak of this to anyone while I might have stopped it. I never thought he would truly harm a youngling or any of our kind."

"Traitor!" Leda yelled, baring her teeth and flashing crimson.

"It is no proof!" Neo lunged toward Aja.

Kronus blocked him, meeting Neo's gaze. "You would attack a female?" he asked in a low voice.

"They spoke of using needler venom to taint the food," Aja said, glaring at Neo.

"This is proof of nothing," Neo repeated, face ablaze with fury as he stared at Kronus. "Two more traitors, too fearful of action to be of any benefit to our people."

"The only traitors I see are you," Kronus replied, lifting his chin to indicate Neo and the kraken gathered behind him. "You have harmed our own kind. This is not worth our blood."

"The scanner detected the unique toxin of the blue needler in all the afflicted," Arkon said. He was met with several confused looks. "The computer confirmed they were poisoned by needler venom."

"Now we are to take the word of some human-built machine?" Neo demanded.

"*We* were built by humans," Dracchus said. "We live in a place built by humans, on a world settled by humans. Were it not for humans, we would not exist."

Neo turned to face Dracchus. The cords stood out on his neck, and his eyes were wild. "They have served their role, and now they are only a threat to our kind. But *we* are the superior creatures. *We* need never suffer at their hands again!"

"Nothing you say will change his mind," Larkin said. She tilted her head back to meet Dracchus's gaze when he turned his head toward her. "I think he broke on that ship. Words aren't going to fix that."

Dracchus clenched his fists. His body was in the same state it assumed while in wait during a hunt; senses heightened, muscles thrumming, blood hot. But what would be accomplished by a fight here? Violence had only worsened this situation. It wouldn't change any minds now.

"Our accusations have been made." Dracchus faced Neo and the group of kraken that supported him — nearly twenty able bodies, nearly twenty of their species, lost to this madness. "Our people should not have their lives threatened by our own. We have always worked together for survival. This action is far beyond what can be tolerated. It cannot be forgiven."

Neo narrowed his eyes. "What are you saying?"

Ector moved forward, placing himself between Neo and Dracchus. "It is clear that your prejudice against the humans has changed you all. You have become a threat to human and kraken alike." He turned toward the rest of the gathering. "The time has come for action. We must make this decision together. You have heard the accusations, heard the evidence provided, and you know those who have acted.

"If you support Neo, do so now. If you believe that killing the humans, at any cost, is the correct path, swim it with him. It does not befit us to hide our true allegiances like cowards."

In the tense silence that followed, three of the kraken in the group behind Neo broke away and went to the edge of the larger crowd, looks of disgust and shame on their faces. No one else moved; Leda, Garon, and Orphus maintained their positions behind their new leader.

Ector nodded, a sad look in his eyes. "I leave it to you, my people. An act like this cannot go unpunished. By the old ways Neo and his followers claim to preserve, such harm to females and younglings would mean death."

"No!" Neo shouted, triggering a great commotion. Skin flashed crimson on all sides, kraken lunged forward, and a desperate fight nearly erupted.

"Enough!" Dracchus roared over the cacophony. Silence fell over the gathering as he approached Neo.

"I challenge you," Neo growled. "I challenge you for leadership, for dominance, for our lives!"

"No," Dracchus replied evenly. "Your right to challenge me has long since passed. You are not worth the effort I would expend to kill you."

Neo and his followers railed, raising claws and bearing teeth. To either side of Dracchus, other kraken formed a line — Jax and Arkon, Brexes and Vasil, Rhea, dozens of others. Randall and Larkin joined the line, shoulder-to-shoulder with the kraken around them.

"Had your plot succeeded, I would have slaughtered each of you with my own hands," Dracchus said. "But our numbers are already diminished. Our people have suffered enough, and those willing to live in peace, those willing to adapt and work together, will suffer no more by your doings. You are banished."

"You cannot do this!" Leda cried, shoving another kraken aside to come forward. "I am a female!"

"You are a bitter female filled with hatred," Vasil said. "No male here is willing to have you."

Leda's skin flared, and she turned her eyes on Larkin. She lunged toward the human, claws poised to attack. Before Dracchus could make a move, Larkin extended her arm, pointing the barrel of her pistol at Leda's face. The female kraken halted abruptly.

"You cannot kill me," Leda snarled.

"I'm not feeling quite as merciful as my mate, so I suggest you back the fuck off," Larkin said.

Anger and pride collided in Dracchus, one fueled by the brazen attempt to harm his mate, the other by Larkin's quick, cool response.

Leda growled, but eventually drew back, eyes narrowed on Larkin.

"This is because of them!" Neo thrust a finger at Macy. "The hunters would never have come had we killed that human slit in the beginning, and our people would not be divided!"

Jax growled. "It is not too late for you to face the old punishment, Neo."

"This is no longer your home," Dracchus said, "and you are no longer our people."

"And what of Kronus?" Garon demanded.

Dracchus swung his gaze to Kronus, who had remained in his earlier position with Aja just behind him.

"Do you stand with them, Kronus?" Ector asked.

"No," Kronus replied, "but I cannot deny my part in this. I will accept the same punishment."

Voices stirred throughout the crowd, some filled with regret, others with shock. Dracchus met Kronus's gaze; the ochre kraken's eyes were filled with many emotions, but foremost among them were shame and humility.

"So be it," Ector said.

"And you, Aja?" Ceres asked.

The female glanced at Neo and Kronus, then focused her attention on Ceres. "I will stand with the humans…for peace."

"You are all traitors!" Neo snarled. "You turn your backs on our ancestors by befriending those who enslaved us, all to shove your cocks into their filthy slits! You taint our blood, and we will not—"

"Leave. Now." Dracchus finally allowed his skin to turn crimson. "Should any of you show your faces here again, it will be at the cost of your life."

Growls and curses followed as Neo's groups shoved their way out of the room, filing through the door.

Orphus turned and glared at the crowd. "You will pay for choosing humans over your own kind," he vowed.

The kraken nearest to him shoved him into the corridor, and a portion of the crowd broke off to ensure the banished found their way out of the Facility.

"I was sure a fight would break out," Larkin whispered after releasing a shaky breath.

The line of kraken dispersed, and Jax returned to his mate, taking her in his arms. "It would have been ended swiftly," he assured her.

"Not without injury," Larkin replied, holstering her pistol.

Dracchus extended an arm, covering her cheek with his hand. She looked exhausted — dark circles under her eyes, pink blotches on her cheeks, her hair drawn back and tied hastily, leaving loose strands around her ears and temples.

Exhausted, but still beautiful.

"For all their bluster, they are cowards," he said. "The chances of them fighting ended once they realized the numbers that would oppose them."

She placed a hand over his and turned her face into his palm, kissing its center. "I would have fought beside you regardless."

He smiled. Whatever she'd gone through, Larkin's spirit was far from broken. "I know, female."

Dracchus lifted his gaze from his mate, and only then realized that the other kraken were looking at him expectantly, some with open curiosity on their faces. Though they'd all known of the presence of humans, relatively few had likely seen more than a glimpse of one. Fewer still were likely to have seen any such interaction between human and kraken.

"This is nothing to fear," Dracchus said as he drew Larkin into his arms. "This will not destroy our kind. It will not destroy who we are. We can only be stronger for it." He looked over his shoulder — Aymee and Arkon, Jax and Macy, Randall and Rhea; all were nearby with their younglings, standing together unafraid, unashamed.

"This is the way forward," he continued, facing the crowd again. "For myself. For my family. The conflict we have known is not the fault of these or any other humans. It has been carried in our hearts for generations, and they have made us face it. Befriend them or do not. Appreciate them or do not. But they do not deserve hatred. They are our people, too."

"Everything has changed," someone said in the crowd. "We cannot go back to the lives we knew, not after this."

"But change can be good," Ceres said gently.

"For good or ill, change must be faced head-on." Dracchus looked into Larkin's eyes. "Together."

He returned his gaze to the crowd, searching their faces. Though these events had begun well over a year before, Dracchus realized that *this* was the turning point. *This* was the moment when the kraken faced all that had happened and all that would happen. There could be no more denial.

"Our kind have long preferred solitude," he said, "but we have always drawn together to survive. Now, we must come together to adapt. We must come together to ensure this change is one that benefits our kind. We must create a future worth having, for the younglings yet to come."

CHAPTER 22

LARKIN TRACKED THE GULPER AHEAD AS THE FISH DRIFTED IN AND out of the seaweed. Movement in her peripheral vision caught her attention. She smirked to herself. Ikaros, anticipating the coming kill, was settled beside her, ready to dart forward.

A few weeks ago, she could never have imagined this scene — she lay on her stomach on the rocky seafloor, harpoon gun propped before her, hunting fish with her brother and a trained prixxir. If she'd dreamt of this, she would've shaken her head and called herself a fool.

She refocused on the gulper, inhaled, and fired. The harpoon shot through the water in a flurry of bubbles. It impaled the gulper, pinning it to the seafloor.

"Four out of four!" Randall declared through the diving suit's comm system.

Ikaros chirruped and raced to retrieve the fish.

Randall swam to her side and turned his head toward her, grinning behind the mask. "You're making me look bad in front of the big guy. Guess some things never change."

Larkin laughed and lifted her gaze to Dracchus, who was

drifting on the current nearby. He nodded, offering her a smile, and raised three fingers.

Three more before we head home.

She was tempted to miss a few shots just to make this last a little longer. This was only the second time he'd taken her out of the Facility. It'd been two weeks since the banishment, and while things had been relatively peaceful, tension lingered in the air. She couldn't quite place it, but she knew Dracchus felt it too; an instinctual sense that things weren't done.

Ikaros swam back to her, carrying the skewered fish by the harpoon. She took it and scratched under the prixxir's chin, handing the catch to Randall, who removed the harpoon and placed the fish in the net with the other six they'd caught. Randall had missed three out of five shots before deciding it was easier to retrieve harpoons that weren't launched into the thick seaweed. Larkin had been mildly disappointed that he'd forfeited so early.

"Macy cooks gulper in some kind of winefruit sauce, and it's delicious," Randall said, handing her the harpoon. "We should see if she's willing to make some."

Larkin reloaded the gun. "If it keeps Aymee out of the kitchen, I'll even beg her." She looked and Randall and grinned. "She would have made a terrible wife."

Randall laughed, shaking his head. "Not like you're any better."

"At least my cooking is edible. We'd all starve if we were depending on her."

"She would've made a great wife," Randall said. "Would've kept my figure trim."

Larkin snickered. "I think Rhea is doing a fine job of that."

She couldn't be sure, but it looked like he blushed as he turned away. "I am *not* having that conversation with my sister."

"Just making small talk," she said, settling back into position.

She scanned the vegetation ahead, seeking out the little flashes of orange that meant a gulper was swimming through the stalks. Ikaros lay beside her, tail wiggling in anticipation.

"So, how are things between you and him?" Randall asked.

Larkin glanced at Randall from the corner of her eye. "Great. He's…really great," she said, distracted but genuine. She pulled the trigger, skewering another gulper. She turned toward Randall as Ikaros went to collect it. "It's just…"

"Too big?"

"Randall!"

"You started it!"

"You really want to know how big—"

"No! *Hell* no!"

Larkin sat up, laughing. "Yeah well, let's just say he puts you and every other guy to shame."

"I'm your brother, Larkin. You're only supposed to talk about my dick when you're making fun of me to your friends."

"Your friends were my friends, Randall."

He grinned, but the expression faded suddenly. She knew where his mind had gone — some of the men who'd betrayed him had been their friends, had been people they'd joked with around campfires, who they'd trudged through muddy swamps and cloying forests alongside.

Her attention shifted to Dracchus. His head was tilted, and he had a curious look on his face. He made a series of quick signs. Larkin's understanding of kraken sign language wasn't anywhere near deep enough to translate.

"What did he say?" Larkin asked.

"He wants to know what we're talking about."

"Might as well tell him."

Randall rolled onto his side. He pointed at Dracchus, and then lowered his hands to his pelvis, pantomiming wrapping his hands around a rather girthy object. Larkin doubted it was real sign language, but Dracchus seemed to get the gist of it. He shook his head with a frown, moved his hands down, and made an even larger circle with them.

"Is he serious?" Randall asked. "Fuck. Please don't answer that."

Larkin made no attempt to contain her amusement. She laughed so hard her sternum hurt.

Ikaros arrived with the harpooned gulper. The prixxir treaded water, whiskers twitching as he watched her laugh.

She blinked the tears from her eyes. "Oh, I missed you, big brother."

"Yeah, well...kraken commander says you need to bag two more. Better get back to work."

Larkin accepted Ikaros's offering and loaded up a fresh harpoon while Randall tended to the catch.

"So, what were you really going to say before?" he asked as she resumed her watch.

Her smile slowly faded, and she sighed. "He hasn't *touched* me since I was poisoned. He treats me like I'm glass, bound to crack and shatter at any moment."

"He could break concrete as easily as glass," Randall said. "He's just worried about you, Elle. You were *really* sick, even with the antitoxin."

"I know, and I get that." Another shot; another gulper. Ikaros sped away. "But I've been fine for days now, and he still won't." She looked at Randall. "Not sure why we're having this conversation. You are my brother."

"Yeah, but that doesn't mean I never give half-decent advice. Did you...did you tell him?"

She didn't need him to clarify his meaning. "I did."

"How'd he take it?"

"It shocked him, I think. Maybe even hurt him. God, Randall, just *seeing* him with those kids..."

"You're not taking anything away from him, Elle," Randall said firmly.

Larkin drew in a deep breath, and once again blinked away moisture from her eyes. "He's assured me he's fine with it, but part of me still grieves because I'll never be able to give him that." She turned her head toward Ikaros as he returned. "He left me after I told him."

"That son of a—"

"I understand why he did. Not going to lie, it hurt, but I kind of laid it on him. It's...not an easy thing to accept, especially for his kind, when they already have so much trouble reproducing. But...Dracchus chose me. He came back, and chose me, and as dedicated as he'd been before that, he was ten times more devoted afterward."

"And then you got sick." Randall took the harpoon from Ikaros this time, handing a free one to Larkin.

"Yeah," she said, reloading the gun. "I know that hit him hard. It hit everyone hard, but I'm not dead."

"No, you're not, and you're the one who had to suffer through the pain. But we both know him, Elle, pretty damn well. Think about how that affected him."

"He's so damn noble," she said affectionately.

"And he hates being idle. The whole time you were sick, he was kicking his own ass because he *needed* to do something to help you, and he couldn't. He tried to hide it, but he was too much of a wreck to pull it off. You almost died, and he was powerless to influence it one way or another."

Larkin looked up at Dracchus again. He swam over the swaying seaweed, his form cast in shadow by the rays of sunlight streaming through the surface. "I love him, Randall."

He sighed. "Shit."

She turned her head to stare at her brother. "That's not helpful."

"Okay, okay. You want some real advice?" His gaze flicked toward Dracchus. "Things have been off-kilter lately with all the stuff that's gone on, but normally, the kraken are all about challenges. Most of them happen between males, but sometimes, when a female is really interested, they'll dance for the male."

"You're telling me to dance?" she asked lamely. "That's your sage advice?"

"Trust me on this one, okay? That's the way his people have done things. It *will* get his attention."

"So, like, in the water?"

"Well…that's how they usually do it."

Larkin lined up her shot, focusing on another gulper. "I'm a damn ranger. What do I know about dancing?" She pulled the trigger.

And missed.

Ikaros chirruped questioningly.

"Fuck," she growled.

Randall whistled. "Little dancing got you that scared, huh?"

"Oh, shut up, Randall."

He passed her the other harpoon. She loaded it and skewered another gulper without a word.

"Done!"

Ikaros bolted toward the fish.

"What, you imagine my face on that one?" Randall asked.

Larkin rolled her eyes and stood up to survey their surroundings. The rocks upon which they'd positioned themselves were slightly elevated over the rest of the terrain. Straight ahead were stalks of seaweed, as thick as the jungle. Behind and to her right, the rock fell away in step-like formations, with various sea creatures scuttling in the crevices. To the left was a steep drop-off of almost thirty meters. The sandy seafloor at its base was lost in darkness from her vantage.

"What are we going to do, Randall?" she asked, frowning.

"Eat some fish tonight?"

"I mean about the rangers. About Dad."

Randall was silent as he collected the final fish from Ikaros and bagged it. Dracchus made another pass overhead, looking from side to side as though watching for danger.

"We're going to have to talk to him sooner or later," Randall finally said. "It's the only way we can get him to stop. Fuck, he's doing this for *us*. It's got to be us to end it, right?"

Larkin nodded. "I'm worried about him, especially with Neo and the others prowling around out here somewhere. We can't stay down here forever, anyway. There has to be something, some way, to bring humans and the kraken together."

"You're right. And he," Randall gestured toward Dracchus, "is the guy you have to convince. If you can get him to agree, he stands the best chance of getting the others to consider it."

"I'll talk to him."

"You should do your dancing first," Randall said with a smirk. His eyes followed movement behind her, and his smirk broadened into a grin.

Larkin turned. Dracchus was there, his amber eyes aglow in the sunlight, his smile somehow fierce and gentle at once. He signed; Larkin caught *good*, but the rest was too fast.

"You did good," Randall translated with a laugh, "but I just wasted air."

"Sounds about right," Larkin replied.

Randall made a series of gestures to Dracchus, and the two went back and forth a few times before Randall tied off the net full of fish, strapped his harpoon gun to his wrist, and gathered the spare harpoons.

"What was all that?" Larkin asked.

"Told him I'm going to head back so you two can have a private lesson on *sign language*." He offered an exaggerated wink.

"Guess you'd better practice your shooting while we're at it, huh?"

"Ouch." Randall called Ikaros to his side with another gesture, and swam backward for a short distance, smiling at her. "I missed you, sis!"

"See you later." Larkin watched Randall swim away. "Sam, cut off all outbound communication." She slowly exhaled and turned her attention back to Dracchus.

He stared at her with slight confusion — and a touch of anticipation — on his face. What had Randall actually told him?

More importantly, what the hell was she about to attempt?

"Damnit," she muttered, setting the harpoon gun down.

Dracchus didn't need to sign his question; it was communicated perfectly through his expression.

What are you doing?

Larkin held his gaze and began moving; a soft swaying of her hips, twisting them side to side. The suit would leave little to his imagination.

She'd never felt particularly feminine. She'd grown up mostly around men, in the wilds, wearing the same clothes and doing the same work. Yet here she was trying to tempt her mate with a sensual display, feeling utterly ridiculous.

"Damnit, Randall, you better be right."

The confusion on Dracchus's face faded as he trailed his gaze down her body, and a new gleam joined the sunlight reflected in his eyes.

Encouraged, Larkin stepped closer to him, rocking her hips, and settled a hand upon his chest. His hearts thumped against her palm, muted by the suit, and she marveled at his color in the soft rays of light from above.

She walked around him slowly, trailing her hand over his shoulder until she reached his back. He turned his head to watch her over his shoulder as Larkin skimmed her fingers down his spine. He shuddered, arching his back and tilting his face upward. She took satisfaction in the reaction she'd elicited from him.

Dracchus flashed maroon as he spun to face her. He caught her arm and slowly raised her hand, pressing her palm to his face. She knew he was thinking the same thing as her — *I wish our skin was touching.*

Dracchus rose off the bottom, sliding his hand along her arm as he swam around her. His tentacles brushed over her legs, her hips, her backside and abdomen; he circled leisurely, and she could almost feel him looking through the suit to see the body beneath. His eyes were amber flames each time their gazes met.

He rounded her again, and again, and her heart sped, her breath quickened, her anticipation built.

"Elevated heartrate detected," Sam said. "Do you—"

"Shut up, Sam," Larkin growled.

Dracchus's claws grazed her shoulders and trailed along her arms. Tingles ran across the surface of her skin, heightening her desire. Her aching nipples hardened, constricted by the suit, and her sensitive flesh was suddenly aware of the faint thrum of the suit's internal energy field.

He took both her hands as he came to her front. Continuing his slow spin, he drew Larkin upward, lifting her off the bottom. Sunlight flashed and flickered around them, and the ocean sparkled.

Colors pulsed over his skin. At first, she thought it was a trick of the constantly shifting light, but as the colors moved faster, she realized it was *him*. He was kaleidoscopic, beautiful, exotic. Dozens of colors and patterns flashed over him, flowing with liquid smoothness. She was transfixed by him.

And then he released his hold on her.

Her momentum carried her through one more rotation. She laughed and turned her head to follow his movement, and her heart stilled.

Dracchus was circling her again, but he did so now in a rhythmic spin that gained speed as he moved, tentacles spreading and twisting. The colors on his skin blurred hypnotically. Larkin moved her arms and legs absently, subconsciously maintaining her position; all her focus was on him, and she turned her head to follow his progress.

As his tentacles flared out, one of them slipped around her waist and pushed her into a spin of her own before sliding away. Shafts of sunlight danced overhead while Dracchus dominated her periphery vision, his hue changing to every color, to no color, and back again with every heartbeat.

He settled his hands on her hips and pulled her against him.

The whole world spiraled around them, but Dracchus remained constant. Solid. *Real.*

She laughed, looping her arms around his neck, and met his eyes.

He held her gaze as they swam; she knew, instinctually, they were heading toward the Facility. Toward *home.*

Larkin smiled, wrapping her legs around his waist as she caressed the back of his neck.

His hands slid down over her backside and along her outer thighs. The scintillating colors on his skin faded, leaving only a rich maroon. He dipped his head forward, pressing his forehead to her mask.

By the time they reached the Facility, Larkin's patience was exhausted. She wanted her hands on Dracchus, wanted her lips on him; she needed to touch him, to *feel* him, *now.*

"Do you require entry?" Sam asked.

"Yes!" she said before he finished speaking. The light above the door flashed green and Dracchus pulled them into the chamber.

He lifted her head over the surface of the draining water, and she hurriedly removed the mask, yanking the hood down to free her hair. She dropped the mask to take his face in her hands and pressed her mouth to his.

"I need you," she said against his lips. "Now."

"In our den," he growled.

"Too long." She bit his lower lip, then soothed it with her tongue; he tasted like the sea.

"No one else will see *my* female." Dracchus slammed the button the instant the light turned green. Before she realized what he meant to do, he tossed her over his shoulder and charged through the open door.

Larkin's shriek turned into laughter as he hurried along the corridor. She watched his tentacles moving beneath him, covering distance faster than she'd ever thought possible. Flattening her hands on his back, she smoothed them down his waist to caress what would've been his ass, if he were human.

"Enough, female," Dracchus said, giving her rump a smack.

Larkin gasped; pleasure followed the brief sting. His hand remained on her backside, massaging it, heightening her arousal.

When they finally reached their room, Dracchus set her on her feet and yanked her suit off before the door had fully shut. Bared to his hungry gaze, she leapt upon him. He took her in his arms as their mouths met in another fiery kiss.

There was dizzying motion, and suddenly, the wall was at her back. Dracchus leaned into her and deepened the kiss, caging her with his arms and pinning her with his body. His hard shaft brushed beneath her backside. She arched, rubbing her nipples against his chest, and that little bit of contact sent flashes of bliss straight to her core.

Dracchus inhaled deeply and groaned. He drew back his head, and Larkin glimpsed his kiss-swollen lips before his hands untangled her legs from his waist, cupped her backside, and lifted her up the wall until her thighs settled over his shoulders.

She cried out when his mouth fell over her sex. He stroked her with his tongue, lapped at her, tasted her. Larkin grasped his head, her only anchor. Closing her eyes, she tilted her head back, submitting to the euphoria he bestowed upon her. His fingers curled over her thighs and spread them wider while his tongue delved deeper.

"Dracchus," she moaned when his lips found her clit. He latched on and Larkin's entire body tensed as he brought her to a swift, blistering climax.

He turned away from the wall and lowered her slowly, letting her sex slide over his chest, kissing up her belly and between her breasts until their mouths met. She wrapped her legs around his middle as he carried her toward the bed. She tasted herself on his lips, but it was *him* she wanted on her tongue.

Dracchus dropped her onto the bed and moved to follow her down, but Larkin held a hand to his chest, stopping him.

"Lie on your back," she said.

He paused, holding himself over her on one arm, and gave her a smoldering, quizzical look, but he allowed her to guide him down onto his back when she exerted a bit more force.

Larkin sat up, meeting his gaze as she slowly trailed kisses down his chest and abdomen. She smiled at the brush of a tentacle over her thigh. The closer she came to his pelvis, the lower Dracchus's brow dropped.

She curled her fingers around his dark shaft as much as she was able. It was steel and velvet, alien and beautiful, glistening with its own lubricant. Her hand glided easily along its length. With her other hand, she brushed the four pinky-length tendrils around his base. Recalling the pleasure the little tendrils had provided sent a fresh rush of heat through her, wetting her inner thighs further.

His cock twitched at her touch, and his muscles tensed. The entire bed shifted as he put his arms to the sides and grasped the bedding.

"I have burned for your touch, female," he growled. "I *need* you."

"In a moment," she replied. "You made me wait this long, you can wait a little longer."

"Larkin," he warned.

She flashed him a grin and held his gaze as she dipped her head toward his cock.

His eyes widened; given their sharp teeth, it wasn't likely that kraken females ever did anything like this. Still, he didn't stop her as she opened her mouth and lowered it over him.

He was too large for her to take any more than his head, but his tentacles writhed when she closed her lips around his crown. She sucked and teased him with her tongue, stroking his shaft and tendrils with her hands. The hint of sea salt in his taste was spiced with something more exotic, something sweet, and she greedily took as much as she could.

Dracchus groaned and arched his back to lift his pelvis toward her. One of his tentacles curled around the back of her thigh and slipped between her legs, caressing her sex.

Larkin moaned around his cock and spread her knees wider, undulating over his tentacle. The ridges of his suction cups stroked and sucked her folds and clit, flooding her with pleasure, intensifying her need.

She tore her mouth from his shaft when she came, panting out his name. Her sex clenched, hollow, empty, her slick ran down her thighs, her arousal scented the air.

"*Now*, female," Dracchus growled, wrapping a tentacle around her waist.

She climbed on top of him, still gripping his length, and lowered herself upon him. The head of his cock entered her. Biting her lip against the pressure, she moved up and down, taking him in a little at a time as he stretched her.

Dracchus's hands brushed along her thighs, the light grazing of his claws sending delightful thrills across her skin.

She needed him inside her, needed to be filled by him, needed to join with him and be overwhelmed by the electrifying connection they shared when their bodies came together.

Larkin flattened her hands on his abdomen and raised her pelvis. As though he knew her thoughts, Dracchus slid his hands to her hips. She bore down upon him, lent strength by his hands, and he thrust upward to meet her.

There was a pinch as he filled her completely. She panted, fingers curling over the hard muscles of his abdomen, nails raking his soft skin. It was pleasure, it was pain, it was breathtaking.

Dracchus stilled his hips as she adjusted, but his hands soothed her, his tentacles caressed her, and his eyes possessed her.

She rocked against him, relishing the slow glide of her sex around his shaft. His tendrils stroked her with every downward pump. Euphoria spread through her, gathering at her core in a molten mass that demanded *more, faster, harder!* Her body obeyed the call.

His skin burned her from the inside out, and she focused on the thrust of his steel length, pushing deeper, *deeper.*

Larkin fell forward, bracing her hands on his chest, as the sensations overwhelmed her.

Dracchus claimed control. His strong hands tightened on her hips, pulling her down with increasing force and speed. Larkin leaned her weight into the heels of her hands, digging her nails into his flesh, needing to relieve the pressure, yet yearning for *more.*

He was unrelenting, wild, desperate.

"Please," she begged, unsure of whether she was asking him to stop or to push harder.

He only moved faster, baring his teeth. The ferocity of his visage belied the adoration in his eyes. He stared at her as though she meant the world to him.

Her body shuddered and the dam broke, allowing wave after wave of pleasure to crash through her.

"I love you," she rasped before she cried out in bliss. Her inner muscles tightened around his cock, fluttering and pulsing, seeking to draw him impossibly deeper and lock him in place. She collapsed upon his chest, and he wrapped his arms around her, sheltering her while she came undone.

Heat blossomed inside Larkin as Dracchus roared his release. His tentacles wound around her legs and pulled her down into his final thrust and held her in place. The rapid beating of his hearts washed over her. He growled, pumping shallowly in the aftermath, the minuscule pulsing his shaft echoing through her like the aftershocks of an earthquake, the small tendrils at his base gently caressing her sex. She trembled against him.

She kissed his chest and closed her eyes. No matter what

happened beyond these walls, she was at home in his arms; *he* was her home. Her comfort, her security, her sanctuary.

He moved his hands down her back, his touch impossibly light, impossibly gentle. Larkin stretched an arm up to cup his cheek with her palm.

"You danced for me," he said.

"Wasn't much of a dance. I'm terrible at it."

"But you did it for me."

Larkin inhaled, taking in his scent — their combined scent. "Yeah. For you."

"I love you, Larkin." His voice was so low that she felt his words more than she heard them; they were a rumbling in his chest, rising from the deepest parts of him.

Larkin raised her head to meet his eyes. His face was grave, his gaze intense.

"You are my mate. I want you to be mine forever, in the way of your people," he said.

Warmth and joy swelled in her chest. She smiled and stroked a thumb over his cheek. "Dracchus, would you join with me?"

"*Join.* That is what you call it?"

"Yes. Join with me and I will be yours."

"I am yours, as well. I will join with you, female." The bed groaned softly as Dracchus sat up. He guided her legs to either side of his waist, maintaining the connection between them as he moved, and supported her back with his tentacles. He took her face in his hands. "What must we do, to follow your ways?"

Larkin wrapped her arms around his neck and brushed her lips against his. "Just love me, Dracchus."

"Always."

CHAPTER 23

DRACCHUS WOKE TO DARKNESS SO THICK THAT HE QUESTIONED whether he'd opened his eyes or not. His vision adjusted quickly, aided by the muted glow of the room's nighttime lights. Larkin was tucked against his side, sleeping soundly, head resting on his arm. He lifted his head and scanned the shadows in the room.

Nothing seemed amiss.

He eased back down and closed his eyes. Larkin's slow, steady breathing mingled with the Facility's faint ambient hum, which was audible now only because of the relative silence. He filled his lungs with a deep inhalation and released it gradually, waiting for sleep to reclaim him.

Larkin's scent teased his nostrils, and he drew her a little closer. She stirred with a sigh and stretched her arm across his chest. Such a small, innocent movement, made without her awareness; it reminded him of her softness, her heat, her taste.

He was tempted to wake her. He'd spent the last five days making up for their lack of intimacy during her recovery. It hadn't been easy for him; his worry for her health and safety had been the only thing making him refrain over those two weeks, and her dance — her inexperienced, clumsy, beautiful dance — had shattered his remaining resolve.

For now, he'd let her sleep. No matter what she claimed, he knew she wasn't fully recovered from the poisoning. Morning would have to be soon enough to get his taste of her.

Dracchus pushed aside his desire, his thoughts, and focused on his own breathing.

Something scraped against the door.

He sat up, turning his head toward the sound.

"What's wrong?" Larkin placed a hand on his shoulder and pulled herself into a sitting position.

The sound came again — claws against metal? The thickness of the door restricted the passage of sound from one side to the other, making it difficult to identify.

"Is that Ikaros?" Larkin asked, slipping out of bed and reaching for her clothes.

"I will check," Dracchus said. He slid his tentacles onto the floor and crossed the room. Randall sometimes took Ikaros out during the late hours of the night, and the prixxir had probably just pawed at their door, hoping they'd go hunting.

The door opened silently at the touch of a button. Dracchus narrowed his eyes against the bright corridor lights.

"Good, you're awake," Randall said.

"Damnit, Randall, what the hell?" Larkin appeared next to Dracchus, fully clothed in a shirt and pants. She shielded her eyes with a hand as she scowled at her brother. "It's the middle of the night."

Dracchus looked over Randall. He wore only a pair of pants, his hair was tousled, and his cheeks and jaw were darkened by a short growth of hair. He clutched a pistol in one hand. Ikaros was beside him, staring down the hallway, whiskers and spine fin raised.

Dracchus frowned.

"Ikaros was acting up," Randall said, turning his head from side to side to glance down the corridor. "I thought he wanted to go out at first, but I think this is more. I think someone's prowling these halls."

Larkin moved away from Dracchus.

"Did you find anyone?" Dracchus asked.

Randall ran his free hand through his hair. "No. But something doesn't feel right."

Having donned her boots and belt, Larkin returned. She drew back the slide of her pistol to confirm the round in its chamber. "Let's check it out."

Before either Dracchus or Larkin had exited the room, Ikaros growled, sinking to bunch his shoulders defensively, attention on something down the hallway.

Randall turned his head in the same direction. "Oh, shit."

Dracchus moved through the doorway and halted abruptly when he saw what the two were focused on.

Kronus stood in the center of the corridor, four doors away.

Larkin stopped beside Dracchus, aiming her pistol at Kronus. "What are you doing here?"

Kronus lifted his hands, displaying empty palms.

"You accepted the terms," Dracchus said, advancing toward Kronus. "You know what it means to have returned."

"I did, and I do," Kronus replied. He met Dracchus's gaze. "The warning I must give you is worth the risk."

Dracchus stopped a body's length away from Kronus. Randall, Larkin, and Ikaros fell into place on Dracchus's sides.

"Here for more threats?" Dracchus asked.

"No. I cannot allow the past to repeat itself." Kronus's expression was strained. "I will not remain idle while more innocents are harmed."

"So you sneak into the place we sleep in the middle of the night?" Randall demanded. "That's a bit too similar to shit your supporters have pulled on me for my liking."

"What are you talking about, Kronus?" Larkin asked.

"The others have rejected their banishment," Kronus replied. "They are coming now to reclaim the Facility."

The words didn't sound right, couldn't be true, but there was no deception in Kronus's haunted eyes. Dracchus had known something like this was inevitable, that a movement birthed of hatred could only end in violence. *This* is what he'd sensed coming over the last few weeks. It was oddly relieving to have something to justify the dread that had been burning in his gut, low and steady, since the banishment.

"All of them?" Dracchus asked.

Kronus nodded. "Their time in the wilds has made them bold. Successful hunts have made them believe they are the superior group, that they can best you and take this place back."

"Don't they remember that *everyone* stood against them?" Larkin asked.

"Their belief seems to be that killing all of you will turn the rest back to the proper way."

Dracchus clenched his jaw. "How long?"

"They'll be here soon. I came once I knew they meant to carry through with this plot."

"How was it you managed to leave?" Dracchus demanded, moving closer. "Did they not question your sudden departure?"

"I have been watching them without their knowledge." Kronus frowned and ran his tongue along his teeth. "Neo would likely have them kill me if he knew I was so close."

"I'll go alert the others," Larkin said.

Dracchus caught her by the arm as she moved away, and she turned to face him.

"Dracchus, you better not—"

"Tell them to gather weapons and younglings and return here," he said. "Go as quickly as you can."

Larkin's features eased, and she stepped closer to place a kiss on his lips. "I will."

He released her and watched her run down the hallway.

Randall made a clicking sound with his mouth, and Ikaros took off behind Larkin, following her around a turn in the corridor.

Once she was out of sight, Dracchus felt an almost undeniable pull to call her back, to go after her, to do *anything* but let her go beyond his reach.

She is a warrior, he reminded himself.

Larkin had faced danger before, had experienced at least two brushes with near-death — one of them at the hands of the kraken who was coming to kill them all. Dracchus didn't have to like the thought of her being in danger to acknowledge that she was a survivor.

She stands with me.

He swung his gaze back to Kronus. "Go. Before one of the others sees you."

Kronus's brow creased and his frown deepened. "I violated my banishment. My life is yours to take."

"There will be enough bloodshed soon, Kronus. I have no desire to add to it without good reason."

"I will remain."

Dracchus stared at the ochre kraken. What should he make of this? Another lurking betrayal?

"Your suspicion is founded," Kronus said. "I've no love for you, or the humans you have allowed to dwell in our home. But I owe my life to two of them, and as I said...I cannot allow the past to repeat. I cannot allow younglings and females to be harmed."

"You are with us, then?"

"Yes. After, if I yet live, you may take whatever action you choose."

Dracchus nodded.

"I need to let Rhea know," Randall said, "and get something out of our room." He hurried to his door and opened it. The lights were on inside.

Dracchus followed as far as the doorway, pausing just outside;

he didn't trust Kronus to go inside, and wouldn't risk looking away from the ochre kraken for even a few moments.

Randall spoke to Rhea in soft tones, too low for Dracchus to make out the words. The female looked at Dracchus and frowned. She wore the expression with equal parts uncertainty and fury.

"They will not come here without facing the consequences," she said.

"They knew that already," Dracchus said. "We will shelter the younglings in your den."

Randall crouched on the far side of the bed and rummaged through something Dracchus couldn't see.

Rhea straightened, a hint of red on her skin. She looked down at Melaina, who stood as tall as Rhea's middle. "Will they go so low as to slaughter younglings?"

Dracchus glanced at Kronus; the ochre kraken stared down the hallway, seemingly oblivious to his surroundings, but had not moved from this position. Satisfied, Dracchus turned back to meet Melaina's wide-eyed gaze.

"Whatever they are willing to do," Dracchus said, "we will allow no harm to the young. You are strong, little one, and you will be safe here."

"What about everyone else?" Melaina asked. There was a hint of fear in her voice, but she stood as straight as her mother, and her concern was for the others. Though she was not his youngling, Dracchus took pride in her.

"They will be here soon, and the small ones will need to see your strength. They will see your bravery and know there is no reason to fear."

Melaina smiled and nodded.

Voices in the hallway called Dracchus's attention away. He moved toward the sounds.

Ikaros rounded the corner first, followed by Larkin and then the others — Macy and Aymee, carrying their half-asleep younglings, and then Jax and Arkon. The two male kraken cast skeptical glances at Kronus but said nothing.

Larkin and the prixxir moved directly to Dracchus, and he drew his mate into a tight embrace, overwhelmed by an unexpected sense of relief. She squeezed him back.

"Now what?" she asked.

"Damn it!" Randall's frustrated voice — accompanied by a *thump* — drew everyone's attention to the doorway.

Randall clenched his jaw, backed up, and turned sideways to pass through the door with a long, cloth-wrapped bundle in his arms. He knelt once he was in the corridor and set the bundle down, unraveling it to reveal six long guns — *rifles*, as the humans called them.

Larkin broke away from Dracchus and picked up one of the weapons, inspecting it with confidence and familiarity.

"How long have those been in your den?" Dracchus asked. He'd shown Randall how to access the weapons and diving suits he'd hidden away, but he'd thought it had been with the understanding that they'd only be taken when necessary.

"When I reorganized the mess you made of that cabinet, I couldn't fit everything back in," Randall replied with a smirk that said he hadn't tried particularly hard to make anything fit.

Dracchus grunted; now was not the time for this discussion, partly because his gratefulness would undermine the annoyance he was meant to display.

"So, what's the—"

Macy's words halted when Ikaros growled — a deep, undulating, menacing sound. The prixxir stared down the corridor from which the others had just come, slowly backing toward Dracchus and the others. The growl ceased, and Ikaros stood with whiskers and spine fin raised. In the ensuing silence, Dracchus became aware of another sound — the uneven rhythm of tentacles moving quietly along a metal walkway, barely audible above his own breathing.

"Get the younglings inside," Dracchus commanded in a low voice, "and lock the door."

Macy and Aymee hurried past him with Sarina and Jace while Jax, Arkon, and Kronus moved to stand beside him.

Dracchus's hearts beat thunderously, and an uneasy energy suffused his limbs. Arkon handed him a spear. He grasped it with both hands.

Months ago, Arkon had shown him recordings of the uprising. The walls and floors of this building had been splattered with blood. Foolishly, Dracchus had told himself it would never happen again, despite the tensions and disagreements that had been escalating among his people.

"We are the shield," Dracchus said to the kraken beside him. "Randall and Larkin will shelter behind us and fire between our bodies."

"Ikaros, to Melaina," Randall said.

The prixxir looked toward Randall with wide eyes, whimpered, and scurried into the room.

"We're here, too," Aymee said.

Dracchus glanced over his shoulder to see Aymee in the hallway, holding one of the rifles. Rhea was beside her with a spear in her hand. The door to the den slid closed.

"Aymee..." Arkon's voice was breathless, overflowing with concern.

"Macy's staying with the kids, and that's only because she's pregnant. We *all* need to fight for the lives we've made here." Keeping the barrel pointed at the floor, she raised the rifle and checked the chamber. "Promise I won't shoot Randall this time. I hope."

Randall chuckled, Larkin snickered, and, despite everything, Dracchus smiled. His chest was tight, *full*, but it wasn't merely anticipation, wasn't merely concern — it was affection. It was *love*. These were his people, and he didn't want any of them to come to harm. He shifted his gaze to Larkin. Her eyes were bright, intense, brimming with emotion. She dipped her chin in a nod and made a simple sign.

With you.

Dracchus returned the nod and looked ahead.

Neo turned the corner at the head of a pack. At least eight kraken followed him in a tight cluster, too tightly packed for him to count. All displayed crimson skin.

Dracchus met Neo's eyes as the banished kraken halted.

The air, normally clean and comfortable, grew thick and oppressive, charged with palpable, electric tension. Both groups stared at one another in silence. Were they frozen by the weight of the moment? By what was to come? Frozen by fear, or hatred, or both?

A few of Neo's bunch held harpoon guns. Several more wielded spears. They were only six doors away. Larkin had said the doors were each four meters apart; it was not much distance for a kraken to cross.

"You may leave now with your lives," Dracchus called. He spread his tentacles slightly wider, mindful of the humans behind him as he coiled his muscles like springs, ready for the fight.

Neo wasted no breath on a response. As one, he and his followers charged.

Gunfire deafened Dracchus. He felt the heat of the rifles on his sides, felt the air displaced by the screaming projectiles, and the vibrations of the small explosions pulsed across his skin. Flashing lights came on along the corridor, accompanied by a loud, blaring sound.

"Firearms discharged in Cabins Hall C," the Computer announced loudly. "All active security personnel be advised, firearms discharged..."

Crimson-skinned kraken reeled in pain, their blood splattering the walls and floor — just as human blood had, more than three hundred years ago. Only two attackers fell.

The thump of harpoon guns blasted down the corridor, and

long missiles shimmered under the overhead lights as they sped toward Dracchus's group.

Dracchus batted one aside with his spear. Another hit the floor and slid behind their line, clattering into the wall before it lost momentum.

The third hit someone to Dracchus's right; a pained grunt was the only sound marking the impact, too indistinct for him to know if it had been Arkon or Jax.

Another burst of gunfire dropped two more kraken.

Dracchus ran his gaze over his enemies. He knew all their faces, all their names, but they were so far gone to rage that he couldn't put any of them together. The only certainty was that these were too few to account for all the kraken who'd been banished, even with four of them down. The others either hadn't come or were approaching from another direction.

The computer continued repeating its warnings. "All non-security personnel, please remain where you are or seek shelter in the nearest lockable room, as detailed in this facility's emergency procedures. This is not a drill. Firearms discharged in Cabins…"

"Jax!" Dracchus shouted. He could barely hear himself over the cacophony. "Take Randall and Rhea, guard our flank!"

Jax nodded and fell back, granting Dracchus a brief glimpse of the large gash on his arm.

Dracchus, Arkon, and Kronus broadened their stances to cover some of the newly opened space as the first of Neo's group crashed into the line.

Crimson limbs thrashed and flailed in a frenzy. Claws tore Dracchus's skin, a spear sliced across his ribs, and he was hammered by tentacles and fists. The crimson-skinned attackers were attempting to scramble over him.

They mean to strike the humans first.

To strike my mate.

Roaring, Dracchus lowered his shoulder and heaved, shoving the foremost attackers backward. Arkon and Kronus thrust their spears into the stumbling kraken, but it didn't halt the next charge. One of the attackers leapt high.

Dracchus jabbed his spear up with one hand, burying it in the kraken's shoulder. He extended his other arm simultaneously, closing his free hand around his foe's throat. Dracchus swayed backward with the kraken's momentum.

Garon, he realized. This was Garon, his face contorted in uncontrollable fury.

A similar rage blazed fully to life inside Dracchus. He'd grown to adulthood with many of these kraken, had hunted with them. And all that had ceased to matter.

A pistol appeared in Dracchus's peripheral vision, barrel angled upward. The slender fingers gripping it were familiar to him.

Larkin squeezed the trigger. The projectile entered Garon's skull between his eyes. The body jerked once and went still.

Dracchus tore his spear free and hurled the carcass toward its fellows. The aggressors were no longer kraken. They were wild beasts, no better than razorbacks in kraken skin, and they were threatening Dracchus's people.

The body hit two of the attackers, knocking them backward, and Dracchus charged into the gap.

He thrust the head of his spear into one kraken's chest, planting it deep. Clutching the shaft with both hands, he swung, slamming the kraken into one of the other crimson-skinned monsters. Claws and blades raked his skin, but he was beyond pain.

Gunshots and alarms drowned out all other sounds. Two crimson beasts hurled themselves through the projectiles, surging past Dracchus, dragging themselves forward over their fallen comrades. He spun to pursue them. Arkon and Kronus were already battling opponents of their own, and Larkin and Aymee had fallen back slightly, guns to their shoulders, still firing.

The acrid tang of gunfire and blood overpowered all other scents.

Kronus twisted, thrusting his spear upward as one of the attackers swung along the wall. The head of the spear punched through the kraken's abdomen and burst out the back, embedding itself into the metal plating. The kraken halted abruptly, body folding around the weapon.

The kraken's shocked, agonized face was suddenly familiar — Orphus.

The maneuver left Kronus undefended; his original foe stabbed him in the side. Pain tightened Kronus's features as he swung backhand. His fist caught the other kraken's jaw. The crimson-skinned attacker reeled, and Kronus threw himself at his opponent, taking him down in a mass of writhing tentacles.

The other charging attacker leapt off the wall and grabbed the ceiling rails, hurling himself toward the humans.

Larkin pivoted, dropped to a knee, and fired twice at the oncoming kraken. She rolled aside as the attacker crashed to the floor, but the injured kraken scrambled back up.

Someone hooked an arm around Dracchus's from behind. Dracchus leaned forward; he needed to protect Larkin, to reach her, but his foe dragged him back and used Dracchus as an anchor to lift himself off the floor. Tentacles caught Dracchus's other arm. The attacker threw all his body weight into pulling Dracchus's arms backward and apart, threatening to topple the big kraken over.

Shoulders wailing in protest, Dracchus remained upright, dragging himself forward.

Ahead, Larkin raised her pistol to shoot the kraken who'd charged her. Seemingly unaffected by the bullet wounds already bleeding on his torso, the kraken caught her leg with a tentacle and pulled her feet out from beneath her. Aymee hammered the butt of her gun into the back of the attacker's head as Larkin hit the floor.

Beyond Aymee and Larkin, Randall, Rhea, and Jax — both kraken bloody — battled more of the exiles, who'd come from the other corridor.

Two more attackers hurtled past Dracchus.

He roared. The sound burst from his chest and ripped out of his throat, vibrating back into him as it reverberated off the walls.

Arkon stabbed his opponent in the face and turned, skin flashing red. He tackled the closest of the two charging kraken, knocking them into one another. All three hit the floor.

Dracchus clenched his fists and bent his arm as much as he could before slamming his shoulder — and his foe's head — into the wall. The grip on his arms loosened.

Arkon loomed over the kraken he'd tackled, straining as he battled the tentacles wrapped around his arms to bury his claws in the other kraken's neck. His arms were covered in blood and gore, but his foe continued struggling.

Kronus was still down, wrestling with his original opponent; his tentacles encircled the attacker's neck, slowly squeezing the life out of the crimson-skinned kraken.

The beast who'd charged Larkin had Aymee pinned against the wall.

Arkon roared Aymee's name, but he couldn't disengage from his foe.

Dracchus slammed the kraken on his back into the wall again, and again. Something crunched in Dracchus's arm, but he didn't relent until the hold loosened enough for him to break free. He shrugged the other kraken off his back.

Larkin jumped atop the kraken holding Aymee. She slammed her knife into his neck four times, twisting the blade on the final stab. The kraken swayed backward and released Aymee, who dropped to her knees. Larkin hopped away from the dying kraken, allowing him to collapse, and bent to collect her rifle.

Rhea had another female against the wall. Keeping the female pinned with a forearm on her throat, Rhea sliced open the female's abdomen with her claws.

The female's skin reverted to its normal shade as her life faded; she'd been Leda, once.

The second kraken Arkon had knocked down pulled himself to his feet. He turned to look at Arkon and Kronus, both of whom remained occupied, and met Dracchus's gaze. The hatred in his eyes was unmistakable.

Neo.

Dracchus lunged forward.

Neo turned and leapt toward Larkin. Dracchus's hands closed around two tentacles, halting Neo in midair. The crimson-skinned exile hit the floor hard, clawing for purchase as Dracchus dragged him closer.

A distant *thump*, and dull pain bloomed in Dracchus's lower back. He didn't relinquish his hold on his foe, his *enemy*, the monstrous creature who sought to do his family harm. Who sought to do *Larkin* harm.

Turning onto his back, Neo twisted his tentacles around Dracchus's arms. His abdomen flexed as he bent to lift his torso, swiping his claws wildly. Fresh gouges opened on Dracchus's chest; he didn't feel the sting of his wounds, only the warmth of his own blood as it flowed from them.

Larkin and Aymee fired over his head at targets down the hall; more of Neo's followers were behind him. Past the human females, Jax was tearing out the throat of another kraken. Rhea and Randall turned in Dracchus's direction. They were flanked by several more kraken.

They were surrounded and being overrun.

Dracchus buried his claws in Neo's tentacles.

Rearing back, Dracchus swung Neo into the wall. Neo's grip didn't ease, so Dracchus swung again, this time in the opposite direction. The impact was powerful enough to vibrate the floor.

Neo sagged, tentacles loosening, and landed atop one of his fallen companions in a heap. Dracchus fell upon him immediately, trapping his foe's tentacles beneath his own. Neo thrashed and struggled as Dracchus clamped a hand on his throat and shoved his head down to the floor, bending the crimson kraken over the body below.

Ignoring the claws shredding his forearm, Dracchus drew back his fist and hammered it into Neo's face.

Thwap.

Neo's struggle's wavered. Dracchus struck again.

Thwap.

Again. And again.

Head stuck between the solid floor and Dracchus's fist, Neo's desperate thrashing weakened with each successive blow. Something cracked wetly under Dracchus's hand.

Dracchus struck again, kept striking until Neo's arms fell limp and his struggles ceased, until his own hand was dripping with blood.

He shoved himself off the corpse and turned to the new wave of attackers. Larkin had her back to them. Had she not noticed them?

The other kraken flowed past her, and just as Dracchus tensed to intercept them, recognition broke through the haze of battle. He knew these kraken, too.

Vasil, Brexes, half a dozen other males. Even old Ector. They continued along the corridor, engaging the few crimson-skinned kraken who remained behind Dracchus.

When two of the newcomers dragged Kronus up off the floor, Dracchus halted them with a shout. Kronus's shoulders rose and fell with labored breaths, and blood trickled from at least a dozen wounds on his chest and arms. He stared at Dracchus with a mixture of challenge and resignation in his eyes.

Leave him, Dracchus signed.

Though their brows furrowed in confusion, they obeyed.

Kronus sank down, leaned back against the wall, and closed his eyes.

Dracchus moved toward his mate. His hearts pounded in his ears, louder than the alarm still blaring overhead. A spasm locked his back; he gritted his teeth against the wave of agony as Larkin, panting, finally lowered her rifle. Her eyes widened as they fell upon him.

She covered the small distance between them swiftly, yelling behind her, "Aymee!"

Dracchus cupped her jaw and lifted her chin, checking her neck, her face, her whole body for signs of injury. There was blood on her clothes, but apart from a few superficial scratches, she appeared unharmed. Relief flooded him.

"I'm fine," she said over the alarm, pushing aside his hands to look him over, face strained with worry. She pressed her lips tighter together with each wound she discovered. "But you're a mess, Dracchus."

"I'm here," Aymee said, voice hoarse.

Arkon stood before her a moment later. Frowning, he lifted his hands as though to touch Aymee's neck, which was covered in angry, red marks, but pulled them back before making contact. He said something to her; Dracchus couldn't hear his words over the noise, but she mouthed something like *I'll be okay* in response.

She turned her attention to Dracchus, running her fingers gently over a few of his wounds. Her touch stung.

Hesitantly, Arkon moved to a panel beside the entry to Randall and Rhea's den. He manipulated some sort of control to produce a floating, see-through screen filled with human symbols. His fingers flicked through the symbols with surprising speed — Dracchus couldn't understand how Arkon could tell them apart, or how they held any meaning.

The flashing lights ceased, and the wailing alarm went silent.

"Security alert in Cabins Hall C has been cleared," the

computer announced as though nothing had happened. "Please resume your normal duties."

Dracchus's ears rang in the sudden silence, as though unwilling to forget the cacophony of moments before. He looked down the hall.

None of Neo's followers remained upright. Their bodies were strewn about the corridor in pools of blood. Vasil and Brexes were moving among the fallen, delivering quick deaths to any who clung to life.

A strange, high tone — *beeeeeep* — drew his attention back to Arkon.

Arkon leaned his face closer to the screen. "Macy, it is Arkon. You can open the door now."

Several heartbeats passed. Pain slowly made itself known in new parts of Dracchus's body, introducing him to wounds he hadn't yet noticed. He shoved it aside.

The door opened, and Ikaros bound out, leaping at Randall with enough enthusiasm to knock the human down.

"Easy, easy," Randall said, rubbing the prixxir's side.

Macy leaned through the doorway, peered up and down the corridor, and looked back into the room. "Stay in here. Do *not* come out until one of us comes to get you, okay?"

"Okay," Melaina and Sarina replied in unison.

Macy stepped into the hallway and closed the door. Tears spilled from her eyes as she ran to Jax and took him in a tight embrace, avoiding his wounds. "I was so scared I'd lose you."

Jax returned the embrace. "Nothing will keep me from you, Macy."

"They all came to help us," Larkin said, looking past Dracchus.

He followed her gaze. Even more kraken were in the hallway now, dozens of them. More, perhaps, than had ever been in the Cabins at once. Their conversations were low, their expressions fraught with confusion, anger, and sadness.

Slowly, their eyes began to turn toward him.

"We need to get all the injured to the infirmary," Aymee said softly behind him. "That includes you."

He turned his head to look at her over his shoulder. "I will be—"

"You have a fucking harpoon sticking out of your back!" Larkin snapped, glaring at him. "That isn't *fine*."

The dull pain in his back sharpened, and he was suddenly aware of the weight of the projectile jutting from the wound.

Ector and Vasil approached him.

"This will not be easy for any of us to understand," Ector said. He looked as though he'd aged several more years since the last time Dracchus had seen him, only two weeks before.

"Keep only who you need to clear the hall," Dracchus said. He looked past them, at the expectant crowd. The truth of what had happened, the enormity of it, poked at the edges of his mind, but he would not allow it entry. "Gather in the Mess," he called. "As soon as our wounds are tended, we will address this matter, and we will decide how to move forward as a people."

Slowly, many moving as though in a daze, the kraken began to disperse.

"What about him?" Vasil asked, gesturing to Kronus, who remained in the place he'd taken against the wall.

"He fought alongside us," Dracchus said, "and risked much to warn us of what Neo intended. We will discuss his fate, as a people."

Ector placed a gentle hand on Dracchus's shoulder. "Our people look to you as a leader, Dracchus. You have proven time and again that you will fight for their survival, that you will put their needs before your own. They will all need to lean on your strength, now more than ever."

Those words echoed something Jax said to Dracchus after the decision had been made to allow Macy to stay.

Dracchus was no more comfortable with the implication now, even after so much had changed. "I will do all I can for our people, elder, but I should not lead. They would do better to follow Jax or Arkon."

"You have been leading already, whether you realize it or not," Ector replied gently. "And for now, at least, we are dependent upon you."

Dracchus looked over his surroundings again. Blood and gore bathed the hallway, and the bodies of the fallen were scattered about as carelessly as pebbles on the seafloor. He still couldn't acknowledge this, not yet; he feared the burden might crush him. But he could acknowledge that he'd never wanted it. No matter how tense things had become, no matter how infuriating the behavior of the exiled kraken, *he'd never wanted this.*

His gaze shifted back, over the people gathered behind him. Arkon, Jax, and Rhea embracing their human mates with such quiet relief, such *love.* Ikaros sat with surprising patience beside Randall, gently pawing at Rhea's tentacles with apparent concern. All the kraken bore numerous wounds, taken in the defense of people they cared for.

He looked finally at Larkin, who stood beside him, watching him with apparent concern. She stepped closer to him and settled her hand over his hearts. "I will stand with you. I'll always stand with you."

Dracchus did not know the proper words to express his feelings toward her, if those words even existed. Their actions had always spoken louder than anything either of them could say. He dipped his head and kissed her, letting his lips linger against hers; this small taste wasn't enough.

Had he known the events of this night would occur, he wouldn't have changed a single thing leading up to it. The price had been steep, but *this* was the future of his people, *this* was their way forward — not the bloodshed and loss of life, but his friends, his family. They were the start.

And Larkin…

She was *his* future.

CHAPTER 24

Dracchus moved into the Mess at the rear of their small group. Larkin walked directly ahead of him, with Aymee and Arkon preceding her. The others had already entered after their wounds were treated. Despite Larkin calling him *krullheaded* and several other interesting names, Dracchus had refused any sort of treatment until everyone else had been tended.

The kraken gathered in the room parted to allow Dracchus and his group to pass, and he felt the weight of their eyes upon him. He moved as smoothly as he could given the aches and pains that had come to dominate his body over the last few hours.

He welcomed the pain, if only as a distraction. It was a powerful thing to focus on.

His people were quiet while he moved to the far wall and entered the small space that had been left clear for him. Aymee and Arkon took their places with the rest — Jax and Macy, Rhea and Randall, Vasil, Brexes, Ector and the other elders — at the front of the crowd. Kronus was by himself to one side, staring at the floor. Several male kraken watched him with undisguised wariness and suspicion.

"Uncle Drak!" Sarina shouted when he drew near. Her voice

shattered the prevailing silence. She leaned over Macy's arm, holding her hands toward him.

He took her, and she immediately looped her small arms around his neck and clutched his upper arm with her tentacles. Reaching across his chest, he patted her back, gritting his teeth as the freshly sealed cut on his side disapproved of the movement.

She pressed her forehead to his and blew through her siphons. Smiling, Dracchus did the same. There was something uncharacteristic in her eyes; a glimmer of sadness? He wasn't sure she understood what had happened, but at the very least, she knew it hadn't been good.

"I love you, Uncle Dracchus," she said, nuzzling her face against the crook of his neck and shoulder, clinging to him.

"Love you too, little one," he replied. When he looked back to the crowd, many of them stared at him in open question. Love, still such a new concept to the kraken, perhaps even stranger than the sight of a male holding a youngling as small as Sarina.

"This is the offspring of Jax the Wanderer and Macy, the first human to live in the Facility since the uprising," he called, running his eyes over the crowd. "She is Sarina. She and all our younglings are the future of our kind. They are not defined by their blood, or the blood of their parents, but by how they see the world. And when we do not taint their views early, they are wise enough to see the truth.

"Humans and kraken can exist peacefully. We can share this world, we can even live together and thrive." Dracchus gently pulled Sarina from his arm. She frowned, but went back to her mother willingly. "We cannot ignore what happened tonight. The divide between kraken is not the fault of humans. We are to blame, and we allowed it to widen and plunge us into violence.

"Neo led his exiles into the Facility tonight to kill not only the humans, but all of us who associate with them. Kraken who have done their part for our people for years, some beyond their normal duty. What was the reasoning behind this? Is loving a human crime enough to be slaughtered by our own kind? Does it warrant the killing of younglings, regardless of their blood?"

His hearts thumped in their rapid triple-beat. He drew in a slow, deep breath, and released it with equal measure. Apart from the pain of his wounds, his chest and throat were tight. It was Arkon's place to use words like this, not Dracchus's.

A warm body tucked itself against his side, and he knew it was Larkin without looking. Her presence calmed him somewhat.

"Neo and his group wronged these humans, and these humans are *our* people. When the exiles faced consequences for their actions, they chose retaliation rather than acceptance. They came with anger and hatred in their hearts, and that is how they were returned to the sea.

"And what is in our hearts, we survivors? Confusion. Sadness. Pain, loss, anger. The reasons for what we have done does not counteract the price that was paid. But our people are strong. Our people are intelligent and wise. We will learn from this pain, and together we will move on to the future we have long waited to claim."

Larkin stepped forward. "This war between our people needs to end."

The kraken turned their attention from Dracchus to his mate. Some frowned, flickering glances between him and Larkin.

"I know some of you might still be angry at me for what I've done. I helped the rangers capture your people. I understand that anger. In my ignorance, I believed the words of a man who had betrayed myself and my brother." She gestured toward Randall. "The humans hunting you are doing so out of fear. Fear of the unknown, fear of what might happen, fear of what's already happened.

"I know only enough of your past to know that tonight was a repeated event. The circumstances were different, but the outcome would've been the same. We would've been slaughtered in our beds. The kraken that attacked tonight are the ones humans fear, the ones we called monsters. The ones who we hunted to protect ourselves from what *could* happen.

"For a while, I thought that way." Larkin turned her gaze toward Dracchus briefly. "But I know different now. Macy, Aymee, and Randall know different. There are already people in The Watch who know different. The rest of them need to be shown that they're wrong. They need to *see* with their own eyes that you aren't monsters, but people, like us."

"What do you mean?" Brexes asked, brow low.

"Your people locked Jax away, and beat Dracchus, Vasil, and Neo," someone said from the crowd.

"And your people would have killed me," Macy said.

"We fear what we do not understand," Larkin said gently. "Our people, and yours."

"This is a lesson we try to teach all younglings who hunt with us," Ector said, "but it is often overlooked. Knowing *of* a thing is not *knowing* it. Awareness is not understanding."

"And humans and kraken know little of each other," Dracchus said. "These are not the ones who enslaved us, and we are not the ones who rose against them."

Larkin ran her hands through her hair, tugging it back from her face. "We would have died tonight had it not been for a single kraken who put aside his hatred and risked his life to warn us."

"And, when given chance to leave and save himself, he remained to fight alongside us," Dracchus added. "He shed his blood in our defense."

Larkin turned to face Kronus. "And for that, we thank you, Kronus. You saved us."

All eyes shifted toward Kronus. He looked back at the crowd uncertainly, arms folded across his chest. He kept himself near the wall, with more than a body's length separating him from the others; it was as much space as could be allowed, given the number of kraken present.

"Even though he was cast from his home, Kronus has acted

with honor and selflessness," Ector said. "That is an example we may look upon with pride."

Kronus's skin flashed violet with embarrassment for an instant, and he lowered his head. This was far removed from the outspoken kraken of months before. Had the recent events merely humbled him, or broken him?

"Kronus is also proof that we can change. That we can look upon one another without blinding hatred or fear." Larkin turned back to Dracchus. "Which is why I propose we all go to The Watch."

Shock rippled through the crowd in the form of muttered voices and questioning glances.

"If we go there, the hunters will capture us all," someone called.

"We won't let that happen," Larkin said. "I have chosen my side, and it is with you." She took Dracchus's hand. "I stand with my mate."

Dracchus squeezed her hand and met her gaze. The depth within her eyes was staggering, and he wished, for a moment, that everything else would go away — the other people, his pain, the building itself — leaving only himself and Larkin, so they could hold one another in peace.

"Our father is the one who leads the hunters," Randall said, stepping forward to stand beside his sister, "and as Larkin said, he's driven by fear. The fear of losing his children. He's a good man who's been driven to do terrible things by that fear, but he deserves a chance to change his course. Just like Dracchus gave chances to the others. If we can show him that we are safe, and that our people can exist *together*, he'll stop."

Conversations sparked throughout the gathering. Voices rose above the din, some for the plan, some against; the only consistency was the energy with which the people spoke.

"What do the elders think?" a male shouted.

Ceres moved forward and lifted her hands. The crowd quieted. "We have lived here for many generations without any contact with humans. Our prosperity has always been the product of our toil, and our traditions have helped to ensure our continued existence. But our people have never thrived. Ours has been an existence of constant struggle. We females are few. Our younglings are few. And our people have existed on the edge of disaster since our beginning.

"The humans have given us hope. They have produced kraken younglings. Though we have no guarantee of prospering together, this may be the best hope for our people to finally thrive."

"The dangers cannot be denied," Faro said, "but it may well be time to face those dangers for the chance at something better."

Ector eased forward and smiled. "I speak only for myself in this, but I would like to see the place Macy and Aymee came from at least once before the sea reclaims me."

"Larkin showed us kindness during our captivity," Vasil said, "and I have only seen more of it from the other humans here. I do believe there are others like them."

"Humans already know of your existence," Larkin said. "It is no longer a secret. Show them who you really are and give them a chance to show you who *they* are, too. We're all people. As different as we appear, we want the same thing — to *live*."

"Dracchus?" Ector asked. "What do you say?"

"As all things, it is a risk," he replied after several moments of silence, keeping his gaze on Larkin. "But it is a risk worth taking. Our people have much to learn from each other, and we cannot continue along under constant threat of attack." He looked to the crowd. "I will force no one's choice in this matter. When I have healed fully, I will go to The Watch with my mate. Any who wish it are welcome to join us."

"I will go," Jax said.

Arkon moved forward. "And I."

Ector and the other elders, Vasil, Brexes, and Rhea all came forward one at a time, and then more kraken, males and females alike.

"And I," said Kronus.

Dracchus turned his head to look at the ochre kraken. Kronus's unease was plain in his slight frown and drawn brows, but his gaze was steady.

With a nod, Dracchus turned back to the crowd. "So it shall be. We will face the future together, as we always should have. Let us gather again in five days' time, and we will venture to The Watch and show the humans — and ourselves — that friendship is possible."

DRACCHUS AND LARKIN didn't enter their new den until the sea was already lit by the rising sun. Though the corridor beyond their door looked like all the others in the Cabins, it wasn't *theirs*. The room lacked Dracchus and Larkin's scent, lacked the trinkets they'd gathered over their weeks together, lacked clothing that properly fit Larkin, but it was clean and quiet.

That the other humans and their kraken mates had denned in the three neighboring rooms offered a bit of comfort.

The only comfort Dracchus sought, however, was in Larkin. She led him into the bathroom, removed her clothes, and pulled him into the shower. She maneuvered deftly in the tight space as she washed the remaining blood from his skin, mindful of every recently sealed wound.

Her hands caressed him, but her touch was not meant to arouse; she was letting him know she was there, reminding him *he* was still there, too.

When they finished, she took her time in drying him off. He would have done it himself, but every movement elicited new pain, and the tight skin around his wounds threatened to tear if stretched too far.

Once she dried herself, she donned a shirt and took his hand. "Come to bed, Dracchus."

He followed her gentle guidance. His body was exhausted, but his mind…

The pain was not enough to distract him from his thoughts anymore.

Dracchus eased himself down onto the bed carefully, movements stiff, and draped his forearm over his eyes. He needed to sleep. Needed to fall into that black embrace before everything else rushed to the surface. But it was not black behind his closed eyelids.

It was crimson.

He clenched his teeth against the raw memories, the faces, the blood.

They'd been monsters.

They'd been people.

His people.

The bed dipped as Larkin climbed onto it. She settled herself closer to the headboard than him, slipping her arms around his head to cradle it against her chest. Her hands trailed lightly over his siphon, his temple, his cheek, and her lips brushed across his brow.

"You don't have to be strong around me," she whispered.

He wanted to reply that he would always be strong for her, but the words caught in his throat. Pressure built in his chest, pressure and overwhelming heat, and his body shuddered against it.

"I did not want this," he rasped.

Her fingers continued their slow course over his skin, a constant sign that she was not just with him, she was with him *in that moment*.

"I wanted my people to come together," he continued, each word hurting more than the last as it emerged. "To prosper. To find the same joy and peace the humans in The Watch seem to have. I tried…" He curled his trembling fingers, but the pain of his claws digging into his palms did nothing to steady him.

Larkin took his hand and applied gentle pressure to loosen his grip. She laced the ends of their fingers together and guided his arm down. Cupping his cheek with one hand, she turned his face toward hers.

He opened his eyes. Pulses of black and crimson floated in his vision, a result of how tightly he'd squeezed his eyelids shut, but they yielded slowly to Larkin's face, which was framed by her damp, red-orange hair. She'd dimmed the lights, and the soft glow on her pale skin made her appear otherworldly.

"You are one man, Dracchus," she said, stroking his cheek with her thumb. "You are not responsible for the choices of others. Change takes time, and even the best changes don't come without resistance. You were given a bad situation, and you did the best you could with it. The fault isn't yours."

"They were our people. Whatever they'd done, they were our people. And this wound was dealt to all kraken. How do we take that back? How do we close it?"

"You can't."

He'd known that truth, deep inside, before she spoke it, but hearing it out loud increased the pressure within him tenfold. Were it not for Larkin, were it not for Sarina and the rest of his family, he might have longed for simpler times, for the days when his greatest concern was to ensure Jax was around for the next hunt, or who his next challenge would come from. But if this pain in his hearts was the price for the family that had grown around him, he would pay it again and again without hesitation.

Larkin slid down to curl against his side and wrapped her arm around his chest. Twining his tentacles with her legs, he slipped his arm around her shoulders. He needed to feel her, to hold onto her. His wounds ached, but he didn't care; she would be his balm.

"Time is the only thing that can heal these wounds," she said softly, her warm breath tickling his skin, "but you can help by being there. By carrying on, despite how much it hurts. Whenever you feel weak, I'll be your strength." She kissed him. "You're only one man, but you're not alone."

Dracchus closed his eyes and drew in a deep breath. He focused on her solidness, on the heat of her body, on her scent slowly enveloping him.

The names and faces of the dead kraken drifted through his mind, but he didn't fight them away. He allowed himself to feel the pain of each loss, holding Larkin a little tighter. In time, they faded — not forgotten, but finally ceding to his bone-deep weariness.

"My heart is yours, Dracchus," Larkin whispered as sleep descended upon him. "So long as it beats, I will be by your side."

CHAPTER 25

THOUGH THE WATCH WAS, LIKE MOST EVERY TOWN ON HALORA, relatively small, its waterfront was bustling with activity. Fishermen hauled supplies to and from the boats moored along the gently bobbing dock. A few men seemed to be inspecting some sort of damage to one of the hulls, while others were securing a load to the crane that hauled goods to the warehouse atop the cliff.

Larkin recognized one of the boats — it had accompanied the large ship on its two-week hunt for the kraken. It was the vessel she'd been trying to reach when Neo first attacked her.

"That's my father," Macy said through the suit comm system, pointing toward a burly, bearded man at the end of the dock.

Larkin turned to look at Randall. He treaded water beside her, frowning. "Do you think Dad is there, too?" she asked.

"I don't know," he replied. "Part of me wants him to be, and the other part hopes he's not."

"The scouts said they didn't see any ships nearby," Aymee said. "There's a good chance they all came back here."

"As quick as storms come in during this time of year, they really shouldn't be going too far from port," Macy added.

"Practicality isn't the sort of thing that's been able to stop our father, lately." Larkin's eyes lingered on the dock for another moment before she dipped underwater. The kraken were gathered along the bottom, more than fifty of them, their skin changed to blend into their surroundings. They were nearly imperceptible to the naked eye.

Dracchus reverted to his normal coloring as he rose from the seafloor, looking up at her.

Look for our signal, she signed, moving her hands slowly to ensure her gestures were accurate.

Dracchus nodded and signed with equal care, using the human language. *See you soon.*

Larkin smiled and returned to the surface. "They'll be waiting."

"Let's get this over with," Randall said.

The four humans swam toward the dock together, suits easing their movement through the calm water. Anticipation fluttered in Larkin's chest with increasing strength as they neared their destination.

She didn't know how this meeting would go. None of them did. The kraken and the townsfolk wouldn't be armed, but any rangers in the vicinity would be carrying rifles. It would be up to Larkin, Randall, Aymee, and Macy to keep the villagers from panicking and the rangers from attacking.

They were only fifteen meters away when shouts rang out and people started grouping up on the dock. Randall was the first to reach it, pulling himself up and turning around to assist Larkin, Aymee, and Macy. They looked at one another, then removed their masks and pulled their hoods back.

"Macy?" someone asked gruffly.

Larkin looked at the man as he came forward, recognizing him as Breckett, Macy's father.

Macy smiled wide. "Hi, Dad."

They both ran forward, catching each other in an affectionate embrace.

Breckett lifted Macy off her feet. "Ah, Macy girl, we missed you."

"Missed you, too, Dad." Macy's voice was strained, as though she were on the verge of crying.

"Macy! Aymee!" Another man joined them, his red hair tied back in a ponytail.

"Hi Cam," Aymee replied with a grin.

"That's all you got? Hi Cam? We didn't know if you were dead or alive!" Camrin said, hugging her.

Larkin watched the reunion silently. She knew all too well how they felt. She looked up at her brother only to find his eyes, filled with uncertainty, upon her. She extended her hand and he took it, lacing his fingers with hers.

"We need *everyone* here," Aymee said, withdrawing from Camrin's embrace. "Can you get my parents?"

"You're not leaving yet, are you?" he asked, frowning. "You just got here."

"It's important," Macy said, giving him a quick hug.

"What's going on?" Breckett asked.

"We'll explain soon."

"Is Jax…?"

"He's here," Macy said, lowering her voice so only those nearest to her could hear. "They're…all here."

Breckett's eyes widened. He looked behind him to the gathering crowd, and Larkin followed his gaze with her own.

Her heart skipped when she saw him — Commander Nicholas Laster.

He strode down the length of the dock, armed rangers flanking him on either side, and the townsfolk and fishermen stood aside to allow him past with no shortage of disgruntled expressions. Larkin squeezed Randall's hand.

"Shit," Randall muttered, his tone a confused blend of relief and apprehension.

Larkin hadn't expected him to get here so quickly. She glanced higher and might've kicked herself; how had she missed the lookout he'd posted near the clifftop warehouse?

It didn't matter. Spotting the ranger wouldn't have made a difference.

Her father was here, and he was alive.

"Camrin, go. Gather as many people as you can and get them here, *fast*," Aymee said.

Camrin nodded and ran off, squeezing past the rangers. Nicholas glanced at him for only a moment, barely slowing.

Breckett turned toward the crowd, putting an arm around Macy as Nicholas approached.

"What the hell's going on down here, Breckett?" Nicholas demanded. "I was told people just crawled out of the sea. You pulling some kind of—" His words — and his approach — halted as his gaze swept over Macy and Aymee, finally fixating on the people behind them.

He held Larkin's gaze for several seconds before looking at Randall.

Macy and Aymee shifted aside as he suddenly moved forward. He paused for an instant in front of Larkin and Randall and then took them both into a crushing embrace.

Larkin wrapped an arm around him and squeezed her eyes shut as she turned her face against his shoulder. *This* was her father. This was the man who had been missing from her life for over a year. Tears burned her eyes as she tightened her hold.

Nicholas held them for a long time. Long enough for it to hurt in the best way, long enough for her to feel his tears trickle into her hair.

"I lost you," he whispered raggedly, "I'm so sorry I lost you."

"We're okay, Dad," Larkin said.

"We're here now," Randall added.

He drew back, cupping the backs of their necks with his hands, and looked them over. The tears in his eyes gutted her. "How? Where've you been? How did you get here?"

"We swam," Larkin replied.

"Swam," he repeated and shook his head in disbelief. "Doesn't matter. You can tell me all the made-up stories you want once we go into town and get a hot meal."

"They aren't making anything up," Macy said. "We did swim here."

"And we're not going to town," Larkin added. "Not yet."

Nicholas glanced at Macy as though for the first time, confusion creasing his brow, but he turned back to Larkin without saying a word to the other woman. "What do you mean you're not going to town?"

"We have a lot to talk about, Dad," Randall said.

"And we'll do it in the town hall while we get you two some food and proper clothing. What the hell are you wearing, anyway?"

"They're diving suits. Pre-colony tech. And we're going to talk *here*." Larkin pulled away from her father, taking a few steps back.

"Aymee!" came another voice from the crowd. A man and woman pushed their way through the rangers — Doctor Kent Rhodes and his wife, Jeanette. They didn't stop until they reached their daughter, dragging her into their arms. Aymee released a soft *oomph* and put her arms around them.

"I thought you were dead," Jeanette wailed. Tears streamed down her cheeks.

"I'm sorry," Aymee said. "I wish I could've sent word."

Nicholas had released Randall and turned partly to watch the scene unfold. "These are the missing girls," he muttered.

"That ranger, Cyrus, said they were injured trying to save you from a kraken on the beach," the Doctor said, "but Randall told us you went with him willingly. We knew Arkon wouldn't hurt you, but we didn't know what was happening, didn't know if you were safe. Didn't know where you were."

"Arkon was trying to save me," Aymee said. "Cyrus would have killed both of us if we hadn't left."

"What?" Nicholas demanded. "That's a direct contradiction of Cyrus's report, and I won't have you—"

"Don't you dare talk to me like that." Aymee glared at Nicholas, pulling away from her parents to face him. "You should ask your son exactly the kind of person Cyrus was."

"A monster, Dad." Randall met his father's gaze unflinchingly. "He was insubordinate, violent, made inappropriate advances toward Aymee and several other women, shot me with the intent of assuming command of my unit, and was ready to murder Aymee and Macy to lure out the kraken."

Nicholas's face paled as his features hardened. The nearby rangers — one of whom was Jon Mason, the man who'd run Cyrus's report back to Fort Culver — exchanged uneasy looks.

"You should tell us, Jon," Larkin leveled her eyes on him, "about the drawings Cyrus stole from Aymee's home. Or how about his plans to *relieve Randall of command*?"

"I didn't know where he got the drawings from," Jon said, jaw muscles ticking. "And he sent me home right after shit went down on the beach. I wasn't involved in any of that stuff."

Larkin lowered her brows. "But you knew about it."

Nicholas stared at Jon, betraying his fury only through a slight flaring of his nostrils.

Jon's face reddened. "That wasn't supposed to be how it turned out! I didn't know he was going to shoot him. Randall was too busy chasing local pussy to focus on the mission, and he was fucking us over at every step. How the hell else were we going to get anything done?"

"We were dealing with the unknown," Randall replied through clenched teeth. "I was trying to figure out what the hell it was we were hunting! That means asking questions *before* we shoot!"

"Disarm him," Nicholas said, gesturing to Jon.

Jon Mason's struggles meant little; three other rangers pried the rifle from his hands and divested him of his pistol and knife before they grasped his arms and forced them behind his back.

"I witnessed Cyrus shoot Randall," Macy said. "He and the other men who were with Randall grabbed us and used us as live bait to goad the kraken into an attack. They weren't gentle."

"Take him back into town and restrain him," Nicholas ordered. Two of the rangers hauled Jon along the dock, through the crowd. When Nicholas turned back to Randall, he wore the stoic mask of the commander, that old hardness having returned to his eyes. Larkin knew how much of a sham it was by now. A final, desperate layer of defense against everything that had torn apart the man's life.

"I sent you out here to hunt sea monsters, ranger. How the hell did that turn into a mutiny?" the commander demanded.

Behind him, several more rangers forced their way to the front of the dock.

"Because they're not monsters," Randall replied. "You sent me out here because there was no way the stories were true, there was no way we'd find anything dangerous. Because you thought this was safe. Well, we found the source of the stories, and they're *people*. The only monster was the man you sent along with me."

"They are animals with above average intelligence," Nicholas said. "Elle, explain the situation to your brother."

"I already have," Larkin said. "About how I helped capture them, and how they were tortured."

He glared at her. "I don't care for your tone, ran—"

"It's time for you to shut your mouth and listen," Larkin snapped, stepping toward him. "No more krullshit, Dad, or commander, or whatever you want to be called right now. Those kraken that you had caged were *people*. Intelligent beings who were made by *us*. They share human DNA, they can talk and reason and feel, and all they wanted was to live their lives in peace before you sent Randall out here to hunt them down."

Larkin glanced at Macy, Aymee, and Randall. "We are here to tell you to *stop*. This needs to end. They are not monsters, but they aren't going to remain idle while you hunt them. You are going to stand down, *commander,* before it's too late."

"What the fuck is this?" Nicholas asked in a low voice. "My own children turning on me? You tell me Cyrus was a traitor, and then you try to do the same thing to me?"

"You know that's not what this is," Randall said.

"Just stop this, Dad," Larkin said, tone softening. "You did all of this to protect us, but you went too far. We're safe now. It can be over. Let it be *over.*"

"I've seen what those things can do." Nicholas thrust his arm toward the sea vaguely. "I know what will happen if we…if we just…if we let them go."

"They have never once revealed themselves in all the years I've lived here," Breckett said. "I've worked on these seas nearly every day of my life, and I've never seen them, not until one of them brought my daughter back. We thought her lost at sea during a storm."

"Jax saved me," Macy said. "I would've drowned otherwise."

"This is not the same as what happened to me and Mom," Larkin said gently. "The kraken are not a danger to any of us, so long as we stop hunting them."

Her father's face paled further, save for a wild blotch of red on each cheek. His eyes gleamed. "This isn't about your mother. It's about…"

"Everything has been about her since she was taken from us," Larkin said. "You didn't want to lose the family you had left. I understand, Dad, but it needs to stop. It's changing you into someone we don't know anymore. Just… *Please,* before you lose us both."

He clenched his jaw and averted his gaze, his stance unsteady, uneasy. He offered no response.

"I'm going to show you. *We're* going to show you. Please, just trust me, Dad. Trust me in this." Larkin looked at Randall. "Signal them."

Randall nodded and stepped to the end of the dock. He moved his arms in exaggerated signs, making sure the kraken lookout would be able to see them.

"No weapons," Larkin said, running her gaze over the people gathered. More had come while they'd been speaking to Nicholas, some of them piled in the boats to see around the cluster of townsfolk. "No matter how strange this is going to feel for most of you, *please*. No weapons, no hostility."

The crowd's uncertainty was apparent in their whispered conversations. As far as Larkin could tell, only the rangers were armed; several of them kept shifting their eyes toward her father, who remained unmoving.

Larkin heard a tiny change in the sound of the bay's gently lapping water. The crowd gasped as she turned, keeping herself perpendicular to the humans and the kraken now climbing onto the end of the dock.

Dracchus, unsurprisingly, was first. If Larkin's father noticed, he made no outward sign. The big kraken approached slowly, amber eyes sweeping over the crowd of humans. The rangers raised their rifles as more kraken followed.

Macy and Aymee pulled away from their parents, turning toward the crowd. As one, Larkin and Randall pulled their pistols from their holsters, aiming at the rangers. Aymee and Macy followed suit.

"I *said*, no weapons," Larkin said, stepping in front of Dracchus. From her peripheral vision, she saw her companions do the same, creating a human barrier in front of the kraken. "We will lower ours if you lower yours."

"We have come without weapons," Dracchus said from behind her.

Nicholas finally came out of his trance-like state at the sound of Dracchus's voice. He turned toward Dracchus with wide, angry eyes. "You're the one that took my daughter," he growled, stepping forward.

"Stop where you are, Dad," Larkin commanded.

Nicholas hesitated, gaze dipping to the gun in her hand. "What are you doing, Elle? What are you doing?"

"Protecting them. *This* kraken saved me that night. He might have taken me, but he *saved* me, too."

"Stand aside, Elle. This has gone far enough."

"It has," Randall said. "Order your men to stand down, Dad. Weapons down. We're not here for *this*."

"Are you seriously going to stand for this, commander?" one of the rangers said, stepping forward without lowering his rifle. Christopher Brock, the one who'd beaten Dracchus on the boat. "We need to shoot these fucking things."

Larkin turned her pistol on him. "Your finger so much as twitches in the general direction of that trigger, and I will put a bullet between your eyes."

Brock scowled, glaring at her, but he removed his finger from behind the trigger guard, straightening it along the side of the rifle.

Nicholas turned his head toward his men. "Stand down, rangers."

"This is krull—"

"Stand down!" Nicholas shouted. "Rifles on the dock and back away."

Larkin watched several of the rangers cast each other looks of uncertainty, but they did as they were commanded, slowly lowering their weapons and retreating with their hands held out in front of them.

Once the rangers had moved back, Larkin holstered her pistol; it was the best she would offer while the rangers still carried their sidearms. Randall, Macy, and Aymee did the same.

"These kraken came here to show you there is nothing to be afraid of. They are not the monsters we thought they were. They came to *speak* to you," Larkin said.

"There has been bloodshed between our people in the past,"

Dracchus said, "but there is no need for any more. So long as we remain unknown to one another, there cannot be lasting peace between our people. We come to you today to show you who we are — your neighbors, and not your enemies."

Larkin looked at her father. "You asked us where we've been. We've been with them," she swept her arm toward the kraken. "Living among them, working beside them. Building a family."

"What?" Nicholas's brows fell. He parted his lips to speak, but no sound emerged.

"I'm sure you've heard plenty of rumors about me," Macy said. "That I was taken in the night by a monster, stolen from my friends and family. Only those close to me knew the truth."

Larkin turned her head as Jax, carrying Sarina, moved to stand behind Macy. He put an arm around her.

"This is my mate," Macy said, looking up at Jax. "And our child."

Silence born of shock dominated the crowd for several seconds, and then they burst into conversation — frantic, uncertain, awed conversation. Larkin gritted her teeth when she heard words like *abomination* and *freak* over the din.

Breckett, who'd been standing near Macy, looked at Jax and Sarina. His eyebrows rose high, wrinkling his forehead. "That's... my granddaughter?"

Macy smiled wide and nodded. "Sarina."

Breckett's eyes glistened, and his beard bobbed slightly as though he were moving the mouth hidden within. He stepped closer to Macy tentatively, and a hush fell over the crowd as he reached a hand out to Sarina.

Sarina clutched her father, her wide eyes moving from the crowd to Breckett.

"This is mommy's father," Jax said gently. Removing his arm from Macy, he extended his own hand and touched a finger to Breckett's. "He will not do you harm."

"This is your grandfather," Macy said. "The one I told you about. He's family."

Sarina looked between Jax and Breckett, until finally, she extended a tentacle, brushing the tip over the top of Breckett's hand. "Family?" she asked.

"Yes, child. Family," Breckett said. "Sarina is a lovely name, and you are a lovely girl."

Sarina smiled. "Mommy said it was her sister's name."

The tears flowed from Breckett's eyes, disappearing into his beard. "It was. The sea took her from us a long time ago. But now it brought you."

"Are you sad?" Sarina asked, frowning. "Water comes from Mommy's eyes when she's sad, too."

Larkin glanced at Macy; surely enough, the woman was crying along with her father.

"No, I'm not sad. I am very, very happy to finally meet you, Sarina," Breckett said.

Sarina looked at Jax then back to Breckett before holding her arms out to him. Breckett took her without hesitation, pulling her close. Sarina wrapped her tentacles around his arm and cupped his face with her hands. "Your face is very hairy and tickly," she said.

Breckett laughed; it was a deep, rich sound, and it seemed to affect everyone nearby — the expressions in the crowd had softened, and many were smiling softly as they watched.

"And this," Aymee said, turning her face toward Arkon as he approached with Jace in his arms, "is my mate and son."

Larkin watched as Aymee's parents met Arkon and Jace, their bright smiles warming her heart.

Dracchus settled his hand on her shoulder. She turned to look up at him as he gently guided her aside and moved forward.

Her father looked at him, wide-eyed, and dropped a hand toward his pistol.

Larkin's mouth went dry, and her heart was suddenly pounding. Her mate and her father stared at one another in tense silence, only a few meters of space between them. It would take only an instant for the situation to go wrong. Faster than she could react, she could lose either one of them.

Nicholas clenched his jaw. "You took my daughter from me. Took my son," he said through his teeth, but his words lacked the venom of earlier.

"You put us in cages and beat us," Dracchus said, voice startlingly calm.

"So, what? This is revenge? You had my son for a year, a year of me not knowing if he was alive, if I'd lost my boy. The pain we inflicted wasn't even a fraction of what I've felt."

"Inflicting pain upon us did not ease your own," Dracchus said, "and it did not bring your children back. They were safe under my protection. You taught them to be hunters, to be warriors, and they are both capable. They are both honorable and brave. And they have come back to you today to protect my people.

"I have not forgotten what you did to us. I have not forgotten my days on your ship. They will remain with me for years to come, and what you did drove one of my kind to madness. He attempted to kill my mate more than once because you solidified his hatred." Dracchus twisted his torso, extending an arm to gesture at Larkin. "*She* is my mate. My female. And your actions did *not* protect her."

She met Dracchus's gaze with all the love and pride she felt for him; he'd proclaimed her his in front of all. He smiled at her.

"I am not here to boast." Dracchus lowered his arm and turned back to Nicholas. "I am not here for revenge. I am here because my people, and my mate's people, have suffered enough. Larkin cares for you deeply. Her capacity for love is immense, perhaps endless, and it is something for which I admire her greatly. I forgive you for what has been done, and I am sorry for the pain that we have caused you and your people."

"Enough of this krullshit," Brock growled, lunging forward to grab his rifle and aim it at Dracchus.

Larkin drew her pistol and fired from the hip.

The crowd gasped collectively; several people screamed, and some scattered.

"Fuck!" Brock pulled his bleeding hand to his chest as his rifle clattered onto the dock. He bared his teeth at Larkin. "Bitch! You choose fucking monsters over—"

Dracchus closed the distance between himself and Brock in an instant. The nearby rangers stumbled back from the big kraken, but Brock just looked up. He took Dracchus's fist on his cheek and crumpled, crashing down in a heap.

The other rangers reached for their weapons as Dracchus eased back toward Larkin.

"Stand down, damn it!" Nicholas growled, stepping between Dracchus and his men.

Larkin held her pistol up, daring the rangers to even *look* at their weapons. Jace and Sarina were crying to the side, undoubtedly startled by the loud noise and shouting.

Nicholas glared at his men for a time, and, seemingly satisfied, turned back to Larkin and Dracchus. "Is this all true, Elle? You're this thing's…*mate?*"

Larkin looked at her father. "He's not a thing. His name is Dracchus. And yes, I am his mate. We've joined."

"And this is my mate," Randall called from nearby. Rhea stood with him, Melaina and Ikaros beside them. "My wife."

Rhea moved away from Randall to stand next to Dracchus. She looked at Nicholas. "You have caused our people much trouble, human. But many of our problems began in kraken hearts. It is not too late to come together."

Nicholas looked at Randall, and then at Larkin, his expression unreadable. "You two…you've been…happy, with these…people?"

Larkin nodded. "They've become my family."

"Mine, too," Randall said.

Nicholas's gaze shifted between his children before he finally lifted it to the kraken before him. He studied them in silence as Larkin's heart thumped. "You're keeping them safe? You swear to me, they are safe?" he asked, voice raw.

"I would give my life to protect Larkin," Dracchus said.

Rhea snorted. "No one touches my mate but *me*."

Nicholas's eyes glistened with sudden moisture. "You're taking them again, aren't you?"

"With peace between our people, we all may come and go without fear," Dracchus said.

"Without peace," Larkin said, "we would go and not come back. We can't risk any more lives. As much as we love you, we just can't."

"I stand for peace!" Breckett called. "There's never been trouble between the people of The Watch and the kraken, and I don't see any reason for it to start now."

"As do we," Kent said, arms around his wife and Aymee.

Murmurs of assent rippled through the crowd; these people's lives had been disrupted by the rangers for over a year. They deserved peace, they deserved security, they deserved normalcy. Even if it was a new normal, at least it wouldn't be guided by hatred or fear.

"And me!" called another voice. A woman ran past the rangers, heading straight for Macy. Camrin followed close behind her.

"Mom?" Macy stepped into the woman's embrace, returning it with equal fervor.

"I'm sorry. I'm so sorry," the woman sobbed, cupping Macy's head and pulling her closer. "I missed you so much."

"It's okay. I'm here," Macy said gently, running a hand down her mother's back.

"Madeline," Breckett coaxed.

Madeline raised her head and looked at Breckett. She stilled. She glanced between Macy and Sarina before pulling away. "Is that...? Is it her?"

Breckett nodded. "Our granddaughter."

Madeline covered her mouth with her hands as tears rolled down her cheeks. But instead of going to Sarina, she turned to Jax and wrapped her arms around him. "Thank you," she whispered. "Thank you."

Jax — only a bit awkwardly — hugged the woman back.

Nicholas had turned his head to watch this unfold. He slowly returned his attention to the kraken. He had to tilt his head back to look Dracchus in the eye, but he made no sign of being intimidated. For a few moments, he was the commander and Larkin's father simultaneously.

"You and I have to have a talk, kraken," Nicholas said.

Dracchus's mouth tilted to one side in a smile. "Randall already spoke with me. I am aware of the consequences."

Nicholas nodded stiffly. "We're still going to have that talk. I need to make it *explicitly* clear."

"What is this talk you speak of?" Rhea asked.

"Just some lighthearted death threats, one male to another," Randall replied.

Taking a deep breath, Nicholas stepped past Dracchus, stopping in front of Larkin. "I...I guess I made a mess of things, Elle..."

"We all do crazy things out of fear for the people we love," Larkin said.

He dropped his gaze to the dock. "It's just...after your mother died, and you were hurt... I..."

Larkin holstered her pistol and stepped forward, wrapping her arms around her father. He clutched her against him. "I know, Dad. I know."

"You're so much like her, Elle. I didn't want to lose you, too. I *couldn't.*"

"You didn't lose me. And it's not too late for all of this. Please. Please just give this time. Make peace. He makes me happy, Dad." Larkin looked at Dracchus, meeting his gaze. "I love him."

With deep concentration on his face, Dracchus moved his hands slowly through a series of human signs.

I love you, too.

"Gone for a month and a half, and you fall in love?" Nicholas asked.

Larkin chuckled. "What are you going to do with me?"

Nicholas drew in a shaky breath. "I guess…the first step is to accept that you're not my problem anymore." He laughed, more a relieved sound than an amused one, and held her tighter still, leaning his cheek against her hair. "Come here, Randall."

A few seconds later, her brother wrapped an arm around her. Larkin's chest ached with emotion. She'd missed this so much. Her father, her brother, her family.

Nicholas pressed a kiss to her head and Randall's before he released them and stepped back. He turned toward the crowd. "The kraken are not a threat in the eyes of the rangers," he called, voice echoing over the water. "We will gather our belongings, repair any damage we might have caused, and return to Fort Culver."

He lowered his gaze to the rangers in front of him. "You men have served bravely, and you deserve time with your families. Once the lingering matters concerning this excursion are settled, I will appoint a successor to take my place as Commander. I have failed all of you."

"Commander," Jason Dane stepped forward, "please. This was just a short lapse, sir. You did your best, based on the information you possessed."

A few of them spoke up in agreement.

Nicholas raised his hands, and they fell silent. "It has been my honor to lead you, but I'm not fit for it any longer. Maybe I haven't been for years. Either way, my children are *here*, so this is where I need to be."

A small hand reached up and touched Nicholas's back.

Nicholas turned and to see Melaina looking up at him. Brow creased, he knelt to get closer to her eye level.

"Randall became my father when he fell in love with my mom," Melaina said, glancing between Randall, Rhea, and Nicholas. "Does that mean you are my grandfather?"

Nicholas's features softened. "I guess it does."

"So you have to let your face get really hairy too, right?"

Breckett barked laughter.

Nicholas smiled; it was the most genuine smile Larkin had seen from him in a long, long time. "Maybe. I don't think grandfathers *have* to have big beards, but...I've never been one before. You'll...have to help me figure it out."

Melaina smiled. "I would like a grandfather. I never had a father before Randall, and that's been really fun. A grandfather should be even more fun, right?"

Nicholas looked at Randall, making no attempt to hide the pride in his expression. "I'll try, but I have a feeling that your father's already better than I can ever be."

Slowly, the kraken and human groups moved closer to one another; their interaction began with awed, awkward stares, but soon, tentative conversation began between the bravest on both sides.

Dracchus pulled Larkin into his arms. He raised a hand to her cheek, claws lightly sliding into her hair. The nearby water reflected in his amber eyes, increasing their depth, giving them a sense of motion. "You have created a future for our people to share."

"It's up to everyone to make it a good one, but it's a start." She cupped his face, brushing her thumbs over his cheekbones. "Thank you for trusting us. For trusting in me."

One of his tentacles coiled around her waist, its tip gently stroking her lower back. The rest of the world faded away — the crowd, the voices, the swaying dock beneath her feet. In Dracchus's eyes, she was all there was, she was *everything*.

"You stand with me," he said, voice rumbling in his chest, "and I will forever stand with you. I will be your strength when you do not feel strong. I will be your comfort. I will be your heart." He lowered his head and caressed her lips with his. "Just as you are mine."

EPILOGUE

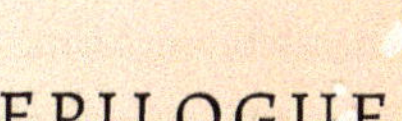

363 Years After Landing

"Hurry up! There's something I want to show you!" Larkin tugged on Dracchus's hands.

He pulled himself up a few more steps along the narrow, spiraling staircase. He'd always felt heavier on land, but he'd never imagined how much worse it would while climbing stairs. No matter how many times he'd seen it from the water and the town below, Dracchus had never realized just how tall the lighthouse was.

"You will be late," he replied. "Your father does not appreciate when you are late for his hunts."

"He can wait. This is important."

They continued upward, moving around the enclosed central shaft — Larkin had said it was an *elevator* that used to carry people to the top, but it had ceased functioning long ago.

Perhaps she should have had Arkon tinker with it beforehand to see if he could repair the device.

By the time they reached the door at the top, Dracchus's

muscles were ablaze. Even when he'd swam for a day and a half without rest, he hadn't felt as drained as he did now.

"Close your eyes," Larkin said, one hand on the door button, the other holding his.

He closed his eyes without hesitation.

The door opened with a soft sound, similar to the sound of the doors in the Facility. It provided him a bit of comfort.

"Duck down a little," she said. "A little more. And turn your shoulders."

His tentacles brushed the doorframe as she led him through. The air in the chamber was different; it bore a faint, metallic scent, and he could almost sense sound attempting to intrude upon the quiet from some unseen *outside*. Larkin's boots echoed gently on the floor as she led him forward.

Another door swished open, and wind hit him immediately. It was cooler than the wind he'd felt as they approached the lighthouse from below, faster, louder. Larkin tugged his hand again. He knew the instant he was in open air.

"A little farther, Dracchus."

Larkin guided his hands to something — a railing — and he closed his fingers around it.

"Okay. Open your eyes."

Dracchus obeyed. He saw the sky first, stained with the vibrant reds and oranges of the sunrise, which were broken only by violet clouds on the horizon. The sea was next as he lowered his gaze, shimmering in the strengthening morning light. Lower still, and he saw the land — and became immediately aware of just how far away it was.

His head spun for a moment, and his stomach churned. He swayed back, away from the railing, but Larkin pressed her hands to his back to steady him.

"It'll pass," she said. "No matter how it feels, you're *not* going to fall."

He closed his eyes and drew in a deep breath. When he opened them again, the sensation renewed itself — his insides lurched as though he were falling — but he tightened his grip on the railing and let the sensation fade.

Larkin moved to his side, slipping an arm around his waist, and pointed out over the edge. "Look over there."

Following her gesture, Dracchus swept his gaze over the fields filled with strange, four-legged animals, over the jungle with its impenetrable plant-life, and to the beach visible beyond. Pale sand ran up to a stretch of rocks, and higher still was a ridge covered in swaying grasses and clumps of vegetation. Along that higher ground, buildings were being constructed — he could *just* hear the human workers, their shouts and hammering little more than whispers on the wind from this distance.

Ten structures in total, all standing along the coast, looking out over the beach and the sea beyond it.

"What are those buildings?" he asked.

"Homes. For the kraken who want to try living on land but aren't comfortable in town yet. That first one," her hand shifted into his field of view, indicating the house on the left, closest to the cliffs that flanked the beach, "is going to be Randall and Rhea's. It'll give them a lot more space for Ikaros and Melaina to play."

Dracchus smiled. Ikaros and Melaina often hurried through the corridors back home, and with the prixxir having filled out to full size, things sometimes felt cramped.

She moved her hand over. "And that one will be Jax and Macy's. She said she loves being near her parents, but they need a little more space, especially with Sarina and Eros getting so big."

"How long have these been hidden from me?" he asked, looking at her.

"It wouldn't have been a surprise if we told you too early," she said, grinning. "Arkon was designing them for months before we started. He wanted to make them more comfortable for kraken.

He's got some sort of system for pumping sea water into tubs in each one, but it only works about half the time."

Dracchus chuckled and shook his head. Leave it to Arkon to come up with such a plan, when the sea was so close to the homes. "Is that why he has been so irritable lately?"

"You know he won't stop until he has everything perfect."

"I know."

Larkin pointed toward the buildings again. "And that one, the little one, is ours." She looked up at him. "I know you want to remain at the Facility with most of the kraken, but we come here so often... I wanted a den of our own while we're on land. It'll give us more time with Sarina, Eros, and Melaina. Jace, too, when Aymee and Arkon visit."

He settled his gaze on the building. It was smaller than the rest, but it was centrally located, and it would be theirs.

Fourteen kraken had taken up permanent residence in The Watch — including Jax and his younglings — and many more visited often. These were first homes built for their kind, far enough away to allow them the hint of isolation that they found so comfortable while close enough to ensure they remained a part of the community.

As more kraken and humans worked together, as more of them lived together, the Facility would become less necessary. Their people were moving on from the past, learning that shelter and prosperity could be found elsewhere, if necessary. Combining fishing efforts with the humans and learning how to use similar storage techniques had already benefited the kraken greatly, reducing the frequency of hunts. That had given them time to expand their knowledge and skills in other directions.

This was more than he could have hoped for. More than he'd dared dream. Not everyone had embraced the changes, but conflict had been at a minimum.

"Would it not have been easier to walk to the houses?" Dracchus asked.

"Hmm." Larkin skimmed her fingers down his spine. "But then I wouldn't have you for myself."

Her touch sent a thrill through him. He turned to face her, dropping his hands to her hips. He ran a tentacle up the leg of her pants and brushed its tip behind her knee, taking in her scent, her taste. Even after a year, his appetite for her was insatiable — it only grew each time they came together. "And now that you have me?"

She positioned herself between Dracchus and the rail and kissed his chest, peering up at him as she kissed down his abdomen. He grasped the railing again, tighter than before. "I'm sure I can think of something."

ALSO BY TIFFANY ROBERTS

THE INFINITE CITY

Entwined Fates

Silent Lucidity

Shielded Heart

Vengeful Heart

Untamed Hunger

Savage Desire

Tethered Souls

THE KRAKEN

Treasure of the Abyss

Jewel of the Sea

Hunter of the Tide

Heart of the Deep

Rising from the Depths

Fallen from the Stars

Lover from the Waves

THE SPIDER'S MATE TRILOGY

Ensnared

Enthralled

Bound

THE VRIX

The Weaver

The Delver

The Hunter

THE CURSED ONES

His Darkest Craving

His Darkest Desire

ALIENS AMONG US

Taken by the Alien Next Door

Stalked by the Alien Assassin

Claimed by the Alien Bodyguard

Saved by the Alien Crime Boss

STANDALONE TITLES

Claimed by an Alien Warrior

Dustwalker

Escaping Wonderland

Yearning For Her

The Warlock's Kiss

Ice Bound: Short Story

ISLE OF THE FORGOTTEN

Make Me Burn

Make Me Hunger

Make Me Whole

Make Me Yours

VALOS OF SONHADRA COLLABORATION

Tiffany Roberts - Undying

Tiffany Roberts - Unleashed

ABOUT THE AUTHOR

Tiffany Roberts is the pseudonym for Tiffany and Robert Freund, a husband and wife writing duo. The two have always shared a passion for reading and writing, and it was their dream to combine their mighty powers to create the sorts of books they want to read. They write character driven sci-fi and fantasy romance, creating happily-ever-afters for the alien and unknown.

Sign up for our Newsletter!
Check out our social media sites and more!
http://www.authortiffanyroberts.com

www.ingramcontent.com/pod-product-compliance
Lightning Source LLC
Chambersburg PA
CBHW070610310726

48982CB00001B/39